The Downfall of the Winterbou

By Patrick Gera

Copyright © 2024 by Patrick Gerald   All rights reserved.

No part of this book may be reproduced, distributed, or transmitted in any form or by any means, including photocopying, recording, or other electronic or mechanical methods, without the prior written permission of the author, except in the case of brief quotations embodied in critical reviews and certain other non-commercial uses permitted by copyright law.

This is a work of fiction.

Names, characters, places, and incidents are either products of the author's imagination or used fictitiously.

Any resemblance to actual persons, living or dead, events, or locales is purely coincidental. First Edition

Content Warnings

This book contains

- Graphic violence
- Sexual assault
- Death
- Profanity

Viper's Den's cottage

*

Prince Charles gripped the reins with one hand, the other clutching Sophia's limp body tightly against him as they rode through the storm. The wind howled, tearing at his soaked cloak, while the rain lashed his face like shards of ice. A dull, throbbing ache from the rock's blow pulsed through his head, each jolt of the horse sharpening the pain. His vision swam, his grip on consciousness slipping, but he forced himself to remain upright.

As Viper's Den's cottage loomed through the fog, Charles made out the shadowy forms of two figures standing guard outside. Their dark cloaks hung heavy with rain, blurring into the night's gloom, yet their steady stances and the well-worn hilts of their weapons betrayed them as men long accustomed to violence. One of them stepped forward, his heavy boots squelching in the mud, and the serpent insignia—a coiled snake—glinted darkly on his cloak.

"Your Highness," the guard greeted him, his tone as cold and steady as the storm. Barely a glance spared for the unconscious princess in Charles's arms, as if such sights were but routine. "Odd hour, Your Highness, to ride with cargo so dear."

Charles's grip on Sophia tightened as a wave of dizziness washed over him, nearly pulling him from the saddle. He swung his leg over the saddle, nearly losing his grip. His boots hit the mud, and his knees buckled, forcing him to brace himself against the horse's side to stay upright. "Aye," he rasped, his voice barely above a whisper. The two guards shifted, moving in eerie synchronization as he allowed Sophia's limp body to slide from his arms. Their hands caught her weight with practiced ease. The guards exchanged a glance, a silent signal, and from the shadows emerged a stable hand, who silently took the horse's reins. The beast, weary and dripping, was led away toward a small, weather-beaten stable tucked beside the cottage.

Inside Viper's Den's cottage, muffled cries and the scrape of metal echoed through the dim, suffocating air. The thick warmth brushed against his skin like damp wool, prickling with an almost palpable tension. As he staggered through the door, his eyes adjusted to the dim glow cast by a single torch flickering in the gloom. He looked up to see a man hanging from the rafters, bound in heavy, rusted chains. His head lolled to one side, his chest smeared with blood, while two Shadow Serpents worked him over, their movements cold and efficient. One held a bloodstained knife; the other pressed a red-hot iron to the prisoner's flesh, the serpent insignia on his sleeve glinting in the torchlight.

The man's limbs thrashed weakly against the chains, a hoarse gasp slipping out as he sagged back down. His breath came in ragged bursts, each one forcing another tremor through his battered form. A flicker of disgust crossed Charles's face, but he quickly buried it. The Serpent nearest to the prisoner leaned in, his voice low and ice-cold. "Thou hast but one more chance. To whom did she bestow the jewels?"

The prisoner's mouth moved, his voice a faint murmur, but no answer came. Without a word, the second Serpent pressed the iron deeper into the prisoner's chest. The stench of charred skin clung thickly to the air, mixing with the sharp, metallic tang of fresh blood. Charles grimaced, the acrid stench thickening the throb in his head as he moved further into the cottage.

The Shadow Serpent barely spared him a glance as they carried Sophia inside and laid her on the rough-hewn table near the fire. Charles's legs wobbled, his hand clenching the back of a nearby chair, his vision flickering as his head pounded mercilessly. The man's groans behind him weakened, but the Serpents continued their grim task, undisturbed by his arrival.

With barely a glance at Sophia's unconscious form, the guards turned without a word, their cloaks trailing behind them as they left, the door creaking open. The cold night air swept in, carrying with it the muffled sound of their footsteps fading into the rain. Only the faint tracks of mud marked where they had stood, quickly blurred as the storm swallowed their steps.

Charles lowered himself into the wooden chair, his breath ragged, his fingers digging into the armrest. The cottage air clung thick and choking, pungent with the tang of blood and charred flesh. The fire crackled close by, its warmth barely touching the cold that settled deep in his bones. Each pulse of his headache sent a fresh wave of dizziness spiraling through him.

One of the Shadow Serpents, Bartholomew turned from his grim work, approaching Charles. In the torchlight, burn scars marked his face. The coiled serpent on his sleeve glinted in the dim glow as he inclined his head. "Lucian Blackthorn is not present, yet we stand ready to serve thee, as ever, Your Highness."

Charles fumbled at his cloak with trembling fingers, drawing a small pouch of coins and letting it fall onto the table with a dull clink. "There's a maiden lost in the woods. Let the beasts feast upon her bones, but I'll send a man to be certain it's done."

The Serpent, Bartholomew gave a nod, the bloody knife still gleaming in his hand. "And what of the princess, Your Highness?"

Charles's gaze flickered toward the fire, though it did nothing to warm him. His jaw tightened, the pounding in his skull blurring his thoughts, making it hard to think. He pressed through the fog clouding his mind. "Cast her into mine own dungeon," he rasped, each word scraping forth with effort. "None shall lay eyes upon her."

Bartholomew inclined his head. "As you command."

Behind them, the tortured man let out a weak groan as the hot iron pressed into his flesh once more. He twisted against the chains, his hoarse voice breaking in desperate pleas. "Mercy... I beg thee... mercy..."

Charles's vision blurred, the stench of burning flesh mixing with the taste of blood on his tongue. He turned his gaze, unwilling to show he noticed. His hand shook slightly as he gripped the armrest, the weight of the journey, his injury, and a gnawing sense of guilt settling over him like a heavy cloak, dragging him deeper into the chair. Pain throbbed in his temples. He blinked slowly, trying to keep himself awake.

Viper's Den, dark and suffocating, seemed to press closer with every breath he took. The firelight flickered unevenly, casting shadows that stretched and twisted along the rough walls, their jagged forms shifting in time with the wind's howling outside. Sophia lay still on the table, her pale skin almost fading into the dim light, while the tortured man's ragged breaths filled the heavy air.

Noor's voice echoed in Charles's mind, soft and unsettling, gnawing at his thoughts. *"Fear not, my liege; this is not the finality of our tale. I shall return in spirit, lingering with thee in every moment of thine affection. Those whom thou dost cherish shall be mine to claim, for whatever thou dost desire, know that my spirit shall seize it as well."* Her words twisted in his head, an icy weight settling over him and tightening his chest with a creeping dread. His jaw clenched against the chill, but the memory lingered, insistent.

He glanced toward the man with the burnt face, his throat tight as he forced the question from his lips. "What dost thou know of spirits?" His gaze lingered on the Serpent's scarred visage, hoping for answers but fearing what he might hear. His hand tightened around the armrest, muscles tense as he awaited a response, his breath held in spite of himself.

The man stilled, his scarred face tightening as he struggled to grasp the prince's meaning, his gaze shifting uncertainly before he spoke. "Your Highness... dost thou inquire of a vengeful spirit?"

Charles's breath hitched, his heart pounding in his chest. His eyes darted to the iron being thrust back into the fire, its surface already glowing faintly red. He looked away quickly, forcing his attention elsewhere. "Yea," he said, his voice faltering. "I doth inquire of a vengeful spectre. Is there... is there some dark sorcery that may yet halt such a force?"

The crackle of the fire filled the silence between them. The iron shifted in the embers, its heat intensifying, glowing hotter with each passing moment. The tortured man stirred, his breath coming in shallow, uneven gasps. He twisted again, frantic, his wrists straining against the chains. "Nay... nay, please!" he whimpered, voice rough from endless cries. His body tensed as the iron was pulled from the fire, casting a menacing red glow across the chamber as it hissed toward his flesh.

The burnt-faced Serpent, his voice low and measured, glanced toward the iron and then back at Charles. "A witch there be, Your Highness... one most skilled in arts dark and foul, who could craft spells to stay such forces—or weave charms yet stronger still." He paused, his voice dropping lower, "Though at a price, no doubt."

The tortured man whimpered louder, his body trembling in anticipation of the iron's searing touch. The prisoner's choked cries echoed as he thrashed, fully aware that the agony was about to strike again.

The tortured man jerked in his chains, his body instinctively pulling back, though there was no escape. A muffled scream tore from his throat the moment the iron bit into his flesh, the sickening scent thickening the air, clinging to everything in the chamber. His body convulsed as the searing heat bit deeper. Charles's gaze briefly flickered toward the man, his face tightening despite himself, before he forced his eyes back to the Serpent.

    Charles remained still, fingers steady despite the chaos around him as he dipped into his cloak pocket, retrieving another pouch of coin. The faint clink of metal barely registered against the backdrop of the prisoner's desperate cries, a sound that grated on his nerves. He turned his focus away, unwilling to acknowledge the man's suffering, even as Noor's threat echoed in his mind. *"I shall return in spirit, lingering with thee…"* The thought sent a chill down his spine, a reminder of the dark promise she had made, but he shoved it aside, unwilling to let it take root. His hand tightened on the pouch, and a flicker of something like hope—though he'd never admit it—sparked in his eyes at the idea of seeking out the witch who could offer him a way to break free from the shadows she cast.

<u>Thorncrest Castle The dungeon – Princess Sophia</u>

Sophia drifted back to consciousness, her senses reeling as she emerged from the suffocating darkness into a waking nightmare. The dungeon loomed around her—a haze of shifting shadows that seemed to writhe with a life of its own. Her eyes struggled against the gloom, each flicker of light punctuated by a relentless pounding in her skull, a metronome to the eerie silence enveloping her.

Tentatively, her trembling hand brushed against the lump on her head, a jolt of pain shooting through her. A sharp hiss escaped her lips, swallowed by the oppressive air. With each small movement, a stabbing ache lanced through her side, drawing her gaze down to a crude, hastily sealed wound that marred her skin. The ragged edges of the injury gaped as though protesting the crude stitching that held them together.

A gasp tore from her throat, reverberating off the stone walls in a hollow, echoing cacophony. No one came. No one heard her cries.

Fragmented memories flooded her mind, sharp and fleeting like splinters of ice. She remembered the sharp crack against her skull, the way the world spun wildly before everything faded into darkness. "Noor…" The name trembled on her lips, weighted with fear, but the dungeon offered only mockery as her voice echoed back at her.

A rustle shattered the silence, sharp and jarring in the stale air. Rigid with fear, Sophia's gaze darted toward the noise. A rat scurried past her feet, its claws scraping against the stone. A wave of revulsion washed over her, compelling her to press her back against the cold wall, her skin crawling with the filth of the place.

Then, from the depths of the shadows, she sensed movement. A soft scraping, like a hand brushing against the stone, followed by a faint rustling that seemed to come from just beyond her line of sight. Her heart raced, pulse quickening with the awareness of unseen presences. Each slight sound—the shift of a body, the barely audible creak of chains—set her nerves on edge. What lurked in the darkness? Each noise made her skin prickle, the unsettling thought of hidden captives lurking nearby igniting a deep-seated fear. What if they were watching her, their own despair mirroring her own?

The air was thick with the stench of decay, every breath a struggle against the oppressive dampness that clung to her. Mildew soaked into her skin like a second layer, and when she reached for her hair, she recoiled at the gritty, matted strands that had once flowed like silk. Her once-golden locks lay knotted and filthy, mud caking them into a grotesque tangle.

Her clothes weighed her down, thick with grime and caked mud, clinging to her as if they were a heavy shroud. The fabric, stained and torn, scraped against her skin, stiff with dried blood, each shift sending fresh waves of discomfort coursing through her. The only comfort came from the cloak draped across her shoulders, its warmth a cruel reminder of the life she had fled. Panic unfurled in her chest—was this some twisted form of rescue, or merely a cruel pause before a darker fate?

Memories of Charles in the forest crashed over her, the image of his bloodstained clothes burned into her mind. Noor... dread coiled tightly within her. Had she fallen to Charles's cruelty? Was she still alive, or had the darkness consumed her too?

Sophia's breath hitched, and she called out again, her voice cracking beneath the weight of her fear. "Charles! Prithee, I beseech thee, grant me my freedom!" The desperation of her plea echoed off the damp walls, swallowed by the stillness that surrounded her. Only silence answered, the empty air devouring her cries.

Each unanswered call stripped away her remaining hope, leaving her hollow. The bitterness of abandonment settled deep within her, pressing down like a lead weight. There would be no savior, no hand to lift her from this pit of despair.

The heaviness of despair pressed upon her, and she curled in on herself, instinctively trying to shield her fragile spirit from the engulfing darkness. Exhaustion clawed at her mind, and with tear-streaked cheeks, she curled against the filthy stone floor. The cold gnawed at her skin, but she had no fight left. Slowly, mercifully, sleep claimed her, offering a brief escape from the nightmare.

<u>A few hours hence.</u>

Sophia's eyes fluttered open, heavy with the weight of sleep, as echoing footsteps reverberated through the dungeon's gloom. Her heart clenched, fear wrapping around her chest like icy tendrils. Was it a savior or a tormentor drawing near? Each slight movement sent a sharp pulse through her side, the ache spreading deeper with every shallow breath—a relentless sting that reminded her of her fragility.

Disoriented and half-awake, she strained to make sense of the shadows that seemed to swirl around her, her pulse quickening with dread. The darkness felt alive, shifting and rustling as if other unseen captives stirred in their cells—the faint scrape of fingers against stone and the soft clink of chains punctuated the oppressive silence, amplifying her sense of isolation. She could almost sense their despair mingling with her own, an unspoken connection that heightened her anxiety.

Each footfall echoed through the stone chamber, driving fresh waves of terror into her heart, tightening her grip on the cold iron bars. She could barely summon the strength to lift her head, her senses heightened as the silence shattered like fragile glass, punctured by a voice that sliced through the stillness. Cold recognition coiled in her chest, dread tightening its grip as she realized who it was.

"Little sister," Charles's voice dripped with false familiarity, a cruel taunt that sent chills down her spine. Sophia's fists clenched, her nails biting into her palms as a surge of fury coursed through her, though her body remained weak and trembling. If only she had the strength to hurl her hatred at him, to spit in his face. But even that small act of defiance was beyond her reach. Her mouth felt parched, her voice stolen by fear.

Charles thrust a torch into the holder outside her cell, and the small flickering glow surged forward, casting wavering light that danced across the rough stone walls. As he came closer, the torchlight crawled over the walls, throwing ugly shadows into every corner. Sophia's mind raced as she stared at the torch, questions flooding her thoughts even as the light brought her no comfort.

He moved nearer, the flickering flame illuminating the dark bruise and gaping gash on his brow, swollen and raw from their last clash. The memory of her desperate strike with a rock flashed in her mind, sharp and clear amid the haze of pain. Despite her body shaking like a leaf, her gaze locked onto his, a mix of defiance and dread swirling in her chest.

As the torchlight brightened, she sensed movement in the darkness beyond her view, the subtle shifts and whispers of captives in their cells—an unsettling reminder that she was not alone in her suffering. The soft rustle of fabric and the faint clinking of chains reverberated in the air, hinting at their presence without revealing their forms. They were there, close yet unseen, their fear intertwining with her own as the warm glow of the torch crept ever nearer.

"Wherefore art thou, Noor?" Her voice trembled, each utterance heavy with desperation. The unsteady torchlight flickered over her pale face, her shallow breaths barely stirring the damp air around her, each movement fraught with weakness. "Why dost thou confine me in this wretched dungeon?" The words slipped from her lips like a whisper, her tone too delicate, too faint to carry the full weight of her fury.

Charles stood before her, separated by the iron bars that cast long shadows across the damp stone floor. His lips curled into a false smile, dripping with mock sympathy. If only he could hold his own words with such ease. Yet, beneath the smug sneer lay a cold tremor of fear, a chill that curled through his thoughts like the touch of a ghostly hand. It was the first life he'd taken by his own hand, the first time he'd truly watched breath slip from another's body. Why, he'd ordered deaths before, signed their fates with the ease of a name on parchment—but to take the life himself?

"If it were not for mine own self, dearest sister," he began, his words soft but threaded with menace, echoing faintly in the oppressive air. "It was by naught but fortune that I didst chance upon thee and that wretched Noor Winterbourne," quoth he, his gaze shifting as if grappling with some feigned truth. He shuddered inwardly at the memory of Noor's last gasping breaths, her words haunting his mind: she had claimed, with her final strength, that it was he—not any outsider—that was the true danger to Sophia. A lie, he told Sophia. "Noor bore naught but ill intent. Had mine intervention not been timely, thou wouldst scarce draw breath this day."

Yet even as he played the part, the shadow of his unease loomed large. Had it not been for the

Shadow Serpents and their discreet handywork, he would not be here now, clean and unburdened. He owed them for making it seem as though the filth and blood had never touched his hands. *"They shall see to it that a witch's craft shall shield me from the spirit of Noor."* He could not bring himself to imagine Noor's face *"Aye, and fortune smiled in that the Serpents cleaned up what was left,"* he murmured inwardly, his gaze steeling with false confidence.

Sophia's eyes blazed with fury. "Is there no end to thy deceit, brother?" Her voice quavered, tears tracing paths down her cheeks, her emotions laid bare. "How canst thou twist the truth so?" She tried to shift her position, but a searing pain in her side forced a cry from her lips, her body betraying her as she slumped back against the wall.

In a tearful whisper, she pleaded again, "What hast thou done with Noor?" Each word was a dagger of fear, stabbing deeper into her heart as she awaited his response.

For a moment, Charles tilted his head, as if perplexed by her inquiry. Then his expression shifted, a wicked grin curling upon his lips. *"Compose thyself,"* he inwardly urged, forcing his lips into a sneer even as his thoughts tugged at his courage. "Didst she not strike thy head with considerable force?" he mocked, his voice laced with a cruel ease. "But fret not—I have dealt with her most decisively." He hoped the witch would see to it that her ghost remained far from him, tethered in some other realm. Such matters were best left to the mystical arts, and he awaited the casting of a spell to bar Noor's spirit from haunting him. "Know that I did this for thee."

Sophia's breath hitched, her body trembling as his words fell upon her like a suffocating shroud. "Wha—what hast thou done?" Her voice faltered, fear coiling tightly around her throat. "Unless thou hast returned her to her kin in a sound state, then thou hast done naught for me!"

Her wrath blazed forth like wildfire, consuming all reason. "Thou shalt not escape unscathed for this foul deed!" she declared, venom lacing each syllable, though the iron bars stood resolutely betwixt her and her quarry.

Charles met her gaze with a cold, unyielding stare, his voice dropping to a low, menacing tone. "Shall I summon Robert Winterbourne for a hunting expedition, dear sister?"

Sophia's blood ran cold at the unspoken threat. Her body jolted forward, fingers clawing at the iron bars, straining to close the distance between them, though the bars held her back, her hands trembling with the force of her frustration. Pain tore through her body as the cauterized wound pulled, forcing a sharp cry from her lips. She recoiled, clutching her side in agony.

"Thou wouldst not dare," she hissed, her voice filled with both rage and terror. Her eyes pleaded with him, though she tried to mask it with defiance. "Brother, I know thou wouldst not."

But Charles only laughed, the sound echoing through the dungeon's cold, suffocating air. "Oh, would I not?" he sneered, malice dripping from every word. *Though surely her spirit waits to accuse me,* he thought, a nervous pang pressing at his gut. He dismissed the thought and fixed his face into a sneer. "Thou shalt obey me, or I will pay Robert a visit."

Sophia's tears welled again, her fear for Robert igniting fresh waves of desperation. "I beseech thee, brother," she whispered, her voice cracking as her defenses crumbled.

Charles's lips barely twitched, his eyes narrowing as he watched her struggle, the faintest hint of amusement flickering across his face. Without another word, he retrieved a leather flask from his pocket and set it on the iron bar just within her reach. The promise of a drink—of relief—hung in the air, tempting her as her parched throat screamed for it.

With trembling hands, Sophia snatched the flask and twisted the top open, the sound like salvation in the quiet. She drank deeply from the flask, the thin ale sliding down her throat, its bitter taste a welcome relief from the dryness that had plagued her.

Charles turned to leave, his steps heavy and deliberate. "Halt! Pray, tarry a moment!" Sophia cried, her voice raw, her heart pounding in her chest. "Leave me not here! I beseech thee, brother!" But the dungeon swallowed her words, offering nothing but the oppressive silence in return.

As his footsteps receded, faint sounds stirred from the other cells. A soft clinking of chains rattled in the dark, punctuated by a shuffling of feet, as though other prisoners shifted in their bonds, testing their restraints. A low, uneven scraping echoed from somewhere to her left—perhaps a hand trailing weakly across the cold stone. Each noise carried a quiet desperation, muted by the thick walls but unmistakable, pressing in on her like shadows creeping closer. Sophia tightened her grip on the flask, feeling their unseen presence, their suffering intertwining with her own in the oppressive dark.

*

In her cell, the faint light outside her door quivered, its flame now a frail remnant of its former glow. The torch, once burning bright, had dwindled over the past hour, shrinking to a faint, sputtering ember that barely held its ground against the shadows pressing in. Darkness gathered in the corners, thick and unbroken, save for the weak light that struggled on, flaring and fading like a final breath. Where it had once cast steady warmth, it now offered only fleeting glimpses, each flicker weaker than the last. As the cold shadows crept closer, they seemed poised, waiting to consume the torch's last ember.

Every inch of her body felt heavy, her limbs reluctant to obey as she shifted, struggling to rise from the cold dungeon floor. Her knees throbbed, bruised from the unyielding stone beneath, and the damp air clung to her skin like a wet shroud, thick with the sour stench of decay. Each breath came shallow and slow, barely disturbing the dense stillness around her. She swallowed, gathering what remained of her strength, and let her voice drift into the darkness, fragile and worn, as though it might crumble with each word. "Is there any soul who heareth me? I pray thee, answer!"

Silence held, stretching taut. Then came the rattle of chains, sharp and deliberate, echoing through the damp, narrow space like a wordless reply. Sophia's heart quickened, caught between dread and the faintest flicker of hope. *"Why dost they not answer with words? Art they spirits, or art they mutes?"*

Desperation tinged her voice as she called out again, her tone faltering yet insistent, reaching into the depths of the cell block. "Greetings! Pray, what be thy names? Why dost thou keep silent?"

A stir rose from the darkness, chains clinking in ghostly rhythm, yet no voice followed, leaving her with only the hollow scrape of unseen movements.

A sudden clank shattered the stillness as the unmistakable sound of a key turned in the heavy iron lock at the dungeon's main door. The lock groaned, reluctant, as metal scraped against metal, the sound deep and resonant, reverberating down the narrow stone corridor. Sophia froze, her body tense, eyes wide as she strained to glimpse whatever moved beyond the shadows. Her breath caught, suspended somewhere between her chest and her lips.

"Is it Charles yet again? Or have the heavens themselves been gracious, sending forth one who might deliver me from this plight?" Her whispered thoughts barely left her lips, as if the chill around her swallowed them whole.

In the distance, a dim glow flickered through the doorframe, the faintest touch of torchlight casting shadows that stretched and twisted along the damp walls. The light wavered, and a shuffle of uncertain feet accompanied it—footsteps that seemed hesitant, as if the figure doubted whether to enter these depths.

The silence shattered further as a footstep echoed down the corridor, slow and deliberate. Each step struck the stones with purpose, filling the corridor with a hollow resonance. Around her, chains from other cells stirred, faint clinks and rattles as though the unseen prisoners, too, responded to the distant approach. The chains moved in sync with the approaching light, casting brief, shivering shapes that melted back into darkness almost as soon as they appeared.

As the visitor's footsteps echoed closer, a restless clamor swept through the cells. Chains rattled louder, the metallic clinking sharper, more desperate, as though the prisoners reached out with every ounce of strength they had. Shadows jerked and shifted, bodies straining against their bonds, pleading eyes following the visitor's every movement, their silent cries for aid trapped behind weary gazes. Each cell seemed alive with a frenzy of restrained movement, the prisoners' chains scraping and tugging as if they might somehow break free.

The visitor paused before each cell, his torch casting harsh light on hollow faces pressed close to the bars, hands trembling as they reached out, only to fall back in resignation. He leaned in, squinting as if to study each face, his own expression darkening with unease. A sigh escaped him—a shuddering, reluctant exhale—his discomfort palpable as he took in the skeletal forms and pleading eyes.

With each step, the clamor softened, prisoners slipping back into the dark as his torch moved on, leaving only silence in his wake. And as he neared Sophia's cell, his pace slowed, steps dragging, haunted by the quiet desperation that lingered in the empty air.

It doth not sound like Charles, forsooth. Were it truly him, he would ne'er make such gasping sounds. The thought flickered through Sophia's mind, a spark of hope piercing her fear. Whoever moved beyond her cell door now might bring some form of aid. She forced her voice into the dark corridor, steady as she could make it. "Hark! Who moveth in this shadowed place?"

The footsteps halted abruptly, the torchlight quivering as though the visitor swung it around, casting wild shapes that leapt and twisted on the stone walls. Silence hung heavy, and then the figure's voice broke through, strained and uncertain. "Pray, who art thou that dost inquire?"

Sophia's heart thundered in her chest, the familiarity of the voice sending a tremor through her. She knew it, yet its source eluded her. A beat passed, thick with anticipation, before she spoke again, her tone resolute. "As I hath asked first, thou art bound to answer first."

The pause stretched, her breath caught as she waited, fingers pressing firmly into the rough stone beneath her, steadying herself for what might follow.

The visitor's posture shifted, his shoulders easing as he took a deep breath, then resumed his steps, his stride more assured. The torchlight steadied, casting firmer shadows that no longer danced wildly along the walls. A subtle shift in tone hinted at a growing self-assurance, his low pitch now laced with an unmistakable strength. "I am Lord Edward Saint-Clair of Ironstone. Now, prithee, reveal thy name to me."

Sophia's breath caught, the name washing over her like a rush of cold water. Her mind raced, piecing together fragments of memory, each one stoking the faint embers of hope. She pressed a trembling hand to her chest, hardly daring to believe, her voice soft yet clear as she called back. "It is I, Sophia Beaumont."

The silence that followed hung thick, as if the very walls held their breath, waiting to hear his response. Finally, as he neared Sophia's cell, he spoke, his voice barely more than a murmur. "Your Highness?"

He paused, gaze lingering on her, a flicker of doubt crossing his features. Yet more hiding, then? But in the dungeons? A jest, mayhap, to taunt the wretches caged within?

He recalled the grim scenes he had witnessed while passing through the dungeon. Other prisoners, locked in iron collars that chafed against raw skin, some muzzled by the cruel iron of the scold's bridle. One or two bore mouths silenced forever, tongues crudely removed, their faces pale in the torch's faint glow.

A warmth spread through Sophia's chest, her lips parting in a small, breathless smile. Her fingers, which had been tightly clenched in her lap, relaxed, reaching forward as if to touch the air between them. Instinctively, she tried to push herself up, shifting her weight in an attempt to rise, though her legs trembled and her body protested. She managed only a slight lift before her strength failed her, leaving her kneeling in a gesture of both respect and eagerness.

Her voice wavered, barely containing her relief. "Oh, Your Grace! Words cannot convey mine joy at beholding thee!"

Edward's gaze swept over Sophia, taking in her disheveled state—the coarse, peasant dress she wore, torn at the hem and stained with mud that streaked the once-plain fabric. Her golden locks, matted and clumped with grime, appeared almost brown, the gleaming strands dulled beneath layers of dirt. Stray strands clung to her face, tangled and lackluster, as if she had battled the elements—or something far worse. Her eyes, though bright with relief at seeing him, held a deep shadow of exhaustion, a look he'd seen only in soldiers returning from the harshest battles.

With a furrowed brow, he reached for the iron latch, intending to open the door. But as he pulled, the door remained rigid, the lock unmoving under his grip. He paused, fingers tightening around the handle, realisation dawning as he tugged again, his movements sharper, more urgent. Yet the door held fast, the lock unyielding.

He peered through the bars, his voice dropping to a low murmur thick with shock and growing anger. *Be she here against her will? Hath some cruel soul locked her within these walls?*

Sophia's eyes stayed fixed on his grip around the iron latch, her breath hitching as he gave it another firm pull. The door didn't budge, the lock unyielding beneath his hand. Her heart sank, a faint tremor rippling through her as his fingers tightened around the handle in a moment of frustrated pause.

"Pray, tell me thou hast the key!" she whispered, the last shred of hope slipping from her voice.

Lord Edward's jaw tightened, a shadow crossing his face as his gaze narrowed. He arched a brow, his voice clipped with irritation. "Pray tell, why should I possess a key?"

Sophia's body quivered, her voice catching as a wave of realisation washed over her—she had been foolish to think he might carry the key. She swallowed, words catching in her throat, barely able to push them out. "'Tis Noor Winterbourne—she was assailed on mine account. I must know if she still draws breath." The memory of Noor, her forbidden love's twin, filled her mind—the maiden who had barely tolerated her, yet had risked her life to help.

Edward's gaze flickered past Sophia, barely acknowledging her words, his expression turning stony. He let her question hang in the stale air, his eyes sweeping the dungeon for any sign of a guard or a key, finding only the gloom that pressed in from all sides. He let out a low, frustrated sigh. "This place be unfit for a princess." he muttered, the words slipping out under his breath as if speaking to the shadows themselves rather than to her.

The torch outside sputtered weakly in its holder, its flame shrinking to a flicker that barely held back the darkness. Meanwhile, Edward's own torch, steady in his hand, cast a sharper, brighter light, sending shadows stretching and twisting across the damp stone walls. Edward's brow knitted, his gaze sweeping around the cell as if searching for answers hidden in its shadows.

"Wherefore art the jailer?" he muttered, a note of bafflement slipping into his tone as he turned to her. "Who wouldst lock thee away, and for what foul purpose?"

Sophia could barely find her voice. Fear and guilt tangled in her chest, making her throat constrict and her heart sink like a stone. "Mine own brother... the prince," she whispered, her voice trembling. Tears gathered in her eyes, blurring her vision as they threatened to spill.

Edward's face twisted, a storm of confusion and disbelief flashing across his features. He felt his mind grapple with the emotional bomb she'd just dropped. "Charles? Why would he undertake such an act?" he pressed, incredulity hardening his tone. "Is this matter naught but a trifling jest betwixt two siblings?"

Sophia opened her mouth to answer, but the words stuck, lodged in her throat, too heavy to release. Her chest tightened painfully, and a single tear slipped down her cheek, quickly followed by another. Her whole body shuddered as quiet sobs overtook her, each one seeming to echo in the dim cell. "By my troth, 'tis no jest, Your Grace! Pray, look upon me—the state I am in is plain for all to see." Edward's countenance grew stern, his eyes narrowing with resolve. "With all due reverence, Your Highness," he spoke, his voice icy and detached, "this matter is none of mine to meddle in. I cannot take part in this quarrel."

Her heart sank like a stone at his words, and her legs threatened to give way. She gripped the iron bars tightly, her knuckles white, the cold seeping into her skin. Her breath hitched, her chest tightening with each shallow inhale, as if the very air had turned against her. Each breath came ragged, the bitter rejection twisting inside her like a knife. "Your Grace… I beseech thee," she whispered, her voice quivering with desperation, yet her plea was scarcely loud enough to pierce the heavy silence.

Edward's jaw tightened, his eyes aflame with fury. "I have journeyed far to court thee," he proclaimed, his voice growing colder, sharper. "It is grievous enough that I find myself pitted against suitors such as King Shepparton of Valoria—king in title alone, but a hog in appearance and character. Yet many of the realms expect us to join in matrimony! Saint-Clair of Ironwood is deemed a fine match, royal title or no! And yet, without so much as a word, thou didst flee! Now I am left to endure the scorn of mine own kin. They say thou couldst not bear even a single day in my company, and I am rendered a jest amongst them."

He exhaled sharply, anger tightening his expression. "The courts endeavor to make all believe that thou hast been taken against thine own will; yet many do not hold this to be true. I myself harboured doubts until I beheld it with mine own eyes this very morn."

His words struck Sophia like a blow, each syllable heavy with bitterness and hurt. "The kingdom revels in my humiliation," he spat, his voice trembling with emotion. "All because thou didst leave me to face the shame alone."

Her fingers twisted the fabric of her gown, an anxious habit she couldn't suppress. *"Didst he lay eyes upon me this morn?"* "The morn? Yet thou didst not utter a word?"

Sophia's heart pounded in her chest, guilt gnawing at her with every breath. She had fled without thinking of the consequences, without considering the pain she had caused. And now, seeing the anguish etched on Edward's face, the guilt weighed on her like a stone, pressing down until she thought she could not bear it.

Her hand moved slowly through the bars, trembling as though the weight of the moment made each inch feel impossible. Her fingers hovered in the cold air, uncertain, desperate for a connection. "Your Grace," she whispered, her voice thick with regret. In a moment of raw emotion, her fingertips grazed his arm—a gesture meant to convey what words could not. "I never meant to shame thee," she whispered, her voice quivering with the weight of her apology.

"I did not mean to cast dishonour upon thy noble name, my lord." She paused, drawing a shaky breath. "Verily, my heart is beset with trepidation at the thought of wedlock. Though we have been acquainted since the days of our youth, yet love hath not graced us. Thou art a most worthy suitor, yet if thou dost refuse mine hand, I am left at the mercy of others—such as King Shepparton of Valoria, or worse, as thou hast rightly warned!"

Edward's eyes lingered on her outstretched hand before shifting to her face. The unspoken silence between them seemed to stretch, thick and heavy, as though the very air grew colder with each passing second. But then, slowly, he stepped back, pulling away from her touch. His face hardened once more, cold and distant, as if he were determined not to let her apology soften him. "As loyalty be mine own, so shall it remain, bound to none save myself." he muttered, his tone final. His eyes flicked toward the guttering torch outside, the last flickers of flame reflecting in his steely gaze.

Sophia's heart sank at his words. The cold iron of the bars bit into her fingers as she gripped them tighter, her voice breaking as she spoke. "Edward, I beseech thee… I shall do all that is required, even as the kingdom would command. If it be thy wish, I shall court thee as a dutiful bride. Aye, I shall wed thee, shouldst thou desire it. But I entreat thee, lend me thy aid, I beg of thee."

Edward's gaze flickered with something—perhaps surprise, perhaps calculation—but he did not soften. "And how dost thou expect me to free thee from this place?" His voice bore a sharp edge, laced with biting doubt. "This dungeon is steeped in shadows and schemes—no guards stand watch, no jailers linger. Wouldst thou have me report thy plight unto the Queen Mother or the King?" *If her presence here be no jest, then who am I to trust as truth?*

Sophia's heart beat as though it would shatter her chest, her voice barely a whisper. "No keeper doth guard this place," she murmured in haste. "It is but a grave for those they would cast aside, that they be forgotten." Should the King and my mother find out, Charles would surely kill Robert, she thought, the weight of her dread pressing down like iron shackles. She could feel the helplessness sinking into her bones. "Alert none as of yet, for I have a matter of greater import to lay before thee."

Edward's eyes narrowed, his grip firming on the torch. He held himself a little straighter, leaning closer, his gaze fixed on her in a quiet demand. A muscle in his jaw tightened, and he studied her intently, the line of his mouth hardening as he processed her words. "What matter doth hold more weight than thy safe escape from this place?"

He stood rigid, his fingers wrapping tightly around the torch's handle, a faint tension flickering in his gaze. Sophia's fingers twisted together, the knuckles white as her mind wrestled to bring forth details. "I entreat thee, venture forth into the forest, I prithee," she pleaded, her voice trembling. "The entrance lieth to the north of Ravenswood; thou shalt see a red cottage." Her brow furrowed, eyes darting as she grasped at scattered fragments in her memory. "As thou dost enter... thou mayst spy trees marked with bloody handprints—they be mine own." Her voice wavered, and she bit her lip, searching her mind as if through a thick fog. "I know not if the rain hath washed them away, yet press onward, straight and true."

She paused, taking in a shaky breath, her eyes unfocused as she strained to remember. "Seek ye out Noor Winterbourne," she continued, each word an effort. "The dark-haired maiden of rare beauty. Thou shalt know her when thine eyes do fall upon her." She closed her eyes briefly, the strain visible on her face, then added, "Hadst thou looked upon me yestermorn, thou wouldst have found her ever at my side."

Her voice grew softer, weighed down by urgency and guilt. "A great debt binds me to her, for she did strive to save me, and now bears suffering for her kindness. I must know if she yet lives."

For a moment, Edward's gaze faltered, his expression a picture of indecision as two opposing emotions duked it out for dominance. "A commoner's life," he muttered, his voice low and tinged with reluctance. *And yet, doth she venture to such extremes?* Though he rarely spared a thought for the lower classes, there had been something intriguing about Noor—sharp-witted, bold, and almost unsettlingly poised for one of her station. A rarity, he'd admitted privately. But why would Sophia risk herself so? "If it be my wish, dost thou grant thy hand in marriage?" he asked, his words deliberate.

Sophia swallowed hard, a knot of dread twisting tighter with each breath. Each word felt hollow, a bitter betrayal of the love she kept buried deep within her for Robert. Her chest ached with the weight of what she was about to say, but she forced herself to speak, her voice trembling. "If it be thy wish, Your Grace," she murmured, barely able to meet his gaze. "I shall wed thee."

The thought of Robert flooded her mind—his face, his touch, his quiet strength—and her breath caught in her throat. But she had no choice. Noor's life was in Edward's hands now. "But prithee," she continued, her voice quivering, her heart splintering with each word, "I beseech thee, aid me in saving her."

Edward's eyes narrowed as her plea registered. Strange, this fixation on a mere commoner, he thought, but he pushed the impulse to sneer aside. *Yet, loyalty remains steadfast, unyielding in its embrace.*
he reasoned. "Thou hast pledged this as a favour, yet I would have thee court me in earnest." His gaze softened, warmth creeping into his eyes. "Many a couple presents themselves together in public, yet shares naught of their intimacies unless they seek an heir. But I desire more than heirs, Sophia." A faint smile touched his lips, edged with hope. "I would know thee as a true companion."

He could hardly admit it, but her plea stirred something unspoken within him. He thought of the way her laughter had once sparked warmth in grand halls, her glances that conveyed a brightness and wit he rarely saw. Yet he saw her hesitation, the unspoken reluctance in her gaze, and a flicker of unease tugged at him. *Would she ever regard me as aught but mere obligation?* he wondered, a bitter taste at the thought.

Sophia's breath caught as Edward's words hung in the air, their weight pressing down on her. A heavy silence settled between them, her throat tightening as she searched for words that would not come.

The air felt heavier, pressing down on her chest, her body tensing as his unspoken longing settled around her like the walls of the dungeon. It wasn't his affection she craved—it was Robert's, and the thought made her chest ache.

Her hand found the fabric of her gown, gripping it tightly as though it might steady the storm within her. She longed to recoil, to escape this moment, yet she remained rooted, bound by the truth of her circumstances.

Each of Edward's words echoed in her ears, louder with every second, until she could scarcely think over the rising storm within her. She wanted to pull back from what he was asking, yet her reality held her fast.

The cold iron bars pressed into her palms, a reminder of her prison—physical and emotional. With a shuddering breath, she lowered her gaze, the flicker of defiance that had stirred within her fading as quickly as it had flared. "If that is what it takes," she whispered, each word heavy, dragging her deeper into a fate she didn't want. She forced herself to look back at him, her expression carefully composed, though her reluctance showed in the tightness of her jaw and the stiffness of her shoulders.

Edward's gaze softened, his lips parting as he took in her response, relief mingling with a cautious hope. *Mayhap, with time, she will come to see me as more than duty,* he thought, though a flicker of doubt persisted. He mentally shoved the worrying thoughts aside, clearing space for a spark of optimism to take hold.

The last remnants of her will crumbled beneath the weight of his expectations. Though her voice held steady, her heart screamed against the words she was about to speak. "I shall... take the time to know thee." she managed, the hollow promise tasting bitter on her tongue.

Edward's face stiffened, his chiseled jawline suddenly more pronounced as resolve etched its way across his features. A lock of dark hair fell across his forehead as he leaned slightly forward, his blue eyes sparkling with determination. "Verily, I shall command the stable lads to prepare mine steed and beseech a few knights to accompany me, so that we may cover more ground."

Sophia's heart raced at his words, panic surging through her like a wildfire. Her head whipped back and forth, the denial etched on her face as her voice ticked up in a pleading staccato. "No soul may know! If Charles were to uncover this, he might decree her demise, and I too shall be doomed!" The fear laced her words, each one spilling out as if she were fighting to keep the truth at bay.

Edward's brow furrowed, a deep crease forming between his eyebrows as confusion washed over his handsome features. "Why? Why would he, a prince, care for a peasant?" His voice was laced with incredulity, the tension in his jaw tightening as he struggled to comprehend the situation. "Surely thou canst not impart such tidings without elucidating the reason."

Panic tightened its grip on Sophia's chest, her heart racing as her thoughts spiraled. As her breathing sped up, the tension in her voice spiked, mirroring the anxiety washing over her face. "Verily, when I am secure, and when all is perchance safe, I shall reveal unto thee then." Her eyes widened, pleading with him to understand the gravity of the moment. "Yet, if Noor is to possess any chance of survival, the swifter thou dost seek her, the better her fate may be."

Edward rolled his eyes, frustration evident in his expression. "I shall venture forth alone, yet heed my words: the more aid I possess, the greater the chance she may be found. The forest is no trifling expanse."

Sophia's heart raced, frustration and fear colliding within her. She clenched her fists, the urge to shout her objections rising in her throat. He spoke the truth; the vastness of the forest loomed large in her mind, and he would need every bit of help he could muster. But the thought of revealing Noor's plight sent icy fingers of dread creeping down her spine. "Pray, do as I bid thee. Speak naught of this to any soul," she urged, her voice steady despite the turmoil roiling inside her.

Eyes locked, her gaze betrayed its frantic scrambling to stay afloat on a sea of composure. The stakes were high, and each thud of her heart echoed her fears, a silent prayer that Noor would survive whatever fate awaited her in the dark woods.

"As you wish, Your Highness, I shall take my leave at once." Edward turned on his heel, determination evident in his stride. However, a sudden burning curiosity from the princess halted him, her voice cutting through the thick air.

"Before thou departest, I prithee, inform me—who else resides in this place? I discerned the sound of chains and movement, yet no words have reached mine ears. Pray tell, who occupies the other cells?"

He paused, half-turned, the weight of her question settling heavily upon him. Edward's glance darted her way, and his facial expression wavered between rapt attention and growing unease. The crystalclear windows to his soul—those brilliant blue orbs—scrutinized her, sparkling with equal parts concern and fascination.

"I know not the identities of those imprisoned here," he admitted, his voice tinged with reluctance. "They do not speak, for it is not in their power; yet when thou dost depart from this place, mayhap I would counsel thee to avert thine eyes from them, for 'tis a sight unfit for a princess."

Sophia's face went pale, a cold wave of dread washing over her. *What dost he mean?* Fear twitched inside her as she heard the unease creeping into Edward's voice, a worry that refused to let go of her concern for Noor. She inhaled deeply, trying to calm the storm brewing inside her.

"Thank thee, Your Grace. I beseech thee, go with haste and return swiftly once thou hast taken Noor to a healer." Her voice trembled with urgency, each word laced with desperation.

"Yea, Your Highness." Without another glance, he turned fully away, the flickering flame of his torch casting a warm glow that pushed back the shadows around him. As he walked, the light danced along the stone walls, leaving Sophia alone in the dimness, her heart racing with worry for Noor.

*

As the hours blurred into one another after Edward's departure, Sophia could no longer tell whether it was day or night. In the dungeon's thick darkness, time lost all meaning, each moment dragging on painfully as she felt more and more ensnared. Though she hadn't seen Rosalind since fleeing, the thought of her loyal handmaiden still brought a flicker of comfort. She knew Rosalind's absence was a blessing—any encounter with Charles would put her at risk—but the isolation gnawed at her. How long had she been down here, alone?

The cold stone walls and iron bars pressed in around her, trapping her in uncertainty. The ache in her injured leg throbbed persistently, a cruel reminder of the wound that had been cauterized while she lay unconscious. Her stomach growled, a hollow echo in the stillness, and she felt the burn of thirst scratch at her throat. The clanking of chains from the other cells echoed around her, sharp and urgent, as if each prisoner was struggling against their bonds, reminding her that she was not alone in her suffering. The sounds of movement reverberated in the air, a grim chorus of anguish shared among them.

Rosalind had always been more than a servant. In her presence, Sophia found quiet reassurance, a place where her burdens could be set aside, if only for a moment. Now, in this desolate silence, Sophia's mind turned to Robert, her forbidden love. How she longed to confide in Rosalind, to share the weight of the feelings she dared not voice aloud.

Each sound at the door set her heart racing. She longed for Edward's return, for some sign that he had found Noor and taken her to safety. But her thoughts were filled with dark imaginings of what might have happened in the forest. How long had she been waiting? Hours? A day? Perhaps the night had come and gone, unnoticed in the endless gloom.

Sleep had evaded her, the hard, cold ground offering no comfort. The freezing air clung to her, sinking into her bones, her body shaking uncontrollably.

The torch that had long since burned out left her eyes accustomed to the darkness. And yet, through the cracks in the stone, she thought she perceived a hint of light—was it a trick of her weary mind? Had dawn finally arrived, or was she simply imagining it? The relentless cold seeped deeper into her bones, each breath growing more labored, and she couldn't tell how much longer she could endure this torment.

The silence shattered with a sudden, jarring sound—the unmistakable clank of the main dungeon door being unlocked. Sophia's pulse quickened, her senses straining to pierce the thick darkness. *Could it be Edward?* She listened intently as the door swung open, the creak of the hinges echoing through the dungeon like a grim herald. Heavy footsteps followed, each step landing with a firm, deliberate weight that sent faint tremors through the stone floor beneath her.

A glow seeped into the dungeon, distant yet distinct, the torchlight casting long, wavering shadows that barely reached her cell. *The heavens be kind; perchance 'tis Edward with Noor,* she thought, clinging to a fragile thread of hope. *Pray she be safe, and they have come to liberate me from this wretched plight.* But as that hope took root, doubt crept in, twisting her stomach. The clinking of armour rang out, sharp and cold, reverberating through the chamber—a sound that set her on edge.

Two figures descended, their steps echoing louder with each stride, the metallic scrape of armour signaling an unfamiliar presence. With each cautious step, the darkness seemed to close in around her, making her skin crawl, and she felt a raw, primal fear seizing her heart in this barren, isolated landscape.

The silence fractured with the dull thud of heavy boots striking stone, each step echoing ominously, growing louder as they drew closer. Shadows stretched and twisted under the approaching torchlight, casting ominous shapes that flickered and danced against the damp walls. In the cells around her, she sensed movement—the faint scrape of shackles dragging along the stone, and the soft, eerie rustle of bodies shifting in the darkness. Though no voices broke the silence, the other prisoners stirred, an unspoken dread rippling through them.

Sophia's heart pounded as the footsteps neared, their weight pressing down on her like a silent threat. The metallic clink of armour mixed with the shuffling chains in the other cells, the noise echoing through the narrow, suffocating space. It felt as though the dungeon itself braced for what was to come, its cold walls amplifying every sound, every small movement, as if mocking her powerlessness.

The footsteps slowed, then stopped just outside her cell. The jingle of keys punctured the silence, and Sophia's breath hitched as the torchlight flared, illuminating her brother's face—Charles. Behind him loomed Sir Tristan Blackwood, his shadow casting an ominous presence as he reached for the lock, his armoured hand steady and unyielding.

The sharp jingle of iron keys shattered the oppressive silence as Sir Tristan reached for his belt, pulling a rough-hewn key from its ring. Charles stood behind him with a look of cold detachment, his disdainful gaze fixed on Sophia. Sir Tristan, towering in his armour and shadow like a dark sentinel, slid the key into the lock, each grating turn of metal against metal echoing through the dungeon and tightening the dread coiling around Sophia's chest.

"Come, sister," Charles spat, his voice laced with contempt. The cell door groaned as its rusted hinges protested.

Sophia's breath caught as she looked to Sir Tristan, who had begun to draw his blade, its cold steel glinting in the dim light. The towering knight, his face impassive, glanced at Charles for approval as the prince sneered in expectation. "The prince hath commanded thee to rise, Your Highness," Tristan said, his deep voice heavy with warning.

Fear clawed at Sophia's insides, her heart racing wildly as she fought to summon her strength. Her legs wobbled beneath her as she struggled to stand, her fingers curling tightly into her palms, grounding herself against the rising wave of panic.

Prince Charles huffed, annoyance twisting his lips into a sneer. "Lift her, fool!" he barked at Sir

Tristan, his hand cutting through the air as if swatting a fly. "Dost thou need a written decree? Get on with it!" His eyes glinted with disdain, impatient for the task to be done, as if the very act of waiting were beneath him.

In response, Sir Tristan slid his blade back into its sheath with a sharp rasp and stepped forward. His massive hand clamped around her arm with an iron grip that made her gasp as pressure surged through her skin. She flinched, his grip pressing hard enough to make her skin prickle beneath her sleeve, as if the warmth of his touch seared straight through the fabric. "Pray forgive me, Your Highness; I merely follow the commands laid upon me," Sir Tristan muttered, his grip unrelenting.

Charles sneered, his eyes narrowing. "Wouldst thou prefer I visit Robert?" he hissed, malice dripping from each word. Sophia's breath seized in her throat, her body tense with dread. A wave of nausea rose within her as her trembling fingers lifted slightly, as if to halt his words before they struck. She shook her head, eyes wide with silent plea, lips parting though no sound escaped.

Sir Tristan yanked her from the cell, dragging her down the dungeon's dark, narrow corridor. Shadows clung to the walls, shrouding the slumped forms that lined her path, chained and broken. She'd heard the faint clinking of chains while confined to her own cell—whispers of unseen lives. Yet nothing had prepared her for the sight that met her eyes.

Pale, hollow-eyed prisoners slumped in the cells, their faces twisted in silent agony. Some bore the Scold's Bridle, iron clamps biting harshly into their skin, mouths forced shut by cruel metal that forbade even the smallest sound. Others were pinned by the Heretic's Fork, iron prongs pressing relentlessly beneath their jaws, eyes wide with terror but void of any voice. Her gaze faltered as it met those who had been silenced even further, their tongues crudely severed, leaving gaping wounds in place of speech. These eyes stared back at her—hollow, pleading, yet hopeless.

A wave of nausea surged within her, each breath coming shallow and fast as if the dungeon air itself was strangling her. *How had she lived above such horrors, blind to the torment that festered here?* This was no home—this was a graveyard, and she was walking through the shadows of lives forgotten. In this wretched place, suffering lurked behind every moss-covered stone, seeping into the damp walls like rot. Her pulse thundered in her ears, each step a forced march through horror, her only escape lying in the distant light of the corridor's end.

Her legs felt like lead, each step an effort. Sir Tristan's hold on her arm remained unyielding as he dragged her up the narrow staircase. The rough stone beneath her feet and the weight of her body pulled her down with every step. Pain flared in her side, and the ache in her head throbbed with each labored breath. Charles and Sir Tristan moved swiftly ahead, neither sparing a glance back to check if she could keep up. Sophia stumbled, her legs leaden with fatigue, each step sending a dull ache through her bones. Her feet ached, and her legs shook, each step feeling more uncertain, as if they might buckle beneath her at any moment.

At the top of the staircase, Sir Tristan gripped the heavy iron door, bracing himself before he pushed it open with a firm, steady force. The door groaned in protest, its hinges grinding as it swung wide, each movement slow and deliberate under the weight of thick metal and reinforced wood. He filled the doorway, blocking most of the light from beyond as his gaze cut through the dim corridor, sharp and unyielding.

Charles gave her a hard shove, his hand catching her just below the shoulder, enough to throw her off balance. Sophia staggered, catching herself against the rough stone wall, her fingers scraping for a hold as she steadied herself. Her breath came in shallow, uneven gasps, her heart pounding as she fought to keep her footing. Behind her, the iron bolt slammed into place with a final, grim snap, sealing away any thought of turning back.

Sir Tristan's grip was unyielding as iron, each tug forward a sharp reminder that there was no escaping his hold. The narrow hallway felt tighter with every step, its looming walls pressing in, dragging her deeper into a place that had once felt like home but now seemed strange, oppressive. Questions swirled through her mind—where was Charles leading her, and what waited for her ahead? But the fear twisting her insides held her tongue.

Several steps passed in tense silence before she could hold back no longer. "Brother," she whispered, her voice barely above a breath, "pray, where dost thou lead us?"

A flickering torch cast a brief glow over Charles's face, catching the raw edges of the wound on his head. The sight of it turned her stomach, the swollen flesh a reminder of their last brutal encounter. He turned to her, his gaze hard and unyielding, distant as though he were looking past her entirely.

"Thou shalt tell our brother, the king, and mother that I saved thee," he commanded, each word clipped and harsh. "And thou shalt speak of this to no one," he added, his tone like a lash. "Not even Rosalind!" The mention of her handmaiden struck like a blow, and his smirk only deepened at the sight of her reaction. "She serves the crown afore she serves thee. Should she be pressed, she will betray thee without a thought."

The words bit deep, but Sophia forced herself to hide her hurt, her face a mask of composure. She clenched her jaw, burying the sting where he couldn't see it.

They continued on, the silence thick between them. Each step flared the pain in her thigh and sent a fresh ache through her head, but she pressed forward. Sir Tristan's shadow loomed close behind, his presence a constant reminder that escape was a fool's hope.

The halls felt hollow in a way she'd never noticed before, as though the castle itself watched them pass in silence. She could hold her question back no longer. Her voice was barely more than a whisper, raw and trembling. "Why dost we creep through our own halls as if we be thieves in the night?"

Charles's reply was swift, his tone as sharp as the winter wind. "No soul shall know of thy return ere I will it," he snapped. "I am taking thee to the healer, but should he pry too deeply, his life shall be forfeit. Speak not out of turn, lest thou find thyself back in the dungeon."

Sophia's pulse quickened, his threats a coiling snake in her chest. The unspoken warning about Robert hung heavy between them, tightening around her heart with every step. She knew she had no choice; every move bound her tighter in the grasp of her brother's power.

*

Sophia's breath hitched as they neared the imposing doors of the grand hall. Fear gnawed at her insides, each step a sharp reminder of the pain throbbing in her side. Sir Tristan's iron grip on her arm never faltered, his fingers digging into her flesh, dragging her forward without mercy.

Her eyes darted around the empty passageway, the absence of guards and servants heightening her confusion. A hasty whisper escaped her, the sentence spinning out into the air like a skipped stone. "Where art the guards? The usher? Where doth mother tarry?" Her voice wavered, but Charles offered no reply, his silence as cold as the stone walls surrounding them.

Sir Tristan gave her arm another hard yank, and she stumbled into the hall. As she jerked suddenly, a searing bolt of pain shot through her injured side, but she choked back a scream, her jaws locked in a fierce determination to show no weakness. Shadows crawled across the stone walls like living things, as if the dim torchlight was awakening secrets the ancient hall had kept hidden for centuries.

Inside the grand hall, the fire crackled in the hearth, casting restless shadows that crawled across the stone walls. Two figures awaited her arrival—Ambrose Thornbrook, the infamous healer from Wound-Ward on Cutthroat Row, and his assistant. Ambrose's reputation was as shadowed as the alleyways of Cutthroat Row itself: he was the healer who patched up rogues and murderers, mending wounds that law-abiding folk would rather ignore. *But why him?* The thought struck her as her heart raced with unease. *Why would Charles choose a healer of Cutthroat Row's underworld instead of one of the royal physicians?*

Ambrose's gaze met hers, dark and intense, assessing her with a precision honed by years of treating men who survived by their wits and blades. Though he stood in the grandeur of the royal hall, his presence seemed to pull in the shadows, as if the firelight recoiled from the reputation he carried. His assistant lingered nearby, a tray of worn, almost menacing instruments in hand, tools that looked more suited to a back-alley clinic than a castle.

Sophia could feel their stares, weighted and unyielding, pressing against her chest until each breath felt tighter. She fought to steady herself, her heart pounding with confusion and a growing dread.

The air was thick with silence. The only sound was the steady crackle of the flames. Ambrose's eyes widened as Charles spoke, his voice sharp and biting. "The princess."

Ambrose and his assistant exchanged startled glances, clearly unprepared for the sight before them. Sophia's gown, once pristine, was now torn and stained with dried blood. Exhaustion was etched on her face, her skin washed out, her limbs quivering like stripped branches in the wind. The healer's breath caught in his throat as he took in the full extent of her disarray.

He had seen wounded nobles before, but the sight of the princess in such a state was beyond anything he'd imagined. Every tear in her clothing, every smear of blood and mud told the story of her ordeal without words.

Ambrose stood frozen, his mouth moving but no sound escaping. His assistant looked equally stunned, standing rigid as if not daring to breathe.

Charles's voice sliced through the air, shattering the silence. "Well?" he snapped, his impatience like a blade. "Get on with it!"

Ambrose rushed forward, his footsteps echoing in the cavernous hall. He dropped to his knees beside Sophia, hands already moving to examine her wounds.

Sir Tristan Blackwood loomed nearby, silent but menacing. His presence filled the space like a dark cloud, his armour barely creaking as he moved. Though he said nothing, his watchful eyes never left Sophia.

The healer worked quickly, his fingers tracing the cuts and bruises on Sophia's arms and side. His assistant stood just behind, holding a tray of instruments, eyes still wide with shock. The hall seemed to close in around Sophia as Ambrose tended to her wounds, the oppressive weight of her brother's presence looming over her like a shadow she couldn't escape.

"Your Highness," he murmured, dipping his head respectfully. With a trained touch, he gently but firmly found her pulse, tuning into the steady beat of her heart.

Despite the tension gnawing at her, Sophia held herself steady, refusing to let her unease show. She drew in a deep breath, an attempt to steady herself.

A wince flickered across Sophia's face as the healer's rough fingers probed the tender bump on her head, sending a stinging pain that radiated through her. Her eyelids clenched shut as she fought the uncomfortable intrusion.

"Pray, what manner of injury didst thou suffer, fair lass?" Ambrose's mutter carried a note of concern, etching lines of worry.

Sophia forced her eyes open, struggling to focus through the haze of pain. She shifted uncomfortably, not sure what to say.

She bit back the truth about Charles, feeling the weight of it press down on her as the healer's gaze lingered, sharp and scrutinizing.

Like a precision instrument, his gaze calibrates on her, slicing through the fog of false innocence, hunting for the flicker of duplicity that would give her away.

"Verily, I must have stumbled and struck some manner of object," she finally said, her voice barely above a whisper. The words sounded feeble and unconvincing even to her own ears.

Ambrose's gaze held on Sophia, his eyes shadowed with quiet scrutiny, as if her words might reveal some hidden truth. "Struck, dost thou say?" he repeated, a note of doubt slipping into his voice. Over them, the prince's cold glare lingered, a reminder that each word carried its own risk. "Canst thou recall how thou didst feel when the blow did land? Didst thou feel dizziness, perchance disorientation?"

Sophia's pulse quickened, her gaze slipping briefly from her brother's sharp stare. "Aye, I felt unsteady, and even now, the ache doth linger," she murmured, swallowing the rising unease. "There is a throbbing within mine head. I... I must have lost mine footing." The words hung heavy on her tongue, as though resisting even the air itself.

Her mind drifted back to dim fragments of her capture—she could scarcely recall how she'd come from the forest to the dungeon. "Verily, it is as though mine own thoughts hath slipped away," she added quietly.

Ambrose studied her a moment longer, a faint, tempered smile touching his lips. "With rest, in time thy mind shall find its way back, and thou shalt be as thou once wast," he replied. But his gaze drifted to the wound upon her leg, his tone gentle yet pressing. "And pray, what of this, Your Highness?" he inquired.

Sophia cast a quick glance at Charles, who stood nearby, arms crossed, his face unreadable. Suppressing her frustration, she forced her expression to remain neutral. "I recall it not," she replied simply, hoping to end his questions.

Ambrose's eyes widened slightly, though he kept silent. How could any noble forget such grievous wounds? The knot upon her head, the deep gash upon her leg—hurts such as these were not easily forgotten. Yet he held back his thoughts, keenly aware of the prince's imposing presence and the unspoken threat that filled the air.

In the dim light, Ambrose's thoughts drifted to countless wounded souls he had tended—the soldiers, thieves, and wayward men who had whispered tales of punishments endured under nobles' orders. Some had cursed the names of princes, yet he was a healer, not a judge. He knew well the lines he could not cross.

"Your Highness," he spoke at last, calm yet concerned. "Be assured thou shalt recover well, yet I must impress upon thee the need for rest, lest thou worsen thine injuries."

Straightening, he met her gaze with quiet resolve. "I would counsel thee to take up a walking staff," he advised gravely, "and to guard thy strength."

Turning to his assistant, he directed, "See that she is given salve for her wounds and head."

The assistant, visibly nervous, fumbled through Ambrose's satchel, his hands trembling as he searched for the vial. The faint clinking of glass echoed through the hall's thick silence, each sound a reminder of the prince's expectant gaze.

At last, he retrieved the vial and moved swiftly to Sophia's side, his hands unsteady as he offered it to her. His anxious glance shifted from Sophia to the prince, as if he, too, felt the silent tension that weighed upon them. With a shaky exhale, Ambrose handed her the vial, his gaze flickering between Sophia and the prince with a wariness that spoke volumes. His fingers lingered just a moment longer than necessary, as if reluctant to relinquish her to whatever fate awaited. Sophia's hand closed around the vial, her fingers clenching so tightly that her knuckles blanched. "Thank thee, I am most grateful," she whispered, her voice thin, stretched taut as a wire.

She kept her eyes lowered, focused on the cold stone beneath her feet, jaw set, the faintest quiver betraying the struggle within. Though she dared not lift her gaze, Charles's presence loomed over her—a silent threat, heavy as a storm cloud. Like a spectral presence, his gaze materialized before her, unmoving and suffocating, draining the warmth from her skin.

Ambrose's assistant, standing a pace behind him, was less composed. His hands fidgeted nervously at his sides, eyes darting between Charles and Ambrose as though unsure of where his focus should lie. His breaths came shallow and quick, almost audible in the charged silence of the hall. A fine sheen of sweat glistened on his brow, and his fingers fumbled with the edge of his satchel, as if he longed to bolt for the door yet didn't dare move a muscle under the prince's gaze.

Ambrose, at least, is no stranger, Charles thought, watching the healer with a calculating eye. He had learned long ago that loyalty could be bought, and Ambrose, for all his dealings with Cutthroat Row's criminals and whores, had earned his trust more than once. In darker hours, when wounds needed tending far from royal eyes, Ambrose had stitched his skin and stanched his blood. They'd even shared a laugh over a tankard of ale in the grime-streaked back room of a Cutthroat tavern. Yet this assistant, this skittish little creature beside him, was another matter.

The boy was a twitching mess, hands unsteady and feet shifting. Charles eyed him with distaste. A stranger, and a fool, he thought, his distrust curling cold and certain in his gut. He didn't know the lad, and he didn't trust any hand to touch the princess who lacked either discretion or courage. Whatever Ambrose saw in the boy mattered little to him. The assistant had done nothing to earn his confidence, and if one wrong word or motion revealed even a hint of indiscretion, Charles would see him gone without a second thought.

Ambrose stepped back, his inspection complete, though his eyes lingered on her, shadowed with concern. "If that be all, Your Highness?" he ventured, his tone cautious, sensing the tension thrumming through the hall. Ambrose's gaze drifted to the jagged wound on Charles's head, raw and clearly visible. He hesitated for a breath, as though he might offer his services for it, but something in the prince's cold expression held him back.

"That shall suffice, thank thee," Charles replied curtly, his impatience in his voice sharp as a blade's edge. A single, decisive movement of his hand signaled the exit, leaving no room for misinterpretation. "The princess requires rest."

Ambrose, catching the command in Charles's tone, inclined his head deeply, signaling the end of his duties. His assistant, casting a final, trembling glance at the prince, scrambled to gather their instruments, his clumsy hands betraying the nervousness he could scarcely contain.

Charles's gaze lingered on them as they exited, the door creaking shut, each step echoing faintly as they departed down the corridor. Alone with Sophia once more, he felt his control settle like an iron clasp. In the flickering torchlight, shadows played across his face, a reminder of the power he held—one that no healer, and certainly no assistant, could ever begin to threaten. The silence in the hall shattered abruptly, an unexpected noise cutting through like a blade from the wooden chests in the corner. Sophia's breath stilled, her eyes widening as the lids creaked open—pushed by unseen hands.

A chill seized her heart, pounding fast enough to drown out her thoughts. She took an unsteady step back, her foot catching on the uneven stone floor, nearly throwing her off balance. "Charles!" she gasped, her voice cracking with terror.

But Charles's face remained unreadable, his expression as still as stone, giving away nothing, as though he'd anticipated this all along. His cold indifference tightened the dread twisting in her chest.

With a low groan, the lids swung open fully, revealing two shadowed figures emerging from within. They rose slowly, unfolding like shadows creeping into the light, moving with a chilling, deliberate grace that seemed to drain warmth from the room. Cloaked and hooded, they stepped into the dim glow, their faces obscured, their every movement exuding danger.

The flickering torchlight caught on the edge of a dark, coiled symbol stitched across their chests—markings unfamiliar to Sophia but steeped in foreboding. Her pulse thundered, hands trembling at her sides as they moved closer, exuding a silent threat that made her blood run cold. Instinctively, she moved back, taking a small, involuntary step behind her brother, despite the gnawing doubt that flared in her mind. Would he even shield her if it came to it?

Cold dread curled through her as questions spun wildly in her mind. "Who art these folk? Why hast they been concealed in this place? Dost thou think they meant me harm?" Her mind raced with a torrent of questions, each one darker than the last.

The figures' every movement was measured, slow, as they advanced, and Sophia's heart drummed so wildly she feared they could hear it. Her breaths came shallow, cold panic gripping her chest, forcing her to look desperately to Charles for reassurance. But his expression was impenetrable, offering nothing but the same detached control he wore like armour. There was no comfort, no hint that he might even care for her safety.

One of the cloaked figures paused, waiting for a signal. And then, a small nod from Charles—the merest tilt of his head—set them in motion. They were no random strangers, no accidental visitors. He had summoned them, hidden away until this very moment.

Charles's gaze flicked to Ambrose's assistant, his brow lowering with a shadowed intent. Though ordinarily he would have had no trouble sending both healer and assistant away, the recent events with Noor had left him unsettled, a rare crack in his trust. His eyes narrowed in distrust as he looked at the assistant, trembling and visibly uneasy. The boy had shown too much fear, too little discretion.

"Handle the assistant," Charles commanded softly, his voice laced with cold finality. "Let it seem as though misfortune hath befallen him."

Sophia's breath froze, her mouth parting in horror as the meaning of his words sank in. "Brother!" she choked, her voice barely a whisper, her mind struggling to process the cruelty of his command.

Her lips parted, trembling, struggling to make sense of what he'd commanded. *"Verily, he cannot mean to… to order the end of a life for mere suspicion?"* She inwardly gasped.

Charles's ire flared within his eyes as he turned sharply toward Sophia, his voice dripping with disdain. "Know thy place, sister!" The words sliced through the air like a whip, a bitter reminder of the lowly station women held in their society. Sophia was in no position to question his authority, especially not after the events that had transpired.

"Count thyself fortunate it is not thy fate," he sneered, his tone laced with acrimony. "After such a pathetic display!" His words were a harsh rebuke, underscoring the consequences of her actions.

He advanced, his presence looming ominously as he leaned closer, whispering in her ear with a venomous hiss. "His blood is upon thy hands. Take heed: when thou standest before the court, thou must artfully explain how thou wert attacked by a commoner and that I, thy gallant brother, did save thee."

Sophia stood frozen, her heart racing as a torrent of emotions threatened to drown her. Tears shimmered in her eyes, unbidden, yet Charles's gaze remained as frigid as winter's breath, devoid of any trace of compassion. Without a flicker of remorse, he turned to the hooded figures, his voice cutting through the air with commanding authority. "Seek out Lucian Blackthorn," he ordered, the weight of his words heavy with expectation. The darkness seemed to stretch and twist around the figures as they rose from the shadows, their hooded silhouettes casting an aura of foreboding as they moved across the stone floor, silent as death.

The figures acknowledged Charles's command with bowed heads, each cloaked form bearing the sinister emblem of the Shadow Serpents: a darkly coiled serpent stitched over their chests, a symbol steeped in secrecy and silent menace. The torchlight caught briefly upon this mark, sending faint glints across the ominous insignia as they moved toward the hall's edge.

Sir Tristan, brow furrowed, awaited his lord's next call. "Inform the guards to resume their posts," Charles instructed sharply, his tone leaving no room for dissent. "And summon my attendant at once."

Tristan nodded, bowing his head in swift obedience before turning on his heel, the metal of his armour clinking softly as he departed, each step echoing with cold purpose.

In that moment, Sophia couldn't decide what was worse: being left alone with her callous brother or in the presence of these cloaked figures, who seemed all too willing to carry out his orders, no matter how sinister they may be.

As the doors closed behind them, a sense of foreboding settled over Sophia like a heavy blanket.

Her hands clasped together, fingers digging into her palms as her lips shaped a silent prayer.

She dared not utter the words aloud, but within the depths of her heart, she pleaded for mercy upon the man they had been ordered to end. With each whispered plea, she hoped against hope that the gods above might grant him a swift passing, sparing him the fate that awaited at the hands of Charles's mercenaries.

Charles lowered himself into his chair with a labored sigh, his movements unsteady, his posture hunched. Suddenly, the world spun, forcing him to brace a hand against his forehead, the pounding ache from his earlier blow throbbing as if his skull were lined with molten lead.

Despite his discomfort, he kept silent, unwilling to betray weakness before his sister. Biting back the pain, he masked himself with indifferent resolve. The blow from the rock in the forest had struck him harder than he dared admit, but he would not falter—not before her.

But Sophia, clouded by her own anguish and fear, took no notice of the subtle signs of his struggle. She eased herself down in the chair beside him, her face etched with anxiety. With a quiet gasp, she lowered herself, each movement strained, her breaths shallow and quickening. The words fell from her lips, trembling as she spoke, "What hath befallen thee, brother? What foul fate hath cast such shadows upon thy soul?" Though she knew he would not offer a sincere reply, the question escaped her nonetheless.

Charles turned his cold gaze upon Sophia, disdain flickering across his features. "Thou art but a princess," he uttered, his voice steeped in scorn. "Thou hast known naught but a paltry share of misfortune." His tone conveyed an air of superiority, as though his suffering granted him an unyielding dominion over her.

Sophia's heart clenched, an ache deepening within her as she struggled to comprehend his words. *How could he understand her pain, her heartbreak, her longing? He knew nothing of the trials of womanhood, nothing of the agony that burdened her heart.* His cruelty cut deeper than any blade.

Her eyes found the fire, the faint warmth flickering there, yet too far to ease the chill gripping her bones.

She ached to move closer, to feel even a semblance of comfort, but even the flames could not thaw the chilling despair that clung to her. With a heavy sigh, her eyes moved toward the narrow window, feeling as though she were still trapped within the cold and unyielding walls of the dungeon.

A lump formed in her throat as her thoughts strayed to Robert. Would she ever see him again, be able to explain her heart to him? Would she find a way to beg forgiveness for Noor's ill fate? The mere thought of never holding him brought tears to her eyes, each tear blurring her vision with a swell of sorrow she could no longer contain.

As her silent tears fell, Sophia turned a disbelieving glance toward her brother, the weight of her grief pressing down, leaving her feeling as trapped and powerless as a bird with clipped wings, yearning for freedom.

"How dost thou dare imply that I know naught of suffering?" Sophia's voice cracked with emotion, raw and fierce, as she lashed out at her brother. "We both bear the weight of our father's loss, the same burden of a shattered heart!" Tears blurred her vision as she spoke, her words spilling out in anguish.

"Thou hast led a life of privilege and freedom," she continued, her voice quivering with barely contained rage. "Whilst I have been forced to endure the suffocating confines of corsets, to be paraded like a prize mare for barter. My desires are trampled underfoot as if they were naught but leaves in the wind."

Her vision blurred with tears, yet she pressed on, her voice growing sharper. "And just when I dared carve out a semblance of independence beyond these walls, thou dost rip it away from me!" Her voice cracked, carrying the raw ache of betrayal, the injustice weighing down upon her heart.

Neither dared meet the other's gaze, too swept up in their own pain to bridge the gap between them.

"Thou hast taken the life of the sister of the man I hold dear!" Sophia's voice trembled on the verge of breaking. Each word was a fresh wound, deepening the ache in her chest. "And now thou hast bound me here, well knowing how it doth torment my soul. I beseech thee," her voice steadied, tinged with steely resolve, "why dost thou persist in this cruelty?"

Charles's gaze flickered with something fierce, his fingers drumming against the table's edge as the firelight flickered over his face. "Our father," he began slowly, savoring the words as though each one were a precious jewel, "proclaimed that I would be a great king, should fortune grant me the chance."

He paused, his eyes darkening with ambition, fingers tightening against the polished wood. "He spake of how I might render our land mightier than any other." His voice lowered, like a secret being borne out of the shadows. "He believed I had the power to force foreign lords to kneel, to make their crowns bow, and their riches pour into our coffers." A cold smile lingered on his lips, the dream of dominion stirring in his gaze.

Sophia felt a wave of nausea rise within her. The brother she once knew was gone, replaced by this stranger who hungered for power beyond reckoning.

"The crown rightly ought to be mine!" he hissed, his eyes burning with an unsettling fervor. "Should the throne elude me, I shall see this land drown in ruin and rebuild from its ashes a realm worthy of a true king!"

"Nay, Charles! The crown hath ever been John's destiny," she whispered, her voice tinged with fear. "He is the firstborn son, the rightful heir. Briarwood's armies are vast, yet many would perish in such a clash! Shouldst thou fail, it would spell ruin for Briarwood, the realm crumbling into dust!"

Her voice wavered, and she forced herself to breathe, to steady the growing dread that clawed at her insides. *Could he truly be willing to take John's life for the throne?*

The weight of dread pressed down upon her, every possibility pulling her deeper into despair. A sickening chill settled over her as her gaze fell upon him, recognizing that her brother—this twisted shadow of the man bound to her by blood—might sacrifice everything in pursuit of a crown.

Sophia's body trembled with the effort of standing upright, feeling as if her legs would betray her and collapse beneath her. She fought to remain steady, loath to show any hint of weakness before her relentless brother.

Charles's expression hardened, his ire only deepening as she dared question his resolve. "He may be the firstborn, but our father knew where the kingdom's strength lay!" he spat, a hint of desperation lacing his words. "I have labored more than any other to deserve that throne!"

Sophia met his gaze, her heart thundering as the weight of his fury bore down upon her. She felt the force of his ambition pressing in like a storm, yet a fire sparked in her own eyes as she held her ground. Despite the terror gnawing at her, she refused to shrink back, facing him with all the courage she could muster, even as his voice rose like a tide that threatened to drown her.

Just as the tension thickened, the door creaked open, drawing all eyes as Charles's personal attendant stepped inside. Charles snapped instantly, his voice sharp as a blade. "Who art thou? What dost thou seek?"

Baldwin Honorcrest, the prince's loyal attendant, entered with a purposeful stride, his arms cradling an unexpected guest. Midnight, Charles's sleek and enigmatic cat, settled comfortably in Baldwin's hold, her dark eyes mirroring the quiet mystery of the hall. As Baldwin's gaze shifted to Sophia, shock visibly cracked his otherwise composed expression. *The princess? She yet lives?* For a brief moment, confusion flickered in his brow, but he kept silent, well-acquainted with the wisdom of keeping to his station. Whatever had brought the princess back to these walls, the air between brother and sister hung thick with unspoken tension.

"Your majesties," Baldwin murmured, bowing low, the cat pressed to his chest. "Midnight hath been groomed as per thy wishes."

A flicker of warmth softened Charles's cold eyes, an expression rare and fleeting. Yet, as quickly as it had come, the moment vanished. With razor-sharp intensity, his eyes cut through the quiet, shattering the serenity of the moment. "Feed her!" he barked, the order snapping like a whip. "And send a messenger to summon our brother and the Queen Mother—forthwith." The weight of his command darkened the hall, casting a shadow over Baldwin as he lowered his head in silent obedience.

Sophia's heart pounded as dread coiled within her, the chill of suspicion tightening around her thoughts. *Why doth Charles summon our mother and brother? Could it be that he meaneth to bring them harm?* The notion sent a creeping fear along her spine, rooting her to her seat, helpless beneath Charles's calculating stare.

Baldwin, sensing the urgency, tightened his grip on Midnight. He backed away, each step measured and precise, as if mindful that the slightest misstep might rouse the prince's wrath. Midnight's tail flicked lazily, unaware of the tension, her gaze coolly surveying the room as Baldwin reached the door. Without another word, he slipped into the corridor, the echo of his retreating steps fading into the darkened hall.

With a sudden, menacing pivot, Charles turned his gaze upon Sophia. "Thou must needs put on a grander display for our brother and mother, lest they perceive thy shortcomings as treasonous folly," he commanded, his tone laced with threat. Sophia bit her lip, nodding, her heart heavy with foreboding.

A storm raged within her. If only she could summon the courage to speak against him, to let slip his treacheries for all to know. *Could he truly believe he was untouchable in his web of lies, so certain of his cunning?*

A flash of rebellious spirit ignited in her chest. "Even thou canst not be so heartless?" she challenged, her voice trembling with the weight of her fears for her loved ones. Their eyes clashed, the world around them fading as time stood still in that charged moment. "It doth trouble me to ponder that thou wouldst take a life, yet our brother? Our mother?" Confusion twisted her features. "Surely, thou wouldst not be so bold as to attempt such a deed?"

A chilling smirk crept across the prince's lips. "Oh sister," he replied, a dark chuckle escaping him. His mirth was stifling, wrapping around her like a thin sheet of frost, a warning to keep her distance. "I desire not to end their lives," he proclaimed, rising to his full height. He sauntered toward the roaring fire that danced in the hearth, his silhouette flickering against the flames. Rubbing his hands together, he continued, "Nay, I desire for our brother, the king, to witness as I seize the kingdom from him."

His voice dripped with cold satisfaction. "Softly, I shall lay claim to all that he doth possess." The flickering firelight accentuated the dangerous glint in Charles's eyes, casting an eerie glow upon his features.

Summoning all her strength, Sophia rose to her feet, pain echoing in the hushed hall with each labored breath. Like quicksand, the headache dragged her down into its dark cycle. But an alluring glow—weak yet resilient—brightened the surrounding fog, hinting at an escape from the numbing chill that seeped into her bones.

Exhaustion fell away as she reached the fireside, the gentle heat working its magic to thaw her frozen limbs and still her racing thoughts. It was a blessing she had deemed impossible after the torment of the cold dungeon night. With her eyes squeezed shut, she let the fire's radiant heat wash over her, its soft flames seeming to whisper sweet nothings in her ear.

But then, her gaze—a storm of resentment and defiance—locked onto Charles. Hate roiled within her heart, bold and unwavering. "Dost thou not fear that I would spill all thy secrets?" she spat, the challenge clear in her tone.

Charles gazed into the flickering flames, his countenance as blank as a winter's night, void of any remnant of compassion. At length, he spoke, his voice a cold whisper that cut through the air. "Thy foolish fondness for the peasant lad hath sealed thy silence." He paused, the weight of his words settling like a thick fog. "Shouldst thou choose to defy, not only shall the boy's life be forfeit, but our brother shall also bear the burden of sorrow." He smirked, "Our brother's heart."

At this, a sharp pang gripped Sophia's heart, as if a vice had tightened around it. The notion of Robert facing such a dire fate was a torment too cruel to endure. Yet a question spilled forth from her lips, tinged with confusion. "Our brother's heart, thou sayest?" she murmured, bewildered. Who had captured King John's affections? Her mind raced through the tangled web of courtly intrigues. Could it be the Duchess De Valois, Madame Élisabeth, the one rumored to have caught King John's eye? But what use would her downfall serve Charles's dark designs? Could her brother truly hold affection for the Duchess? Sophia had never warmed to the haughty lady, whose Francian accent grated upon her ears.

How curious that Madame Élisabeth, having dwelt in Stowshire since her youth, spoke not the tongue of Briarwood with any grace! The duchess had sought the king's hand since her betrothal ended in bloodshed, and now, it seemed she might ascend to the throne. Surely, the court would not countenance a queen who spoke so poorly of Briarwood's tongue!

In a realm rife with whispers and misinterpretations, the truth of courtly romances lay shrouded in uncertainty.

It had not occurred to her that Charles could be speaking of Mary Winterbourne. Though she knew the king and Mary had crossed paths once, the depths of Charles's plots to ensnare King John's heart with Mary remained a secret to her.

A dull throb blossomed in her head, making the effort to think a burdensome task. The fog that clouded her mind dulled her senses, and soon, the spinning world began to weigh heavily upon her. Desperation led her to grasp at Charles's arm, seeking stability. Yet, he offered no comfort; his sneer spoke of disdain, leaving her feeling small and insignificant.

"Brother," she breathed, her voice naught but a whisper, "I beseech thee for sustenance." Her words stumbled forth, and with great toil, she lowered herself to the floor, each movement a valiant struggle against her frail strength. "I vow to submit to thy will," she promised, her voice trembling like a delicate leaf in the mind.

The air thickened with her plea, a delicate request for a moment's respite from her torment. Time itself seemed to pause, the crackle of the fire echoing in the silence as the siblings stood in confrontation.

Charles's expression remained a mask, betraying nothing of the thoughts churning within. A brief crease formed on his brow, revealing the weight of his thoughts. After a moment, he broke the silence with sharp, measured words. "The servants shall call upon us for our repast." he declared, his tone unyielding.

In the stillness of the grand hall, the flames danced in the hearth, casting a warmth that wrapped around them, a soft, inviting glow that seemed to whisper of comfort and solace.

As moments lingered, the flickering light lulled Sophia into a drowsy state.

Like a haven from the day's struggles, the warmth encased her, its comforting heat thawing the frost of fatigue that had gripped her body. The chill that had seeped into her bones from the dungeons began to fade, replaced by the soothing glow of the fire. In the silence, her body relaxed, releasing its pent-up energy as the shadows played hide-and-seek around her, their gentle whispers nudging her towards a rejuvenating rest.

She felt herself surrendering to the gentle lull of slumber, her eyelids growing heavy as the fire's soft heat cocooned her like a tender blanket. Gradually, she drifted, slipping into the hazy realm where dreams beckoned with tender whispers.

*

<u>An hour hence</u>

The suddenness of Sophia's awakening was akin to a tempest breaching the calm of a still pond. Her eyes flung open, the loud and heavy knock upon the door shattering the tranquility that had wrapped her in slumber's embrace.

As she blinked rapidly, attempting to cast off the vestiges of her dreams, Sophia surveyed the grand hall, her mind momentarily adrift in confusion. The crackling fire still danced merrily in the hearth, casting flickering shadows that played upon the ancient stone walls. Yet, that peace was no more; the intrusion loomed heavy, like a storm cloud threatening to break.

Despite the disruption, Charles remained resolute, his gaze locked upon the flames as he commanded, "Enter!" His voice rang through the hall with an authority that seemed to bounce off the very stones.

The door groaned upon its hinges, swinging wide to reveal Baldwin Honorcrest, the attendant who had earlier brought forth Midnight. At the sight of the familiar figure, Charles's icy demeanor thawed just a touch, a hint of warmth flickering in his stern visage.

"Your Majesty," Baldwin announced, his tone laced with respect yet edged with urgency. "Midnight hath been well fed."

A fleeting softness washed over Charles's stern features, a hint of warmth breaking through his usual reserve. "Bring her hither," he commanded, his tone firm yet laced with a gentle affection that seemed to light his eyes.

Baldwin approached with swift, purposeful strides, cradling Midnight with care before placing her into Charles's outstretched arms. The moment their eyes met, a silent bond formed; Charles held the cat against his chest, a rare softness enveloping him. "There, there, Midnight," he murmured, his voice low and soothing.

His fingers sank into Midnight's fur, brushing through it with a tenderness that belied his often harsh demeanor. Midnight nestled against him, purring softly as if she recognised the solace of his embrace. The flickering warmth of the hearth cast dancing shadows across their forms, wrapping them in a cocoon of comfort—a fleeting glimpse of love shared in the quiet of the grand hall.

For a brief moment, Sophia beheld a side of her brother seldom revealed—a man who lavished care upon his pet, the firelight casting a warm glow upon the intimate scene.

Baldwin stepped back, offering the prince and princess a measure of privacy by the hearth. Clearing his throat softly, he pierced the silence that had settled in the hall, announcing, "Whene'er it pleaseth thee, Your Highnesses, your repast doth await." His voice bore the weight of formality, echoing gently through the chamber.

Charles's gaze shifted from the fire to Baldwin, intensity sparking in his eyes. "We desire to feast at once," he declared, then turned his gaze to Sophia, before returning to Baldwin with renewed urgency. "Assist the princess to her feet, forthwith!"

"Aye, Your Highness," Baldwin replied, nodding respectfully. His tone was soothing, imbued with kindness as he gracefully knelt before Sophia, extending his arm with a gentle flourish. "Permit me, Your Highness," he offered, his eyes gleaming with empathy. "Verily, it is an hour to bid thee welcome home, Your Highness. I am certain that the Queen Mother and the King shall find relief in thy return. I know well that Rosalind doth miss thee greatly."

Weary yet grateful, Sophia accepted Baldwin's hand, finding solace in his support as she rose from the floor. With delicate guidance, he draped her arm over his shoulder, offering steady assistance as they began to traverse the hall together, following in Charles's wake. Their footsteps fell into a rhythmic cadence, even as Sophia's mind swirled in pain, each step a labour against the haze that threatened to engulf her. Yet amidst her discomfort, the promise of sustenance and a moment of respite called to her like a beacon in the gloom.

*

As they proceeded along the corridor leading from the grand hall to the morning banqueting chamber, Charles came to an abrupt halt, his piercing gaze fixing upon Baldwin. The passageway, lined with towering stone walls, bore a chill that clung to Sophia's skin, each echo of their footsteps reverberating through the vast, dimly lit space. Charles's voice cut through the still air, sharp as the edge of a sword. "Pray, summon forth my latest chambermaid," he commanded, his words resonating against the walls with an authority that left little room for question.

Baldwin's expression faltered, doubt creeping into his features. "Your Highness," he stammered, "the chambermaid hath yet to arrive." His voice was tentative, hushed against the background of faint, distant murmurs and the occasional clink of a servant's tray echoing from beyond the corridor's stone archways.

Charles's brow knit in irritation, his frustration bubbling beneath the surface. "She hath yet to arrive?" he demanded, his tone sharp as a blade. The torches along the corridor walls sent wavering light across his stern features, shadows shifting with each flicker of the flame.

Baldwin's shoulders stiffened as Charles's gaze bore into him, the unyielding scrutiny as silent yet powerful as the stone around them. "I know not why, Your Highness," he murmured, his voice thin and wavering like a branch buffeted by a harsh wind. "But I shall seek her forthwith."

Inwardly, thoughts unfolded that he dared not speak aloud: *Foolish she is, indeed, to forgo her shift. Yet I cannot wholly blame her; the servants within these walls hold her in disdain. This realm of his madness hath become a tempest she is ill-equipped to weather. What strange obsession drives thee to fixate upon her? An enigma, wrapped in a veil of dread, she surely is.*

Charles's gaze hardened as he observed Baldwin assisting the princess, his fingers drumming impatiently against his side. The corridor stretched ahead, flanked by narrow windows through which cold morning light filtered, casting a bluish glow that mingled with the torchlight, making shadows stretch and twist across the stone floor. With a clipped, unyielding tone, he commanded, "Go with haste now! I desire her presence before me at once!" The order rang out, leaving no doubt of the prince's simmering impatience.

Sophia's pulse quickened, her heart thudding as her brother's command echoed down the corridor. She felt a sudden desperation as Baldwin began to withdraw, her grip tightening around his arm in a silent plea. Her breath grew shallow, each step forward pressing painfully upon her trembling legs as they moved toward the vast archway leading to the banqueting hall. Words tumbled from her lips before she could stop herself, her voice strained with the weight of her own exhaustion.

"Pray, dear brother," she managed, struggling to keep her tone steady, "grant me this favour. Baldwin aids me in my walk; permit him to escort me first, and thereafter, he may seek out thy chambermaid."

Her gaze darted to Baldwin, hoping he might understand her silent plea—a few moments longer to keep her upright, a brief mercy to regain her strength before they reached the vast oak doors of the morning hall. She couldn't shake the dread gripping her chest, the fear that one wrong word might see her support taken away in an instant.

Charles's voice sliced through the chill air, his tone both commanding and relentless. "I have bestowed my command," he hissed, impatience dripping from his words. "Baldwin shall depart forthwith!" His eyes bore into the attendant, the torchlight casting a steely gleam upon his face as he dared Baldwin to defy the royal edict.

With a swift nod, Baldwin moved aside, ensuring Sophia's stability before hastening off to fulfill the command. Alone, Sophia struggled to find her footing, her visage twisting in pain as her legs quaked beneath her. She reached out a trembling hand to the nearby wall, pressing against the cool stone for balance as she continued down the corridor. Each step was a trial, her movements slow and labored, as if every inch forward was a battle against the overwhelming weakness threatening to engulf her.

As she forced herself along the corridor, each step sending fresh jolts of pain through her legs, a loud growl erupted from her stomach, reverberating in the corridor's silence. Hunger gnawed at her, a relentless reminder of her missed meal. Fatigue and longing for sustenance clouded her thoughts, and, despite herself, her mind drifted to simpler comforts.

Her brother's schemes, the precarious circumstances surrounding them—these concerns faded to the background as she imagined the satisfying taste of a warm meal filling her empty stomach.

As Sophia limped along, her mind settled on her favourite dessert: strawberry shortcake pastry tarts. The thought of those delicate pastries, bursting with sweet strawberries and cream, made her mouth water. She could almost feel the buttery crust crumbling beneath her teeth, the tangy burst of strawberry sweetness—until a pang of regret struck her heart.

Dread washed over her, mingling with an unwelcome memory. The very dessert that had sparked joy now triggered a painful recollection of the day before. She recalled Noor in the cooking quarters, their attempt to swipe a taste of the pastries foiled by Lord Edward's sudden arrival. A residue of that moment clung to her, a steady throbbing ache in her chest that radiated outward as she replayed the forest encounter in her mind. Poor Noor. How desperately she wished to shake off these haunting thoughts.

Sophia's heart fluttered with an uneasy rhythm, her steps faltering as she cast a furtive glance over her shoulder at Charles. *Wherefore had Edward not returned?* she thought. Her voice, unsteady and betraying her unease, rose before she could stop it. "Pray, tell me, dear brother, wherefore art Lord Edward Saint-Clair?" Her words hung in the still air, laden with a tremor of emotion.

Charles narrowed his eyes, suspicion creasing his brow as if amused by her feigned affection. His expression, sharp as winter's bite, held no warmth. "Why dost thou inquire of his grace?" he demanded, each word like a blade. He remained oblivious to the true weight of her inquiry, unaware she had sent Edward forth to seek Noor.

Fear coiled about Sophia's throat, tightening like a noose as she searched for a response. She wished she had held her tongue, saving her inquiry until after they'd broken bread together. But now it was too late. And as Charles shifted the cat in his arms, he continued, his tone filled with brotherly condescension. "With Briarwood being among the wealthiest and most puissant lands of the realms, we are as precious gems to those who seek union. Our fates are sealed, for thou art bound to wed one of import, and many a powerful suitor shall vie for thy hand. Though it pains me to confess it, dear sister, thou art indeed fair. Such beauty shall surely attract the attentions of many suitors. Yet, be wary, for most shall not treat thee with the kindness thou deservest. There are those among them who would seek to ensnare thee, to exploit thy noble title for their own ends."

A chill crept down Sophia's spine at his words. He spoke truth, yet the thought of being reduced to a mere title for a stranger's ambition stoked an ember of rage within her. Her fists clenched at her sides, and with a steely edge to her voice, she muttered, "Black-hearted villain, fit only for the gallows, like thee, brother?"

Charles's lips twisted into a smirk, though a hint of unease shadowed his gaze, a trace of his recent misdeeds lingering. Just yesterday, he might have taken pride in such a remark, yet the memory of Noor's death haunted him, casting a shadow that weighed heavy upon him. He could only cling to a dim hope for redemption in the days yet to come. Returning to their conversation, he said with an indifferent shrug, "Lord Edward Saint-Clair mayhap be one of thy better choices." A flicker of amusement crossed his face as he recalled the wretched King Shepparton of Valoria and many other suitors Sophia had attracted.

"I can scarce see thee as Queen Shepparton," he mused, nearly laughing at the thought of the old, leering king, whose bulk nearly burst his garments and whose jowls shook when he spoke. Shepparton, whose breath reeked as sour as his reputation, was known as much for his wealth as for his unseemly gaze upon younger maidens.

Sophia shivered at the mention of King Shepparton, her mind recoiling. Respectful suitors? Why settle for a title when her heart yearned for something real, for love? Her affections lay with Robert Winterbourne, yet Charles's assessment was not unfounded. As she resigned herself to her noble fate, she recalled her few exchanges with Edward, finding comfort in the memory that perhaps, of all her suitors, he might not be the worst to consider.

The very idea that Charles would offer her counsel stunned her. For a fleeting moment, he almost appeared human, a faint echo of the brother he once was. Yet she knew better; any warmth would vanish as quickly as it had come.

"Lord Reginald Hawkecliff hath made request to court thee," Charles remarked, his tone too casual for the weight of the words. The name alone sent a shiver through her spine, conjuring images of a man feared for his brutality—a man rumored to have beaten his late wife to death and taken pleasure in the horrors of battle. Whispers spoke of his mistresses, many of whom had ended their lives after a single night in his company. The very thought knotted her stomach, and she struggled to keep her expression steady.

"His Majesty, our brother, didst put an end to Lord Reginald Hawkecliff's request straightaway." Sophia shivered, a question lingering unspoken in her heart. Had Charles held the reins of power, would he have accepted such a dreadful match for her?

As they approached the doors to the royal breakfast banqueting hall, the guards stationed outside inclined their heads with a familiar yet hesitant respect, their eyes lingering on her bruised face and peasant's attire. Recognizing her disheveled appearance, they exchanged subtle glances, struggling to reconcile this battered figure with the princess they had once dutifully served. One of the guards stepped forward to push open the heavy wooden doors.

The scents of roasted meats and fresh bread filled the sunlit hall, stirring Sophia's hunger. She could not deny the gnawing emptiness in her stomach, even as her heart grew heavier.

With a great effort, she hastened to the long table and, without waiting for formality, seized a piece of warm bread. She bit into it eagerly, relishing how the warm bread softened on her tongue. For a moment, the comfort dulled the ache within her. Just then, Roderick the Usher approached, a familiar yet shocked expression crossing his face as he held a chalice in hand. He poured the wine with a flourish, though his hands trembled slightly, and his gaze kept flickering back to her mud-streaked hair and bruised skin. Could it truly be the lost princess, seated once more in royal breakfast banqueting hall?

Charles rolled his eyes at his sister's unroyal behaviour. *She hath dwelt among the common folk for far too long! Ere she took flight, she starved not, but bore herself as a true princess should.* With Midnight in hand, he strode to his seat, making a pointed cough that resonated through the hall, a subtle signal for Roderick to attend to him.

Sophia lowered herself into her chair, acutely aware of the quiet awe she stirred in Roderick. He lingered for a moment, pouring wine with a trembling hand, his gaze flitting between the chalice and Sophia. Disbelief danced in his eyes as he traced the bruises and grime marring her face, searching for the princess he had once known. Now, she seemed a stranger.

Suddenly, Charles snapped, "Shall I take mine own seat, like some commoner? Or art thou ready to serve thy prince?"

Roderick jolted upright, shock widening his eyes. Without hesitation, he rushed to Charles's side, pulling the chair out with urgency. He then quickly moved to the seat behind, ensuring Charles had a place to set Midnight down beside him.

Charles stood beside his chair, a flicker of anticipation in his gaze. After a final glance at Sophia, he lowered himself into the seat with a soft creak, adjusting his weight as he gently lifted Midnight from his lap. Cradling the cat, he placed her beside him, ensuring she was comfortable against the armrest. Midnight purred softly, her body sinking into the plush fabric as Charles leaned back, a satisfied smile creeping onto his lips while his fingers resumed their gentle stroking of her fur, warmth flooding his demeanor.

"Good girl, Midnight," he murmured, his voice low and soothing. "Rest thee well, my dear." Her contented purr deepened, and she nestled closer, relishing his affection.

His attention shifted to Roderick, who approached with the chalice in hand. As Roderick poured the wine, the deep red liquid glimmered in the sunlight streaming through the hall, capturing Charles's interest. Once the chalice was filled to the brim, Roderick stepped back, bowing slightly, his eyes darting to Sophia with a mix of awe and respect.

Sophia's fingers trembled as she reached for the polished silverware, the weight of its elegance feeling foreign against her unsteady grip. Each movement sent a jolt of pain through her leg, and the remnants of her concussion clouded her thoughts, making the simple act of reaching for the fork feel monumental.

With a deep breath, she steadied herself, focusing on the ornate fork gleaming in the light. As she grasped it, a shiver of uncertainty ran through her, but she pressed on, her resolve hardening against the wave of weakness. The platter before her held a vibrant array of roasted meats and fresh bread, and she willed herself to fill her plate.

Her hand shook as she transferred a slice of succulent lamb, the fork nearly slipping from her grasp. The sound of metal clinking against the wooden table echoed softly in the royal breakfast banqueting hall, a reminder of the grandeur that felt so far removed from her current struggle.

Charles took a slow sip of wine, savoring the rich flavor before even considering the platters spread before him. As the warm liquid slid down his throat, he felt the pulsing ache in his forehead, each throb a reminder of his recent injury, as if the pain were keeping time with his heartbeat.

The chalice clinked softly against the table, a sound that broke the silence, but his tense features told a different story—shoulders sagging under the burden of his thoughts. He reached for a fork, his hand steady despite the dull throb echoing in his head. Carefully, he speared a few tender pieces of lamb, placing them on his plate with deliberate slowness, silent questions churning in his mind. *I pray the Shadow Serpents have seen fit to arrange for the witch to weave her dark enchantments posthaste.*

His fingers brushed against the edge of the woven breadbasket, and with a moment of hesitation, he grasped a piece of warm bread, its crust crackling softly beneath his touch. Bringing it to his lips, he savored the moment before breaking off a chunk, the aroma of fresh bread mingling with the lingering scent of wine.

Both of them delved into the feast without exchanging words, the silence thick and stifling, punctuated only by the clatter of utensils against plates and the occasional grumble from Charles. Sophia kept her eyes downcast, attempting to ignore the throbbing in her head, but soon a wave of nausea crept over her, and the bright hall felt as though it were slowly closing in.

She discreetly moved her hand to her pocket, retrieving the small vial of ointment the healer had given her. Staring intently at it, she examined the faint, pale liquid within, almost translucent in its hue. Doubt gnawed at her. Should she drink it or apply it to the bump on her head? Her brow knitted as she studied the vial, fingers tapping restlessly against the table. A heaviness settled in her chest, the choice lingering like a shadow over her thoughts.

The thought of ingesting the ointment felt peculiar. What if it were meant solely for external use? The notion of consuming it in front of Charles felt awkward, a fear gnawing at her that he would deem her foolish for misusing it. She could almost hear his condescending tone, the sharpness of his words piercing her uncertainty.

After a moment's hesitation, she carefully placed the vial back in her pocket, her hands trembling slightly. Gripping her chalice once more, she took a sip, her thoughts wandering to the passage of time. Time slipped through her fingers like sand, leaving her anxious and restless. *How long dost thou reckon it will be ere the messenger reaches Ravenstone Castle?*

The messenger's speed would depend on the horse. Though the heavy downpour kept the townsfolk sheltered indoors, the path would remain relatively unobstructed. Yet, he would still face delays while the guards assessed his entry and requested an audience with the king.

Her mind spun like a top, whirling with the thrum of unspoken questions that vibrated through her entire being, each one a silent drumbeat urging her to find answers. How would the king respond to the news of her return? What emotions would surface when he learned of her presence?

Would her brother and mother set aside their pressing affairs and rush to Thorncrest Castle upon receiving the message? Or would they remain at Ravenstone Castle, sending back a cruel, uncaring reply through the messenger boy?

Would she be condemned to spend her days confined within these castle walls until she was forced into a marriage with a stranger? Seeking solace, she brought the chalice of honey wine to her lips once more. The sweet warmth of the liquid briefly soothed the ache within her heart, a fleeting balm against the uncertainty that loomed ahead.

The door swung open, and Maid Elowen stepped inside, her eyes widening as they fell upon Sophia at the table. A gasp caught in her throat, disbelief coursing through her at the sight of the princess, who had been missing for so long and now sat in such a disheveled state. The tray she carried trembled slightly, clattering against the silverware as she hurried forward.

Elowen wore a simple yet functional gown made from sturdy, unadorned fabric that allowed for ease of movement while she went about her daily tasks. The gown was a muted shade of brown, practical for a servant who often worked in the kitchens and storerooms. However, distinguishing her as a royal servant, the dress featured the royal crest—a golden lion—embroidered on the left shoulder, signifying her allegiance to the crown.

"Your Highness!" Elowen exclaimed in a breathless whisper, dropping into a deep bow, her forehead nearly touching the floor. The dishes on her tray rattled, a faint, unsteady chorus betraying her nerves. *So the guards spoke true,* she thought, *Her Highness hath indeed returned.* Relief swept over her, tinged with a flicker of worry.

Sophia caught Elowen's gaze and forced a smile, a facade of happiness that barely masked her unease. "Good morrow, Elowen," she said, her voice steady despite the turmoil inside her.

After rising, Elowen took cautious steps, her hands steadying the tray as she set it down, the aroma of roasted meats and freshly baked bread wafting through the air. With gentle, practiced motions, she began to clear the used plates, her fingers brushing against the remnants of the feast, lingering just a moment longer on the scraps that lay abandoned.

Elowen hesitated, her cheeks flushing as she looked at Sophia, a mixture of hope and disbelief brightening her eyes. *Might I be grasping at a possibility that's too good to be true? The princess dost remember mine own name?* A smile blossomed on her lips, radiant and genuine, despite the heavy tray balanced carefully in her hands. "Your Highness, the kingdom shall rejoice greatly at thy return. 'Tis an honour to serve thee once more. If there be aught I may do for thee, pray, do but ask."

She shifted her weight, the tray wobbling slightly as excitement surged through her, her hands trembling just enough to reveal the fluttering exhilaration within. Each word she spoke was steeped in reverence, her heart pounding at the realisation that the lost princess had returned.

As Sophia considered the maid's eager offer, a tumult of thoughts swirled in her mind. "Mayhaps a dagger could serve me well... Aye, one swift strike, and this wretched prince would trouble me no longer. But can I prepare to bear the responsibility that cometh with wielding such a formidable weapon? Dare I plunge it deep and rid myself of his cruel shadow?" The weight of uncertainty clung to her, like a dark cloud overshadowing the moment.

She forced a smile, thin and fragile upon her lips. "Elowen, thou art most kind. I am greatly grateful for thy service." The words tasted bittersweet, a hollow echo of the warmth she yearned for yet could not truly embrace.

"Knowest thou where Rosalind might be? I have missed her dearly." Even as the words escaped Sophia, a chill prickled her skin. A frosty intensity emanated from Charles's gaze, suffocating her thoughts like a vice.

His shadow loomed large, its dark contours a warning that one misplaced phrase could unleash his pent-up anger.

Elowen's brow furrowed thoughtfully, her expression shifting as she considered the question. She bit her lip, searching her mind for any sign of Rosalind. "I know not where Rosalind might be, yet I shall send for her anon," she replied, her voice steady and untroubled.

"Mine thanks to thee," Sophia said softly, her voice sincere, a faint smile gracing her lips as she acknowledged Elowen's kindness.Elowen dipped into a graceful curtsy, her fingers gripping the tray firmly to steady her hands. Rising to her feet, she wore a gentle, pleased smile, her eyes sparkling like pooled sunlight on a winter morning. She took a last, reverent glance at the princess before turning to leave, her steps light and quick, as if carrying a cherished secret.

Charles tilted his head back, letting the last drop of wine linger on his tongue before setting the empty chalice down with a pointed clink. Sophia caught his eye, and a suggestive smile crept upon him. "At least the servants didst miss thee. I wonder if Mother and our brother shall react in like manner?" he drawled, his words dripping with mockery.

Without missing a beat, he flicked his eyes to Roderick, a silent demand in his raised brow, his fingers drumming expectantly against the chalice, waiting for the immediate attention he felt owed.

At the table, Roderick stood nearby, his attention on the prince. With a steady hand, he poured wine into Charles's chalice, the rich crimson liquid arcing smoothly into the cup, catching the flickering candlelight as it filled to the brim.

A sharp knock echoed through the hall, slicing through the stillness. Roderick's hand stilled midpour; he set down the wine with a brisk precision and quickly crossed the hall, his steps swift and assured.

Reaching the door, he pulled it open in one smooth motion, revealing a tall figure cloaked in deep purple, the royal hue draping over his shoulders with an unmistakable air of authority. The lion's crest on his chest caught the light streaming through the high windows, a proud symbol gleaming against his noble frame.

"Sir Tristan Blackwood," Roderick's voice broke the quiet, carrying through the hall as Tristan stepped forward, his figure outlined by the interplay of firelight and the pale daylight streaming through narrow windows. The hearthlight danced over the stone walls, mingling with the pale daylight streaming in through the high windows. A soft gleam played across Tristan's armour and the rim of the chalices, catching brief highlights in the quiet hall.

With a practiced bow, Tristan allowed his cloak to sweep low over the floor, his expression resolute. "Your Highness," he spoke, his voice low but steady. Leaning closer, he continued, his words intended for Charles alone. "The Shadow Serpents have seized the witch, as required for the casting. The gathering is set for this eve."

A tense stillness hung between them, the subtle crackle of the fire the only sound in the hall. Firelight flickered across Tristan's face, casting faint shadows on his brow as he exchanged a brief glance with Roderick, whose stance remained stiff, attentive.

"Mine thanks to thee, Sir Tristan." Charles's words broke the quiet, his tone a mix of relief and something unsaid. He lifted his chalice, pressing the cool metal to his lips for a lingering sip. Yet, even as the warmth of the wine spread, a chill clung to his thoughts—Noor's dark promise, like a shadow lingering in the play of fire and daylight.

The thought of the witch's involvement flickered in Charles's mind, a faint spark amidst the gathering gloom. If her magic could indeed deflect the looming troubles, it felt like a fragile shield against the darkness threatening to engulf him. Leaning back in his chair, he felt the tension in his shoulders ease, as though the very air had shifted, lightened by that small but significant assurance.

As Sir Tristan took his leave, a wave of unease swept over Sophia. She shot a quick glance at her brother, her brow furrowing. "What is it thou seek'st? What news doth Sir Tristan bear?"

Charles turned to her, a mocking smile tugging at his lips, as if her worry were mere jest. "Sir Tristan doth bear news of matters that concerneth not a princess." He lifted his chalice, taking a leisurely sip of the deep red wine, savoring the moment as though it were a fine delicacy.

With a casual flourish, he set the chalice on the table with a soft thud, the sound ringing hollow in the weighted air. "Word of thy return shall soon be carried far and wide, spreading across the land. Suitors may well hold for a time of grace; yet doubt it not, they shall come swiftly upon thee ere long. What course dost thou intend to take?"

Sophia rolled her eyes, irritation sharp in her gaze. *How doth he speak of such matters, after all that hath transpired? How can his tongue prattle on, as though naught hath changed, and now he speaketh of suitors?* Frustration simmered, settling in her chest like a stone dropped into still water, weighing her down. "Mayhaps, if the suitors dost truly seek mine favour, I shall have them see thee to thine end." Her words dripped with sarcasm, but beneath, a tremor of anxiety lingered, a reminder of the torment that throbbed just beneath their gilded façade.

Charles laughed, a rich, carefree sound, as if her words were no more than a gentle breeze against the storm of his ambitions. "Thy friend, Princess Shorwynne of Valefort—would she not make a fine bride?" His tone was teasing, yet a flicker of seriousness lingered in his eyes. Shorwynne was a prize in beauty, and though Valefort was neither as powerful nor as rich as Briarwood, it was still a worthy land to be bound with.

A chill crept through Sophia at his suggestion. "Thou meanest to court Princess Shorwynne?" Her voice trembled, betraying her shock. They were friends, in a manner, seeing each other only at grand events. Valefort lay a considerable journey away, a crossing of the sea that turned perilous when the gods were unkind. A princess seldom traveled unless necessity demanded it. Though they shared similar duties and exchanged missives, those missives often vanished into the ether, responses taking months to arrive.

"Surely, Princess Shorwynne, in all her grace and beauty, hath suitors of far greater standing than thee!" she retorted, her eyes narrowing. "Dost thou think her so foolish as to even cast a glance upon thee?" Her words dripped with the venom of sibling rivalry, an insult cloaked in feigned concern.

Charles merely chuckled, his handsome features undisturbed, charm radiating from him like sunlight. "All these high-born suitors thou dost speak of—yet why dost thou count the likes of King Shepparton, Lord Reginald Hawkecliff, and such amongst them?" His smile was disarming, the kind that could turn heads and stir envy, even as ambition swirled within him like a restless tide.

Sophia knew he was right; at least she had garnered the interest of Lord Edward Saint-Clair, a handsome man from a powerful and wealthy family—a modest consolation in a world where her pride might have withered long ago. Yet her heart belonged to Robert, a commoner whose strength and kindness ignited a fire within her—a love forbidden by the unyielding divide of their stations. The memory of Edward's proposal to wed for love lingered like a bittersweet echo, tempting yet overshadowed by the truth: it was a union born of duty, not desire.

"Wouldst thou wed Princess Shorwynne in public, merely to sire heirs? Or dost thou seek to take her as thy wife, that thou might love her truly?" Her words hung heavily in the air, daring him to confront the truth.

Charles regarded her as though she had spoken madness, disbelief flickering in his eyes. "Thinkest thou me fit for a loving husband? Canst thou truly see me bound to but one?" Mockery danced on his lips, yet beneath it lay the unmistakable yearning for freedom—a longing that could never be tamed by the confines of marriage.

Sophia's heart raced as she met her brother's gaze, a knot of dread tightening in her chest. "If thou hast grown weary of thy wife or found her of no further use, wouldst thou have slain her?" The question slipped from her lips like a whispered prayer, laden with unspoken fears. Her fingers trembled as she reached for her chalice, seeking solace in its coolness, her breath catching as she awaited his response.

Charles's expression shifted, a flicker of contemplation crossing his features. He leaned back, reaching across the table to place another slice of meat on his plate, his movements unhurried yet deliberate. For a brief moment, his jovial façade wavered, revealing a mind at work, weighing the implications of her words. *Kill my wife? Nay, not with mine own hands. Should her death be required, let it fall to another—a Shadow Serpent, mayhap. Yet, the dungeon might suffice. Surely, it need not come to such a final end... or so I hope.*

"Wouldst thou truly think that his grace, Lord Edward, or whosoever thou dost wed, might harm thee, should they tire of thee?" Charles leaned forward, a glint of mischief in his eye. "I expect, if they desire to cling to the title and wealth thou dost bring, they would bide their time ere disposing of thee." His tone dripped with sarcasm, each word twisting the knife as the tension grew between them.

A chill crept through Sophia at his words, and for a moment, Shorwynne's face flashed in her mind. The thought of her friend being bound to Charles filled her with an unexpected pang of dread. *What fate would await her if he tired of her, as he has others? Would he cast her aside just as easily?* Sophia's mind whirled, caught between the unsettling truth in his words and the desperate hope that Edward might be different. Yet a flicker of doubt lingered, casting a shadow over her heart.

With a cold, tantalizing cruelty, Charles leaned in closer, his gaze piercing through her defiance. "Or mayhap thou wouldst flee in unlawful folly with that peasant lad thou seemest to favour. Dost thou fear that, once thou art too old to bear more, the natural savagery of his kind would prevail? Would he leave thee and thy child to freeze and starve in some wretched place like Mudlark Alley, forsaken while he takes a younger maiden to his bed?"

His words cut like daggers, each one laced with venom, twisting deeper with each syllable.

Sophia's chest tightened, her pulse quickening as she met her brother's gaze with a defiance she could barely contain. "Verily, brother, any maiden—or even Princess Shorwynne herself—wouldst need be in the depths of desperation to seek thy favour," she spat, her voice sharp as steel. "I pray that, in their wretchedness, they end thee whilst thou dost slumber."

Her words hung in the air, sharp and biting, but Charles only raised an eyebrow, a low chuckle escaping him. Rather than taking offense, he seemed amused, his lips curling into a smile as if she'd offered him a jest. He leaned back, shaking his head, his eyes gleaming with satisfaction as though he relished her failed attempt to wound him.

Charles's hand hovered over the table before he gripped his knife with calm deliberation. With a sudden thrust, he drove the tip of his knife into the meat, his eyes on her as the chalice beside him trembled. For a moment, the knife stayed embedded, vibrating as if daring him to fling it across the table at his sister. His gaze fixed on Sophia, cold and unblinking, as he drew the blade back slowly, each movement adding to the strained quiet between them.

"Thou dost mistake my harshness for insult, sister," he said, his voice steady but carrying an ominous edge. "Mark my words—one day, thou may'st thank me, for 'tis a cruel world in which we dwell." He sliced off a piece of meat with precision, his gaze never leaving hers, as though studying her reaction.

Sophia forced herself to hold his gaze, her heart pounding. She managed a slight smile, her lips barely lifting. "Truly, brother, 'tis strange that the court favours Madame Élisabeth for John and not thee. Have they looked so far that they overlook thine own merits?"

Charles's knife paused mid-air as he chewed, his eyes narrowing. Her own words lingered uneasily, and a faint prickle of dread crept in beneath her defiance. Her brother's darkness mirrored that of Élisabeth—a match that sent a chill down her spine.

They had been sparring for some time now, each dig sharper than the last. Their exchange had soon drifted to the subject of Charles's imagined reign, Sophia mocking him with thinly veiled disdain. "How long wouldst thou wear the crown before the people rise against thee, or some reckless fool—greedy like thyself—decides to steal it?" Her words dripped with scorn, but before he could respond, a commotion erupted from the corridor.

"Get thy hands off me!" The sharp cry, unmistakable in its familiarity, sliced through the hall, jolting Sophia. A rough scuffle followed, a jarring mix of grunts and hurried footsteps. Her heart pounded as the grand doors flew open with a resounding crash, making the walls shudder, sending a shiver down her spine.

The guard shoved Mary Winterbourne into the hall with ruthless force, his grip like iron, dragging her as if she were quarry brought to slaughter. She stumbled forward, her wrists bound tightly, terror stark on her face. At the same moment, Sir Tristan Blackwood stepped in behind them, his expression unreadable as he took his place by the door, having waited outside for the summons. Sophia's stomach twisted, a cold dread tightening in her throat. She watched, horrified, as Mary struggled with every step, her body straining against the bonds. Each ragged breath, each muffled cry, was a fierce defiance against the fate being forced upon her.

Baldwin staggered in just after Tristan, gasping for air, his face pale and damp with sweat. "Your Highness," he stammered, his voice thin with dread as his gaze darted nervously between those gathered. "I beseech thee, forgive our delay… She would not come willingly." His words fell like a curse, plunging the hall into silence thick with dread.

Sophia's mind raced, flashing back to Charles's casual order to bring a maid forward. Her stomach knotted with regret and helplessness—how had she let herself ignore the precarious web of deception that held them all? After Noor's tragedy, she'd hoped Charles might finally leave the Winterbourne family in peace. Yet here was Mary, another pawn in his merciless game.

Mary's silence was a thunderous defiance. Her blazing eyes locked onto Charles, her hatred fierce and unyielding. The tension between them crackled like a storm on the edge of breaking. Her clenched jaw, the unbreakable resolve in her gaze, the tight set of her shoulders—each was a promise that she would never serve him, not now, not ever.

Charles continued his meal with an infuriating calm, spearing a piece of meat and lifting it to his mouth as though the turmoil before him were no more than idle entertainment. He barely looked her way, his gaze flickering dismissively to Mary before returning to his meal, her rage beneath his notice, as inconsequential as the morsels on his plate.

Unaware of Noor's fate, Mary's anger remained fixed on Charles alone. Had she known the full truth, she might have lunged for the guard's blade, struck down the prince then and there, unleashing chaos.

Charles chewed slowly, his fork and knife clinking against the plate with deliberate precision. Without looking up, he addressed the guard, his voice as cold as steel. "Teach this insolent knave the reverence due to royalty." The royal banquet hall fell silent, an air of tension thickening as the guards and knights stood by, faces impassive, trained to endure the prince's cruelty without protest. Roderick kept his gaze down, his jaw clenched as he held his stance. Baldwin's fingers twitched slightly, his discomfort barely concealed as he kept his posture rigid. Sir Tristan, ever dutiful, remained still, his unease masked by an unreadable expression. They had witnessed Charles's merciless ways before, yet beneath their stoic exteriors, reluctance simmered, bound by duty rather than respect.

The guard delivered a swift, brutal blow to the back of Mary's knees. "Thou art to curtsy with swift obeisance in the presence of royalty, without hesitation or delay! Dost thou not know thy place?"

Mary's legs buckled, hands stretching out to catch herself, but another shove sent her sprawling onto the cold, polished floor, the impact echoing across the hall.

With a soft, deliberate clink, Charles set his fork down, his gaze locked onto Mary, a predatory smile curling on his lips. He lifted his goblet and took a slow sip, savoring the moment as though it were a fine delicacy. "Ah, much improved," he drawled, letting the words linger, each syllable a calculated strike.

Sophia's throat tightened, her eyes dropping to her lap, her cheeks burning with shame. She felt the weight of her silence pressing her down, her breath catching in her chest. Even without meeting his gaze, she felt Charles's mocking stare sear into her. The weight of her silence pressed down on her, turning her stomach. She clasped her hands tightly, unable to look at Mary, knowing the truth would soon unravel.

Charles's twisted smile widened as he leaned forward, casting a cold gaze upon Mary. "Come hither, my sweet," he sneered, his voice dripping with mock affection. "Permit me to present thee to the princess." His gaze flicked toward Sophia, the malice in his eyes unmistakable.

"And tarry not," he added sharply, his voice taking on a more commanding edge. "Ready one of the chambers with all speed. My sister hath been grievously assailed by a wretched commoner." His tone turned to feigned sorrow, though his eyes glittered with satisfaction. "She doth require time for her mending."

Sophia's heart clenched, dread coiling tightly around her chest. She kept her gaze on her lap, every fiber of her being willing herself invisible. She knew the moment was coming—Mary's eyes would find her, and with them, the crushing realisation of who she was and the tangled web of lies that had ensnared them all.

A surge of desperation rose within her, the urge to scream, to tear through Charles's web of lies, to end this twisted farce. But the words caught in her throat, swallowed by the bitter knowledge that it was too late. She was bound by the silence she had chosen, and now Mary, Noor, and the entire Winterbourne family were ensnared in the venomous feud between her and Charles.

The weight of shame pressed down upon her, anchoring her gaze to the ground. This was her doing, and the cost had grown heavier with each passing moment. The thought of Mary learning the truth about Noor's fate gnawed at her, each unspoken word a stone upon her heart, binding her further to a destiny she could no longer control.

How would Mary and Robert react when they learned that Charles had slain their beloved sister—and all because of her? The guilt pressed down upon Sophia like a stone, each breath more shallow than the last. She could already see in her mind the devastation that would strike the Winterbournes, their hearts riven asunder by the cruel hand of fate. With every fibre of her being, she longed to turn back the wheel of time, to undo the grievous wrong she had wrought—but such hopes were naught but whispers on the wind, lost in the darkness that had taken root.

Mary's gaze shifted toward Sophia, and disbelief twisted into bitter disappointment. *Robert's lover, Sophia, Noor was right, as she always is. And what now, I wonder? Death, perhaps?*

Sophia's golden hair, usually a soft and tangled mess, now bore streaks of mud, clinging to her cheeks like shadows of deceit. A dark bruise marred her jaw, and her cheeks, usually so vibrant with warmth, looked hollow and battered. Here she sat, surrounded by platters of food, her bruised and dirtied face at odds with the gleaming royal banquet hall. Mary could barely reconcile the woman before her with the one who had stayed at their cottage, laughed by their hearth, and woven herself into Robert's life. Now she was here, a princess—an impossible truth wrapped in grime and bruises.

The silence between them spoke louder than words. Sophia kept her gaze lowered, each averted look a silent confession. Why wouldn't she face her? There she sat, bruised and smeared with mud, her tangled hair falling over her eyes, looking more like someone dragged from the battlefield than a princess.

"Your Highness," Mary rasped, summoning her courage, though bitterness laced her tone. Her legs quivered as she sank into a trembling curtsy, her body screaming in protest as she lowered herself before the princess.

Her gaze slid toward Charles, rage kindling in her heart like a spark upon dry tinder. She yearned to scream her defiance, to let fly the words that burned within her: *I will not serve thee, nor any of thy blood!* But the weight of his threats bore down upon her, relentless as iron. She knew that to voice her rebellion would mean a public reckoning at his hand, her punishment delivered before them all. So she swallowed her fury, masking her defiance with the guise of submission.

Inside, Mary's heart raged, her resolve roiling beneath the weight of fear and anger. Only last night, she had plotted their escape—she and her kin, far from Ravenswood and the twisted grip of the prince. Yet Noor's absence now cast a shadow most foul, gnawing at her very soul. She and Robert had passed a sleepless night, dread pressing down upon them like an anvil. Charles's threats still rang in her ears, the menace creeping ever nearer.

Her thoughts drifted to Charles's cryptic words about Noor serving Edward Saint-Clair. Hope flared for a fleeting moment—had Noor taken refuge with the lord? But just as swiftly, that hope faded. Noor had little regard for lords such as Edward; the thought was naught but folly.

Steeling herself, Mary hesitated before addressing Charles. "Your Highness," she began, a tremor in her voice, "might I make bold to suggest aiding both the princess and Lord Saint-Clair? Hath he yet awakened from his slumber?"

Charles's eyes narrowed, a faint twitch at the corner of his jaw betraying him ere he forced it still. Silent moments passed, thick with tension, his gaze like a blade cutting through the air. "Lord Saint-Clair ventured out late and hath not returned," he replied, his tone clipped and cold. He took another slow sip from his chalice, dismissing her with a sharp flick of his hand. "Prepare the princess's chambers. Be gone."

Mary's throat tightened, but she held his gaze, her lips pressed into a thin line as she fought to keep her voice steady. "Your Highness," she said softly, "my sister hath not returned home since yestereve."

Charles's gaze hardened, a flash of ire in his eyes as her unspoken accusation hung between them. She sought answers—answers he could not yield. His mask of composure faltered, and for a heartbeat, guilt simmered beneath his control. Yet he pressed it down, burying it beneath a show of calm. "The chambermaid hath been dismissed," he said, his voice striving for command, though a slight tremor betrayed him. "Escort her to the princess's chambers," he ordered the guard. For an instant, uncertainty flickered in his eyes—a crack in his cold veneer—ere he turned away, eager to end the exchange before it unraveled further.

Mary's entire body quaked beneath the guard's iron grip, his rough handling sending sharp jolts of pain through her slender frame. She struggled, desperate tears spilling down her cheeks as she twisted against him, her breath coming in ragged gasps. "Your Highnesses!" she cried, her voice thick with anguish, each word weighted by the despair that clung to her. "Pray thee! Speak but truth! Say only that she was dismissed, and no ill hath befallen her!" Mary's pleas rang through the hall, a sorrowful echo that seemed to cling to the cold stone walls.

Sophia kept her head bowed, her gaze fixed upon her plate, for she could not bear to meet Mary's eyes. Guilt weighed down on her, each of Mary's cries slicing deeper, cutting at the fragile threads holding her together. Remorse clawed at her throat, tightening it as though bound in chains. She tried to summon words, but they caught in her chest, knotted in the heaviness of her regret. She swallowed hard, her insides twisting, the bitter taste of guilt rising with each of Mary's desperate pleas. Her hands shook in her lap; she pressed them down, forcing herself to stay still as dread twisted inside her.

Charles, his patience stretched thin, cast an irritated glance toward Mary's weeping. Her display of raw emotion was an unwelcome disruption, especially in the presence of his guards and attendant. He could not allow the truth of Noor's fate to slip with so many ears listening. "Thy sister hath been dismissed," he stated, his tone sharp with finality. "'I am told she hath departed of her own will, perchance to seek comfort within some tavern.'"

He had no certainty in his own words, for the truth lay buried in the blood-soaked soil of the forest. The image of Noor's lifeless body flashed in his mind, the weight of it still heavy on his hands. Panic surged within him, unbidden. "Be gone!" he barked, his voice laced with the memory of the blood that still haunted him.

For a brief moment, a flicker of hope stirred in Mary's heart. In the chill of his tone, she found a hesitant reassurance that soothed her frazzled nerves and patched over the holes in her battered heart. She clung to the thought that Noor might have sought refuge elsewhere, as if grasping at smoke with trembling hands. The doubt lingered, but the prince's explanation, however thin, was enough to soothe her fraying nerves. Perhaps Noor rested in a tavern even now, weary from the day's trials but safe. It was a fragile comfort, but in the storm of uncertainty, it was enough.

Squaring her shoulders, Mary turned to the guard, her voice steady though her heart quaked. "I shall go willingly," she said, her words firm. "Thou needst not drag me hence."

The guard looked to Charles for permission, and with a curt nod from the prince, he released his hold on her. Charles, his expression unreadable but his approval clear, watched as they made to leave. Just before they could depart, he spoke once more, his voice cold and commanding, punctuated by the sharp stab of his fork as it pierced the meat on his plate with chilling precision.

"Mary!" Charles called, his voice sharp and laced with cruelty. "Thy earnings shall be docked for thy tardiness this morn and thy unpermitted departure yestereve," he declared, each word heavy with threat. "If thou leavest early again without my leave, expect consequences most severe."

As the guard released her arm, Mary's emotions churned beneath the surface—anger, frustration, and fear twisted together like a vine of poison ivy. Yet outwardly, she remained composed, her expression a mask of brittle calm. Her fists clenched by her sides as she forced a smile that felt foreign on her face, concealing the storm raging within her. A fire burned in her chest, urging her to speak her mind, to lash out at the prince for his cruelty. But she swallowed the words that threatened to spill from her lips, knowing well that defiance would bring only greater punishment.

"It shall not come to pass again, Your Highness." Mary murmured, her voice strained with barely concealed resentment. Her words were brittle, breaking under the weight of her anger, yet she curtsied with what grace she could muster. Her steps were swift as she retreated from the hall, the sound of her feet echoing against the cold stone floors, the guard trailing silently behind her like a shadow.

As her figure disappeared down the corridor, Charles's lips curled into a smirk, his gaze shifting to Sophia, amusement flickering in his eyes. "Ever the silent witness, art thou not, sister?" he taunted, his voice dripping with mockery. "Or hath thy tongue abandoned thee entirely?"

His words hung in the air like a challenge, his tone a cruel jab at her silence. He watched, transfixed, as her hands quivered, ever so slightly, like the first whispers of a summer breeze, hinting at the quiet storm brewing beneath her surface. "Dost thou have no message for thy beloved Robert?" he added with a sneer, his condescension cutting deep. Sophia's body trembled with weariness, her head heavy under the strain of all that had come to pass. Yet it was not merely exhaustion that troubled her, but the relentless cruelty Charles seemed intent on wielding. She looked at him, disbelief mingling with sorrow in her gaze, her voice soft and strained as she murmured, just loud enough for his ears alone, "Brother... why dost thou summon a Winterbourne here? Why dost thou insist she know my true title? And to what end dost thou seek to humiliate her so—compelling her to curtsy as though she were but a drudge, docking her earnings, seizing her meager coin? Such matters bear no weight upon thee, yet they hold the world to one like her."

Her gaze flicked upward, briefly, her eyes narrowing with a glint of anger, as though silently imploring, *Consider all that hath befallen of late.*

Barely above a whisper, her voice softened further, kept low enough that neither Baldwin nor the usher would catch her words. "Thou must understand," she continued, sorrow and frustration threaded through each word, "they shall not cease their search for Noor." Her quiet plea held a desperate hope that he might grasp the gravity of what lay ahead.

Charles waved his hand with a dismissive flick, his gaze steady and cool. "Let them search," he said, his tone like ice. "They shall find naught." The certainty in his voice masked a thin edge of unease. He had put the matter in the hands of the Shadow Serpents, trusting them to sweep away all trace of what he had done. And yet, the memory of Noor lingered like a shadow he couldn't quite escape, her lifeless eyes haunting him in the quiet moments.

He straightened, his jaw set, pushing the thought aside. He had made his choice, and the serpents would see it buried. Tears welled in Sophia's eyes, her brother's callousness settling upon her like a shroud. For a fleeting moment, before Mary's arrival, she had dared to hope that Charles might still harbor a glimmer of compassion, some faint remnant of reason to which she could appeal. But that hope lay extinguished now, crushed beneath the weight of his indifference. She pushed her plate aside, her appetite lost, the very thought of food turning her stomach.

Baldwin, the prince's attendant, stepped forward with a respectful bow, his tone deferential as he addressed his liege. "Your Highness, might I fetch a walking stick for the princess?" His gaze briefly flicked to Sophia's injured leg, a silent gesture acknowledging her discomfort.

Charles waved a hand with lazy indifference. "Aye, fetch it," he replied, his thoughts already drifting elsewhere. It would serve him well if their mother and brother believed he had shown some semblance of concern for Sophia's recovery.

Baldwin bowed low, his movements deliberate and dignified, an unspoken display of respect. With quiet grace, he withdrew from the hall, leaving the siblings alone with the unspoken tension that hung heavily between them.

*

Twentieth minute hath passed

It had been about twenty minutes since Baldwin had left to fetch the walking stick. Sir Tristan stood watchfully near Charles, his stance rigid and unmoving, a constant sentinel close by the prince. Roderick lingered along the far wall, hands clasped behind him, his gaze respectful but distant. Sophia and Charles sat at the table, their contrasting demeanors evident. Sophia sat slumped, her shoulders heavy, her gaze drifting to the plate she could scarcely bring herself to touch. Across from her, Charles leaned back, a faint smirk playing on his lips, his eyes flickering with something close to satisfaction.

A soft rustling signaled Baldwin's return. He entered with a quiet confidence, moving lightly across the hall as he approached, a walking stick resting in his hands. The stick gleamed, the polished dark wood catching the light, while intricate silver vines twisted up its length, meeting at a rose-shaped handle—a finely crafted piece, elegant yet strong, something only royalty would hold.

Baldwin bowed, lowering the stick before Sophia. "Your Highness," he murmured, his voice soft, a glimmer of warmth in his tone. "For thy comfort, should it please thee."

Sophia nodded in acknowledgment, her fingers curling around the polished wood, the solid feel of it grounding her. "Mine thanks, Baldwin," she replied, barely above a whisper, as though any louder might shatter the delicate calm she clung to.

Charles's eyes never left her, his gaze sharpened with a hint of amusement. He noted her grip tighten around the stick, a faint curve forming at his lips as he leaned forward, his tone laced with feigned concern. "Sister, hath recent troubles wearied thee so?" His voice was gentle, but his words held a mocking edge, each syllable falling with the weight of an unspoken jest.

Sophia held his gaze, her voice steady, determined not to let his words unnerve her. "Aye, brother, 'tis so," she said, forcing a calmness into her tone. "Yet 'tis a weariness shared by all who serve thee," she added, her gaze flicking briefly to Baldwin, who now stood back with lowered eyes, silent once more.

Charles chuckled, the sound low and deliberate. His gaze shifted to Baldwin, then to Sir Tristan, who stood nearby with a barely perceptible nod, mirroring Charles's approval. "Indeed, 'tis only the most loyal who endure such strain. Mayhap 'tis good fortune that such loyalty endures… lest it prove… lacking."

Sophia's fingers traced the delicate silver inlay, each curl a point of focus as she fought the twist in her stomach. The tension in the hall pressed down on her, thick and stifling, each word seeming to hang in the stillness, the quiet murmur of the fire the only ease in a hall so fraught.

Sophia's head swam, memories rushing in disjointed fragments, each one leaving her dizzier than the last. The sharp, tearing pain of Charles's blade biting into her leg surged up, followed by the hollow blackness that had overtaken her as she'd been struck down. She remembered coming to in the cold, damp stone of the dungeon, her leg a mass of raw, burning flesh—cauterized, though the agony felt like anything but healing.

Her breath caught as more images pressed in, each vivid and haunting. Charles's taunting smirk, his icy dismissal of Mary's pleas, the edge of malice in his threats toward Robert—and then the sight that had sent her stomach lurching: hooded figures slipping from the dark chest in the hall, like spectres summoned from fevered nightmares. And Noor—her heart twisted as Charles's chilling words echoed in her mind. Noor's fate lay veiled in his lies and cruelty, a dark hint of something final, something unspeakable.

Was it truly so? Each twisted moment, a truth unto itself? Her hand trembled around the chalice. A cold splash of wine across her face—would it snap her out of this nightmare? Would the madness dissolve, or only deepen, pulling her further into the chaos that threatened to consume her?

Charles's gaze slid toward her, a subtle narrowing of his eyes and a tightening at the corners of his mouth betraying his disapproval. His brow arched slightly, a silent reprimand, as if to remind her of her place and the indiscretion of speaking so boldly, even in a whisper, before the servants. His jaw set, a faint shadow of irritation playing across his features, though he masked it well.

He leaned in close, his voice slipping to a murmur that barely crossed the space between them. "Ah, Princess, thou needst not trouble thyself with such matters," he said smoothly, his tone shifting as if the topic held no worth. Then, with a faint smirk, he continued, "Yet I must inquire—what didst thou and the peasant boy occupy thyselves with during that time when all the kingdom did fear that thou wert taken against thy will?"

Sophia's heart lurched, a cold wave of dread sweeping over her, her pulse quickening as her eyes darted toward Roderick. The usher stood close enough to catch a stray word, his stance rigid and attentive, as if awaiting command. Panic flashed across her face as she clutched the walking stick, her fingers instinctively tightening their grip like a lifeline.

Charles's eyes glinting with a cold, almost sinister light as he lowered his voice to a near whisper, each word laced with a barely veiled threat. "Thou knowest, sister," he began, the chill in his tone cutting through her like a blade, "'tis the common folk who suffered most. Taxes and other burdens were raised to fund the extra search parties." His words lingered, heavy with implication, each syllable a carefully crafted warning. He seemed to savor her growing dread, his gaze never wavering, his expression hard, unyielding.

A slight smirk tugged at the corners of his mouth as he continued, the weight of his manipulation pressing down on her, making her feel caged. "Without mine threats of having Robert slain, should the court discover—well, he is as good as dead, and thou wilt be despised by all. They would see thee as a stain upon the royal line, an errant princess who abandoned her station, and the folk would cry for retribution. So, question not nor meddle with mine affairs. Can I confirm we're clear on this point?

A heavy stillness surrounded them, weighed down by the fierce intent in his eyes, which never wavered, never looked away.

Sophia's face paled, her lips parting ever so slightly, yet her gaze remained fixed upon her brother, wide and uncertain. He said it, and her face shut down, every muscle tense, her lips squaring off against the pain. Shoulders slumped, she gripped her walking stick with whitened knuckles as though it alone kept her steady.

"But we are among the wealthiest and most puissant lands in all the realms, with a great host at our command and much riches to our name," she murmured, her voice low and strained. "Why, then, must the lowborn bear the burden?"

Charles's laughter filled the hall, cold and biting, echoing off the stone as he leaned back, flicking his hand dismissively toward their chalices. A mocking smile curled on his lips. "It is true, we possess wealth and command our own army, yet thou knowest little of the toil of coin. Thou caredst not for the lowborn when thou didst wear the finest of gowns, bedecked with diamonds that could feed a family for years. The wine alone thou hast consumed this morn could have been enough to cure a man sorely injured."

He gestured pointedly to the goblets before them, and Sophia's heart seized as her gaze dropped to the chalices. Her stomach churned, each sip now souring in memory as she thought of the cost others had borne for her luxury. A shadow of dread flickered across her face.

Charles went on, scorn thick in his voice, a glint of cruel amusement in his eyes. His lips curled ever so slightly, not in a smile but in something darker—a sneer that played at the corners of his mouth, as though the very words tasted bitter on his tongue.

"Thou art so troubled by the plight of the low-born, but what of the army, when they are sent to flee in battle? "Pray, when they return, bearing the spoils of a won skirmish, claiming that which the vanquished hath left behind, have they thought upon the kingdom or town from whom it hath been taken? Any treasure, arms, or goods seized in battle are regarded as the royal property, with the soldiers allowed naught but a portion. And if a skirmish or battle bringeth territorial gain, the newly conquered lands shall be deemed the crown's own possession. Or when a man falls in battle, never to return, leaving his kin to starve, bereft of coin to see them through? Do not feign care for the low-born now, for thou hast reaped the fruits of others' toil and sacrifice all thy days!"

The sunlight spilling through a nearby window caught his expression, casting a sharp contrast between light and shadow on his face, emphasizing the disdain that etched itself into every feature. His eyes glinted with a harsh, unfeeling amusement as he went on, voice biting. "Whether it be by direct taking from their pockets, or by the labour that they dost give, this land wouldst be naught. Our family's title, naught. Our wealth, perchance, dwindling to naught."

In the daylight, every furrow of his brow and the cold mockery in his gaze became more distinct, leaving no doubt of the contempt that coursed through his words.

Sophia's mouth closed, her throat tight as she struggled to swallow the growing despair and guilt his words stirred within her. Her chest tightened, and she lowered her gaze, unable to meet his as the truth, bitter and unyielding, settled upon her.

A sudden, resounding knock shattered the tense quiet, and both Charles and Sophia's heads turned sharply toward the door, their expressions taut. Roderick straightened immediately, casting a glance at Prince Charles for direction.

Charles's gaze lingered on the door as he gave a curt nod. "Pray, discover who it be," he commanded, his tone edged with restrained authority.

Roderick moved swiftly, his steps measured as he opened the door. William, the steward, entered, his face set with a solemn composure. He approached the table, stopping just short of it, and bent into a low bow.

"Your Highnesses," he intoned, his voice carrying both clarity and weight, "the King and Her Majesty draw nigh to the gates."

Sophia's heart quickened, though she felt far from ready to face anyone. Even so, the thought of seeing her mother and brother John, was a small comfort compared to remaining alone with Charles. She grasped her walking stick with one hand, the edge of the table with the other, and tried to rise. Yet as she pushed herself up, a wave of dizziness swept over her, forcing her back down into the chair.

"Now, now, sister mine," Charles said smoothly, his tone laced with mock gentleness. A selfsatisfied glint lit up his eyes. "Remain seated."

Turning to William the steward, Charles issued his command with cool authority. "Bid the king and our mother know that we await them here."

William bowed low, then quietly withdrew, leaving Sophia to settle back into her chair, the walking stick still clutched tightly in her hand. Her stomach churned as the heavy silence filled the hall.

Sophia's thoughts drifted to what might follow. She pictured her mother dismounting and heading straight for her chambers to shed her riding attire, no doubt eager to don something more suited for court. John, however, she could envision leaping from his horse, casting aside his cloak to the nearest servant, and striding indoors without delay.

Her fingers tapped nervously against the table as she strained her ears, hoping to catch even the faintest sound of footsteps from the corridor. The waiting gnawed at her insides, a cruel twist of anticipation and dread.

Charles, sensing her unease, took a slow sip from his chalice, his gaze lingering on her. The warning signs had been there all along, courtesy of Robert's would-be adversary. Each lingering glance felt cold and calculating, a silent warning that left her stomach twisting. She could feel the invisible chains he held over her, over everything she cherished, tightening with each unspoken threat.

The queasiness that had begun earlier grew stronger, and Sophia felt her head swim as the dizziness returned. With trembling hands, she reached for her chalice, taking a hurried gulp to steady herself, though the wine did little to calm her nerves.

The silence stretched between Sophia and Charles, thick and oppressive, settling like a dense fog over the hall. The fire crackled softly in the hearth, casting long, wavering shadows across the chamber, but neither sibling moved nor spoke. They sat across from each other, each lost in their own thoughts, as if they'd been waiting in this quiet tension for an eternity.

Sophia's eyes drifted over the silverware and the lavish platters, now seeming gaudy and excessive, each item a stark reminder of the wealth and ease she had accepted without a second thought her entire life. Her hand instinctively cradled the polished wood of her walking stick, her fingertips tracing every groove of the ornate design. Only now, after months spent hiding and surviving among the common folk, did she feel the weight of all she had once ignored—the coin taken from those who had so little, the wealth that filled the royal coffers at the expense of others.

Across from her, Charles sat with the same unreadable expression, his gaze fixed upon her with an unwavering calm. His fingers tapped idly against his chalice, the faint sound punctuating the silence, as though marking the passage of the long, slow minutes. The faint, barely-there smirk that played at his lips seemed to mock her, each moment stretching into a reminder of the truths he'd pressed upon her, truths she could no longer dismiss.

<u>Ten minutes hence.</u>

Ten minutes passed in this quiet standoff, the space between them feeling colder, more weighted with each heartbeat, as if both awaited the arrival of something that would shatter the stillness.

A distant rumble echoed through the stone corridors, growing louder with each passing moment. Sophia's breath caught as the heavy doors shuddered, anticipation thickening the air. At a nod from Charles, Roderick moved swiftly to pull them open, stepping back with the utmost respect.

William, the steward, entered first, bowing deeply before announcing, "Your Highnesses, His Majesty the King and Her Grace, the Queen Mother." Torchlight flickered as Sir Eadric, the king's knight, followed, his armour catching the light. Behind him moved Alaric Stonebrook, the king's personal servant, alongside the queen mother's attendants and Rosalind, Sophia's handmaiden, all clad in royal colours of deep purple adorned with the lion rampant crest.

The king and queen mother entered together, a formidable presence as they stepped through the doorway. At their arrival, Roderick immediately bowed low, his posture respectful. Charles rose from his seat with a composed expression, while Baldwin and Sir Tristan Blackwood offered their deep bows, laced with deference. Even Sophia, though unsteady, clutched her walking stick with one hand and the table's edge with the other, inclining her head in reverence as best she could, the weight of their presence unmistakable.

King John's steps, measured and resonant, echoed like thunder, each one an unspoken proclamation of his authority. The very air seemed to yield, bending to his will as he crossed the threshold, his gaze sweeping over the hall. The queen mother moved with regal purpose, her gown flowing like a dark tide, but her eyes, wide and filled with fear, found Sophia instantly.

Sophia's breath stilled as her eyes met her brother's. Though he was the sibling she had once loved most, in this moment, he was her king. The amethysts in his crown glinted in the daylight, casting a cool gleam over his brow and lending an even graver cast to his face. Would he be angered? Disappointed? Sophia's chest tightened as her thoughts jostled within her, scattered like leaves caught in a sudden, fierce wind.

John's face remained set, his countenance as unyielding as carved stone. Behind him, the faint clink of Sir Eadric's armour and Alaric's soft steps faded into the background. The flickering torches responded to his approach, casting faint shadows in rhythm with his steps. The air felt heavier, harder to draw, and even the cold stone beneath Sophia's feet seemed to pulse with the gravity of the moment. The smooth wood of the table bit into her palms as she clutched it, fighting to still the panic that threatened to overwhelm her. The king's gaze moved slowly over Sophia, his brow tightening with each mark of weariness etched upon her face. His hand clenched briefly at his side, then released, his fingers trembling under the weight of all the unspoken questions that lingered there. She was transformed from the sister he remembered—her once-bright features shadowed by exhaustion, her garments worn and stained, a silent testament to what she had endured. "By God's grace," he murmured, his voice low, as though uncertain of the reality before him.

"Sophia?" His expression softened slightly, a glimmer of relief flickering in his eyes. "I can scarce believe mine eyes, for it seemeth thou hast chosen a new hue for thy hair," he added, his tone laced with a gentle jest as his gaze lingered on the mud-caked strands that dulled her golden locks to a murky brown.

For a brief moment, a warmth crept through the hall, the jest breaking the tension, and a faint smile tugged at the corner of his mouth. Yet beneath the humour lay a glimmer of relief—she lived, and she stood before him.

Sophia's heart fluttered, though her aching head dulled any joy. She took an unsteady step forward, each movement sending a fresh wave of agony from her wounded leg. The brightness in her eyes dulled, and her smile began to sag, like a flower whose petals had started to droop. The king reached out, steadying her in a warm embrace, though even this could not hold her steady for long.

As they parted, the king's expression darkened, his nose wrinkling at the scent of sweat and blood clinging to Sophia. His gaze shifted to Charles, and his eyes narrowed as he took in the dark bruise shadowing his brother's forehead, the faint swelling at his temple. The king's eyes lingered on Charles's injury, his gaze steady and questioning. His voice remained controlled, though an unspoken weight pressed behind his words.

"Brother," he said slowly, the weight of authority underlying his tone, "thou hast done well. The kingdom shall rejoice at her return."

Charles inclined his head, but the faintest twitch of discomfort betrayed him under his brother's scrutinizing gaze.

The queen mother's gaze followed her son's, and she moved forward as Rosalind, Sophia's handmaiden, came to Sophia's side, her hands trembling as she gently reached out. The queen mother's fingers hovered over Sophia's injuries, her expression a blend of horror and tenderness. "Sophia!" she gasped, her voice raw with emotion. Her hand reached forward, but seeing the wound, she faltered, her face blanching. "By heaven! What horror hath befallen thee?"

Sophia swayed, strength fading fast. She raised a hand weakly, her fingers trembling, but her legs gave way, and she sank back into the chair as the pressure in her head pulsed, blurring her vision once more.

"Mother… I… prithee, I beg thee, do not make such a fuss." Her voice was barely more than a whisper, fragile and worn, yet her plea sliced through the thick air.

The king's gaze shifted to her, piercing and unyielding, his voice taut with restrained wrath. "What else hast thou suffered, sister? What more did they do to thee?" His tone was low, almost a growl, as he glanced toward Charles. "What more did they do to thee? Who hath taken thee, dear sister?"

Sophia's lips parted, but no words came. The pounding in her skull made it impossible to think, the edges of her vision swimming. Rosalind, who had rushed in with the queen mother, quickly raised the chalice from the table and held it to Sophia's lips. "Drink, milady," Rosalind whispered softly, her voice calm but urgent. Though she happened to arrive at the same time as the king and queen mother, she had received message from Elowen to come at once.

"Who hath taken thee, dear sister?" The king's patience thinned, and his voice grew cold. "Where did they make thee dwell? What foul deeds did they visit upon thee?" "A simple hanging will not suffice for such treachery. These traitors shall stand trial, and once found guilty, they shall meet the sword. Their houses shall burn, and with them, their name shall be forever erased!"

The queen mother's expression darkened, anger now replacing the fear in her eyes. "To the sword, for it is but kind; they ought to meet their end with slow and grievous suffering!" she spat, her hand slamming the table. The sharp crack of her fist striking the table reverberated off the stone walls, lingering in the heavy air. Every head in the room turned slightly, the noise rippling through the space like a physical force, cutting through the tense silence. The startled flicker of glances betrayed the weight of the moment, all eyes drawn to the sudden, fierce display. "They shall bear the weight of this grievous deed. No mercy shall be bestowed upon them."

Sophia winced, her breath shallow as she struggled to keep her thoughts straight. Fear gnawed at her, not for her life but for the truth she held back. Could she reveal that she had left willingly? That she had lived among the common folk, forsaking her duties as a princess? And Charles—how could she betray him now, knowing the wrath it would bring?

Charles, sensing the growing tension, puffed out his chest, forcing a confident tone. "Fear not, Your Majesty," he declared, his voice steady but hollow. "The wretch who did her harm is dead. I saw to it, with mine own hands."

The Queen Mother's gaze softened, her lips trembling as she placed a hand on Charles's arm. "Charles," she whispered, her voice thick with emotion, "thou art a true son unto this family. I thank thee, for protecting thy sister."

Yet as Charles stood there, basking in the queen mother's approval, the lie weighed heavily in the pit of his stomach. Sophia's stomach churned, bile rising in her throat as she watched her mother praise Charles for a lie. Sophia's chest tightened, her stomach churning as the praise for Charles hung in the air, making her feel as though the hall was closing in around her. Her hands clenched, the urge to speak clawing at her throat, yet she couldn't force the words out. How could her mother not see it? How could she not sense the deceit dripping from Charles's lips? Sophia longed to speak, to tell the truth, but her tongue stayed still, heavy with the weight of fear. Her heart hammered in her chest as she imagined the storm that would follow her confession—Charles's wrath, her mother's scorn, and the consequences that would surely fall upon them all.

King John's voice broke through the tense silence, a thunderclap in the still air. "Hold thy congratulations!" His words cracked like a whip, his fury rising.

John's eyes locked onto Charles, unblinking and hard, his intensity enough to make the air between them feel like it was thickening. Charles shifted slightly under the weight of it, as if feeling the pressure tighten around him.

"He hath sought vengeance without trial!" John's voice filled the chamber, each word landing with brutal force. He shifted his gaze to their mother, anger flickering in his eyes. "Such matters are not for thee or Charles to decide. They must be brought before the court! What if an innocent soul hath faced the executioner?"

The hall fell into an uneasy stillness, as if the very stones held their breath. The queen mother, Victoria's eyes darted between her sons, the tension in the hall coiling tighter with each passing moment. John's hand moved to his temple, his frustration palpable. "Speak plainly, Charles," he demanded, his voice low and dangerous. "What hast thou done? What actions hast thou taken?"

Charles shrugged, a smirk playing at the corner of his lips, a glint of arrogance flashing in his eyes. "I hath handled it." he said, his tone laced with indifference. "There is naught to worry about."

"Thou darest!" John's voice thundered, his eyes ablaze with fury. "Thou art bound by the laws of this kingdom, as am I! Thou art no tyrant to act as judge and executioner!" Sophia watched the fire in her brothers grow, her heart clenching. John was right, but could he tame Charles's hunger for power? She feared not.

As the tension reached its boiling point, a knock echoed through the chamber, sharp and sudden. John's gaze darkened further, shooting daggers at Charles before gesturing for him to answer. Charles nodded curtly, calling out, "Enter."

A sharp knock echoed through the chamber, and after a brief pause, Roderick stepped forward, easing the door open with a low bow. Another steward, Margaret, and a senior servant entered, their heads bowed in deep respect. "Forgive the intrusion, Your Highnesses," the senior servant said, casting a nervous glance at the simmering tension. "Sir Edward Saint-Clair hath returned. He approaches the castle on horseback, riding with great haste."

Sophia's heart leapt, her pulse quickening at the mention of Edward. Her breath caught, and for a moment, the chaos around her faded. She moved to rise, eager to greet him, but her mother's arm shot out, barring her path.

"And where think'st thou art going?" Queen Mother Victoria's voice was cold as steel, her gaze sharp as a blade. Sophia froze, her excitement snuffed out in an instant.

"I... I was but making to greet Lord Edward." Sophia replied, her voice wavering, her hands trembling at her sides.

Victoria's eyes narrowed, suspicion flickering across her features. Sophia had never shown interest in Edward, nor in any suitor before. "Thou shalt not meet anyone in such a state," she snapped, her gaze sweeping over Sophia's disheveled appearance with disdain. "Thou art a princess of this kingdom, a reflection of our house. Look at thee! Filth and ruin."

Sophia's breath caught as Queen Victoria's gaze flicked to Rosalind, her fingers snapping with sharp authority. "Draw a bath for the princess, and do it swiftly," she commanded, her voice slicing through the air like a blade. "Gather the maids—she will need their aid with that hair of hers. These rags," she spat, her nose wrinkling in disgust as she pointed to Sophia's tattered clothing, "burn them, and see to it that the ashes are carried far from hence. Even fire shall not cleanse them of their stench."

Sophia's heart sank, her hand trembling as she looked to Rosalind for reprieve. Her eyes pleaded silently, though she knew none would be granted. The weight of the moment pressed on her chest, suffocating her. She turned toward her mother, summoning the last of her courage. "I shall take the bath, Mother," she said, her voice steady despite the tremor in her limbs. "But afore all else, I must parley with Lord Saint-Clair." Her heart pounded as she spoke his name, her thoughts racing ahead to the news she feared about Noor.

Victoria's gasp pierced the hall, sharp and quick, her face blanching as if the very suggestion had knocked the air from her lungs. "Most certainly not!" she cried, her voice trembling with shock. Her fingers tightened around the edge of the table, knuckles white. She looked at Sophia as though she were seeing a stranger. "Look at thee, child! Thou art covered in filth—thy hair matted, thy appearance so ragged I hardly know thee. A princess? Nay, thou look'st no better than a peasant dragged from the mire!"

Her eyes snapped to Rosalind with a steely command. "Prepare the bath! At once!" The sharpness in her tone left no room for question. Then, as she looked back at Sophia, the hardness softened in her gaze, replaced by a flicker of maternal concern. Her voice, though gentler, still held its edge. "My dear, thou dost not wish Lord Saint-Clair to behold thee thus. I know thou art weary, but some dignity must be maintained."

Sophia's frustration simmered beneath her composed exterior, her calm concealing the storm within. Her voice, low and resolute, cut through the air. "Mother, I am fully capable of deciding for myself." The boldness in her tone drew startled glances from the servants and courtiers alike. Sophia's gaze locked onto her mother, steady and unyielding. She stood tall, her chin slightly raised, her resolve unwavering as the tension between them thickened. "Lord Saint-Clair hath traveled far, and it would be unjust for me to make him wait. I will greet him now."

Victoria's brow furrowed, her lips parting as she turned to King John, her posture tense with expectation. The delicate lace of her gown was no match for the iron-like pressure of her clenched fist, betraying the mask of composure she wore like armour. "John, make thy sister see reason."

John shifted uncomfortably, scratching the back of his neck, clearly uneasy with the confrontation. "Mother speaks true," he said at last, though his tone was hesitant. "Thou hast been through much, sister, and… thy appearance bears the marks of it."

He moved toward the head of the table, gesturing subtly for his mother to join him. Turning back to Sophia, his expression softened, concern coloring his voice. "There is no need to strain thyself further, Sophia. Lord Saint-Clair would understand if thou didst rest."

Sophia's hand reached for the walking stick beside her, her grip firm despite the slight tremor in her fingers. "If I am to wed Lord Saint-Clair," she said, her voice unwavering, "then he will see me at my worst sooner or later."

John's gaze flicked to the walking stick, the sight of it underscoring her vulnerability. His brow furrowed, worry deepening. Did she not see her state—how her very struggle to stand was proof of her need for rest? He took a slow sip of honey wine, using the moment to gather his thoughts. When he spoke again, his voice was gentle. "Hast thou sought the aid of a healer, Sophia? It may be best."

Sophia let out a long, heavy sigh, her patience worn thin. "Oh, indeed," she replied, her tone laced with sarcasm, "Charles hath so graciously seen to it that Ambrose Thornbrook attends me." Her gaze sharpened on Charles, bitterness flashing in her eyes. She reached into the folds of her gown and casually produced a vial Ambrose had provided, a token of the treatment she had received hours after her waking. The cauterization of her wound, performed while she lay unconscious, was yet another decision forced upon her. Her jaw tightened, resentment simmering at the thought of choices made without her consent.

Caught off guard, Charles blinked, his smug expression faltering for a heartbeat before he composed himself, his face settling into a mask of calm. His brow lifted ever so slightly, and his mouth curved into what passed for concern, though the sharpness in his eyes betrayed him. "Indeed," he said, his voice measured, though he lifted his chalice as if to close the matter. "Sophia's health, 'tis of the highest import." He took a long drink, feigning composure, but the shift in the room did not go unnoticed.

Victoria's gasp echoed through the hall, her features twisted with disbelief. "Ambrose Thornbrook?" she repeated, her voice dripping with horror. "Ah, so now we deign to mingle with healers who tend to criminals and outlaws, all for thy sister?" Her words cut through the air like a blade. "By all means, let her wallow in the mud with the swine and sup from their very troughs!" She cast a sharp glance at Charles, her outrage evident, making it clear how deeply his failure stung—how dare he not arrange for a royal healer for Princess Sophia. "Ah, perchance we ought to break bread with these criminals and grant them entry into our very homes! A most splendid idea, is it not? Surely, nothing could go awry with such a *wise* decision."

Sophia's frustration gnawed at her, concerns for Noor pressing heavily with each passing moment. Her pulse quickened as she spoke, her tone even but laced with urgency. "Your Majesty, my liege," she said, her voice calm but resolute. "Pray, allow me to demonstrate to Lord Saint-Clair that I shall ne'er keep him in wait, should we join in union."

King John's eyes softened as he glanced between his mother and sister. As he let out a slow sigh, a conflicted blend of emotions seeped into his tone, resignation subtly taking center stage. "If thou art so insistent upon seeing him ere thou retire, then let it be. But I too agree with Mother—thou must not present thyself in such a state. Recall, thou art a princess, not some common beggar."

His gaze shifted to Charles, who appeared preoccupied with his drink, barely hiding his indifference. John's voice sharpened, commanding attention. "Charles, what of her chambers?" Charles lowered his chalice with exaggerated slowness, a smirk playing on his lips. "In the west wing, upstairs—the second chamber on the left, as ever," he drawled, his voice oozing with indifference. "Though, seeing as she dresseth like common muck, might Her Highness wish to lie with the swine this eve?" His words lingered in the air, dripping with venomous disdain, daring anyone to challenge him.

John's patience waned. "Mock me not, brother, or I shall have that chalice spilled upon the floor ere thou canst even blink!" John, ever aware of the castle's layout, knew well enough where Sophia's chambers lay. His tone shifted, stern and pointed. "Has her chamber been prepared? If thou hast time to send for a healer from Cutthroat Row, then surely thou hast ordered her bath to be drawn in her private chambers?"

Charles let out an exaggerated sigh, his eyes rolling with such theatrical disdain that it seemed a performance. "Ah, a chambermaid hath been dispatched to prepare the chamber," he began, feigning concern. "But alas, there's a tragic issue with her precious private bath." He waved a hand dismissively, his tone sharp with mockery. "So, the princess will simply have to manage with another, if she can bear such an inconvenience." His smirk curled at the edges, clearly savoring the moment.

The king's patience snapped. "Dost thou turn every trifling matter into a spectacle?" His voice grew sharp with vexation. "Would it slay thee to offer a simple answer, unadorned by such folly?"

A sardonic grin tugged at Charles's lips, his eyes gleaming with mischief. "Ah, but Your Majesty, I cherish every chance to bask in the brilliance of thy royal ire," he replied, his words dripping with sarcasm.

Sensing the rising tension and eager to leave, Sophia interjected with polite urgency. "Pray forgive me, but Lord Saint-Clair doth await. May I be excused?"

John paused, his hand hovering over a roll on the table. For a fleeting moment, mischief sparked in his eyes, and he toyed with the idea of flinging it at Charles, if only to wipe the smirk from his brother's face. But the impulse faded, and he regained his composure. Turning to his sister, his tone was calm but firm. "Rosalind will see to thy bath. Only after thou art refreshed and presentable may thou see Lord Saint-Clair."

Sophia's shoulders sagged with disappointment, but she nodded in acknowledgment, gripping her walking stick tightly as if drawing strength from it. She and Rosalind performed a curtsey, though Sophia's movements were slow, each shift of her weight unsteady and taxing. As they turned toward the door, her steps were halting, her legs trembling with the strain, and her knuckles whitened around the stick's handle. Rosalind moved close, a steadying presence at her side, catching her arm whenever she faltered. Each step felt heavier than the last, her body resisting, but Sophia pressed on, her resolve etched in the tight set of her jaw.

As the king's gaze circled the hall, his even tone sliced through the air, silencing the murmurs and drawing every ear to his words. "Sir Eadric, between the guards posted at the doors and the knights within these walls, I am well-protected. Attend to the princess and see her safely to the bathing chamber."

Sir Eadric inclined his head in a sharp nod, his obedience precise, then lowered himself in a fluid bow. Rising swiftly, he moved to Sophia's side, his steps purposeful. Extending his arm, steady and unwavering, he offered silent support, his eyes meeting hers with quiet assurance as he waited for her to take it.

Shadows of Betrayal and Bonds Unbroken Sophia and Rosalind

Chapter Sixteen

Inside the bathing chamber, Princess Sophia steadied herself on Rosalind's shoulder, her grip firm as pain flared through her wounded leg. Pale daylight streamed through a narrow, high-set window, casting soft, dappled patterns across the chamber and mingling with the faint scent of drying herbs.

Elowen stood quietly by the steaming tub, sleeves rolled and a fresh gown draped over her arm. She poured the last of the hot water, creating wisps of steam that rose around the room. She glanced at Sophia with a small, respectful nod. "The water is prepared, Your Highness." she murmured, a warm familiarity in her tone.

Sophia offered a faint smile in thanks, letting the weariness ease from her shoulders. As Elowen left quietly, Rosalind moved forward, her hands deftly unfastening the ties of Sophia's gown. The worn fabric slipped from her shoulders, gathering at her feet. Sophia's hands twitched as she attempted to assist, urgency in every tremble, though her weakened limbs betrayed her.

Rosalind, calm and steady, loosened the last ties with practiced hands, guiding Sophia toward the bath. Sophia gripped the wooden rim, lowering herself carefully, the heat of the water reaching her skin in gentle waves. As she sank into the bath, a quiet sigh escaped her, the warmth sinking into her muscles, soothing away the stiffness and strain.

Rosalind dipped a clay pitcher into the bathwater and lifted it gently over Sophia's head, pouring warmth that spilled down and washed away the travel's grime. "May I?" she asked, holding a cloth and bar of lavender soap with quiet reverence.

With a small nod, Sophia allowed Rosalind to continue. Rosalind's hands moved with care, the cloth tracing over Sophia's shoulders, easing over every tense muscle. "Thou hast been sorely missed, my princess," she murmured, her voice a gentle hum within the chamber.

Sophia closed her eyes, letting the familiar rhythm of Rosalind's touch carry her away from the worries that had haunted her for days. "I wish I couldst have brought thee with me." she whispered, a note of relief in her voice. "To have thy care once more... 'tis a peace I have long been without."

Rosalind's hands stilled for a moment, her voice softening. "It is ever mine honour to serve thee, Your Highness." she said, a tenderness in her tone. "Forgive me, my lady, if I do overstep, but I hold thee as kin—though no blood doth flow 'twixt us, our loyalty doth bind us strong. Each day thou wert away, I found no peace, only sorrow, for worry filled my heart."

Sophia reached out, placing her hand over Rosalind's, their fingers briefly intertwined in the warmth of the water. "Thy words dost touch mine very soul, Rosalind," she murmured, a tear slipping down her cheek, her voice but a whisper. "I pray our bond doth endure beyond this mortal coil." Rosalind's eyes glistened, though her hands continued their task with gentle precision. "Thou art eager to meet Lord Edward Saint-Clair," she observed, a smile gracing her lips. "Allow me to finish, and thou shalt be on thy way."

Sophia drew her hand back, her fingers trailing over the water's surface as she considered whether to reveal what weighed upon her heart. She trusted Rosalind fully, yet a deep hesitation held her tongue, her memories pressing upon her as heavily as the ache in her wounded leg.

Rosalind, ever attuned to Sophia's mood, watched the flicker of emotions across her face, her gaze shifting from Sophia's eyes to the seared wound. She dipped a cloth into the warm water, wringing it out slowly as if waiting for Sophia's words. "What hath happened to thee, Your Highness?" she asked softly, her tone gentle yet searching, her eyes silently pleading for answers.

Sophia's eyes shone with unshed tears, and her voice grew faint as she began. "It feels as though I live within the lines of some ill-fated tale," she murmured. "It began like a fevered dream, clouded with confusion and loss, and then… I met Robert Winterbourne." She paused, drawing a slow breath as memories surfaced. "Not a nobleman, but he bore the heart of a knight, though he was only a commoner by name. I gave him mine own heart, and he, his to me. But now..." Her voice caught, and she gripped the edge of the tub, struggling against the tide of emotion. "Now, it feels as though 'tis been torn asunder, ripped from me so cruelly."

Rosalind remained quiet, her hands working with gentle diligence, scrubbing away the dirt and strain of Sophia's journey. Each stroke carried a steady rhythm, the warm cloth moving over Sophia's arms and shoulders, grounding her even as her fears took shape in her words.

Sophia's voice dropped, her gaze distant as she recalled the forest. "I felt it there—a shadow, unseen, creeping behind me, watching every step. Each snap of a branch set my heart racing, though mine eyes saw naught but shadows. It was as though the very trees closed in, enclosing me in their dark embrace."

Rosalind's hand paused briefly, but she quickly resumed, her strokes remaining steady, the cloth moving carefully over Sophia's skin. She offered no words, letting Sophia speak freely, the gentle scrubbing a quiet comfort between them.

"It was but my own fears," Sophia continued, a faint flush on her cheeks as she let out a small, wry smile. "Yet 'twas then I met Robert Winterbourne, and the poor lad nearly lost his wits upon seeing me."

Sophia's gaze softened as she thought of the Winterbournes, a bittersweet ache rising in her chest. Her secret weighed heavily, a guilty pleasure tied to the memory of Robert. "How could I tell them?" she whispered, her voice rough with regret. "How could I reveal that I am the princess?" She lowered her gaze, her words barely above a murmur. "How can I, who hath known plenty, speak of such things to those who have known want?"

Rosalind's expression softened, and her hand lingered on Sophia's shoulder for a moment, the cloth resting gently as she offered silent reassurance. "Thou didst not choose to be born a princess, nor didst thou seek such a life," she said gently. "Though thy burdens differ from theirs, they are no less real. I do fear thy path ahead will hold yet more trials, but I pray thou findest the strength within thee."

A soft smile touched Sophia's lips as her hand reached for Rosalind's, gratitude shining in her gaze. "Thou art so full of understanding, Rosalind," she whispered, leaning into the warmth of her friend's touch.

Rosalind's lips curved into a small, playful smile, a spark of curiosity lighting her eyes. "Then tell me more of thy ventures, my princess," she teased, her voice light and familiar. "What tales dost thou carry from thy wanderings?" Her words were filled with affection, a reminder of the bond they shared, stronger than titles and rank, grounded in years of friendship and trust.

Sophia's voice dropped, her gaze distant as she recalled the forest. "I felt something there—a shadow, unseen, creeping behind me, watching every step. Each snap of a branch set my heart racing, though mine eyes saw naught but shadows. It was as though the very trees closed in, embracing me in their dark silence."

"It was but my own fears," Sophia continued, a faint flush coloring her cheeks as a wry smile touched her lips. "Yet 'twas then I met Robert Winterbourne, and the poor lad nearly lost his wits upon seeing me."

Her gaze softened at the thought of the Winterbournes, a bittersweet ache rising in her chest. The weight of her secret pressed on her heart, a guilty pleasure tied to the memory of Robert. "How could I tell them?" she whispered, her voice rough with regret. "How could I reveal that I am the princess?" Her gaze dropped, her words barely above a murmur. "How can I, who hath known plenty, speak of such things to those who have known want?"

Rosalind's expression softened as her hand lingered on Sophia's shoulder, the cloth resting gently as she offered silent reassurance. "Thou didst not choose to be born a princess, nor didst thou seek such a life," she said softly. "Though thy burdens differ from theirs, they are no less real. I fear thy path ahead will hold yet more trials, but I pray thou findest the strength within thee."

A soft smile touched Sophia's lips, and her hand reached for Rosalind's, gratitude shining in her gaze. "Thou art so full of understanding, Rosalind," she whispered, leaning into the warmth of her friend's touch.

Rosalind's lips curved into a playful smile, a spark of curiosity lighting her eyes. "Then tell me more of thy ventures, my princess," she teased, her voice light and familiar. "What tales dost thou carry from thy wanderings?" Her words held affection, a reminder of the bond they shared, one stronger than titles or rank, grounded in years of friendship and trust.

Princess Sophia's voice trembled, though her words were firm as she addressed Rosalind. Her face paled under the weight of what she had seen. She spoke softly, yet the horror was evident in her wide eyes, as though the memory itself sought to escape her lips.

"I... I ventured to Mudlark Alley," she began, her gaze dropping to the floor before flickering back to Rosalind, "and I pray thee, think it not what one might imagine. 'Twas worse still. The very cobbles are stained with human waste, and the stench—God help us—'tis enough to drive a soul mad. Folk, poor souls, left to wither and die, their bodies cast aside to rot where they fell." Her voice faltered, sorrow shadowing her features. She took a steadying breath, but the image of the alley lingered, a darkness too grim to shake.

Rosalind's breath caught as she took in the cruel marks on Sophia's skin. Raised welts, bruises dark as night, marred her tender skin, a visible trace of violence. Horror and sympathy registering on her face, the princess's expression held her gaze captive. "Mudlark Alley doth explain thine injuries, Your Highness."

Sophia's lips parted, as if to correct Rosalind, but she let it go. A small pause in her gaze betrayed a fleeting thought, her hand instinctively finding the tender spot on her arm. A smile softened her expression as she returned to thoughts of Robert, her voice taking on a tone both fragile and fierce.

"Robert hath shown me much," she murmured, her fingers absently brushing the marks on her arm as if they, too, were memories etched deeper than flesh. "He taught me how to endure beneath the canopy, to listen as the forest speaks, to seek shelter, though it be crude and cold. And in that place, I was not the princess burdened with kingdom and court." Her gaze glimmered with a quiet defiance, a spark ignited by freedom's touch. "For once, I was unbound. I loved as I pleased, and for the first time, it was mine own heart guiding me."

In her memory, the tavern's rowdy din swirled around her—chalices clinking, boisterous laughter, the smell of stale ale and smoke. It was a world far removed from her own, yet within its rough embrace, she had found a strange, fleeting comfort. Sophia's voice faltered, her eyes fixed on Rosalind, as if confessing a crime.

"I have fallen in love with a peasant," she whispered, each word a defiance against her royal blood. Her breath hitched, hands curling into tight fists. "I, a princess, bound to duty and crown, yet my heart… my heart belongs to him."

Rosalind's hand flew to her mouth, her eyes wide. "A princess cannot wed a commoner," she whispered, almost as if hoping to banish the thought.

Sophia's gaze dropped, her face pale. "I know it well," she replied, her voice breaking. "To love him is to hold what I can never keep, to grasp at shadows that will vanish as dawn breaks." Her fingers trembled as she spoke, as though trying to seize the impossible, her memories slipping further and further from her grasp, leaving only the ache of what could never be.

Rosalind's hands slowed, a faint tremor betraying her empathy. Though she continued her task, the tenderness in her touch said what words could not, each motion a quiet expression of the sorrow she shared with her princess.

She had always known the struggle of Sophia's having to wed for duty, but hearing it laid bare tugged at her heart. Rosalind's hands paused briefly when Sophia spoke of Noor and Charles, the tragedies pressing down upon them both. The sadness in Sophia's voice echoed Rosalind's own, and together they bore the weight of that grief in silence.

When Sophia spoke of her dealings with Edward, the regret in her tone was unmistakable. Sophia's shoulders sagged, her head dipping slightly as though a great weight had settled upon her. Her eyes, once bright with resolve, now seemed dulled, flickering with the struggle she carried in silence. Each movement felt slower, as if her very thoughts had grown too heavy to bear. Rosalind continued her work, gently washing Sophia from head to toe, her expression mirroring the emotions Sophia revealed.

"I only wish I had been at thy side in these trying times," Rosalind sighed, her voice heavy with sorrow as she rose to fetch another soap for Sophia's hair. "Though it may seem hard to believe, these trials will make thee stronger in the end."

Just as Rosalind prepared to wash Sophia's hair, a sharp knock on the door interrupted their moment of quiet. Sophia's eyes met Rosalind's, a flicker of curiosity and apprehension passing between them. Rosalind set down the soap and moved toward the door, her soft footsteps the only sound in the chamber. She opened the door just a crack to find a servant holding clean garments.

With a nod, Rosalind accepted the dress and undergarments, closing the door swiftly. A faint smile touched her lips as she turned to Sophia, holding up the fresh clothes. "Now, Your Highness, whilst thy heart may belong elsewhere, perchance Lord Edward shall grow upon thee." Her tone was gentle yet earnest. "I have had the pleasure of serving him in thy absence. He doth possess a charm about him."

Rosalind placed the garments on a nearby stand, her eyes thoughtful. "Shouldst thou not feel for Lord Edward as he might wish, thou needn't worry overmuch," she said. "Fulfill thy duty as promised, and, should it come to it, speak plainly of thy feelings. Make clear that while marriage may bind thee, love may not."

Returning to the bath, Rosalind resumed her task with a contemplative sigh. "Many noble unions do not begin with love, yet in time, they endure. Perchance thou and Lord Edward might come to an understanding—a display of unity for the world, yet in private, thou art free to follow thy heart's true desire."

Sophia's breath caught at the suggestion. "Rosalind," she began, her voice laced with surprise, "thy mind worketh in ways I cannot fathom. But Robert… he would ne'er accept such an arrangement. To see me wed to another—especially a lord—whilst he remaineth hidden like some secret… it would break

Robert. Besides, I feel as if His Grace, Lord Edward, doth yearn for love." There was a flicker of hope in her words, a faint glimmer that somehow, love might yet endure.

Rosalind picked up the wooden bucket, swirling the water with soap as she prepared to wash Sophia's hair. "I know not Robert, and mayhap he shall loathe the thought at first, but in time, he might come to see the advantage of being a secret love. He would want for naught, shouldst thou grant him an allowance. It is more common than thou might think."

"Should he refuse to accept it, unless thou dost flee again, thou wilt have to wed with title and put Robert from thy life," Rosalind mused quietly. "I've heard tales—whispers of alliances forged in noble halls. Even thy parents, 'tis said, did not begin with love."

"Aye, my mother oft told me so." Sophia's heart clenched at the thought, her mind turning to the painful truth of her situation. "What fate shall befall when Robert doth learn of Noor?" she asked, her voice quivering. "Shall he ever look upon me again? How could he e'er forgive me for the falsehoods, for the secrets I hath kept?"

Rosalind paused, her hand hovering over Sophia's head as she positioned the wooden bucket for the rinse. "Only time shall tell, my princess," she said softly, her words carrying the weight of both wisdom and comfort. "Art thou ready?"

Sophia took a deep breath, her body tensing as she braced for the water. "I am prepared," she whispered.

Rosalind carefully and poured it over her hair. The water ran through, loosening the mud tangled from the forest's damp paths, the gentle warmth tracing over her scalp and shoulders. Each pour seemed to lift a bit of the journey's weight from her, allowing Sophia to ease under Rosalind's careful hands. Rosalind filled the bucket again, pouring another soothing stream, then a third, until the water ran clear and her hair lay smooth and soaked.

Once the last of the mud had rinsed away, Rosalind gathered Sophia's wet hair, lifting sections to squeeze out the excess water, letting droplets slip back into the tub. Sophia closed her eyes, finding a rare moment of release in the rhythm of Rosalind's steady hands.

At last, Sophia rose from the tub, and Rosalind worked swiftly, drying her with linen cloths before helping her into the gown. The comfort was short-lived as the corset's laces drew taut, each pull pressing the stiff fabric into her ribs—a reminder that even here, her station clung to her like an unseen weight.

Once dressed, Sophia extended her arms, letting Rosalind fasten the final ribbons. Her mind raced, each moment away from Lord Saint-Clair gnawing at her patience. Rosalind had just bent to pull on her scuffed shoes when a knock, sharp and unmistakably commanding, cut through the quiet chamber.

Before Sophia could respond, the door creaked open, and both maidens stilled. The Queen Mother, Victoria, swept in, the air seeming to chill in her presence. Candlelight cast deeper shadows across the stone walls, and Sophia straightened, her gaze locking on her mother. Her fingers twitched at her sides, a coiled tension gathering low in her gut, heavy beneath her mother's imperious stare. "Mother?" she managed, struggling to smooth the edge from her voice. She could already feel her plans slipping further from reach.

Victoria's entrance was regal, her chin held high, eyes narrowing as she assessed her daughter and Rosalind. Without a word, both dipped into low curtsies, though Sophia's bow held a brittle stiffness.

In her hands, the Queen Mother held a small box, its jewel-encrusted surface catching the light. She extended it toward Sophia, her voice warm with a practiced affection. "My dear Sophia," she said, her tone smooth, almost too pleasant. "I bring thee a gift, one most fitting for this joyous occasion." Her eyes glinted as she offered the box, holding it as though it contained some rare treasure.

"Joyous occasion?" Sophia echoed silently, her heart sinking further. She forced a polite smile as she took the box from her mother's hands, though the weight felt foreign and unwelcome. "Thou art most gracious, Mother," she replied. "Yet, I must away—for Lord Saint-Clair doth await. Might I open this at a later hour?"

Victoria's eyes softened, a flicker of concern passing over her face before vanishing beneath a composed smile. "Thou canst not spare a moment for rest, yet thou must spare one to see what I've brought thee," she replied, her tone gentler now, a hint of persuasion softening her earlier command. Her gaze fell to the ornate box in her hands, a small, satisfied smile tugging at the corners of her lips as if admiring a prize hard-won. Her fingers traced the jeweled edge, the pride in her choice apparent without a word. "I wish for thee to wear these when thou dost meet his grace. Indulge me, child."

Resigned, Sophia forced a smile and pried open the box, revealing a pair of elegant white ankle boots, their leather so fine it glistened, adorned with delicate jewels and embroidery. They were fit for royalty, crafted with meticulous care, yet as Sophia's eyes lingered over the intricate details, her heart sank. These were shoes for show, not for walking—certainly not for one with a wounded leg.

Rosalind, quick to catch Sophia's silent plea, knelt to help her put on the boots. Their eyes met briefly; Sophia's frustration was plain, while Rosalind's gaze offered a quiet reassurance.

Victoria, meanwhile, settled into a nearby chair, her hand resting lightly on Sophia's shoulder, her thumb tracing the fabric of her daughter's dress with a motherly familiarity. "I admire thy dedication, my child," she said softly. "But remember, thou must not push thyself too far. There is no glory in courting whilst thou art unwell."

Sophia clenched her teeth, though the warmth of her mother's touch softened her impatience. "Yes, Mother," she replied, her voice quieter now, her frustration carefully subdued. "I shall take my rest only once I have met with Lord Saint-Clair."

Victoria's expression shifted, her eyes narrowing ever so slightly. "I would have thee well, Sophia," she said, a brief tenderness slipping into her voice. "Not only for this court but for thine own sake."

Sophia nodded, though inwardly her thoughts strained for freedom from this conversation. The sooner her mother left, the sooner she could meet Edward—and be done with the day's endless formalities.

But Victoria wasn't finished. "And, Lord Saint-Clair is not the only suitor who awaits thee. Dukes, Marquises, Counts—they all seek thy hand. Some were so vile, their very faces might have sent thee fleeing!" She laughed, a cold, dry sound that barely touched her eyes, as though the thought amused her. "But the Earl of Embrian… now, there is a man of true worth."

The mention of the Earl sent a chill down Sophia's spine. "The Earl of Embrian?" she repeated, disbelief coloring her voice. "Surely, thou dost jest, dear Mother. The man is..." Her voice wavered, barely hiding her distaste. "Is he not already bound in wedlock? And moreover—he is as broad as a cart, Mother! 'Tis naught short of a marvel that his poor steed doth endure such burden beneath him!"

Rosalind's shoulders trembled as she bent lower, stifling her laughter. She knew better than anyone the full extent of the Earl's repulsiveness, and Sophia's polite words did little justice to his grotesque nature.

Victoria's lips pressed into a thin line, though the flicker of amusement in her eyes betrayed her thoughts. "Thou art far too harsh, Sophia. The Earl is a man of fortune and position."

Rosalind, still fighting a smirk, finished lacing the second boot, glancing up at Sophia with a look that seemed to say, *Our work is done here.*

"The Earl is a man whose lady hath departed this life, my dear," Victoria continued, her voice softening yet firm. "Though he may lack in youthful charm, he doth possess both kindness and wealth." Her gaze flickered for a moment as if weighing her next words. "And shouldst thou outlive him—who can say? Perchance joy may yet find its way unto thee."

Victroia drew a breath, her expression shifting as her thoughts turned to His Grace. "As for Lord Saint-Clair," she began with poised grace, "his house doth indeed offer a noble match. Yet, heed my counsel—for whilst thou hast been absent, many a high-born maiden across the realms hath cast her eye upon him. All the wealthiest and titled ladies seek his favour, each hoping to capture his regard. Fair is he, both in countenance and fortune, and suitors flock to him as moths are drawn unto the flame." Victoria's gaze lingered on Sophia, her fingers brushing the fabric of her own sleeve in a thoughtful gesture, as if carefully choosing her next words. "I hath heard tell that even House Valefort wast eager for Princess Shorwynne to court him," she remarked, her tone measured, almost cautious. "'Tis said that, upon the very breath of thy vanishment, they did send word to House Saint-Clair with an offer most swift."

Sophia's hand tightened around the polished wood of her walking stick, her knuckles paling as she absorbed her mother's words. Displeasure swooped across her face, pulling her lips into a tight, accusatory purse. *Princess Shorwynne? I cannot feign surprise that her kin would forbear no delay in seizing upon action; my own blood would show like haste,* she thought, a faint, wry smile hovering at the edges of her mouth. *Were Shorwynne granted voice in such matters, I could not fault her judgment—for in truth, the field of suitors is naught but vile.*

Her gaze drifted to the floor, the resignation settling quietly into her expression, as if already resigned to the absurdity of their choices.

As soon as Rosalind finished fitting the shoe, Sophia reached for her walking stick and declared, "I must go, Mother." She turned to her handmaiden, gratitude evident in her gaze. "Thank thee, Rosalind."

Victoria rose as Sophia did, her expression gentle yet resolute. "Beyond these chambers stands one of our most steadfast guards. Shouldst thou desire it, he shall bear thee forth to Lord Saint-Clair," she offered sincerely, concern woven into her tone. It was clear she wished to spare her daughter any further strain, especially with Sophia's wounded leg.

Sophia blinked, her breath catching as her mother's words sank in. Her eyes darted to Victoria, brows knitting together, unsure whether to respond. For a brief moment, surprise flickered across her face, and though she managed to keep her composure, the weight of her mother's unexpected offer tugged at something deep within her. The thoughtfulness did not go unnoticed, especially as she dreaded the painful walk ahead.

Victoria's response was swift, her tone sharp as she clicked her fingers. "Canst thou not see the princess is ready? Fetch the guard," she commanded, her face filling with slight annoyance as if Rosalind's brief pause had wasted time. *

Rosalind bowed deeply, her voice quick and obedient. "As you wish, Your Highness," she said before hurrying to the door. The sound of the handle turning and the faint creak as it opened echoed softly through the chamber. As she peeked out, she saw five guards standing sentinel—the two who had accompanied her and Sophia earlier, along with three more in the Queen Mother's service. Their postures were rigid, faces solemn, as though the weight of royal duty pressed upon them. There was no sign of Sir Eadric, who had actually carried the princess here. He must have returned to the king.

Her eyes darted to a tall man nearby, one who looked important—a knight.

"Sir Hector!" Victoria's voice rang out, crisp and commanding, prompting immediate movement. At once, the largest knight stepped forward, his approach purposeful and precise, his presence looming over the rest.

Rosalind's eyes flickered with hesitation as Sir Hector drew closer, his towering frame casting a shadow over her. She quickly pulled the door wider and stepped back with a nod.

As Sir Hector entered, Rosalind closed the door softly behind him. She turned to face Sophia just as Sir Hector bowed low. "Your Highnesses," he intoned, his voice deep and respectful.

He wore the royal colours of deep purple, the tunic embroidered with golden threads tracing the lion rampant, the family crest of the crown. On his shoulder, Sophia's personal crest—a rose, delicately embroidered in silver—stood out, marking him as her sworn protector. His leather jerkin, polished to a high gleam, added to his imposing aura. The longsword at his side, with its hilt etched in both lion and rose, seemed an extension of his vigilance. As he shifted slightly, the blade caught the light, a glint reminding all of his readiness to defend the princess at any moment.

Victoria's face softened, a brief flicker of melancholy crossing her gaze as she turned to Sophia and asked, "Thou dost remember Sir Hector?" she asked, a note of nostalgia in her voice. The impressive figure looming before her caught her attention, its magnitude arresting. "He did once serve as protector to thy father, the late king," she continued, her gaze lingering on Sophia. "Many moons ago, long ere thy time," she added with gentle wistfulness, "the Marshal didst journey far afield to seek Sir Hector. Many a tale of his valor hath graced our ears." Pride tinged her voice. "And he didst not disappoint."

Sophia's brow furrowed in brief confusion as she greeted the knight. "I do remember thee," she said, her words careful. In her childhood, Sir Hector had been a distant figure—dutiful and ever-present but strictly professional. He'd been a sentinel of her father's court, one whom she'd known well enough to doubt he would give her the freedom that Sir Thomas had. She glanced quickly at her mother, as if to ask, *Why doth he bear mine crest upon his shoulder?* "Prithee, where is Sir Thomas?" Her previous guard had understood her well, allowing her the space she desired. But Sir Hector's unwavering stare unsettled her, his vigilance pressing heavily upon her, as though he would report her every step directly back to the Queen Mother.

An uneasy silence filled the chamber, tension hanging in the air. Victoria's expression stiffened slightly, as if taken aback by the question. "My dearest, he hath been dismissed," she replied, a hint of discomfort in her tone.

Sophia's voice wavered, hurt and confusion widening her eyes. "What! Mine ears must surely deceive me! Didst thou say he hath been dismissed?" Her words slipped out in a strained whisper, as if she struggled to voice them. "On what grounds was he dismissed, pray tell?" Her voice shook, disbelief twisting her expression. Sir Thomas had been her protector since childhood, a steadfast presence through all the turbulence. She clenched her fists as her heartbeat picked up. *Did they truly think to dismiss him, as though he were but a common trinket? Had they but re-assigned him within our ranks, I would not be so bereft.* The thought of him cast aside so coldly gnawed at her heart, a raw ache tightening in her chest.

The silence that followed was heavy, pressing down on the room. Sir Hector stood rigid, his face unreadable, his gaze fixed somewhere just above her shoulder, as if he too knew he was here as an outsider, replacing one who had been trusted. Rosalind's eyes darted to the floor, a tension crossing her features as she awaited the Queen Mother's reply.

Victoria's expression softened, just slightly, her gaze flickering before she cleared her throat. "Thou wert lost under Sir Thomas's watch, my dear," she said quietly, the words both soft and final, each one carrying the weight of her decision. "He hath failed in his duty to safeguard thee."

As the weight of her mother's words settled heavily in the chamber, Sophia's heart clenched. The thought of Sir Thomas—so steadfast and loyal—cast aside on her account gnawed at her conscience. She could picture his face in her mind's eye, his brow furrowed with concern, always at her side. Now, dismissed for her folly. Guilt clung to her like a second skin, her hands tightening as if to steady herself. But there was no time to linger on it now. The burden of duty called her forth.

She swallowed hard, turning toward Sir Hector, her voice catching under the strain of unspoken regret. "Sir Hector," she began, her words tinged with sorrow, "Wilt thou escort me to Lord Saint-Clair?"

Sir Hector, a figure of strength and duty, inclined his head with surprising gentleness, the furrow of his brow softening in quiet understanding. Wordlessly, he stepped forward, his hands steady as he gathered her into his arms. The coolness of his armour contrasted with the warmth of his embrace; his grip was firm, unyielding, yet mindful of her injured leg.

Victoria rose with the grace of a queen, her gaze fixed on her daughter as she turned to the handmaiden. "Rosalind, unbar the door," she commanded, her voice cutting through the stillness with authority.

Rosalind dipped her head swiftly, her fingers trembling slightly as she reached for the handle. The heavy door creaked open, revealing the dim stone corridor once again. Faint daylight filtered through narrow slits in the thick walls, casting thin beams across the five guards standing at attention. A chill lingered in the air, seeping from the stone and adding to the solemn atmosphere, their breath faintly visible in the cool light.

*

The narrow spiral stairs twisted beneath their feet, each step echoing faintly against the stone walls. The castle's damp air clung to the cold stone, while thin streams of sunlight trickled through narrow windows, streaking across the steps. Shadows bent and shifted with every turn, the dim light warping their figures as they descended.

At the front, two guards led the way with measured precision, their armour softly clinking with each step, swords hanging ready at their sides. Behind them, the Queen Mother followed with regal poise, her gown whispering against the stone steps, the delicate fabric brushing the damp surface as she moved. Though the staircase was narrow, she held her chin high, her eyes fixed ahead, unflinching.

Sir Hector followed close behind, bearing Sophia in his arms. His every movement was steady, though the strain of carrying her down the spiraling stairway grew more apparent as they descended. The daylight from the narrow windows cast his silhouette long against the walls, and Sophia clung to his shoulder, her pulse quickening with each downward step. The walls pressed in as if the air itself was tightening around her, and her leg ached with every slight shift in Sir Hector's arms.

Rosalind and the Queen Mother's attendant came next, their steps light, though Rosalind's gaze flickered between Sophia and the winding stairs, ever watchful. Two more guards brought up the rear, hands resting on the hilts of their swords, sharp eyes scanning the shadows as they descended.

At last, the base of the stairwell appeared, opening into a corridor lit by beams of sunlight pouring through high windows. The cold shadows clinging to the stones were chased away by the light, and

ahead, the grand doors to the banquet hall stood tall, their polished wood gleaming in the midday sun. Two sentinels, armoured and rigid, flanked the doors, faces betraying no emotion as they watched the Queen Mother's party approach.

Victoria paused before the doors, her brow furrowing as she turned to Sir Hector and Sophia. "Sophia," she murmured, her voice firm but quiet, "Thou must needs walk from hence."

With a subtle nod, Sir Hector eased Sophia down, guiding her to stand. The weight of her body felt foreign, her legs trembling beneath her. Pain shot through her wounded limb, and she bit down hard on her lip, willing herself to endure it. Rosalind swiftly presented the walking stick, hands steady as she held it out before the princess, her eyes filled with quiet understanding.

Sophia's fingers wrapped around the smooth wood, her knuckles pale as they gripped it for support. She did not speak, but the silent exchange between her and Rosalind conveyed more than words could. Her lips parted slightly in a weak smile—an acknowledgment of the aid she was too exhausted to voice aloud.

"Thou hast my thanks," she whispered, the words barely escaping her throat, strained and breathless. Each step felt like a battle, her body heavy and uncooperative, breath shallow as the walking stick bore most of her weight.

Victoria's gaze swept over the guards, her eyes sharp with command. Without a word, the sentries at the grand doors moved with practiced precision, stepping aside in perfect unison. One guard stepped forward, grasping the heavy door's iron handle, pulling it open with a slow creak. Sunlight burst into the dark corridor, flooding it with golden warmth.

"Her Highness the Queen Mother, and Her Highness the Princess," the guard bellowed, his voice reverberating through the hall. The announcement cut through the stillness like a call to arms, and as the door swung fully open, every eye inside turned to watch them enter.

Victoria stepped forward first, her regal bow to the king both dutiful and affectionate. Her son's gaze flickered briefly toward her, his chin dipping almost imperceptibly in response. It was a small gesture, but enough to signal his understanding. Behind her, Sophia's walking stick tapped faintly against the floor, though to her, each sound echoed like a hammer striking stone. Her vision blurred, and the pain in her leg sharpened with every step, yet she pressed forward, eyes set ahead, searching for Edward.

Edward sat at the far end of the hall, dressed in the deep brown of his house. The emblem of his family—the oak tree—was emblazoned on his tunic, each branch and leaf rendered in such striking detail that it appeared forged from iron.

Edward's shoulders sagged, his usual strength absent. His arms hung loosely at his sides, each movement slower and heavier, as if his body resisted the exhaustion pulling him down. The toll of sleepless hours showed in every line of his posture.

Sophia's steps faltered as she neared the grand table, her bow to the king slow and careful, her body betraying her exhaustion. "Your Majesty," she said, her voice taut, each syllable laced with the effort to keep herself upright. Her heart pounded—not from respect, but from the gravity of the moment and the knowledge that Edward's news awaited.

She turned to Lord Edward, managing only a strained "Your Grace." Her gaze held urgency, a silent plea for a private word, for answers that only he could give. She dared not look in Charles's direction; the mere thought of his eyes on her sent a shudder through her spine.

Sophia could feel Charles's gaze on her—sharp and relentless, like a cold wind cutting straight through her.

Her shoulders drew back as she straightened, spine lifting with quiet resolve. Her fingers tightened around the walking stick as if bracing against an unseen force. The room's air seemed colder, though she dared not glance in Charles's direction; the intensity of his unyielding stare seemed to seep into her skin.

Edward pushed himself up from his seat, his hand dragging across the table for support. His tunic hung awkwardly, askew and dirtied from the night's labors, with bits of leaves stubbornly clinging to his hair. Dark circles shadowed his eyes, and he blinked slowly, as if sleep fought to claim him with each breath.

He looked as though he had carried a heavy burden for far too long, his posture sagging beneath its weight.

"Your highness, Princess Sophia," he began, his voice thick with fatigue as he raised a hand to rub his eyes. Blinking away his exhaustion, he forced a weary smile, bowing his head slightly. "Thou art a welcome sight to mine eyes, though I wish it were in better times. 'Tis said thou hast endured much hardship."

She clung to the walking stick, her body swaying as she fought to remain standing. "Thou art too kind, Your Grace," she murmured, her voice barely more than a breath, the effort of speaking pulling at her dwindling strength. Her mind whirled with questions she dared not voice here. She silently question *Noor—hath he found her? Pray, tell me, is she safe?*

"I must beg thy forgiveness for my absence," she continued, each word trembling as her strength faded. "I would... strive to make a renewed impression, when this frail form doth permit."

Edward's lips tightened, his gaze weary yet soft as he looked at her. He nodded in acknowledgment. "There is naught to forgive," he replied, his voice steady despite his own fatigue. "Thou hast endured much, far more than any should. It is I who am sorry for thy hardship." He glanced briefly toward the king and added, "When thou art well, I would be honoured to court thee properly."

Sophia's fingers whitened as her grip on the walking stick tightened. Her body screamed in pain, yet her face remained impassive, chin lifted, her will as strong as her limbs were weak. She locked eyes with Edward, her silent plea unmistakable— *Pray, I beseech thee, speak unto me at once!*

Edward's eyes met hers for a fleeting moment, the unspoken question hanging heavy between them. Without a word, he lowered his head, the slow, deliberate motion speaking louder than any words. His search had yielded nothing.

Sophia's breath hitched. Her fingers curled tighter around the walking stick, her knuckles paling as her knees wavered beneath her. The weight of the moment pressed against her chest like the iron bindings of a corset. She shifted her stance, forcing herself upright as the faint glimmer of hope within her was extinguished, snuffed out like a candle caught in a sudden draft.

Her lips parted, a silent gasp escaping as her face paled further. The realisation stabbed at her, sharp and unrelenting: Noor—gone? The thought twisted in her chest like a blade, yet she held her composure, her breathing shallow and uneven, her chin lifting as though sheer will alone could keep her standing.

Edward's voice, soft and careful, broke through the tension. "Wouldst thou allow me to accompany thee on a short walk, Your Highness?" His words were an offering, a quiet shield from the prying eyes of the court.

Sophia's lips trembled as she parted them to speak, but before the words could escape, another voice sliced through the air.

"Nay, she must take her rest." The Queen Mother's tone was firm, a command wrapped in care. She stood close to Sophia, her silver hair catching the morning light that filtered through the narrow windows above. "Her frame is ill-suited to bear such a burden."

Sophia, her body trembling under the strain, dared a quiet plea. "Dearest Mother, I pray thee… grant him leave to escort me unto mine chambers. Sir Hector shall attend us, trailing close behind. Should I falter, he may lend his aid." Her words, though soft, carried a resolute strength that defied her frailty.

The Queen Mother's sharp gaze lingered on Sophia, her lips pressed thin, before shifting toward King John at the head of the table. Her face betrayed nothing as she turned to him, waiting for his word. Across the table, the king paused mid-drink, his chalice hovering near his lips. He looked to Sophia, the silence stretching as he weighed her request.

"If 'tis Sophia's wish," he said at last, his voice steady, though the lines on his face betrayed his worry.

Sophia inclined her head, her voice firming slightly. "Aye, it is mine wish, Your Majesty."

The king's attention turned to Sir Hector. "Sir Hector, thou hast served our kin with steadfast loyalty. Guard her well, and let no harm befall her."

The knight bowed low, his polished breastplate glinting in the daylight. "I shall, Your Majesty."

King John's gaze flicked back to Sophia. "Very well. Lord Saint-Clair, attend my sister. Sir Hector shall remain at thy side, though at a respectful distance."

Sophia, leaning heavily on the walking stick, managed a weak curtsy. The movement nearly undid her, but she steadied herself with a deep, uneven breath. "Thank thee, Your Majesty," she whispered, her voice thin but unwavering.

Edward bowed in turn, his motion slow and deliberate, before stepping closer to her. He offered his arm, and her trembling fingers clasped it firmly, her need for support more than physical. As they began their slow journey from the hall, she leaned into him, every step an unspoken battle against her own body's betrayal.

The guards pulled open the heavy oak doors, their hinges groaning in protest as a shaft of sunlight spilled into the hall. The golden warmth brushed Sophia's face for the briefest moment before the cold hallway beyond swallowed them. The chill bit at her exposed skin, but it was nothing compared to the weight of despair pressing on her chest.

Behind them, Sir Hector and Rosalind followed at a measured distance, the knight's boots echoing on the stone floor. The grand doors closed with a low, resounding thud, sealing the whispers of the court behind them.

As they moved further into the corridor, Sophia's steps faltered, her legs trembling, but she pressed on. Each step carried a quiet strain, her legs trembling under the effort, the ache creeping like a shadow that refused to lift. Yet her face remained calm, her chin lifted as she locked her grief behind a mask of regal composure.

*

Sophia's footsteps echoed through the narrow corridor, each one slower and more labored than the last. The walking stick bore most of her weight, her fingers gripping it tightly as her legs threatened to give out beneath her. The cool stone walls seemed to press in around her, amplifying the sound of her every step, the faint shuffle of her gown, the soft rasp of her breath. Beside her, Lord Edward moved in near silence, but the fatigue hung visibly upon him—his shoulders slightly hunched, his eyes heavy with weariness. The once-ornate tunic, now dirtied and askew, whispered of long hours and little rest.

The silence between them was thick, broken only by the soft click of their shoes against the floor and the distant echo of Sir Hector and Rosalind trailing behind. Sophia's mind raced, but she dared not speak, the fear of Charles overhearing their conversation lurking at the back of her thoughts like a spectre. His words still echoed in her mind, chilling and venomous: *If thou speakest, I shall ruin thee.* Every step felt like a gamble, her brother's threat tightening her chest and sealing her lips.

Edward glanced sideways at her, his brow furrowed as though debating whether to speak. He finally cleared his throat, his voice soft, wavering. "Your Highness… if I may be so bold… thou dost look… different." His words hung awkwardly in the air, his eyes briefly darting back to Sir Hector. "Clean," he added, confusion creasing his brow. His voice lowered, barely a murmur as he asked, "How didst thou escape? What happened in the dungeon?"

Sophia's breath hitched, her chest tightening as she thought of Charles. The memory of his hands on her arm, the cold glint in his eyes as he whispered his threat—*Speak and Robert dies*. She glanced behind her, making sure Sir Hector and Rosalind were far enough away. Leaning slightly toward Edward, her voice dropped to a whisper. "My brother," she began, her lips trembling as she spoke, "His watch is ceaseless; ever doth his gaze linger upon me. I may not speak with freedom." Her eyes darted again to their followers. "Thou must be careful," she warned, her voice trembling with urgency. "Speak thou naught of this to any soul."

Edward's jaw clenched, his concern growing. Edward's gaze lingered on her, his mouth tightening slightly. His hand twitched as if he wanted to reach out but hesitated, her warning hanging heavy between them. The urge to offer help stirred within him, but the danger in her warning held him back. *If I were to court her, aye, even wed her, might I not shield her from the machinations of Prince Charles? His Highness is not without frailty—aye, that infernal cat, Midnight, doth hold sway over him as no man ever could. 'Tis a trifling creature, yet it doth reveal a chink in his armour. Moreover, my family doth lay claim to lands that His Highness coveteth, yet no boon nor bargain could I strike, save it be tethered to the princess's hand in marriage. Fie upon it, for a favour so bound is no favour at all, but a chain.* "Thou hast my word," he replied quietly, his voice firm yet tinged with hesitation. "I shall hold my tongue. Yet surely, the king—thy brother—might lend thee his aid?" He searched her face, hoping for some sign that he might help, but seeing only the deep fear that held her captive.

Sophia's heart pounded in her chest, her thoughts swirling with uncertainty. Could she place her trust in King John? Would he stand as her protector, or would he cast his lot with Charles? The memory of her brother's threats was fresh in her mind, the image of Robert's life hanging by a thread. "I cannot," she whispered, tears welling in her eyes. "Thou shalt not speak of this, neither to him nor to any other. To do so would imperil thee—aye, greatly imperil thee."

They turned a corner, the dim light of the corridor casting long shadows across the walls as the stairwell loomed ahead. Sophia's gaze swept the hall, ensuring once more that they were not overheard. Her voice, barely above a whisper, trembled with fear. "Lord Edward… what didst thou find?" Her breath quickened, the anxiety knotting her stomach. "At the banquet hall… thy nod… what did it mean?"

Edward's face tightened, the memory of their earlier encounter gnawing at him. He had seen the pain in her eyes then, and now, standing before her, he could feel the weight of her desperation. *I should have searched harder,* he thought bitterly. *If I am to win her hand, how can I fail in such a simple task?* His voice, hoarse with exhaustion, wavered. "Your Highness," he began, hesitant. His throat felt dry as he searched for the words. "There was not a trace of the peasant to be found." He used her station rather than her name, hoping it would ease the weight of his news, but in truth, disappointment gnawed at him. His fingers tightened unconsciously at his side, recalling the sight of blood-soaked mud and the unmistakable marks left by something—or someone—being dragged. He had stood there, recalling the signs, his gut twisting in frustration.

Though he would never admit it, he had expected more of her. The blood in the earth told a grim story, yet something about those prints spoke of resistance. *She must have fought*, he thought, with a begrudging sense of admiration he had not wanted to feel.

Sophia's body tensed, her knuckles white around the walking stick. "What meanest thou, no body?" she breathed, dread creeping into her voice.

Edward's face twisted with regret. "Blood hath been shed." he admitted quietly, the words bitter on his tongue. "There wast much of it, yet no body to be found." He shook his head slightly, the memory still fresh. "The ground lay drenched, yet 'twas as if it had been... scoured pure, as though some hand had come for her ere the deed was sealed."

Sophia's breath hitched again, her mind reeling. The image of Noor's broken body, lying somewhere unknown, flashed before her eyes. The thought did twist her within, fear and guilt gnawing at her as a ravenous beast wouldst upon its prey. "Might it be possible," she faltered, her voice a mere breath as though fearing the weight of her own words, "that she yet liveth?"

Edward's eyes flickered with uncertainty. "I cannot rightly say, Your highness." he replied softly, his hand instinctively reaching out toward her arm. His fingers hovered just above her sleeve, hesitant. *Could I have perchance overlooked aught?* "But 'tis clear something terrible hath happened."

Sophia's lip quivered, her breaths ragged as she fought to hold back the tears welling in her eyes. The weight of it all was unbearable. She had sent Noor to her doom, and now the consequences pressed down on her like a heavy shroud.

Edward's voice softened further. "Milady, thy strength hath been tested beyond measure." His hand gently rested on her arm, though the gesture was hesitant, unsure if she would accept it. "Thou dost not need to bear this alone."

Her composure broke. With a sudden sob, her body sagged against him, her hand clutching desperately at his sleeve. The tears flowed freely now, soaking into his tunic as she buried her face in his shoulder. Edward stood still, his own heart aching for the broken princess in his arms. He whispered softly, "Shouldst thou wish it, as per our accord, I shall continue my search for answers, Your Highness... I do swear it."

From his earliest days at court, Edward had watched Sophia from afar, the weight of his father's words ever-present in his mind. He had been but a boy of ten when the seed was first planted—that one day, he might court the princess. Since then, every glance across crowded halls, every formal greeting, had carried that unspoken possibility. But now, with her trembling in his arms, those distant imaginings felt more certain than ever.

Edward's breath caught, his gaze drifting briefly to the floor before returning to her tear-streaked face, the weight of unspoken words pressing between them. "I saw thee yesterday," Edward began, his voice deliberate, each word heavier than the last. "Thy companion... she is no common peasant. I have seen warriors aplenty, and there is a strength within her unlike that of the ordinary folk." A hint of admiration crept into his tone, something he had not expected to feel.

Sophia's eyes met his, a flicker of hope sparking amidst her despair. His hand moved gently, brushing a damp strand of hair from her face. Her body trembled against him, each breath labored and shallow. Her legs wobbled, weakened by fear and exhaustion, barely able to hold her up. "How much blood can one lose afore hope is gone?" she whispered, her voice fragile.

Edward exhaled, his jaw tightening as the fatigue of the long night weighed heavily on him. "I know not, milady," he said softly, each word slow and deliberate. "The night hath been long... but thou must rest. When strength returns, I shall seek her again. Mayhap the healers have found her." His voice carried the weight of exhaustion, the promise firm though faint doubt lingered beneath it.

Sophia nodded weakly, her body sagging further into his. She could barely stand, her strength fading with each shallow breath. Yet Edward's steady presence, his quiet words, gave her just enough resolve to hold herself upright.

From the shadowed curve of the stairwell, Mary Winterbourne stood watching. Her hand pressed flat against the rough stone, its chill grounding her as she strained to make sense of what she saw. Edward's arm lingered around Sophia's shoulders, steadying her, but the closeness between them struck Mary like an ill-timed blow. The way Sophia leaned into him, her fingers clutching the edge of his tunic, unsettled her deeply.

Mary's thoughts turned sharply to Robert. His easy smile, his unguarded trust—how would he react to such a scene? The image of him, so unaware of what unfolded now, made her stomach twist. A flicker of heat rose in her chest, though whether it was anger or dread, she could not tell. Her fingers curled against the stone as though bracing against some invisible force.

Her lips tightened, her breath catching briefly. *What game is this?* she thought. Edward was but a suitor, was he not? And yet, this closeness seemed too practiced, too natural to be happenstance. A tangle of questions knotted in her mind as she stared, silent and unmoving, her pulse quickening at the sight.

Mary stepped back into the shadows, the curve of the spiral staircase forcing her to tread carefully. The uneven stone beneath her feet was cold, the tight coils of the stairwell disorienting. She hesitated, glancing back at Edward and Sophia. Whatever words passed between them, they were too heavy for her to interrupt, though the weight of the moment pressed on her like a stone.

Her gaze lingered a moment longer on Edward's hand, still resting against Sophia. She pulled back further into the shadowed stairwell, her mind spinning with the consequences of what she had seen. *Robert deserves better than to be blindsided by this,* she thought, the bitter taste of unease curling on her tongue.

Without thinking, she stepped back, her fingers digging into the stone wall, searching for something solid to hold onto as her world tilted with the realisation.

Without a sound, Mary slipped down the spiral staircase, each step quick but deliberate as she sought the cover of the shadows. She knew they would come this way—Sophia, Sir Hector, the handmaiden, and the guards—and they could not see her. Pausing a few steps below the turn, she pressed herself against the cold stone wall, her breathing shallow, her body rigid with tension. The narrow windows cast sharp beams of light on the steps above, but here in the curve of the stairs, she was hidden. She waited, heart pounding, listening for the faint echoes of their approach.

The muffled sound of footsteps grew closer, the soft rustle of fabric announcing the princess's ascent. Mary's pulse quickened, her back pressing harder against the stone as she strained to remain silent. The warmth of the day crept through the walls, but it did nothing to soothe the cold dread curling in her chest. As they passed, she caught fragments of their voices, though she dared not move, not even to breathe.

The royal party continued upward, the sound of their ascent fading. Only then did Mary allow herself to exhale, her body slowly unwinding from the tension that had gripped her. The air still felt heavy, charged with the weight of what she had witnessed.

Mary's thoughts collided violently, her mind a storm of confusion and anger. Sophia and Robert... The memory of her brother's love for the princess slashed through her like a knife. How could she hold another man? It was as though Robert had been wiped from Sophia's life, discarded like he never existed. The sight of Sophia leaning on Edward sparked something raw and fierce in Mary's chest.
"Hath she forgotten him so swiftly?"

The anger twisted into something darker, but another thought gnawed at her relentlessly. Wherefore doth Noor remain? She had hoped her sister had found safety—perhaps even taken refuge with Lord Edward. But then... Charles had claimed Noor left for a tavern. *"Hath he lied?"* Or spake he the truth? Edward's face flashed in her memory, his expression weary, drawn from exhaustion. Hath he spent the night at the tavern with Noor, or hath some graver misfortune befallen them?

A tightening unease coiled within Mary, gripping her stomach like a vice. *"Where doth Noor linger?"* The thought gnawed at her relentlessly. *"Hath Sophia, Lord Edward, and Prince Charles plotted together in some twisted jest?"* Each unanswered question circled like a predator, her mind clouded by the sharp edges of doubt and fear that only seemed to deepen with every passing moment.

Mary lingered a moment longer, her fists clenched as she leaned into the rough stone. The weight of everything she had witnessed and suspected pressed down on her, as heavy and unyielding as the walls themselves.

As she descended the steps further, her pace quickened. She had to escape, unnoticed. But even as she hurried along, her mind raced with conflicting thoughts.

Suddenly, rounding a corner, she collided with an unexpected figure.

The impact struck her hard, stealing the breath from her chest. Her feet faltered, the world beneath her shifting unsteadily, as though the ground itself were tipping. Before she could fully lose balance, firm hands gripped her shoulders, steadying her, holding her upright as her surroundings blurred.

Mary blinked, startled, and her gaze lifted to meet that of a man garbed in a purple tunic. Her breath hitched as her eyes fell upon the royal crest embroidered on his chest—a golden crown adorned with amethysts, perched atop a lion's head. The emblem was unmistakable, marking him as a knight of the king's guard, or perhaps one even closer to the crown.

Her heart pounded as she lingered on the crest. *The king's knight?* she wondered, her gaze tracing the intricate details of the lion. Though he wore no crown himself, she knew only those of the highest ranks bore such marks. Yet, there was a warmth in his manner, a softness in his eyes that seemed illfitting for a man of the king's station. *A noble knight, then,* she thought, her mind spinning. *Trusted by the royal family, no doubt.*

"Forgive me, good sir knight," Mary gasped, her voice trembling as she scrambled to regain her balance. "I saw thee not."

The man's expression brightened, a warmth settling in his features as if her presence delighted him. "Thou needst not apologize," he replied, his smile soft but full of charm. "Though I had not expected to meet thee in such a fashion. I have awaited this moment longer than thou knowest."

Mary's pulse quickened, confusion swelling in her chest. *What dost he mean by such words,* she wondered, her breath catching in her throat. As his voice lingered in her mind, she dared to study his face more fully. *'Tis he,* she thought, her breath catching. *The handsome and charming nobleman.* A man of station and grace, whose presence lingered in her memory longer than she dared admit. Recognition stirred within her as she recalled their meeting upon her first day as chambermaid—a man both handsome and charming, yet unsettling in his allure. *A knight of the king's guard...* Handsome as he was, trouble often followed such men, and she had no desire to be ensnared by it.

Her eyes flickered to the floor, and her hands fisted into the fabric of her dress, as if seeking anchor amidst the rising tide of her unease. *I cannot linger here... not with him.* Clearing her throat, she spoke softly, barely above a whisper. "I should take my leave, my lord," her voice wavered, the weight of his presence pressing down on her. "Once again, forgive mine clumsiness."

King John's pause stretched longer than expected, a flicker of surprise crossing his features at her response. Few women, if any, had declined a moment alone with him—let alone twice. His usual composure slipped for a brief second as he processed her reluctance.

Recovering, a cautious smile tugged at the corners of his mouth. "If thou canst bear it," he began lightly, his voice laced with curiosity, "mayhap I might accompany thee to wherever thou art bound? My attendants could use a brief respite."

Mary's heart thundered within her chest. *Why doth he insist? Hath he not maidens aplenty vying for his favour, or matters of greater import than to trifle with me so?* The unease that had begun as a faint whisper now roared within her, each moment weighing heavier upon her mind. *Would refusal stir his ire? What am I to do?* Her lips quivered, and though she forced a response, it came laden with reluctance.

"It would be an honour, my lord," she spoke, her voice straining to hide her discomfort. Hastily, she added, "Though I am but bound for the next chamber."

King John glanced toward his attendants, who waited at a respectful distance. With a flick of his hand, his voice rang with quiet command. "Thou art dismissed." The men bowed and disappeared down the stone corridor, their footsteps fading into the quiet.

Mary watched them leave, uncertainty gnawing at her. *Should I curtsy?* she wondered, her eyes flicking back to the crest on his tunic—the royal purple, the golden crown resting atop the lion's head. *The king's personal knights?* A chill crept down her spine, though the warmth in his gaze did much to counter it. The weight of his rank pressed invisibly between them, a silent force that made her skin prickle. Though he spoke with warmth, there was an unmistakable authority in the way he stood, the crest on his chest gleaming with significance. The very air around him seemed to shift, a reminder that men of his kind could bend the wills of others with a mere word.

A faint smile tugged at her lips, though her heart continued to pound. "Thou commandest much loyalty, my lord," she remarked, her tone light, though her thoughts were still heavy. *Powerful and kind? Such a contrast to the cruelty of the prince.*

King John's laughter echoed warmly, filling the cold corridor with its richness. In his eyes, a playful gleam danced, as though he held a secret only he could share. *She doth not know who I truly am,* he mused, finding her innocence refreshing amid the games of the court.

"One can only hope," he replied with a chuckle, "that one day, I might command thy loyalty as well." Beneath his words lingered something deeper, a note of longing, though she remained unaware of his true identity.

Mary's shoulders tensed at his words, the weight of his gaze heavy. "I am but a humble chambermaid, my lord," she murmured, her voice small. "Thou wouldst have no reason to remember me." There was a quiet resignation in her tone, a soft acceptance of her place in the world. *Why would such a noble man take an interest in me? Dost he require aught of my service?*

A flicker of confusion crossed King John's face. His voice softened, sincerity lacing his tone as he said, "I forget not a face such as thine." His gaze held hers, lingering with unspoken depth.

Her cheeks flushed, warmth spreading from her face to her ears. His words, simple as they were, left her feeling exposed, vulnerable. *Beautiful?* she thought, the word foreign on her tongue. "Beautiful?" she whispered, the question barely audible as though testing the word for the first time.

Without a sound, Mary's fingers fidgeted nervously with the edges of her apron, a subtle sign of her growing unease. A subtle discomfort crept up her spine, a feeling she couldn't quite shake. Though she had faced unwanted advances and suggestive remarks before, there was something about this moment that unsettled her, something different that lingered in the space between them. This nobleman, one of the king's knights as she assumed, was offering her sincere compliments and companionship, something she was neither expecting nor prepared for. *Surely, he hath no intentions to lay with one of such low standing as I?* Mary's thoughts churned as she cast a furtive glance at him, heart fluttering with uncertainty. *Doth he offer his company so freely to all the maids? Or perchance, he doth seek to vet me? Ensuring the royal family be served by none but the best?* Her thoughts swirled in a flurry of uncertainty, her heart racing beneath her chest.

As she stood there, her cheeks flushing with a soft hue, a faint, almost foolish smile tugged at her lips. A servant passed by, his face etched with shock as his gaze flickered between Mary and the man by her side. In all his years of service, the king had never afforded him so much as a passing glance, let alone such company. Bowing his head in reverence, the servant quickened his pace, yet his curiosity lingered in his gaze, leaving Mary with a sinking feeling as though she had been caught doing something improper.

The momentary warmth that had blossomed within her dissipated like morning mist, replaced by a familiar shame that weighed heavily on her chest. *Who am I to stand here with him?* Straightening her back, she fought to regain her composure, her voice tinged with resignation as she spoke. "I truly must take my leave, my lord," she said, her eyes lowering as her unease settled in.

Yet, in the king's ears, her words twisted in the space between them, and what he heard was not "I" but "we." A grin spread across his face, the warmth of his smile unmistakable. "Lead the way, then?" His voice carried an eagerness that left Mary reeling, her heart pounding louder in her chest.

She swallowed, her thoughts turning to Noor. *Surely, she hath returned to the cottage by now, mayhap after a night of drinking...* she reassured herself, though the nagging worry gnawed at her resolve. She took a few careful steps back, recreating the distance between herself and the knight. "It is this way, my lord," she answered softly, gesturing toward a chamber not far from the servant's quarters, her voice as composed as she could manage.

As they began walking, an awkwardness hung between them like an unseen weight. Mary's mind raced with questions. *From what noble house doth he hail? Why hath he such a retinue?* Yet, her fear of offending him held her back, and she said nothing.

King John, sensing the tension, broke the silence. "So," he began, his voice light but with genuine curiosity, "how hast thou found thy new role as chambermaid?"

Mary hesitated, her shoulders stiffening as thoughts of the prince flared within her. "As well as one can when serving the royal family," she replied, bitterness seeping through her words before she could catch herself.

A flicker of anger danced in her eyes as she spoke, her frustration with Prince Charles bubbling to the surface. "I would rather serve pigs than continue this service," she muttered under her breath, her voice trembling with barely restrained emotion. Her fingers clenched tightly around the fabric of her apron, her eyes glistening as she fought the rising urge to break down. "Between thee and me," she whispered, her words bitter and laced with quiet desperation, "I long to be rid of this place."

The king's eyebrows arched in surprise at her boldness, a chuckle escaping his lips. "Is the royal family truly so terrible?" he asked, amusement mingling with curiosity. A slight lift of his brow accompanied the faint curl of his lips, an unspoken acknowledgment of the boldness in her words. His gaze lingered on her, as if savoring the rare honesty she offered—a contrast to the polished flattery he was accustomed to. Surely, she must have known who he was by now? Yet her words held no caution, no fear of consequence.

Realizing the weight of her words, Mary stiffened. *What if this knight is close to Prince Charles?* Regret gnawed at her, but she forced a smile, hoping to mend what had been spoken. "It is not terrible, my lord," she lied, her tone attempting to be light, though her eyes betrayed her uncertainty.

The king nodded, though he sensed the lie beneath her words. Hoping to distract her from her discontent, he offered something unexpected. "Hast thou seen the secret garden within these walls?" he asked, his voice softening with a hint of nostalgia. Few knew of the hidden refuge, and fewer still were allowed within its gates. The garden had long been his refuge, a quiet haven where the weight of the crown seemed to ease from his shoulders.

Mary's brow furrowed in confusion. "A garden, my lord? Within the castle?" Her voice betrayed her uncertainty. She had toiled in the fields outside the walls, but she had never heard of a garden within.

The king's eyes brightened as he spoke of the garden. "Aye," he said, his voice rich with memory. "Tucked away from prying eyes. 'Tis a place of solace." He extended his arm toward her, his smile inviting her to follow.

Mary's heart raced. She felt a tug, a yearning to see this hidden world he spoke of. Yet the servant's gaze from earlier, the silent reminder of her place, lingered in her mind. She hesitated, her hand trembling slightly. "I thank thee for thy kind offer, but I must tend to mine duties," she murmured, her voice unsteady. "Prince Charles will not take kindly if I neglect his chambers."

King John's smile widened at her words, his amusement evident. "Thou needst not fear him," he reassured, his voice soft but confident. "He is but the host in King's stead." He chuckled, thinking of his younger brother's airs. "I shall tell him myself that 'twas I who detained thee."

Mary's eyes widened in disbelief. "Thou wouldst speak so to the prince?" Her voice carried a note of astonishment, the very idea that someone could speak to Prince Charles in such a manner seemed impossible to her. But beneath her disbelief, hope flickered. *Could this man truly have the power to shield me from the prince's wrath?*

With a playful gleam in his eye, King John gave her a knowing smile. "My fair maid," he said lightly, "I speak to the prince however I see fit." His confidence radiated, and Mary felt the weight of his authority press upon her like the gentle touch of a cloak.

A nervous laugh bubbled from her lips. "But, my lord," she stammered, "wilt thou not face trouble for such boldness?"

King John shook his head, his smile never wavering. "Fear not, I shall have a word with the king if needs be," he said, his words rich with hidden meaning. His warmth remained, but something in his tone suggested that his position was far more secure than she realized.

Mary's mind raced. The mere mention of the king filled her with dread. *Would he truly stand by me if I anger the prince?* Doubt gnawed at her, but as she gazed into his eyes, there was something steady, something sure that made her want to believe him. "Art thou sure thou canst withstand the prince's wrath?" she asked, her voice quiet, unsure.

"Fear not," he repeated, his voice gentle. "I am not one to be trifled with, especially not by the likes of Prince Charles." He extended his arm once more, his gesture one of reassurance. "Whenever thou needst a shield, consider me thine."

A warmth blossomed within Mary's chest, her cheeks flushing as his words sunk in. For the first time in longer than she could remember, she felt seen—truly seen. She nodded shyly, a soft smile curving her lips. Something had shifted between them, an invisible thread pulling her toward him, as though the very air around them had drawn them closer.

What is this? she wondered, her heart fluttering as if caught in some enchantment.

As they walked together, the corridors seemed to stretch endlessly, each footfall echoing with an unease Mary could not shake. Each stolen glance toward him sent a flutter through her chest, her pulse quickening with each step they took side by side. *Wouldst thou say this is how Robert felt upon first meeting the princess? Enchanted by her charm and fair countenance? Am I naught but a fool, as my brother hath been before me?* The question gnawed at her, for it had been years since any man stirred such feelings in her chest—since the innocent days of her childhood, when she'd fancied the baker's son, a fondness that ended with the bitter taste of heartbreak. After that, she had sworn to shield her heart, to never let it be laid bare to another.

Yet now, walking beside this man of rank, her pulse fluttered traitorously beneath her ribs. *He seeks naught but a passing moment of kindness,* she reminded herself, *a fleeting distraction from the burdens of his station.* And though she repeated it in her mind, the warmth of his presence stirred something deeper within her.

As they passed the head chambermaid, who offered a nod laced with confusion, Mary averted her gaze, heat prickling the back of her neck. The servants, guards, and attendants they passed seemed to linger with their stares, judgment simmering behind their eyes. *What doth they think?* she wondered, feeling the weight of whispers that had yet to be spoken. She knew all too well that Rumours would soon swirl through the castle like smoke, and it would not be long before Prince Charles himself heard of her peculiar companion. Fear coiled in her stomach, her breath hitching as she imagined the fury that would soon be upon her. Her heart pounded, each beat a reminder of the storm she knew was coming. Her fingers curled into fists at her sides, her breath coming in shallow, uneven pulls as she prepared for the inevitable storm that would soon follow.

As they neared the entrance to the private quarters, once held by the late king, Mary's chest tightened with dread. It had been made clear when she first arrived—those halls were forbidden to her kind. The royal family had decreed it so, wishing to keep their father's memory undisturbed.

Her hand moved of its own accord, brushing against his arm as though seeking an anchor. "My lord," she stammered, her voice barely above a whisper, "we are not permitted within... 'tis not allowed." Her eyes darted nervously toward the guards stationed nearby, their presence a silent reminder of the boundaries she was never to cross. Panic swelled within her, and her pulse quickened like a rabbit caught in a snare. *I must turn back. I cannot be seen here, not with this royal knight.*

The man beside her chuckled softly, a jest on his lips. "Mayhap we should fight our way in?" His tone was light, but as his gaze met hers, the humour died on his tongue. Mary's wide-eyed terror froze him in place, her fear so palpable that it stole the air from the corridor.

The warmth in his eyes dimmed, yielding to a somber gravity. With a quick flick of his fingers, he addressed the guards, his voice firm yet calm. "Let us pass."

The guards, without hesitation, stepped aside, their heads bowing low. Mary's breath caught in her throat, her heart hammering as she realized just how easily he wielded such authority. *Who is this man that even the king's sentinels obey him so readily?*

As they walked together, the corridors seemed to stretch endlessly, each footfall echoing with an unease Mary could not shake. Each stolen glance toward him sent a flutter through her chest, her pulse quickening with each step they took side by side. *Wouldst thou say this is how Robert felt upon first meeting the princess? Enchanted by her charm and fair countenance? Am I naught but a fool, as my brother hath been before me?* The question gnawed at her, for it had been years since any man stirred such feelings in her chest—since the innocent days of her childhood, when she'd fancied the baker's son, a fondness that ended with the bitter taste of heartbreak. After that, she had sworn to shield her heart, to never let it be laid bare to another.

Yet now, walking beside this man of rank, her pulse fluttered traitorously beneath her ribs. *He seeks naught but a passing moment of kindness,* she reminded herself, *a fleeting distraction from the burdens of his station.* And though she repeated it in her mind, the warmth of his presence stirred something deeper within her.

As they passed the head chambermaid, who offered a nod laced with confusion, Mary averted her gaze, heat prickling the back of her neck. The servants, guards, and attendants they passed seemed to linger with their stares, judgment simmering behind their eyes. *What doth they think?* she wondered, feeling the weight of whispers that had yet to be spoken. She knew all too well that Rumours would soon swirl through the castle like smoke, and it would not be long before Prince Charles himself heard of her peculiar companion. Fear coiled in her stomach, her breath hitching as she imagined the fury that would soon be upon her. Her heart pounded, each beat a reminder of the storm she knew was coming. Her fingers curled into fists at her sides, her breath coming in shallow, uneven pulls as she prepared for the inevitable storm that would soon follow.

As they neared the entrance to the private quarters, once held by the late king, Mary's chest tightened with dread. It had been made clear when she first arrived—those halls were forbidden to her kind. The royal family had decreed it so, wishing to keep their father's memory undisturbed.

Her hand moved of its own accord, brushing against his arm as though seeking an anchor. "My lord," she stammered, her voice barely above a whisper, "we are not permitted within... 'tis not allowed." Her eyes darted nervously toward the guards stationed nearby, their presence a silent reminder of the boundaries she was never to cross. Panic swelled within her, and her pulse quickened like a rabbit caught in a snare. *I must turn back. I cannot be seen here, not with a king's guard.*

The man beside her chuckled softly, a jest on his lips. "Mayhap we should fight our way in?" His tone was light, but as his gaze met hers, the humour died on his tongue. Mary's wide-eyed terror froze him in place, her fear so palpable that it stole the air from the corridor.

The warmth in his eyes dimmed, yielding to a somber gravity. With a quick flick of his fingers, he addressed the guards, his voice firm yet calm. "Let us pass."

The guards, without hesitation, stepped aside, their heads bowing low. Mary's breath caught in her throat, her heart hammering as she realized just how easily he wielded such authority. *Who is this man that even the king's sentinels obey him so readily?*

They entered the private quarters, and the silence felt heavy, oppressive. Every inch of the room seemed drenched in memory, as though the air itself held echoes of the past. Dust clung to the furniture like a shroud, the hearth cold and untouched for what seemed like years. Mary shivered, her fingers brushing against the back of a chair, leaving a faint trail in the dust. Her heart pounded louder, matching the weight of the room's stillness. She felt as though she were trespassing into a world where she did not belong.

As her fingers nervously brushed the edge of the chair, he caught the subtle tension in her movements. The way her shoulders tightened, the slight tremor in her hand—he saw it all. His expression shifted, the teasing spark in his eyes dimming as something gentler took its place. He caught her shifting in her seat, a small betrayal of her tension, and her restless fingers stilled for an instant as his gaze lingered. Though he remained quiet, the flicker of understanding in his gaze spoke louder than words. Instead, his presence seemed to ease, offering reassurance without words. "Fear not," he murmured, stepping closer, his voice a gentle balm against the room's coldness. "Thou art safe with me."

She dared to meet his gaze, her heart betraying her with a flutter of warmth at his words. His proximity was intoxicating—too close, too warm, too real. The stillness around him was alive with tension, as if the air itself was reverberating with an unspoken message that left her on edge. There was something about the way his gaze lingered—steady, unwavering—that stirred something deep within her. Her heart raced, unsure whether to be soothed or wary, as though his very nearness could strip away the walls she had carefully built.

"Why did they allow us entry?" she asked softly, her voice trembling despite herself. "I thought only family could enter here. Were you close to the late king?"

A shadow passed over his face, but he quickly masked it with a smile, one that didn't quite reach his eyes. "Aye," he replied after a pause, his tone carrying a weight that spoke of deeper ties than he wished to reveal. "The late king was like a father to me." He paused, his gaze distant for a moment. "And I, in turn, was like a son to him."

Mary nodded, though her curiosity burned hotter now. *A knight hath served both the late king and the rightful king now upon the throne. Surely, they must trust him well, for no man doth rise to such rank without proving his worth and loyalty. Such a position is not bestowed lightly, and I must weigh his every word with care.* she wondered, her confusion only deepening. But she did not dare press further, not yet.

As they moved deeper into the quarters, she could no longer resist asking the question that had lingered on her mind. "Forgive me for asking, but... art thou here to court the princess?"

He blinked, then laughed—a rich, warm sound that echoed off the stone walls. "Court the princess?" His eyes sparkled with amusement. "Nay, fair maiden, the thought of such is quite... absurd."

Mary's cheeks flushed at her boldness, but she managed a smile, relieved that he did not take offense. "I thought as much," she muttered, her embarrassment softened by his laughter. *Would not a knight of such standing be worthy?* The question gnawed at her, her lack of understanding of court life leaving her uncertain. *Perhaps I know far less than I thought of such things.*

"Come," he said, gesturing toward the corridor ahead. "There is much more to see than the king's office and bedchamber. The garden awaits, and I daresay it shall lift thy spirits."

As they walked toward the garden, Mary felt the air grow lighter, her earlier tension fading as his playful tone wrapped around her like a warm cloak. She couldn't deny the way her heart responded to his presence, how each word he spoke seemed to draw her further into his orbit. *Why doth my heart betray me so?* she wondered. *Surely, this is naught but a fleeting fancy...*

But when his hand brushed against hers as they passed through the door to the garden, and she felt the warmth of his touch linger on her skin, she knew it was more than that.

He steered her through the garden gate, where warm light spilled through the foliage like the first rays of dawn, and the air was heavy with the sweet perfume of blooming flowers. It was a place untouched by the sorrows of the world beyond, a secret haven hidden from the eyes of all but the privileged few.

"Is it not most wondrous, dost thou agree?" he asked, watching her as she gazed around in wonder.

Mary nodded, her breath stolen by the sight of such beauty. "Aye," she whispered, her voice filled with awe. "'Tis unlike anything I've ever seen."

He stepped closer, his voice dropping to a murmur as he said, "And yet, not so breathtaking as thou art."

Her heart skipped a beat, the words sinking into her like a whispered secret. Turning to him, she felt the warm colour rising up her neck and flooding her face, while her breathing faltered, snagged on some invisible hook. *What manner of feeling be this?* she wondered, her thoughts swirling in confusion and something else—something far more dangerous.

The tension between them was palpable now, the air thick with the unspoken. She felt drawn to him in a way she could not explain, and though her mind warned her to tread carefully, her heart seemed to care little for caution.

As they wandered deeper into the garden, the sounds of the castle fading behind them, he gestured toward a bench nestled beneath an arch of flowering vines. "Shall we sit?" he asked, his tone softer now, as though the world itself had hushed for this moment between them.

Mary hesitated for a brief moment, her heart thudding in her chest, but she found herself nodding and following him to the bench. The warmth of the sun filtered through the leaves, casting a golden glow over them both as they sat in a companionable silence. She felt the weight of his gaze upon her, and though she tried to resist, her own eyes strayed to his face, drawn by the quiet intensity of his presence.

His nearness was both comforting and unsettling, a paradox she could not easily unravel. He spoke little, but when his hand brushed against hers, resting between them on the bench, the jolt of his touch sent a shiver down her spine.

"Milord..." she began, but her words trailed off, lost in the breathless space between them. She could not finish the thought, for even she did not know what she meant to say.

He turned toward her then, his gaze locking with hers, and in that moment, it was as though the rest of the world had fallen away. The warmth of his hand against hers, the quiet pulse of life in the garden around them, all seemed to fade into insignificance beneath the weight of that gaze. For the first time, Mary felt as though someone truly saw her, not as a servant, not as a mere chambermaid, but as something more.

"Mary," he murmured, her name slipping from his lips like a secret. Hearing her name upon his lips unsettled her, stirring a feeling she had long kept hidden beneath years of duty and modesty. She had spent so long hiding her heart, shielding it from the pain of the world, and now, in the space of a single afternoon, it felt as though those walls were crumbling.

Before she could stop herself, she looked away, her gaze falling to the ground as her thoughts whirled in a chaotic dance of fear and longing. She knew she should rise, should end this before it went any further, before she lost herself entirely in something she could not afford to feel. Though every rational thought urged her to turn away, to end whatever had begun between them, the idea of walking away from him now twisted something deep in her chest, a heaviness she couldn't quite bear.

"I should... take my leave." she whispered, though her heart rebelled against the words even as she spoke them.

He did not release her hand. Instead, his thumb brushed lightly over her knuckles, sending another shiver through her, and when he spoke, his voice was quiet, steady, as though he, too, understood the fragile balance between them. "Stay," he said softly, his words more a plea than a command. "Only for a while longer, I pray thee."

Mary's breath caught in her throat, her heart pounding in her chest as she met his gaze once more. There was no mistaking the longing in his eyes, a reflection of the same desire that stirred within her, and for a moment, she wondered if it was possible to simply exist here, in this moment, without the weight of the world pressing down on them.

In that instant, the magic halted, and reality rushed back in.

The sound of approaching footsteps shattered the delicate stillness between them, and Mary's heart lurched as she turned toward the path, dread clawing at her insides. The figure approaching was unmistakable: Prince Charles, his expression darkening as he drew nearer, his every step radiating barely concealed fury.

"Brother," Charles greeted with a thin smile, though his tone was laced with an unmistakable edge. "I had not expected to find thee here."

Mary froze, her pulse quickening as the reality of the situation crashed over her. *Brother?!* The word struck her thoughts like a sudden blow, unsettling and impossible to ignore.

The man she had been walking beside, the man who had looked at her with such warmth, was not a knight at all. He was the king.

Her breath caught in her throat, her heart hammering wildly in her chest. *The king?* She had been sitting with the king, unaware, speaking to him as though he were a mere noble knight. Her heart lurched, and for a moment, it felt as if the very stones beneath her feet had shifted, unsteady and uncertain.

"I see I have chanced upon a moment ill-timed." Charles continued, his gaze flickering between them, the tension in his voice barely contained. "Pray, what brings thee to the garden this day, brother?"

The king's gaze remained steady, his expression calm, though Mary could feel the shift in the air around them. "I was merely enjoying the garden," he replied smoothly, though the subtle tension in his voice did not escape her notice. "Mary was kind enough to accompany me."

Charles's eyes narrowed, his smile thin and sharp. "How fortunate," he drawled, his tone dripping with sarcasm. "A chambermaid's company is not something thou dost seek every day."

A torrent of emotions crashed through Mary: disbelief, embarrassment, and a twinge of betrayal. *How blind have I been?* The stolen glances, the shared words—what seemed like moments of connection now twisted into something cruel, mocking her for her naïvety.

The weight of realisation settled in her chest like a stone. Every servant's gaze, the head chambermaid's strange look, all made sense now. Of course, it was only royalty who could move so freely through such private halls. The truth hit her with the force of a cold wind, sharp and unforgiving.

Why hath he concealed his identity? The question gnawed at her. They had spoken of the royal family; she had asked of the king, and yet he said nothing. Each conversation now felt laced with hidden intent. Why had he not spoken plain?

Her gaze flickered desperately between the king and the prince, her thoughts spinning like a cornered animal seeking escape. Her stomach twisted painfully, the air thick and cold in the secluded garden, chilling her even beneath the fur cloak she wore.

Foolish girl, she berated herself. How easily had she fallen for his gentle words? For the softness in his gaze that now felt like a snare? The weight of her own folly pressed upon her like a suffocating blanket. Robert had fallen victim to the lies of the crown, and now she stood in his place, ensnared by the same deceit.

King John's lips curled into a self-assured smile, his eyes gleaming as he regarded Charles's sudden entrance. There was no mistaking the subtle glint of superiority in his gaze. Charles's presence here was out of place, and John sensed the tension simmering beneath his brother's forced calm.

The king, keen to his brother's discomfort, spoke with an air of regal confidence, his words heavy with authority. "Thou seemest unsettled, brother," he remarked, his tone edged with mocking amusement. It was clear that John relished the control he wielded, finding satisfaction in rattling Charles's composure.

Charles's expression hardened, his jaw clenched as he bowed stiffly. The polite mask he wore barely concealed the resentment brooding beneath his sharp gaze. "What is my chambermaid doing here?" Charles demanded, his voice low and brimming with indignation.

At that, Mary flinched. Her body moved instinctively, rising from the bench in a rush, her limbs stiff with fear. She kept her head low, her voice quivering as she didst strive to find the proper words. 'Your Majesty... I-I knew not...'" she stammered, each word trembling with shame. Her hands twisted together, her fingers cold despite the cloak's warmth. The urge to flee gnawed at her, but her feet remained rooted to the ground. She had stepped too far, and now there was no escaping the consequences.

A quick glance at Charles's thunderous face sent her heart into a spiral. His dark eyes didst fix upon her, unspoken fury smoldering within. *He shall have me dismissed—or worse.*

Before Charles could speak again, King John's voice cut through the tension with ease. "Thy chambermaids, brother?" His eyebrow arched as he gestured lightly toward Mary. "Dost she not serve the entire household? Or art thou in the habit of claiming servants as thine own now?" There was a teasing curiosity in his voice, but the sharpness beneath it was unmistakable.

Charles's calm broke for a moment, a flicker of anger crossing his features. "She hath been derelict in her duties," he bit out, his gaze never leaving Mary. "Late this morn, and now found within our departed Father's quarters, which is no hour befitting a maid." His tone was harsh, a clear signal of his displeasure. "This insolence must be corrected."

Mary's breath caught in her throat, her entire body trembling beneath the prince's gaze. She had heard of his temper, and the very idea of suffering its brunt terrified her.

A soft chuckle escaped the king, a sound full of amusement that only further ignited Charles's anger. "Surely thou hast greater concerns, brother," John mused, his tone light but with an underlying rebuke. "Our sister hath returned—surely her safety is a far weightier matter than a chambermaid's alleged insolence."

Charles's face twitched with barely controlled fury, his eyes narrowing at the king's dismissal of his complaint. But John's next words carried a command that could not be ignored.

"This maid," he said, his voice firm, "was here at my request." His eyes bore into Charles, leaving no room for further argument. "Thou knowest well that the guards would not allow her entry without mine own word. Let this matter rest."

Charles's jaw tightened, his fists clenched at his sides, but he remained silent, the command of his elder brother unchallenged.

Mary, still trembling, glanced up from the ground. A flicker of astonishment lit her eyes. *He hath kept his word.* The king's protection, though unexpected, brought a small sense of relief, yet dread still clung to her heart. *But how long before Prince Charles seeks retribution?* Her stomach churned with the thought, knowing full well how the prince held grudges like bitter wine.

She swallowed, her throat dry as she spoke. "Your Majesty, thou art kind," she said softly, her voice faltering as she felt the weight of Charles's gaze still burning into her. "His Highness... treats me well." She forced the words past her lips, though each syllable felt like a lie.

The tension in the air thickened, and Mary's heart raced. "May I be excused?" she whispered, her voice barely more than a plea as her eyes darted between the king and Charles, praying for some escape from the storm brewing between them.

Charles's anger flared like a smoldering fire brought to life by the wind. His visage twisted with wrath, and a guttural snarl tore from his throat. 'My chamber doth require thy tending!' he roared, his voice thundering through the halls like the very heavens' own fury.

The king, watching his brother with a discerning eye, saw through the outburst. There was more to Charles's fury than a simple maid's dereliction. "Mary, thou art excused," the king said gently, though his eyes remained on his brother. "Charles and I shall speak now." His tone left no room for argument.

Mary hesitated, then nodded quickly. With trembling hands, she gathered the folds of her skirt and gave a shallow curtsy, her movements awkward and stiff. She turned and fled as quickly as she could, her footsteps light and hurried as she disappeared down the path, leaving behind the tense silence between the two brothers. The bushes blurred past Mary, her steps frantic and unsteady as the pounding of her heart echoed louder than the rustle of leaves around her. Each breath came ragged, each hurried footfall amplifying the urgency that gripped her chest. The oak door loomed ahead, though it felt like an eternity before she finally reached it.

Her hand shook as it found the latch, her fingers curling tightly around the worn wood as though it were the only thing tethering her to the earth. For a moment, she paused, her eyes fluttering shut, her chest heaving with suppressed emotion. *Steady thyself,* she whispered inwardly, though her trembling limbs betrayed her command.

With a sharp intake of breath, she pushed the door open, the soft creak of wood breaking the silence. The dim corridor stretched out before her, shadowed and silent. The cold air bit at her skin, sending a shiver down her spine as tears welled in her eyes, spilling unchecked down her cheeks. The weight of her shame, her fear, it bore down upon her, overwhelming her in the dim solitude of the hallway.

Her hands fumbled as she closed the door behind her, the wood creaking in protest. She gasped for air, her throat tight as though a hand gripped it. *I must flee,* her mind screamed, the idea of escape pulling at her like a rising tide.

Mary's legs moved before she had time to think, her steps faster, more frantic with each passing second. Her breaths came quick, shallow, as her body hurtled toward the next door. The corridor blurred around her, her pulse drumming in her ears.

A flicker of movement—a torch sconce, dim and unlit—loomed suddenly in her path. With a startled gasp, she swerved, her momentum nearly sending her crashing into it. Her heart leapt into her throat, but she managed to stumble past, her breath hitching as she pressed onward.

Reaching the next door, Mary lunged forward, her arm outstretched, fingers trembling as they brushed the wooden latch. Her heart thundered in her chest, her breath catching in her throat as her hand closed around the rough wood. The door swung open with a groan of protest, the sound echoing down the corridor like a warning.

Stepping into the late king's chamber, Mary's eyes darted around the unfamiliar space, her pulse racing with dread. Dust hung in the air like forgotten memories, cobwebs draped the corners like eerie tapestries.

Her gaze flicked back to the door leading to the garden, dread pooling in her stomach as she waited, listening for any sign of Charles's approach. The silence was suffocating, broken only by the thundering of her own heartbeat.

She forced her legs to carry her across the room, each step feeling heavier than the last as she approached the final set of doors. What lay beyond? Would the guards stop her, or would they let her pass without question? Her hand trembled as she grasped the door handle, the ache in her palm a small anxiety, distinct from the thrum of fear knotting her gut. As the shadows of the new corridor stretched out before her, Mary's eyes widened in surprise. Among the guards stationed outside stood Baldwin, Prince Charles's personal attendant, his expression unreadable as though he had been expecting her.

"Mary Winterbourne," Baldwin's voice broke the stillness, his gaze sweeping over her. His tone was stiff, as if phrased by a committee. "I offer thee mine apologies for this morn," he said stiffly, as though rehearsed, but his eyes betrayed a flicker of something else—remorse, perhaps. "I did act under His Highness's command."

Mary clenched her teeth, a wave of frustration surging within her. Baldwin, like the prince's shadow, always watching, always following. She forced a smile, her lips tight with the effort. "The pleasure is mine, Baldwin," she replied coolly, though her heart was anything but calm. "But I must go."

As she made to move past him, Baldwin's voice halted her. "His Highness hath bid me to ensure thy safety." he said, his tone formal but unwavering.

Mary's frustration bubbled over, her patience worn thin. *Why must I always be watched, always controlled?* She swallowed hard, forcing a tight-lipped smile. "I am quite capable of ensuring mine own safety, I assure thee."

Baldwin hesitated, clearly uncertain. "It was not a request," he said quietly, a touch of confusion seeping into his voice. "His Highness insists."

Her lips pressed into a thin line as she felt the weight of the prince's command pressing down on her yet again. "Very well," she said through clenched teeth, her tone clipped with barely suppressed anger. "I shall attend to his chambers."

With a flick of his arm, Baldwin motioned her forward, his silent presence looming at her side. Though she quickened her pace, hoping to outpace him, Baldwin remained close, his footsteps mirroring hers, an inescapable reminder of the prince's control.

Mary's pace quickened, her steps driven by a sense of urgency, yet no matter how fast she moved, Baldwin kept stride, his presence a constant, unwanted shadow. Frustration tightened her jaw, a pressure cooker waiting to blow its lid. *Must I forever be bound by their whims?* she thought bitterly. She longed for a moment of peace, a moment to breathe without the weight of royal eyes upon her.

As Mary hurried past the cold glares of the castle servants, she felt the weight of their judgment pressing down on her like a leaden cloak. The news of her encounter with the king had spread like wildfire, each whispered word distorting the truth further, like the twisted echoes of a tale passed from ear to ear. Now, the servants' accusing stares followed her every move, each glance more damning than the last.

Her face flushed with exertion, beads of sweat forming on her brow, her clothes clinging uncomfortably to her skin. The murmurs behind her felt like a thousand needles pricking her back, each one driving the shame deeper.

Mary's eyes welled with unshed tears as she cast a glance at Baldwin. Her brow furrowed, lips trembling ever so slightly, and though she blinked rapidly to hold back the flood, the faint tremor in her breath betrayed the sorrow she fought so desperately to conceal. Baldwin's gaze lingered, his steps faltering as the subtle cracks in her composed mask revealed the storm within.

"Whenever there is a hint of scandal, people may scowl and whisper about thee," he began, his voice gentle, laced with a hint of resignation. "But fear not, a new scandal is always just around the corner." His words carried a weight of understanding, as if he'd long witnessed the fickle nature of court gossip.

He paused, taking in a shallow breath as he struggled to match her hurried pace. After a moment, he continued, his voice tinged with an attempt at reassurance, "Thy scandal will soon fade into the background." It was a weak comfort, but it told Mary that Baldwin could be an unexpected ally in these unforgiving halls.

If only it were that simple, Mary thought. Rumours might be fleeting for some, but not in her case. This was different. The prince's reaction to finding her with the king had been sharp, his eyes alight with something far darker than mere irritation. If word of their encounter spread further—twisted by the tongues of those eager to embellish—she knew it could enrage him beyond measure. And when Charles was angry, no one was spared his wrath. Trouble would surely find her doorstep, dragging her family down into the storm as well.

Worry gnawed at her like a festering wound, each step she took heavy with the thought of Charles' looming fury. It felt like carrying a satchel full of stones—each one a weight, slowing her thoughts, dragging her deeper into the mire of fear. The last thing she wanted was to bring calamity upon her loved ones, yet that very possibility hovered above her, as real as the cold glares of the servants and the disapproving whispers that followed her every step.

*

As Mary and Baldwin approached the prince's chambers, the two guards stood tall, their stern gazes fixed ahead. Though their faces betrayed no emotion, Mary could feel their eyes tracking her as she neared. The weight of her newness to this royal household pressed down on her. She had only been a chambermaid for a few days, but the tension of her duties already felt immense.

Baldwin, a figure well-known and respected within the castle walls, took charge. "Good morrow, Aldric, Gareth," he greeted with a tone both familiar and authoritative. His ease of command came naturally after years of loyal service. "The chambermaid is here to see to His Highness's quarters, as commanded."

Aldric, an older guard with a weathered face and a gray-flecked beard, gave a curt nod. "Aye, Baldwin," he replied, his voice a deep rumble. His eyes flicked briefly to Mary, assessing her with the sharp eye of someone who had seen many new servants pass through these halls. Another slight nod, his way of silently acknowledging her as the new maid.

Gareth, younger and fresher in his post, cast Mary a curious glance before turning to Baldwin.

"Dost the prince require aught else this morn?" he asked, his tone formal but betraying a hint of nervousness, as though eager to prove himself.

"Nay, Gareth. The maid shall see to his chamber," Baldwin said firmly, cutting off further inquiries. He offered a polite nod, signaling the end of the exchange.

As the guards stepped aside, Mary felt the weight of their attention linger on her. She maintained her composure, but inwardly, her heart raced. The responsibility that came with serving the prince's chambers was no small burden, and each time she entered, the pressure weighed heavier. She could almost feel the walls watching her, as if even they knew she was still learning to navigate the strict expectations of royal service.

Baldwin pushed open the heavy oak door, revealing the disheveled interior of the prince's chamber. The bed, with its finely embroidered silks and furs, lay in a state of disarray. Pillows were scattered on the floor, and the rich blanket trailed off the side of the bed. The hearth, long since cold, stood in stark contrast to the warmth it had once provided.

"Thy work awaits, Mary," Baldwin reminded her softly, his eyes briefly scanning the mess. "Do what needs be done. I shall wait without."

Just as Mary was about to begin, the sound of footsteps echoed in the corridor. Turning toward the door, she was surprised to see a maiden striding forward with purpose, her cloak swaying with each step. The sight of her fine attire, rich in texture and elegantly cut, marked her as a servant of noble rank—though one unfamiliar to Mary.

Baldwin's face, typically marked by the disciplined composure of his station, betrayed a flicker of warmth at the sight of the approaching figure. His lips twitched upward, a rare glint of light sparking in his eyes, though he quickly schooled his features into a more reserved mask, mindful of the guards watching nearby. His posture straightened, hands clasping behind his back with the practiced ease of a man well-versed in courtly manners, yet the eagerness in his voice was unmistakable. "Rosalind! Thou art returned at last. Thou hast been sorely missed."

Rosalind, the princess's handmaiden, approached with a playful glint in her eye and a nod of acknowledgment to Baldwin. "Baldwin Honorcrest ," she began, her lips curling into a teasing smile, "mine day is at last made, now that I hath laid eyes upon thee." Her tone was light, but her voice carried the familiar weight of authority, a hint of amusement woven into her greeting as if she enjoyed the banter between them. After a brief exchange of glances with the guards, she lowered her voice. "I have urgent business with the chambermaid."

Mary's brow furrowed in confusion as Rosalind spoke. She had heard whispers of the princess's trusted handmaiden, but this was the first time she had encountered her. What urgent business could this noble servant possibly have with her, a mere chambermaid?

Baldwin, ever composed, gave a respectful nod and stepped aside to allow Rosalind entry. He glanced at Mary with a look of reassurance before quietly stepping out, leaving the two maidens alone.

Rosalind took a moment to assess the chamber, her gaze lingering on the unkempt bed and the cold hearth before turning her attention to Mary. Rosalind's posture was straight and poised, her chin held high as she entered the chamber with purpose. Every step she took was deliberate, and though her face revealed no hint of emotion, the very air seemed to shift with her arrival, as if the space itself recognised her significance. Even without a word, the way she commanded attention, the slight lift of her brow and the graceful movements of her hands, spoke of a woman who carried more than just simple messages—she carried influence.

"I am Rosalind," she said, her voice measured but not unkind. "I serve Her Highness, the princess." Mary's chest tightened at the mention of the princess. *What business hath the princess with me?*

The thought gnawed at her, though she kept her silence, her posture stiff as she awaited Rosalind's next words.

"The princess wishes to speak with thee," Rosalind continued, her tone now holding a touch of secrecy. She reached into her cloak and withdrew a small, folded piece of parchment, holding it out toward Mary. "This concerns thy brother, Robert."

Mary's hand hovered over the parchment, her breath catching in her throat. The very sight of it filled her with unease, as though it carried with it the weight of consequences she could neither predict nor control.

The moment her fingers brushed the parchment, a subtle but undeniable heaviness settled over her. Though light in form, it seemed to press into her hand, a quiet weight that carried far more than ink and words. Unease crept through her chest, tightening with each heartbeat, as though the simple slip of paper bore the weight of untold truths she was not prepared to face.

Hath this missive the power to undo Robert? Doth the princess declare him unworthy, and that she is to wed a noble? Nay, I shall not be the bearer of such grievous tidings. Folk like us hath no need for such missives, nor use for the ink of nobles. Weartnot deemed worthy to be taught the ways of reading or writing—was the princess mocking us, then? Her hand withdrew, fingers curling away from the offered note, as though the parchment itself carried the sting of insult. She could not take it. She would not be part of this.

"I must needs decline," Mary said, her voice firm, though her heart pounded in her chest. "I have no dealings with Her Highness. Bid her leave me and mine in peace."

Rosalind's brows drew together for the briefest of moments, surprise flickering across her face before she quickly masked it. "The princess's request is not a burden," she said softly, though there was an urgency in her tone. "She merely seeks to speak."

But Mary's mind was already set. She turned from Rosalind, crossing to the narrow window with purpose. With a sharp twist of her wrist, she unlatched the iron-fastened shutters, pushing them open to let the cold daylight flood the stone chamber. The stone walls caught the sunlight in pale patches, illuminating the heavy wooden beams above. "I serve His Highness, the prince," she declared, her voice tight with frustration. "I hath no part in the dealings of the princess. Mine duties lie with the prince and the chambers I am bid to serve."

Rosalind's fingers, deft and practiced, folded the linen missive once more. The soft fabric creased beneath her touch as she tucked it back into the folds of her cloak, her movements smooth and deliberate, concealing the message as though it had never been offered. 'Very well,' she murmured, though the weight of disappointment coloured her tone. 'Shouldst thou reconsider, I am ever within reach.'"

Without another word, Rosalind turned, her cloak trailing behind her as she made her way toward the door. She paused only briefly to glance back at Mary, her gaze lingering for a moment before she exited the chamber.

Left alone, Mary exhaled sharply, the tension of the encounter still lingering in the air. She closed the shutters with a forceful push, the wooden clatter echoing her frustration. The prince's bed, still unmade, beckoned her to continue her duties, but her thoughts were elsewhere, clouded by unease.

Mary's childhood fantasies of Thorncrest Castle now seemed like distant illusions, taunting her with their cruel irony. In those early days, living under the shadow of its towering walls, she had believed that serving the royal family would be a coveted honour—a way to touch the grandeur and nobility that had always felt so far removed from her life. Now, standing as a servant within those very walls, she found the reality far colder than her dreams.

Confined under the service of a prince she despised, the weight of her fate gnawed at her spirit. With every passing moment, the chasm between her present reality and the dreams of her youth seemed to widen, mocking her once-hopeful heart. The realisation settled heavily upon her—how foolish she had been to long for the approval of the nobility.

The crackling of the fire at the hearth did little to warm the cold that clung to her. Her eyes flicked to the disheveled bed—furs and silks, discarded as though their opulence meant nothing to the prince. The very thought of that bed filled her with a revolting mix of sorrow and disgust, gripping her stomach like a vice. There was no sanctuary for her in this chamber, only reminders of the man she had come to loathe.

Her chest tightened as her gaze lingered on the fur blanket crumpled at the foot of the bed. The chill in the air tempted her to wrap it around herself, but the thought of being ensnared in anything touched by him sent shivers through her. Her jaw tightened as she faced the hearth once more, forcing the thought from her mind. Better the cold than the stain of his presence upon her.

Kneeling before the hearth, she fed the flames, her hands moving with automatic precision as her mind wandered to a different time. The warmth of the fire couldn't reach the bitterness festering in her chest. The finely-carved stones lining the walls, once symbols of wealth and power, now seemed to mock her discontent, every flicker of shadow a cruel reminder of how far she had fallen. Her thoughts returned to her life in Ravenswood Town—a place that, though difficult, had been hers. It had been a life of labour and struggle, but she had felt free then. The love of her parents, the comfort of a home that, no matter how modest, had belonged to her. Mudlark Alley had been cruel, but nothing compared to the cold grip of Thorncrest Castle. Here, every corner of the stone fortress felt like a cage, and she was trapped within it.

As she adjusted the fire, the faint sound of the door creaking open caught her attention. Her heart stuttered, and she stiffened, straightening quickly as the familiar click of the latch echoed in the chamber. The prince.

Charles entered with slow, measured steps, each thud of his boots against the stone floor making her feel smaller, more vulnerable. Her fingers curled into the fabric of her apron, knuckles paling as she drew a slow breath. Only then did she turn to face him, her gaze steady despite the tension humming beneath her skin. Her hatred simmered just beneath the surface, but she knew better than to let it show—not yet.

Her apron straightened with trembling hands, Mary curtsied, though her mind was far from submissive. To her surprise, Charles's face wasn't twisted with the usual disdain or anger. His eyes were distant, clouded with confusion. He seemed... lost.

A flicker of satisfaction sparked in her chest. *Had the king chided him, perchance?* But she quickly stamped down the feeling. This wasn't the time to grow complacent—Charles could turn on her in an instant.

Her gaze lingered on him, muscles tightening beneath her skin. His eyes swept the room, never settling, never meeting hers. The knot in her chest coiled tighter with every second his gaze passed over her, unnoticed. He seemed distant, his thoughts somewhere far beyond the stone walls, oblivious to her presence.

Why hath he come? she wondered, the tension in the room growing heavier with each passing second. His presence alone felt suffocating, and the air in the chamber thickened, pressing in on her chest. She longed to flee but knew there was nowhere to go. Thorncrest Castle was both her prison and her captor's stronghold.

Finally, his eyes landed on her, but the fire she had expected never flickered in his gaze. His lips parted, but the words were slow to come. "The king is most enraptured by thee." he muttered, his voice lacking its usual sharpness. "Thou wert meant to be mine! What worth hast thou now? I shouldst have thee slain!"

Mary's throat tightened, her pulse quickening as she forced the words past trembling lips. 'But I am thine, my liege.' The weight of the lie pressed heavy on her chest, each breath a struggle. She could feel the cold grip of fear creeping up her spine, yet still, she spoke. 'He may wear the crown, but in truth, thou art the one fit to rule.' Her hands trembled ever so slightly, though she clasped them tight to keep the tremor hidden.

"Thou art most fair of visage and wise beyond measure, truly the leader Briarwood doth deserve." Her voice trembled, though she forced a smile to linger upon her lips. Her hands, clasped too tightly, betrayed the fear she sought to conceal. She took a half-step back, eyes darting for a moment before returning to his. "How might I be of service to thee, my rightful king?"

As Mary adjusted the fire, the faint sound of the door creaking open caught her attention. Her heart stuttered, and she stiffened, straightening quickly as the familiar click of the latch echoed in the chamber.

Charles entered with slow, deliberate steps, each thud of his boots against the stone floor making her feel smaller, more vulnerable. Her fingers twisted into the fabric of her apron, knuckles whitening as she forced herself to draw a breath. She dared not look at him until she was sure her face wouldn't betray the fear twisting in her chest. Slowly, she lifted her gaze, daring to meet his eyes, though only for a brief moment.

Her trembling hands smoothed the folds of her apron before she curtsied. Though her head bowed low, the tension in her body betrayed her unease. To her surprise, Charles's face wasn't marred with its usual contempt. His eyes, usually filled with sharp disdain, seemed clouded and distant. He appeared distracted, his thoughts elsewhere.

Had the king reprimanded him? A small warmth stirred in her chest, but she pressed it down before it could reach her face. Now was not the time for foolish hope. Charles's temper could turn in an instant.

She watched, wary, as his gaze wandered, barely acknowledging her. Her heart beat louder in her ears, each passing second tightening the knot of anxiety coiled in her chest. His hand drifted absently toward his side, fingers brushing the hilt of his dagger.

As she gazed at the blade, its slight sheen in the dimness provoked an unsettling sensation, like a winter breeze inside her.

Before she could react, his fingers clamped around her wrist, sudden and unforgiving.

The force of his grip sent a shock of pain surging up her arm. Her breath caught, sharp and ragged, as the cold edge of his blade grazed her skin. The room seemed to close in around her, the air thick with her mounting terror.

She willed herself to pull away, but her body betrayed her, rooted to the spot. Her wide, panicked eyes searched his for any sign of mercy, but his gaze remained hard, a dangerous intensity burning behind the cold calm in his voice.

"For what reason were thou slinking in my brother's shadow?" The question, spoken softly, carried the weight of accusation, pressing down on her like a suffocating hand.

He asked the question, and the room went still, as if time itself was holding its breath, waiting for her response to unfold. She parted her lips, but no words came.

She swallowed, the dryness in her throat making it harder to speak, while her heartbeat quickened in the uneasy quiet.

She managed only a stammered response. "I... I sought him not, Your Highness. He did insist that I accompany him." The truth trembled on her lips, her voice barely steady under the weight of his anger. Each word, though honest, felt fragile, as though they might break under the intensity of his gaze.

Charles's face darkened, his grip tightening painfully around her wrist. "Thou takest me for a fool?" he snarled, the sharpness in his tone cutting through the air. "I saw thee, like a snake, twisting thine words to charm my brother."

Her heart pounded, fear knotting in her stomach as her eyes darted to the blade, its edge gleaming under the dim light. She forced herself to remain still, though every fiber of her being screamed to flee. "I would never dare, Your Highness. I swear it—I knew not who he was." Her voice faltered, the plea thin and trembling. "When he didst insist that I walk beside him, I didst think him naught but a noble knight, a man of the king's own guard, and not the king himself."

Charles's disbelief was unmistakable, the scorn in his glare scorching her as if she had spoken something laughable. "Thou expect me to believe such a thing?" he sneered, though the pressure on her wrist began to lessen. He released her, though his eyes never wavered from her trembling form.

Swallowing hard, Mary forced herself to continue. "I swear it, my lord. I knew not to whom I spoke," she murmured, head lowered in feigned submission. Her hands, clasped tightly together, shook despite her efforts to hide it. "He was lonely, my lord. I sought only to offer him words, nothing more."

Charles's grip on the dagger eased as he took a step back, a smile curling at the corners of his lips, though it held no warmth. "Thou claimest ignorance," he said, his voice low and dangerous. "Convenient." His eyes narrowed, the faintest hint of amusement dancing within them. "Thou shalt prove thy loyalty now. Serve me, and none else."

Her heart raced, a mixture of fear and resignation crashing through her. "I am ever thine, my lord," she whispered, her words quiet but steady, a forced smile pulling at the edges of her lips. Inside, she could feel the panic rising, her mind screaming to flee.

She inhaled softly, her fingers relaxing just enough to feign calm. "Thy brother doth not bear the kingly countenance as thou dost, my lord," she murmured, her tone laced with soft flattery. "It is thou who commands presence... who holds the bearing of a true ruler."

Her words lingered in the air, and she saw the change in him almost immediately. A flash of pleasure lit up his face, sparkling in his eyes for an instant. "Aye," he replied, his voice thick with pride. "Thou speakest wisely."

His gaze softened, though the smirk that played upon his lips remained sharp. "It seems thou hast some wit after all."

Relief and guilt twisted together in her chest. She had placated him, but at what cost? As he began to pace, lost in thought, her mind turned toward the king—his kind voice, his gentle presence. She yearned for the safety he might offer, but here she was, trapped in a web of Charles's making.

But her fleeting comfort was quickly shattered as Charles spoke again. "There shall be a celebration for mine sister's return, and it shall be held but a few days hence, he announced briskly. "Thou shalt attend. Wear something desirable."

The mention of the ball left Mary cold. She had never been to such an event, and the thought of it filled her with dread. It was no place for someone like her—a commoner from Mudlark Alley amidst nobles in finery she could never hope to afford. Her thoughts remained on her duties and the long day ahead, her body yearning for rest after the gruelling hours of toil.

More than anything, she felt the tug toward the cottage, a persistent whisper at the edge of her thoughts. She needed to see Noor, to know her kin were safe. Every moment spent away gnawed at her insides. The thought of them, left unguarded, twisted her heart in knots. She could not rest—not until she knew they were secure.

Charles's command settled over her like an iron shackle, dragging her down with an unbearable weight. Her throat tightened as her lips parted, but her words barely escaped, thin and strained. "I possess naught that befit such an occasion, my lord," she murmured, desperation edging her voice. She longed for her bed, for peace, for even a moment of respite.

Charles waved his hand dismissively. "It mattereth not. A gown shall be provided. Baldwin will see to it."

Her breath hitched at the mention of Baldwin. Of course, Charles would not leave her without his ever-watchful guard. "As thou commandest, Your Highness," she murmured, bowing her head in a quick curtsy before retreating toward the door.

Behind her, Charles's fingers drummed against the hilt of his dagger, each beat deliberate, as though savoring the scheme he was weaving. "Thou shalt win mine brother's heart," he murmured, his voice low and calculating, "and once it is broken, thou shalt be mine."

Mary's stomach churned violently. Her fingers twisted the fabric of her maid's uniform, her breaths catching in uneasy rhythm. The very notion of breaking the king's heart—a man who had shown her rare kindness—sent a cold wave of nausea through her. She swallowed hard, forcing the bile down as her gaze darted to the floor.

Worse still was the thought of belonging to Charles. Her skin crawled at the idea, her body betraying her with the faintest tremor that she hid within the folds of her skirt. She could not bear the thought of his touch, of the malice in his gaze, the cruelty lurking beneath his every word. Her breath hitched, but she held herself upright, her expression revealing nothing. When she finally found her voice, it emerged as a near whisper. "If it be thy will, Your Highness," she said, her throat dry. "Yet... what end dost thou seek?"

Charles stiffened, his fists clenching at his sides. His voice cut through the stillness, sharp and unrelenting. "Before I made thee chambermaid, thou wert naught but a field servant." His words dripped with disdain, each syllable sharp and biting. With every step, the atmosphere soured, weighted by the menace of his approach, until she felt suffocated, her breathing tight. "Dost thou mistake my generosity for thine own empowerment?" His tone rose, trembling with anger. "How darest thou question me?"

Mary's fingers twitched, her breath catching as fear gripped her. She forced her voice steady, though it trembled at the edges. "Nay, Your Highness, thou hast been most generous indeed." Her lips quivered, but she managed a smile, her gaze fixed on the floor. Inside, she prayed for distance, for the space between them to grow. "Wouldst thou have me return to mine duties?" she asked softly.

Charles's eyes flicked over her, narrowing in irritation. His jaw tightened, and a muscle in his cheek twitched as though her presence alone grated on him. "Aye," he snapped. "When the hour doth draw near for the ball, someone shall come fetch thee." He dismissed her with a flick of his hand, turning away as though she were nothing more than a tiresome burden.

Mary dipped into a practiced curtsy, her movements smooth despite the tension coursing through her veins. Rising quickly, she turned toward the door, her steps hurried but measured.

Her fingers hesitated over the latch, trembling when they brushed the cold metal. For a moment, she hesitated, the weight of Charles's gaze pressing into her back. Then, with a shallow breath, she pressed down and slipped through the door. The soft click as it closed behind her brought no relief, the tightness in her chest remaining unshaken.

The corridor stretched before her, its emptiness offering no solace. At the far end, Baldwin stood like a sentinel, his presence a grim reminder of her lack of freedom.

The Return No Eyes Witnessed

The servant quarters hummed with restless activity, though the air hung heavy with tension. Within the dim, low-ceilinged chamber, the warmth of the hearth did little to thaw the unease that clung to every soul. A pot of pottage bubbled sluggishly over the fire, its thin aroma mingling with the damp smell of straw and smoke. Servants bustled about, their hands busy with wooden bowls and coarse bread, yet their tongues could not help but wag.

"None did spy her enter," muttered a laundress, her hands red and raw from wringing a shirt into the bucket at her feet. "Yet here she is, hale and whole. 'Tis a tale queerly spun."

"'Tis said she was hidden in the woods, stolen by brigands," replied the cook's assistant, scraping charred bits from an iron pan. "Howbeit none did hear their boots nor see their tracks."

At the hearth, a young scullery maid stirred the pottage, her eyes darting toward the others. "The stable lads claim the gates were unbarred at cock's crow. Mayhap she was smuggled in afore the dawn."

"Foolish talk," snapped the head cook, her voice sharp as the cleaver she wielded. "Keep thy thoughts to thyself, lest thou wish to feel the steward's switch." Her words did little to still the whispers that curled like smoke in the warm, cramped room.

A boy crouched by the hearth, feeding kindling to the flames. "What if she was never stolen at all?" he said in a low voice, glancing over his shoulder. "Mayhap she left of her own will."

"Hold thy tongue, fool," hissed the maid at his side, her gaze darting toward the door. "Speak such again, and 'twill be thy hide hanging on the steward's post."

Despite the cook's glares, the murmurs persisted. Even as trenchers were piled high with coarse bread and the pottage ladled into waiting bowls, the servants' unease rippled through the room. A stable hand, newly returned from his tasks, leaned against the doorway, his face pale. "'Tis ill luck, I tell thee. Horses stirred ere dawn, but no riders did pass the gates. She is returned, aye, but the shadows cling close to her coming."

"Enough of this!" barked the cook, slamming her cleaver onto the worn wooden table. "The pottage shall burn whilst ye prattle like magpies. Get thee to thy tasks!"

Yet even as the servants fell to silence, their hands busy with bread and bowls, the questions hung unspoken in the smoky air. The warmth of the hearth could not banish the chill that seemed to seep from the very stones. *She is returned,* the room seemed to whisper, *but who knows the truth of it?*

The low murmur of voices filled the smoky servant quarters, the clatter of wooden bowls and scraping of ladles the only other sound. In the doorway, the stable hand leaned against the frame, his wiry frame casting a long shadow across the rush-strewn floor. His gaze flicked between the bustling servants, his expression uneasy as though their whispered words carried something heavier than gossip.

The door creaked wider, and he turned sharply, stepping aside as Ysabeau entered, her plain gray dress catching the faint light of the hearth. She moved with an unhurried grace, her hands clasped loosely in front of her.

"Good morn," she said, her voice light yet cutting through the room like a knife.

The stable hand dipped his head awkwardly, muttering, "Morn." The laundress near the hearth paused mid-wring, glancing up with narrowed eyes before offering a curt nod. A scullery boy stirred the pot slower, barely looking over his shoulder as he murmured a faint reply. The atmosphere shifted, attention drawn to Ysabeau's composed figure as she glided toward a stool near the fire.

Lowering herself onto the wooden seat, she smoothed her apron, the gesture so casual it betrayed none of her purpose. She took the chipped goblet left by another servant, sipping it slowly before letting her words slip into the uneasy quiet.

"I wast present when Her Highness wast brought within," she began, her voice calm but heavy with meaning. "She lay unconscious."

The stable hand stiffened in the doorway, his fingers tightening on the frame as if the weight of the words had struck him. The laundress froze, the linen falling limp in her hands as her lips parted in shock. Beside the hearth, the scullery boy dropped his spoon into the bubbling pot, his face going pale as he turned to gape.

"Unconscious?" the scullery maid whispered, her hands trembling as she clutched the edge of the table. "Was she... harmed?"

Ysabeau tilted her head ever so slightly, her gaze sweeping over the room. "Little was spoken," she replied, her tone measured, "save that she had been assailed or cruelly beaten."

A sharp intake of breath rippled through the gathered servants. The laundress crossed herself hastily, her murmured prayer barely audible over the low whistle the stable hand let out, his face pale as he muttered, "Who would dare such a thing?"

The scullery maid's eyes darted around, as though the shadows themselves might give an answer. "Cruel, thou sayest," she whispered. "Could it be...?" She trailed off, fear rooting her words.

Ysabeau remained still, her hands folded neatly in her lap, her expression a mask of calm. She had planted the doubt, the questions. Her fellow Shadow Serpents might wish for her to implicate Noor Winterbourne, but Lucian Blackthorn's silence stayed her hand. He had not given the order, and she would not act without it. What little he had seen of Noor intrigued him; Ysabeau knew he intended to recruit the girl, not cast her as a scapegoat.

The servants' whispers began anew, filling the smoky warmth of the room. Ysabeau let them stir, their unease thickening as speculation grew. She watched the stable hand edge further into the room, his brow furrowed, and the laundress wring the linen until it twisted like rope.

She smiled faintly, her purpose fulfilled. Let them stew.

Ysabeau

The castle bustled with an energy that was neither calm nor controlled. Servants moved through the winding halls with their usual tasks, yet their footsteps slowed whenever they passed one another, heads dipping close to exchange hurried whispers. In the courtyard, guards stood at their posts, their voices low as they muttered betwixt shifts. From the laundry to the armoury, the same thread of unease wove its way through the day.

Ysabeau moved amongst them, as silent and unassuming as a shadow. She passed a pair of chambermaids sweeping the long gallery, pausing just long enough to murmur, "'Twas a commoner who dared raise his hand to Her Highness, or so the tale doth go."

The older maid gasped, her broom faltering as she made the sign of the cross. "God preserve her!" she whispered. The younger maid clutched at her apron, her face pale. Ysabeau's measured steps carried her onward before either could find more words, her expression a mask of calm.

Near the armoury, a pair of guards leaned against the wall, their helms tucked under their arms. Ysabeau approached with deliberate ease, her voice low enough to be swallowed by the clink of metal. "'Tis said a baseborn knave did strike her down, leaving her near to death."

One guard straightened, his face hardening. "A baseborn knave, thou sayest? Such insolence would not go unpunished."

"Aye, bold—or desperate," Ysabeau replied, her tone smooth as silk. She slipped away before more could be said, the sound of their muttering following her through the narrow halls.

By midday, the castle buzzed like a hive, each new servant or guard passing the tale, their voices growing louder with every telling. "A peasant smote her!" growled a stable hand as he pitched hay. "Left her for dead, or near enough!" muttered a page as he carried a bucket of water. "The villain fled into the woods, they say!" snapped a guard as he adjusted his belt by the gate.

Ysabeau moved through it all with measured purpose, her steps soft and her words softer still. She never lingered in one place, nor spoke more than a sentence or two, yet her message spread like wildfire. Though her orders were clear, she took care to keep her words cautious. The tale took on a life of its own, for no name had passed her lips—not yet.

As the sun dipped low, bathing the castle in long shadows, the murmurs grew. "What villain wouldst dare such a deed?" whispered a laundress as she wrung out linens. "Would God allow such wickedness?" muttered a boy sweeping the stairwell. Even the servant quarters, hushed and smoky, seemed alive with voices slipping through the walls like restless spirits.

Ysabeau listened to it all, her expression unchanged, her work already taking root. Yet as she moved through the stone corridors, her thoughts lingered on Lucian Blackthorn. His intent remained unspoken, and until his word came, Noor Winterbourne's name would remain hers to keep. For now, she would let the castle stew in its own imaginings.

<u>Viper's Den's cottage and the witch</u>

<u>Later that eve.</u>

The night bit deep, the kind of cold that sank into the bones and turned each breath into a ghostly wisp. The sky sagged under the weight of thick clouds, choking out the moon's pale light. Prince Charles and Sir Tristan Blackwood rode side by side, their horses' hooves crunching on the frost-bitten trail. Shadows stretched across the narrow path, clawing at their cloaks as if the forest itself sought to swallow them.

Charles's expression was hard, his gloved hands clenching the reins as though they might anchor him against the cold and fatigue. Beside him, Tristan rode in silence, his sharp eyes scanning the tree line. The faint glint of his sword's hilt promised readiness, though he betrayed no outward tension.

The forest was unnaturally still. No bird calls, no wind—only the crunch of hooves and the occasional creak of saddle leather broke the oppressive quiet. It was a silence that pressed on them, heavy and watchful, as if the woods held its breath.

When the Viper's Den came into view, the cottage loomed crooked and jagged against the horizon, warped shutters barely concealing a faint, flickering light. Charles slowed his horse, his eyes narrowing as two cloaked figures emerged from the shadows. Their dark garb blended seamlessly with the night, but the coiled serpent crest on their tunics marked them as Shadow Serpents. Their movements were deliberate, their silence brimming with menace.

One stepped forward, his boots crunching the frost. "Your Highness," he greeted, his voice low and smooth, carrying a dangerous edge.

Charles glared, his usual arrogance dulled by exhaustion. "Hath Lucian Blackthorn shown his face?" His words were sharp but slurred, his weariness seeping through. Dismounting, he stumbled, shoving the reins at the second guard without so much as a glance.

The Shadow Serpent gave a slight shake of his head, his eyes flicking uneasily toward the darkened tree line. "Nay, your Highness."

Tristan dismounted smoothly, his hand resting lightly on the pommel of his sword. His eyes flicked to the serpent crests on their tunics, tracking their movements with a steady wariness.

The prince faltered as his boots sank into the frozen ground, his grip on the saddle tightening to steady himself. Tristan moved closer, his voice low. "Your Highness, allow me to assist thee."

Charles waved him off, irritation flickering across his face. "Save thy breath, Tristan," he muttered, though his wavering steps betrayed his state.

Tristan said nothing, his jaw tightening as he gestured to one of the Shadow Serpents. "See to the horses," he ordered curtly.

The guard gave a sharp nod and took the reins. With deliberate motions, he led the restless mounts away, their prancing steps gradually slowing as they vanished into the darkness of the stable's waiting interior.

Charles stumbled again, and this time Tristan's firm hand caught his arm. "Lean upon me, sire," he said, his tone quiet but commanding. "The serpents within will note thy strength, not the moments thou thinkest to conceal."

The prince snorted but allowed the knight to steady him. They approached the warped door, the faint light within flickering like a warning. Behind them, the Shadow Serpents resumed their posts, their cloaks melding seamlessly into the dark.

Tristan's hand hovered near his sword as he pushed open the door. The air inside was thick and damp, heavy with the scent of smoke. It clung to them as they stepped into the dim room, a presence almost as oppressive as the forest outside.

Shadows danced across the uneven walls, cast by the fire sputtering in a crumbling hearth. Its flames licked at the darkness but failed to chase it away, their meager light glinting off cruel iron tools scattered across the chamber.

A rough-hewn table sat near the fire, its surface scarred by deep gouges and dark stains that bore witness to unspeakable acts. Above it, chains dangled like forgotten whispers of agony, swaying faintly as if moved by unseen hands. In the corner loomed the silhouette of an Iron Maiden, its spiked doors ajar as if waiting hungrily for its next victim. Nearby, a rack stretched taut, the wood warped and splintered from use, its rope frayed but still strong enough to do its work.

Charles stepped inside, his boots crunching over stray fragments of stone and frost-crusted mud dragged in from outside. The heat from the fire barely reached him, its crackling a faint, mocking counterpoint to the chill that clung to his shoulders like a shroud. His gaze swept the room, lingering for a moment on a bloodstained whip coiled like a serpent on the floor.

The two Shadow Serpents stepped forward from the gloom, their movements smooth and deliberate. Bartholomew's scarred face caught the firelight, the web of burn marks twisting his features into a permanent grimace. He bowed low, his disfigured hands resting briefly on the pommel of his blade in a gesture of deference. Beside him, Roric Darkmane mirrored the movement, his long black hair falling forward to frame his face, shadowing his sharp, angular features. The serpent insignia on their tunics gleamed faintly in the dim light, as though alive.

Bartholomew's rasping voice broke the silence, low and deferential. "Your Highness, the preparations are as thou commanded. The hag doth await in the chamber yonder."

Tristan's gaze lingered on the tools of pain that adorned the chamber before shifting to the Shadow Serpents. His hand rested near the hilt of his sword, the movement instinctive and steady. Charles shrugged off the frost clinging to his cloak with a sharp motion, his shoulders stiff as he stepped closer to the fire. The warmth barely reached him, its crackling filling the silence but offering little comfort against the deep chill of the chamber.

The fire popped, and a stray ember leapt into the air before winking out on the cold stone floor. The faint echo of chains creaking in the shadows filled the room as Tristan stepped closer, his eyes narrowing at the Iron Maiden's gaping maw.

Tristan led the way, his boots creaking against warped wooden planks that seemed to sigh under his weight. The corridor smelled of damp timber and cold wax, the faint light ahead dancing along the crooked walls. Charles followed closely, his cloak brushing against splintered beams as the air grew heavier with each step.

As Tristan shoved the door open, a warm, honey-coloured light spilled out, bathing him in its soft glow. The warped wooden walls seemed to close in, their uneven boards stained dark from years of smoke and damp. A ring of candles burned low on the floor, their flames arranged in a precise hexagon. The wicks sputtered faintly, casting shifting shadows that made the room feel alive, crawling with unseen things.

At the center of the hex stood Agathe, the hag.

She was a hunched figure draped in tattered robes, their layers mottled with grime and decay. Stray threads and scraps of fabric trailed from the hem, brushing the floor like fingers of the dead. Her claw-like hands hung at her sides, her gnarled fingers twitching in time with the flickering flames. Around her neck dangled a knotted cord, weighted with crude charms of bone and iron that clicked faintly as she moved.

Her milky-white eyes caught the dim light, blank yet disturbingly aware. She tilted her head toward the prince as he entered, her cracked lips curling into a smile too wide, too deliberate.

Charles stepped forward, his boots creaking against the uneven floorboards. He did not flinch at the oppressive air, nor at the way the shadows seemed to recoil from the hag's presence.

Agathe wheezed, each breath scraping from her chest like iron dragged across stone. Her hunched frame stayed motionless for a moment, save for the faint twitch of her gnarled fingers, their movement echoing the flicker of the candle flames. Her head tilted toward the prince, sightless eyes clouded yet disturbingly aware. A low, guttural laugh rattled out from her cracked lips, curling in the heavy air like smoke. "I doth sense a presence of royalty," she rasped, her words brittle and precise, "and a spirit cloaked in shadow."

In truth, Agathe was no witch. She had been deformed and blind from birth, her twisted form and milky eyes casting her as a pariah in the eyes of the villagers. Many treated her like a disease, their revulsion born of ignorance and fear. Whispers followed her wherever she went—witch, curse, plague—

and, in time, she embraced the name they had given her. If they would see her as a monster, then a monster she would become.

Years of rejection had honed her remaining senses to sharpness. Agathe had learned to navigate the world through the sounds and scents most would overlook. She could distinguish the faint scrape of a blade being drawn, the hesitance in a man's step, the deference laced with fear in a whispered tone. The Shadow Serpents had told her of their purpose—a vengeful spirit to vanquish—and of the arrival of a royal figure. When Charles first entered the cottage, Agathe had pressed her ear to the splintered door. "Your Highness," one of the Serpents had said, the words confirming what her instincts had already guessed.

Now, as the prince's presence brushed against her like a shifting pressure, she straightened slightly. Her knotted cord of bone and iron charms clicked faintly with the motion. The sputtering flames hissed, the uneven warmth of the hexagonal ring of candles failing to dispel the damp chill that clung to the warped walls. As he drew near, her ears caught the rhythm of his steps and the soft intake of his breath, hesitant and measured.

Agathe's nose twitched as the faint scent of fur and musk wove through the damp air. Beneath the acrid bite of smoke and the chill of the room, it lingered—subtle, but unmistakable. Memories swirled to life, sparking a weak, sad smile on her parched lips as her fingers tightened around the cord at her waist. Whispers and rumors long buried began to bubble up, each one a ghost brushing against the edges of her mind.

If mine memory doth serve, 'tis said that one of the royal family cherisheth such a beast—one upon which they dote with much love. A creature so adored, it might serve as a vessel for mischief or worse.

Tilting her head slightly, she drew a deep breath, her gnarled fingers twitching at her sides. She let the moment hang, her milky eyes fixed blindly on the prince as her words came measured and deliberate. "Mine senses tell that the spirit doth seek to take hold of a cat. Doth this bear meaning unto thee?"

Charles's face drained of colour as her words pierced the air. His lips parted, the edges trembling as though forming words he could not bring himself to say. Then, in a breathless whisper, it came: "Midnight?" The name carried the weight of dread, his voice cracking as his hand rose, hesitant, before falling limp at his side. His boots scraped faintly against the uneven floorboards as he stepped forward, his gaze darting from the flickering candles to the hag before him, his horror palpable.

"Pray," he stammered, his voice barely above a plea, "dost thou possess the power to rid me of this wretched spirit?" His gloved hand clenched into a fist, the leather creaking as the question hung heavy in the chamber.

Agathe tilted her head again, her smile deepening, the scars on her face pulling it into something grotesque. She said nothing at first, her fingers brushing the bone charms around her neck, each faint click echoing like a heartbeat in the silence. The flames in the hexagonal ring of candles sputtered, the shadows they cast twisting and curling along the warped walls like living things.

Agathe stretched out her gnarled hand, the bones beneath her skin shifting like old roots. "Come hither unto me, Your Highness," she rasped, her voice carrying a weight that defied her frail appearance.

Charles froze, his chest rising and falling as though the very air had thickened around him. His eyes flicked to her hand, then to the candles. The flames quivered unnaturally, their movements almost alive, as though stirred by something unseen. The circle of light seemed to press in around him, the flickering shadows crawling along the warped walls. Swallowing hard, he stepped forward. The floor groaned beneath his boots as he reached out, hesitant, until his gloved hand met hers—cold and unyielding, her grip tighter than expected. He stiffened, his breath catching, but she offered no pause, guiding him further into the center of the hex.

The light from the candles shifted again, their flames licking higher with a faint hiss. Beneath her robes, hidden chambers of the candlesticks released bursts of fine powder into the air—her secret, an old apothecary's trick to make the flames leap and dance. A faint wisp of acrid smoke curled upward, carrying a sharp, bitter scent that mingled with the damp air. Her bony fingers brushed against the edge of Charles's cloak. His shoulders tensed as her touch lingered, trailing along the fabric until she found the raised design. Her fingers traced the lion and dagger embroidered there, the crest unmistakable. Her lips, parched and brittle, creased into a subtle, knowledgeable smile, eyes glinting with an unspoken understanding.

Charles faltered as her grip tightened, the warmth of the fire pressing against his back. For a moment, he seemed to hesitate, his weight shifting as though resisting her pull. But the insistence of her grasp left him no choice, and he stepped further into the center of the hex, his breathing shallow.

"Now, my prince," she murmured, her voice soft but carrying a thread of menace, "there remaineth but the matter of coin."

Charles blinked, the words pulling him from his trance. His jaw clenched, and his other hand released hers as it dropped instinctively to his belt. The silence of the room seemed to grow heavier as he fumbled at the pouch tied at his side. The faint jingle of silver pennies broke the stillness as he loosened the string, his fingers trembling. He hesitated, glancing at her twisted smile, before pressing the pouch into her waiting hand. The soft leather yielded to her grasp, then vanished into the depths of her tattered robes, swallowed by the folds of worn fabric.

Agathe shifted her grip, reclaiming his hands in her cold, unyielding grasp. She pulled him firmly into place within the hex, the flickering candlelight casting the pair in shifting gold and shadow. The flames leapt higher again, another carefully timed burst from the hidden powders making them hiss and flare. The air felt heavier now, the warmth of the fire oddly stifling, as though the space around them were drawing closer.

She raised her arms, pulling his hands upward with hers as she began to chant. Her voice was low, rhythmic, and deliberate, rising in power with each verse:

"By pale moon's grace and darkling tide, I summon thee hence, no more to bide. By ash of yew and stone of bane. Depart this place, break thy chain. By root and thorn, by ancient lore. Thy tether sever, haunt no more. Through shadowed vale and starless fen. Return thee now, to naught again. By blood once spilled, by bond unmade. Thy spirit fade, thy power unlaid. Begone, I bid, by sacred plight, Be cast to void, forsake this night!"

Charles's fingers tightened against hers as the flames surged higher, their heat brushing his face. The powder hissed faintly, feeding the fire and sending flickering tongues of light against the walls. The shadows stretched unevenly, shifting with each sputter of the flames, crawling along the warped surfaces like restless things. His breath hitched, his gaze darting between the wild shadows and the hag before him.

The air felt stifling, thick with smoke and the weight of her voice. He pulled slightly against her grasp, but Agathe's bony fingers held firm, unyielding, as she chanted without pause.

With the final word, the flames flared violently, a burst of heat rushing over them before the candles dimmed to a faint, steady glow. Agathe released his hands and lowered hers slowly, her breath rasping in the quiet that followed. A sudden stillness settled over her, and though her sightless eyes remained fixed and unmoving, her lips curled into a delicate, knowing smile. Her posture straightened slightly, as if savoring the weight of the moment, her presence radiating an unsettling certainty.

The chamber was dimly lit by firelight and scattered candles, their flames swaying as though stirred by some unseen breath. Shadows stretched long and restless, crawling over the figures stationed around the chamber.

Sir Tristan Blackwood stood a few paces away, his armoured frame silhouetted against the wavering firelight. Though he remained silent, his watchful eyes betrayed his discomfort, his gauntleted hand resting uneasily on the pommel of his blade. Near the doorway, Bartholomew lingered in stoic stillness, his hood shadowing his sharp features. Roric Darkmane leaned casually against the wall, his posture deceptively relaxed, though his sharp eyes glinted with quiet amusement. The two Shadow Serpents, their presence as still as the grave, seemed to absorb the room's tension, amplifying its weight.

"Thy grace," Agathe murmured, tilting her blind gaze unnervingly toward the prince. "I sense no ill humours nor restless spirits lingering hence. Yet, some shades are of such wrathful might, they oft claw their way back to the realm of the living. I pray 'tis not so in thy case."

The prince's fingers tensed in hers, and though his face remained carefully composed, a flicker of unease crossed his eyes. Agathe released his hand, her gnarled fingers retreating slowly, as if relinquishing control reluctantly. The absence of her touch left the prince unsettled, and his hand fell instinctively to the pommel of his sword, though the gilded weapon offered no real comfort

"In the most improbable event thy spirit be of such potency," she continued, her voice smooth and deliberate, "I urge thee to return anon for another ritual. 'Twould be a shame to leave such matters unresolved."

"Another ritual?" The prince's voice emerged low and taut, a carefully controlled calm masking the faint edge of doubt. "I was told thy methods leave no uncertainty."

"And oft they do, Your Highness," Agathe replied, her lips curving in a faint, knowing smile. "Yet, the realm of spirits is a fickle one. Should any doubts trouble thy sleep, thou knowest where to find me."

Bartholomew shifted slightly near the doorway, the creak of leather breaking the uneasy silence. His hooded gaze flicked briefly toward the prince, his expression unreadable. Roric Darkmane smirked faintly, the faintest twitch of amusement tugging at his lips, as though savoring the discomfort in the room. Sir Tristan stood unmoving, his armoured presence heavy with tension as he observed the exchange from the shadows.

The prince exhaled through his nose, his hand brushing the pommel of his blade as though grounding himself in the tangible. His gaze darted briefly to the corners of the chamber, where the shadows gathered thickly in the flickering light. "I shall not require further counsel," he said, his tone clipped, sharpened with a hint of defiance.

He stepped back, his boots creaking faintly against the worn wooden floor. "Thy gods be kind, Agathe," he added curtly, his tone clipped as though eager to end the exchange. Without waiting for a reply, he turned sharply, his cloak catching on the edge of a chair before flaring behind him as he strode toward the door.

The firelight wavered in his wake, casting the room's occupants in fractured light. Sir Tristan's gaze lingered on Agathe a moment longer, his grip tightening on his sword as though daring her to speak further. Roric and Bartholomew moved only after the prince had passed, their movements deliberate, like predators ensuring their prey had fully departed before following.

The day of the princess's celebration

Chapter Eighteen

The day dragged on, each moment pressing down on Mary like a vice. Her arms trembled under the weight of buckets and linens, her back bent from hours of relentless labor. Pain had settled deep into her muscles, yet it was the knot in her stomach that gnawed at her most, twisting tighter with every passing hour. *Where be Noor?*

The thought plagued her mind like a curse she could not shake. *"Hath she wandered into mischief once more?"* she wondered, her lips pressed into a thin line. Noor's vanishings were not uncommon, yet this absence felt different—unsettling in a way Mary could not name. *"Could she have tangled herself with rogues, or worse, a lord with coin enough to make her forget her sense?"* The notion set her heart to pounding, for while Noor was quick of wit and sharp of tongue, even she could overstep her bounds.

Mary scrubbed harder at the stone floor, the harsh bristles scraping against the surface. Her fingers ached, but her mind would not let the matter go. The gnawing thoughts of where her sister might be refused to quiet. She'd heard whispers from the guards about brawls in Cutthroat Alley and saw their smirks when they spoke of it. It left her with a terrible, clenching fear that Noor might be lying in some dark corner, blood pooling beneath her.

She stopped mid-scrub, the rag falling limp in her hands, and cast a weary glance toward the heavy chamber doors. What if Noor was in trouble? What if she needed help? Mary bit her lip. *"And what canst thou do, Mary? Steal away under Baldwin's gaze and outwit a dozen guards? Nay. I am as caged as a bird in this place."*

Baldwin Honorcrest, The prince's most trusted attendant. The name alone sent a fresh wave of anger surging through her. He was ever there, his gaze heavy and unyielding, a silent reminder of the orders she dared not refuse. She felt his presence even now, though she dared not look over her shoulder. It was as if he expected her to slip away at any moment, to betray some secret she didn't even have.

But it wasn't just Baldwin. The castle itself seemed to conspire against her. Guards loomed in every hallway, their swords jangling as they moved, their gazes sharp and assessing. And over it all hung the suffocating weight of *Prince Charles.* His commands were law, and she was little more than a pawn in his schemes. Mary clenched her fists at the thought of him. His smile, all false charm and veiled malice, turned her stomach. She hated the way he summoned her like a dog, the way his words dripped with power he knew she could not challenge.

And now, there was this ball. The very thought of it made her heart race with dread. She was to stand among the court, their judging eyes upon her, forced to endure Charles's veiled barbs and the whispers of those who thought her rise from maid to companion was born of something sordid. *"God's wounds, I hath no desire to don some silken gown and parade like a prize goat for their amusement,"* she thought bitterly. Yet what choice did she have? To refuse Charles was unthinkable.

The sound of knuckles rapping sharply on the door jolted her from her thoughts. Her heart leapt, half with hope and half with fear. She pushed a stray lock of hair back from her face and turned sharply toward the doorway.

Another servant stood in the doorway, her expression sharp and disdainful. "His Highness commands thee to his chambers," the woman announced, her voice clipped. "A gown hath been prepared for thee."

Mary's stomach dropped. *Of course. The ball.* She glanced back at the bucket and cloth at her feet, longing to stay, to finish her work, to avoid the summons for just a little longer. "I hath not finished here," she muttered, though her voice lacked conviction.

The servant's lips curled into a sneer. "It matters not. Thy tasks shall be seen to by another."

Mary opened her mouth to protest, but before she could speak, Baldwin's voice cut through the air like a blade. "His Highness shall not look favourably upon our delay."

Her breath caught in her throat. She gave a curt nod, wiping her hands on her apron before tugging it off. The servant stepped forward to take the cloth and bucket, her movements brusque and dismissive. Mary caught the glint of judgment in her eyes, the silent accusation that lingered in her gaze. *"Aye, let them think what they will,"* she thought bitterly. *"'Tis not their opinion that chains me to this wretched place."*

Baldwin gestured for her to follow, his expression unreadable. With a heavy heart, Mary stepped into the dim corridor, leaving behind the warmth of the chamber. Shadows flickered on the stone walls, cast by the pale light of the torches, but they offered no comfort. Each step she took felt heavier than the last, her legs dragging as though the weight of her dread had seeped into her very bones.

Each step dragged her deeper into her worries, her thoughts circling without end.

Where had Noor vanished? Was she yet whole? And Robert—no doubt he lingered still in some alehouse, squandering what few coins we might ill afford. The knot in her chest tightened further, her breaths coming shallow and quick. *"I cannot bear this much longer,"* she thought, her teeth clenching. *"I cannot hold the weight of this family while they tear themselves apart."*

As they turned a corner, the door to the prince's chambers loomed ahead. Mary's heart pounded in her chest, her palms damp with sweat. She longed to flee, to run back to the hut in Mudlark Alley where she and her siblings had once been happy, to slam the door against the world and its endless demands. But there was no escape. There never was.

She took a breath, squaring her shoulders and steadying herself as best she could.

Whatever awaited her beyond that door, she would face it. She had no choice. For Noor, for Robert, and for the small flicker of hope she still clung to, she would endure.

*

As Mary and Baldwin tread the stone corridors, each step echoed like a hollow drumbeat, reverberating through the narrow passageways.

The wavering torchlight cast shifting shadows along the walls, their shapes stretching into corners as if mocking her unease. The air pressed in close and cold, heavy with silence.

Her feet dragged against the unyielding stone, burdened as though by iron chains, her heart weighed down with dread she could not name. Each step felt heavier than the last, her skirts brushing faintly against the floor. Though Baldwin walked beside her, his presence loomed larger than the space they shared, his silence suffocating in its weight.

Baldwin's voice broke the stillness, calm yet deliberate. "I know thou dost not wish to attend this ball," he said, his tone measured. "And yet, were it not thrust upon thee, 'twould be seen as an honour most would covet." His words lingered in the chill air, touched with faint warmth that felt ill-placed in the cold corridors. "Prithee, strive to find some joy in it."

A sharp, humourless laugh escaped Mary's lips. "Joy, thou sayest? Nay, I am no guest to revel in merriment. I am but a servant, dressed to suit some jest of the prince."

Baldwin's lips curved into a faint, knowing smirk. "To the other guests, thou shalt appear as one of noble blood. Thy true station shall remain hidden from their gaze."

Her steps faltered, her brow furrowing. "Thou dost feign ignorance of the prince's motives," she said, her voice low but edged with frustration. "Yet thou hast served him and his kin all thy days. Surely thou dost hold some knowledge of what drives him?"

For a moment, Baldwin kept his gaze ahead, his expression unreadable. Silence stretched between them, broken only by the distant crackle of torches. His thoughts churned, restless and dark. *The prince is as mad as he is cunning, a tempest none can predict. The rest of his kin—aye, their motives I might untangle, but they stand apart, untouched by the shadow that consumes him.*

When he spoke, his voice carried a note of caution. "I know not what moves him. Yet I counsel thee: take what joy thou canst from this night. And heed my warning." His eyes flicked toward her, heavy with meaning. "Avoid the Duchess De Valois, Madame Élisabeth, at all costs."

The name made Mary stiffen, but she said nothing. As the corridor bent toward the prince's chambers, the sound of their footsteps deepened, each thud growing heavier, mirroring the weight in her chest. Her breath quickened as the shadows around them lengthened.

Her voice, when it came, was scarcely more than a whisper. "How am I to discern friend from foe in such a place? With whom should I speak?"

Baldwin's response was low, his words deliberate, each one sharp with warning. "See all as foes, yet wear the guise of a friend. In such deceit lies safety, and truths long hidden oft come to light."

"Trust not the hand freely offered," he continued, his tone as steady as a drawn blade. "For beneath its clasp may lie the dagger waiting to strike."

Mary's fingers twitched at her sides, an instinct to flee rising within her. Yet she forced her steps to remain steady, her gaze fixed ahead as the corner loomed near.

Torchlight wavered against the narrow stone walls, shadows shifting with their every step. As they rounded the bend, two guards—Aldric and Gareth—came into view, standing rigid as pikes at their post. Mary's heart jolted, but she masked the feeling, her face calm while her thoughts churned in restless circles.

The air grew thick, heavy with the weight of what lay ahead.

Baldwin's demeanor shifted as they approached. His voice turned formal, clipped with authority. "Aldric. Gareth." He nodded to each, his tone precise, his posture stiff with purpose. Whatever ease he had shown before vanished as they stood outside of the prince's chamber.

The guards responded in kind, their faces stern, their eyes giving little away. Mary felt their gaze linger upon her—just long enough to unsettle her—but she kept her chin lifted and her eyes forward. Baldwin exchanged a brief word with them, something official Mary could not fully catch, though the tone carried authority. Whatever he said, they did not question him.

Baldwin paused outside the chamber, his presence halting without a word. Though he had been her shadow, following her every move, now he left her to venture alone. Without him at her back, an unsettling stillness crept over her. Her shoulders tightened, as though expecting unseen eyes to pierce the silence. Why had he abandoned her at the threshold, after watching her so closely all this time?

As she stepped inside, the silence enveloped her, heavy as a shroud. Only the faint sound of her footsteps echoed in the vast chamber, swallowed quickly by the stillness.

"Your Highness?" Her voice trembled, each word laced with uncertainty. They hung in the air unanswered, swallowed by the oppressive quiet.

Her eyes fell upon the gown laid across the prince's bed, its richness stark against the dark furnishings and heavy tapestries that lined the chamber. The fabric shimmered in the soft light of the hearth, fine and opulent beyond reason. She reached out, her fingers grazing the surface before she drew back sharply. Something clenched in her chest, her breath catching. *How much coin was spent on this? Enough to feed a dozen families through winter, no doubt.*

Her gaze shifted to the bodice, scandalously low and designed not for comfort but to draw the eye. A straitlaced look took over her face, emphasizing the firm set of her mouth. *Surely His Highness doth not expect me to wear this?*

This gown would attract the wrong sort of attention, she thought grimly. The whispers that already sullied her reputation would spread like wildfire. She could hear them now: *The chambermaid dressed like a whore to climb the castle's ranks.*

Beside the gown lay a corset, its black and gold threads catching the firelight. Its intricate laces wound through countless loops, the design as beautiful as it was cruel. Mary frowned at the sight. She had heard tales of such garments, how noblewomen bound themselves until breath came short and ribs ached, all for the sake of a finer silhouette. Maidens of Stowshire would squander fortunes on such vanity.

Her hand brushed the garment, and bitterness welled in her chest. *What I could do with the coin spent on this. A hundred meals for Mudlark Alley's starving, or blankets to keep the cold at bay. But instead—this.*

Her eyes dropped to her own slender frame, worn thin from years of toil. *Softness, I lack, and no excess burdens me. Doth my form offend so greatly that it must be cinched as though I were some plow beast?*

The corset's loops and twisted strings seemed a cruel jest, a silent reminder of flaws she had not known she possessed. She swallowed hard, bitterness rising in her throat. *Is this what Charles desires? That I suffer for his amusement? To be paraded before the court, bound in this accursed contraption, as part of some cruel game?*

An uneasy prickle crawled up her arms, prompting her to glance around the chamber, taking in every object, every shadow, with an air of growing trepidation.

Why hither? Why the prince's chambers? The castle held guest rooms aplenty, yet he had chosen his own. Her heart skipped a beat; the unsettling idea left her goosebumped. *Was I meant to dress here, that he might come upon me unbidden, whenever the thought struck him?*

A faint noise from the corridor startled her. Her pulse quickened as she froze, straining to catch another sound. *Was it him? Was he already approaching?* Her breath caught, her chest tight as her imagination leapt to the worst.

Creeping toward the heavy oak door, she pressed her ear against the wood, her heart hammering in her chest. Muffled voices drifted through, faint but unmistakable. She frowned, straining to make out the words.

Not Charles. That is Baldwin's voice... and a woman's.

As she tuned in, the whispers became sentences. Words like *"Midnight," "privy,"* and *"I shall"* drifted through the thick wood, though their meaning escaped her. The exchange ended as suddenly as it began, leaving the corridor steeped in silence once more.

A sharp knock shattered the stillness, sending Mary stumbling back from the door with a gasp. Her breath hitched, her chest tightening as the jolt stole the air from her lungs. She braced against the edge of the table, its cold solidity grounding her trembling hand. Fingers digging into the rough wood, she struggled to steady herself, drawing in sharp, shallow breaths as her pulse throbbed at her throat.

Her hand lifted, trembled as her gaze flicked to the door. *"Pray, I open the door? Why hath Baldwin been sent hence?"* The question clawed at her. Her fingers hesitated over the worn wood of the handle. *Who doth await me on the other side?*

The hesitation passed. Steeling herself, she tightened her grip and slowly turned the handle. The door creaked open, the sound faint yet jarring in the oppressive quiet. She peered through the narrow gap, her breath held as her eyes scanned the dim corridor beyond.

Ysabeau stood there—the maid Mary had glimpsed only briefly on the day she was dragged into the castle. Their eyes met, but no understanding passed between them. As Mary opened the door further, her gaze caught the fading silhouette of Baldwin retreating into the shadows beyond, leaving her unexpectedly alone with Ysabeau.

The maid stepped inside with measured grace, the soft rustle of her skirts the only sound. Her face remained serene, yet something in her bearing set Mary's nerves on edge. A subtle chill seemed to linger in her wake, pressing against Mary like a breath of unseen frost.

"Good eve'," Ysabeau greeted with a slight nod, her tone polite yet distant. She noticed the anxious glance Mary cast toward the hallway where Baldwin had disappeared. "Baldwin hath been summoned hence. There is but one other trusted to tend to Midnight, the prince's most cherished companion." Her voice was soft, but beneath its surface lay something unreadable.

Unbeknownst to Mary, the original servant entrusted with Midnight's care had fallen ill—part of Lucian Blackthorn's quiet machinations. Ysabeau now moved under his orders, a pawn in a far larger game. Yet Mary, lost in her confusion, remained oblivious to the threads tightening around her.

Mary's breath hitched, cold anxiety crawling over her skin. Instinctively, she reached out, clutching Ysabeau's wrist with trembling fingers. "Hath the man with the silvered locks arrived?"

Ysabeau blinked, her expression calm and unruffled. "I know not of whom thou speakest," she replied, her voice measured and even, revealing nothing. Whatever secrets lay behind her gaze, they remained locked away, beyond Mary's reach.

Mary's brow furrowed. "Surely thou dost remember? He gave thee orders, just before thine own eyes." Her voice wavered, disbelief lacing each word. Yet Ysabeau's serene composure did not falter. If she held any knowledge of the man, it remained concealed beneath her placid exterior.

"Thou lookest pale," Ysabeau remarked suddenly, turning to the prince's table. Her voice was distant, its formality deliberate and measured. "Mayhap some ale shall settle thee." She reached for a finely crafted silver chalice resting on the table and poured a small measure from a ceramic jug. The liquid sloshed softly as she handed it to Mary with quiet assurance.

Mary hesitated, her fingers trembling as they wrapped around the polished chalice. Her gaze flicked between Ysabeau and the drink, unease tightening like a knot in her chest.

Bringing the chalice to her lips, she took a small sip, her eyes never leaving Ysabeau's face, as though searching for a crack in her composure.

"Guests cometh and goeth." Ysabeau said, her tone so neutral it was disarming. "Countenances do fade to mere shadows with the passage of time, most so for those who bend the knee to many a lord." Her words were practiced, meant to deflect. Mary's unease deepened, the maid's words only adding to her confusion.

Another sip passed Mary's lips, but her suspicions only grew. Ysabeau's calm demeanor, though placid, did nothing to ease the unease gnawing at her.

"Thou art to take a bath," Ysabeau announced suddenly, her hand gesturing toward the adjoining chamber. The prince's private bathing room awaited beyond the door.

Mary's stomach twisted. Her gaze shifted to the bathing chamber, unease settling heavy in her chest. Her chest tightened, each breath catching as the weight of what lay ahead pressed down. "Doth His Highness bid me disrobe here, within his own chamber?" she whispered, her voice trembling. "Will he seek to take advantage of me anon?"

Ysabeau's expression softened slightly, though behind her gentle tone, her mind remained sharp, calculating. "Nay, he hath no such desire for thee this night," she said, her voice soothing. Yet there was something in her tone—something Mary could not decipher—that sent a chill through her.

Mary swallowed hard, nodding weakly, though her unease lingered. She was caught in a web of circumstances she couldn't unravel, surrounded by motives she could not yet comprehend. She glanced at Ysabeau again, searching her face for answers, but the maid's calm façade remained unbroken. Whatever Ysabeau knew, she was not sharing it—not yet.

As Mary reluctantly moved toward the bathing chamber, Ysabeau's presence served as a constant reminder of the unseen forces at work. Lucian Blackthord had orchestrated every moment, though Mary remained unaware of the full extent of the intrigue that now surrounded her. Ysabeau, ever calm and composed, guided Mary's every step, ensuring that she followed the path set before her, all without raising her suspicions too high.

The tension lingered in the chamber as Mary glanced back one last time. Her thoughts were a tangled knot of confusion and dread, but she had no choice but to trust in the little she knew. Ysabeau's eyes followed her quietly, the calm of her expression masking the dangerous undercurrents that swirled just beneath the surface. The game was far from over—it had only just begun...

Mary hesitated for a moment, her discomfort lingering like a shadow, but then nodded slowly, accepting the inevitability of the orders. She took a deep breath and moved toward the doors that led to the prince's private bathing chamber, her steps measured and reluctant. Behind her, Ysabeau acted with swift discretion, her movements almost a blur. She returned to the jug, uncapping a small vial of mercurybased poison from her pocket with a practiced flick of her wrist, and emptied its contents into the water. She ensured no droplets were wasted, knowing full well that prolonged exposure or ingestion of the tainted ale would lead to more than just an upset stomach—it would bring about tremors, mood swings, and eventual cognitive decline. The clear liquid swirled silently, betraying nothing of its newfound potency as Ysabeau set the vial aside, her face a mask of composed efficiency.

With a final glance at the now-tainted jug, Ysabeau turned on her heel, her movements smooth and purposeful. She followed Mary into the bathing chambers, her footsteps silent on the stone floor, her expression unreadable as she watched Mary's back, observing every subtle reaction.

Inside the bathing chambers, thoughts of her sister momentarily flickered through Mary's mind. She longed to be home, yet a part of her welcomed the prospect of a warm bath, a luxury that poor folk like her did not have. Her initial introduction to this indulgence had left her bewildered—thrust into heated waters without explanation, simply as a prelude to some unknown event. Now, with the knowledge that it was all in preparation for a grand ball, she approached the steaming tub with a mixture of reluctance and quiet anticipation.

The sour, musty odour clung to her dress like the weight of every chore she had suffered, the stench rising from the fabric as a reminder of the sweat and grime embedded in its threads. Each waft brought back the endless scrubbing, the bending over hearths, and the hauling of buckets. She wrinkled her nose in distaste as she discarded the garment.

Tentatively, Mary dipped her toes into the hot bathwater, a sensation both startling and unfamiliar. Her skin prickled, the heat almost too much at first, making her pull back slightly. Yet, after a moment, she relaxed, allowing herself to release a soft sigh as the warmth spread across her feet and up her legs. The heat kissed her skin, both strange and soothing at once, as though her body had forgotten what such luxury felt like. Slowly, she sank into the bath, the water enveloping her, and with each moment, the tension that gripped her body began to dissolve, though the unfamiliar comfort still left her feeling slightly on edge.

Her heart raced in her chest as she watched Ysabeau carefully, her breath catching in her throat with each passing moment. She hoped against hope to see a flicker of recognition in Ysabeau's eyes, a glimmer of remembrance that might confirm her suspicions. But Ysabeau's expression remained unchanged, her features stoic and impassive, adding to Mary's growing sense of unease.

Ysabeau's response was smooth and convincing, her head shaking in feigned confusion as if she couldn't recall a thing. But in truth, the memory of that encounter lingered vividly in her mind, etched like a scene from yesterday. Lucian Blackthord had never bothered to explain his intentions, leaving her to wonder why he had intervened on behalf of this random maiden.

Her words dripped with false sincerity as she continued, "Pray, forgive mine poor memory." Yet behind her facade of innocence, a web of deceit and falsehoods coiled tightly. "I scarce recall the names of mine own grandchildren"—a blatant lie, for she had neither child nor grandchild—"nor do I remember what I ate yestermorn, let alone who I did bathe." In truth, she recalled in great detail what she had eaten, and her tongue was gilded with falsehoods, each word crafted with cunning to mislead and distract.

Ysabeau's expression remained composed, but the undercurrents of manipulation and half-truths simmered just beneath the surface, unseen by all but herself.

The water splashed softly as Mary shifted in the tub, her movements echoing against the stone walls of the chamber. "Pray, strive to call thy memory forth," she urged, her voice tinged with desperation. "Didst thou not bathe me? Dost thou not remember? Surely, if thou canst not recall the grievous torment I endured, perchance thou dost remember mine face?"

Ysabeau's brows arched ever so slightly, her lips parting as if taken aback by the revelation. The expression of surprise seemed almost practiced—a perfect mimicry that failed to touch the depth of her eyes. For a moment, her face froze, brow tensing, eyes fixed on some invisible point as she recalculated her understanding. "Did I bathe thee? In the castle, thou sayest?" she murmured, her voice carrying a subtle quiver. Yet, beneath the surface, the steadiness of her gaze betrayed her. The corners of her mouth tightened just a fraction, and a shadow flickered across her features—so brief it might have been imagined. The stiffness in her posture hinted at the deceit she wove, each nuanced movement crafted to convince while concealing the truth.

Ysabeau's lips curled, a smirk playing at their corners, though her gaze flickered with something deeper, a tension hiding behind her carefully crafted demeanor. "Art thou not most fortunate, to have twice partaken of a bath within Thorncrest Castle?" Her voice held a forced politeness as she passed Mary the soap and cloths, her hands swift but stiff, as if her mind were elsewhere. Her eyes darted toward the shadows of the chamber, a fleeting glance that betrayed her unease, as though some unseen ear might be listening.

The soap Ysabeau handed Mary was far from the simple, rough bars used by common folk. The soap felt unusually refined in Mary's hand, its surface smooth beneath her fingers, shaped with a precision far beyond the rough, homemade bars she was used to. Its deep ivory hue gleamed faintly in the dim light, a stark contrast to the coarse, misshapen lumps of soap common folk would use. The rich scent that drifted from it was unmistakable, far from the harsh, earthy odors of tallow and lye. The scent that rose from it was rich and fragrant, a blend of rosewater and sandalwood, luxurious oils woven into the very heart of the soap. As Mary rubbed it between her hands, a creamy, thick lather formed with ease, coating her skin in a velvety softness she had never known. The oils left a faint sheen on her fingers, the fragrance lingering like the whisper of a royal garden in full bloom.

The cloths, too, were of a finer make, their soft texture a far cry from the rough linens she was accustomed to. These were finely woven linen, soft yet durable, designed to scrub rather than simply wipe. As she ran the cloth across her skin, its smooth fibers glided effortlessly, cleaning away the grime that clung to her from days of toil. The scent of fresh air lingered on the fabric, as though it had been dried in the open sun, far from the smoke-filled hearths she was used to. Each stroke left her skin feeling cleaner, the dirt lifting away with ease. The very act of bathing in the prince's chamber, with such delicate cloths, reminded her just how distant she was from this life of luxury—a life far removed from her own.

Mary's fingers curled around the cloth, but her gaze remained on Ysabeau, her frustration growing. "Thou must recall the grey-haired man," she repeated, her voice straining with desperation, as if this one thread might unravel the tangled web around her.

The briefest hint of a frown crossed Ysabeau's face before she quickly smoothed it into practiced neutrality. Her eyes, once warm and open, now narrowed ever so slightly. The chamber was dimly lit, with both the flickering candle and the low-burning fire casting long, dancing shadows that shifted across her face, deepening the lines of tension she struggled to conceal. The glow from the hearth mixed with the candlelight, creating a play of light and dark that seemed to thicken the very air around them. Ysabeau inhaled slowly, steadying herself before speaking, her voice low. "Thou wouldst be wise to forget certain matters."

Silence stretched through the chamber like a taut string, each second ticking by deepening the unease. Mary's fingers tightened around the cloth, the fabric bunching in her grip as she hesitated. What could Ysabeau have meant by that? Unsure what to say, she dipped the cloth into the water, but the motion was jerky, lacking her usual grace. The water rippled, disturbed, reflecting her inner turmoil. As she drew the cloth up her arm, her movements were slow and overly precise, as if controlling this small action could steady her spiraling thoughts.

A bead of water slid down her arm, tracing a path over her skin, and she flinched slightly, the coolness a stark contrast to the warmth of the bath.

Ysabeau reached for the wooden bucket beside the bath without a word, her movements cloaked in a quiet purpose that left Mary slightly surprised. She watched as Ysabeau dipped a smaller pitcher into the open bucket, the surface of the water rippling gently under her touch. The warmth from the bath mingled with a cooler draft from the chamber, creating a soft, swirling mist around them.

"Lean thee back," Ysabeau murmured, her voice low and uneven. As she spoke, she wondered how she could convey the fate of Noor to Mary without directly admitting her own knowledge

The awkwardness hung heavily between them. Mary obeyed, her eyes closing with a mix of reluctance and unease as she tilted her head back, exposing the nape of her neck. She could feel the tension radiating from Ysabeau, the air thick with unspoken words and stifled emotions.

Ysabeau's hands were steady, but her heart was not. She raised the pitcher, the water inside catching the flicker of candlelight and casting shimmering reflections on the damp walls. She hesitated for a moment, her gaze locked on Mary's vulnerable form, the pitcher trembling slightly in her grasp.

With a gentle tilt of her wrist, Ysabeau poured the water. It cascaded over Mary's hair, a soothing wave that flowed down her scalp and along the lines of her face. The faint sound of water splashing back into the bath melded with the distant crackle of fire from the hearth.

Ysabeau scooped a handful of soap from the clay jar, her movements gentle as she began working it into Mary's greasy hair. Her fingers moved with practiced ease, massaging the scalp, loosening the layers of dirt and oil that had built up over the long, hard days.

As she lathered the soap through the tangled strands, she started to hum, then softly shifted into singing. Her voice carried the melody of a well-known tune, one that was known across the land, made famous by a renowned song teller. But the words were unmistakably her own, crafted to carry a message that she hoped Mary would impart.

"Young child, young child, O young child," Ysabeau's voice trembled soft beneath her breath, the tune wavering askew. "So small, so pure, so kind," her earnest tone held firm, though her voice wandered painfully off-key, causing Mary to wince.

The jarring notes seemed to slice through the steamy warmth of the chamber, intertwining themselves with Mary's dampened locks. Despite Ysabeau's tender hands, her singing made Mary's ears buzz, a sharp contrast to the soothing motions of the wash.

"A man, a man of mystery," Ysabeau sang on, her voice stumbling as a high note twisted into a plaintive squeal. "He serveth in secret, hidden from sight." The melody faltered yet again, notes clashing in a disharmonious tangle. It was as though the song sought its way but kept tripping upon itself. "Off to the healer's secret lair she goes."

"Her spirit doth wane, her body aches," Ysabeau warbled on, the notes dipping and curling awkwardly. " "Yet in the healer's hands, she may slowly wake."

"And so they fight with all their might," she trilled, her voice straining as the melody crumbled. "To bring her back into the light."

Though the song was sung with no grace, its words held a tale of hope and resolve, hinting at secrets yet unknown to Mary. Ysabeau's expression remained still, though her thoughts lingered on the words of the song, heavy with meaning far deeper than its clumsy melody revealed.

Mary, however, merely thought Ysabeau had gotten the words wrong, misinterpreting the tune she thought she knew so well. She listened, trying not to let her discomfort show, puzzled by Ysabeau's strange choice of lyrics and the earnest but jarring delivery.

Mary continued to scrub the dirt from her legs, casting a curious glance at Ysabeau. Yet, she hesitated to correct her, not wanting to offend or embarrass her.

Ysabeau, satisfied that she had conveyed her warning to Mary in her own unique manner and had fulfilled her duty of escorting her to the bath chamber, felt it was time to depart. Without offering any explanation, she turned to leave, as she did not wish to be caught or questioned by the prince.

The door creaked open, breaking the heavy silence that had settled in the chamber. Mary assumed Ysabeau was going to fetch drying cloths and undergarments. However, when she peeked through the partially opened door, she saw Ysabeau bypassing the neatly arranged clothing on the bed, heading purposefully towards the other door.

A sense of unease washed over Mary as she observed Ysabeau's departure. Surely, she couldn't be leaving Mary alone in the prince's bathing chamber, naked. Mary's heart raced with anxiety, her voice trembling as she called out, "Whither dost thou go?" Her words echoed in the chamber, laden with uncertainty and fear. What was Ysabeau about? Whither was she bound?

As Mary surged to her feet in a frenzy of desperation, the bathwater surged over the sides, splashing onto the floor in a chaotic cascade. The water formed rivulets down her trembling body, tracing her small curves like tears of distress. Each droplet seemed to echo the pounding of her heart, resonating with the intensity of her anxiety.

"Return hither!" she called out, her voice quivering with a mix of fear and desperation, reverberating through the empty chamber like a plaintive plea. But there was no response, only the hollow echo of her own voice bouncing off the stone walls.

Mary's eyes darted around the chamber, her eyes searching frantically for the drying cloths. Panic tinged her expression as her lips parted in confusion, uncertainty swirling in her mind like a stormy sea.

As Mary hovered on the edge of the bathtub, her intention to follow the departing Ysabeau clear in her mind, the door in the other chamber suddenly swung open with a force that startled her. Her heart leaped with hope, expecting the return of Ysabeau, but instead, she was met with the unexpected sight of the prince himself. Baldwin trailed behind him, cradling Midnight, the prince's cherished feline companion, and a female attendant, Annis. Shock and humiliation washed over her as she scrambled to cover herself with whatever modesty she could salvage, her cheeks burning crimson with embarrassment at being discovered in such a compromising position.

With a gasp, Mary recoiled, her hands flying instinctively to cover herself as she scrambled behind the bath, using its wide basin as a shield. Though she was hidden within the adjoining bathing chamber, the open doorway offered no true protection from their shocked stares. Her skin, still slick with water, chilled quickly in the sudden absence of the bath's warmth, and her heart pounded violently in her chest.

Every muscle in her body tightened, her breath shallow as she pressed her back against the cool stone of the tub, trembling. She could still feel the weight of their gazes piercing through the open doorway, and the humiliation surged through her veins like fire. Damp strands of hair clung to her flushed cheeks, and she crouched lower behind the bath, desperate to disappear.

In the main chamber, Baldwin turned pale, his face frozen in stunned disbelief. He spun quickly, turning his back to the scene in the adjoining room. Midnight, the prince's cherished cat, nestled in his arms as he hurried to place her in the cat bed near the hearth. His movements were rushed and awkward, as though eager to distance himself from the unfolding embarrassment.

Annis, standing stiffly by the chamber door, her expression betrayed the judgment she withheld. Her lips pressed into a thin line, her eyes cold as they flicked toward Mary, lingering briefly before darting away. She had heard rumours, whispers that Mary was not as innocent as she appeared, and now this spectacle only seemed to confirm her suspicions.

The prince, however, remained still, his eyes fixed on the scene unfolding in his private chambers. His gaze locked onto Mary's trembling figure, barely concealed behind the bath, and his face twisted from shock to outrage. Here was a mere peasant girl, naked in his bathing chamber—a place reserved only for him—without permission, without cause. His disbelief morphed swiftly into anger.

"How cometh this to pass?!" Charles's voice thundered, filling the space with his fury. Charles's entire body stiffened with rage, his gaze snapping toward Baldwin, the anger in his eyes burning like hot coals. Charles's gaze bore into Baldwin, his eyes narrowing with barely restrained fury. The weight of his stare lingered, sharp and expectant, as though pulling an explanation from Baldwin without a word. A flare of tension crossed his face, as if every sentence hung precariously on the cusp of a stormy outburst. "How dare this happen within mine own chambers?" he spat, the words bitter, his voice thick with disbelief. His knuckles whitened as he clenched his fists, barely holding back the storm of his fury. His face reddened, his lips curling in disbelief. "Explain yourself! How darest thou?"

Mary's heart leapt into her throat as she cowered behind the bath, her voice quaking as she tried to form words. "Th-the maid," she stammered, her tone a mixture of confusion and fear. "She told me—told me I was to come here… at thy command, Your Highness." Her voice wavered as her trembling hands tightened on the edge of the tub, trying to make sense of the accusations now aimed at her.

Mary's gaze flickered toward Charles, searching desperately for a hint of recognition, yet his furrowed brow and tightly set jaw only deepened the pit of uncertainty within her. The hard lines etched across his face spoke nothing of understanding, only cold fury, each glance she stole unraveling what little hope remained in her chest. "The maid washed my hair," she added quickly, her voice almost pleading, as though this simple fact might somehow absolve her of the crime she didn't even understand.

Charles's face contorted with rage, his disbelief written in the sharpness of his features. His brow furrowed deeply, and he stormed toward the jug of ale that rested on his table. His movements were rigid, almost mechanical, as he poured himself a drink, his thoughts swirling in anger and confusion. The memory of his recent actions—taking a life—had left him in a haze of distorted thoughts, his recollections fractured and unreliable.

He drank deeply, his hand trembling slightly as he set the goblet down with a loud clink.

"Baldwin," he snapped, his voice sharp and commanding, though a tinge of uncertainty lurked beneath. "Did I command such orders? Was this folly contrived without mine own knowledge?"

Baldwin's back straightened, and he turned slowly, his face as pale as parchment. "Your Highness," quoth he, his voice strained. "Thy command wast only that I should bring Mary hither to don her garments. Of aught beyond that, I know naught."

Charles's anger only grew at the denial, his chest heaving as he struggled to piece together the fragmented events of the last few days. His fingers drummed impatiently on the edge of the table, his mind a whirl of conflicting thoughts.

"Annis!" he barked, his voice echoing through the chamber. "Fetch her hence and see her made presentable!"

Annis's eyes flickered toward Mary, her lips thinning in disapproval, but she nodded quickly. Without a word, she crossed the chamber to retrieve the drying cloths from a shelf. Her movements were swift and deliberate as she carried the cloths into the adjoining bathing chamber, her face betraying no sympathy for Mary's predicament.

Mary, still crouched behind the bath, glanced up as Annis approached with the cloths. Her face flushed deeply with shame, her eyes wide with panic as she scrambled to wrap the cloth around her wet body, shielding herself as best she could from the prince's burning gaze.

Charles, still fuming, watched as Mary struggled with the cloth. His fury, however, was momentarily overshadowed by the confusion that still plagued his mind.

"They shall require her to be fair of visage, Annis." he said, his voice lowering but still sharp. "See to it she appeareth as though she doth belong in this court."

Annis, expressionless, turned to Mary, handing her another cloth for her hair. She began to work quickly, drying Mary's dripping locks with rough efficiency, her hands moving with a detached coldness that made Mary shudder. The prince's eyes remained on her, watching every movement, his anger palpable in the tense air.

Mary, trembling under the weight of it all, kept her eyes downcast, her hands clutching the cloth as though it were her only protection. Annis's fingers worked through Mary's hair with a firm grip, each pull sending a sharp reminder of where she stood. The roughness of Annis's touch wasn't just in her hands—it was in the way she yanked at the tangled strands, as if to assert her control over Mary, every movement underscoring the divide between them, a silent warning that Mary didn't belong in this world of power and peril.

Charles's hand trembled as it lifted the cup to his lips, unknowingly bringing the poisoned ale closer. His fingers tightened around the goblet's cool surface, knuckles whitening with each passing second, though the tremor that ran through him was not entirely from anger. His body, already feeling the subtle effects of the mercury, quivered ever so slightly as he swallowed the bitter liquid. Yet, his fury had not abated—it surged within him, crashing against the walls of his restraint.

Meanwhile, Mary's hands clutched the edges of the chair with a tight, almost desperate grip. The smooth wood beneath her fingers was the only thing grounding her as Annis's rough hands continued their work on her scalp, tugging at her hair with methodical force. The braids pulled tighter with each twist, making her feel more like an ornament being prepared for display than a person.

The gown, now waiting on the bed, seemed a mockery. Every inch of it was designed to adorn a woman who was far from her station, and each pull of Annis's fingers served as a reminder of just how far Mary had wandered from her world in Mudlark Alley. In that moment, the bitter contrast between this absurd luxury and the grinding hardship of her past gnawed at her insides. The noblewomen who lounged in such silks would never know the pain of lifting buckets of water, the harshness of scrubbing floors, or the ceaseless struggle to survive in a world that turned its back on the poor.

She could hear the rustle of the fine cloth being prepared, but her mind wandered, picturing the nobles who wore such gowns daily, likely thinking nothing of the cost. Her lip curled inwardly. To them, she was but a fleeting entertainment, a joke to be mocked in their gatherings.

Annis's hands moved relentlessly, but Mary barely flinched anymore. Her thoughts drifted, the images of Mudlark Alley and the life she left behind dancing through her mind like ghosts. She imagined her sister, wrapped in rough, worn garments, unaware of the luxuries within the castle. How could Mary ever explain this strange new world, with its silks and ribbons, to someone who had never known warmth beyond the hearthfire of a humble home?

Each tug from Annis brought her back to reality, the discomfort pulling her out of her thoughts, but the prince's presence loomed larger than any discomfort Annis could inflict. Even with her eyes closed, she could feel his gaze on her, as if his eyes were stripping her of what little dignity remained.

"If it be thy will, my liege, might I don a garment now?" Mary's voice broke the silence, tentative yet carrying an undercurrent of desperation. Her words trembled on the air, fragile, as if they might shatter before reaching the prince.

Charles's eyes flicked toward her, his face twisted in disdain. "Well, thou canst not attend the ball in such a state, canst thou?" he sneered, his voice dripping with sarcasm. The mockery was plain in his gaze, a look that regarded her question as beneath him.

Mary wasted no time. She rose swiftly from her seat, her hand outstretched for the gown, eager to reclaim some semblance of modesty. Just as her fingers grazed the soft fabric, Annis's voice cut through the chamber like a whip. "The undergarments must be fitted first."

Her heart sank. The thought of being bound in the tight, suffocating corset, an imposition of a world she barely understood, made her breath hitch. But she held her tongue, knowing that refusal would lead nowhere. She could already feel the weight of the corset pressing against her, its tight strings a reminder of the roles forced upon her.

Mary turned toward Charles, her stomach churning at what she knew she had to do. Lucian Blackthord's words echoed in her mind. She had been instructed to ensnare the prince, to use her charms to bend him to Lucian's will. Her lips parted, the rehearsed words tumbling out, though each syllable felt like a betrayal to herself.

"Your Highness," she began softly, her voice barely more than a whisper, "If I were to forgo my shift, would that not... please thee the more?" Her words were laced with an artificial sweetness, but the bitterness behind them stung her more than any blade.

The sharp gasp from Annis was immediate. She recoiled, her eyes wide, scandal and shock written across her face. The disapproval radiated from her in waves, as though the very walls of the chamber had been affronted by Mary's audacity.

But Charles merely smirked, a slow, calculating grin spreading across his face. "Very well, leave the corset be." he murmured, his eyes darkening with some unspoken thought. He beckoned her closer with a tilt of his head, his breath hot against her ear as he leaned in to whisper, "See that the king is made privy to this."

His command was not a request, but a thinly veiled threat. Mary could feel the weight of his schemes pressing down on her shoulders, the knowledge that she was merely a pawn in a game far larger than herself.

With a forced smile, she turned back to the bed where the gown awaited her. Annis, though clearly shaken, moved forward and began to dress her. The heavy fabric enveloped her, and the laces at the back were pulled tight, constricting her movements with each tug. Mary could feel the cold fingers of Annis against her skin, sharp and unforgiving, as they fastened the final buttons.

The prince's voice sliced through the stillness. "Shoes. Or dost thou think thy bare feet will suffice?"

Annis, without a word, fetched the shoes. Mary's fingers grazed the soft leather of the shoes, a texture so foreign to her that it felt like a distant dream—one that belonged to a life far beyond her reach, far removed from the rough realities she had always known.

As the prince moved to pour himself more ale, his hand trembled slightly, the mercury within the cup beginning to take its toll. Yet he remained unaware, his focus still sharp as he waved for Annis to finish her task. "Baldwin!" Charles barked, the name ringing through the chamber with impatience. "Feed Midnight."

The Princess's return feast Chapter Nineteen

As they neared the grand ballroom, the air thickened with the crescendo of music and laughter, cascading over Mary like a rising tide. Each step felt heavier, her nerves coiling tighter, her breaths shallow under the weight of her unease. How came I to this wretched place? The question echoed in her mind, her anger barely contained behind the composed mask she wore.

Her gaze flicked toward the prince, sharp and accusing, though his back was turned to her. The shoes, beautiful but merciless, bit into her heels with every step, a cruel reminder that this world was not hers. Ahead, the towering doors of the ballroom grew closer, their gilded carvings glinting in the light, heralding the spectacle beyond. Her heart raced, pounding in her chest like a war drum.

The guards snapped to attention as the prince approached. With practiced precision, they pulled the doors wide, unleashing a torrent of sound—music, laughter, and conversation weaving together in a cacophony that struck Mary like a blow. She faltered, blinking at the blinding opulence that sprawled before her.

The ballroom was alive with light and motion, a world so foreign it seemed almost unreal. Lavender and rosewater scented the air, replacing the sour stench of spilled ale and unwashed bodies she knew too well. Silk and velvet spun across the floor, shimmering under the glow of chandeliers that hung like gilded stars. Mary's breath hitched. This was no mere hall—it was a stage, and she an unwilling performer thrust into its glaring spotlight.

"Behold His Highness, Prince Charles, and his most esteemed companion!" The herald's voice rang out, cutting through the music like a blade.

A wave of silence swept the room as every gaze turned toward the doors. Whispers rippled in their wake, a sea of curious and calculating stares. Mary froze, her cheeks burning as the weight of their attention bore down on her. Instinctively, she raised a hand to shield her face, but the prince was quicker. The prince seized her hand, steady and unrelenting, anchoring her in place. His smile remained steady, a mask of royal poise that offered no refuge.

"Stand tall and hold thy head aloft," he murmured, his voice low but commanding. "His words cut through her rising panic, steadying her just enough to keep her upright, though her pulse still hammered in her chest."

Banners in deep purple lined the walls, bearing the family crest—a lion rampant, fierce and unyielding. Above them, the princess's own mark—a delicate rose entwined with the lion—gleamed softly in the flickering light. Mary stared at it, willing herself to find strength in the ornate display, though it felt as distant as the stars.

The nobles bowed and curtsied, their motions a symphony of grace and precision. Silken gowns fanned out like petals, while men's polished shoes glided across the floor. Yet beneath their reverence, she saw it—the flicker of curiosity, the glint of suspicion. She was no princess, no noblewoman, yet here she stood, arm in arm with the prince. The questions in their eyes burned hotter than the chandeliers above.

At the far end of the hall, King John broke from his conversation, his gaze locking briefly on his brother. His smile was swift, a flash of courtly warmth that didn't reach his eyes. Prince Charles returned it, their exchange wordless yet heavy with unspoken rivalry.

Then, with a subtle nod from the prince, the nobles straightened, the formal stiffness of their bows melting into an undercurrent of anticipation. The hall stirred to life once more, but Mary remained rooted to the spot. Her chest tightened, her pulse thundering as the gilded world spun around her. The respect they feigned in their bows and polite smiles felt like a dagger's edge—shallow, fleeting, and always ready to turn.

The unexpected show of respect left Mary momentarily unsettled. She knew it was meant for the prince, not her, but being in the spotlight rather than the shadows was disorienting. Caught in an odd haze, she struggled to reconcile the surreal experience.

The prince leaned in, his tone sharp and impatient as they navigated through the crowd. "Cease thy gawking and set thy feet to moving!" he hissed, his words snapping her out of her daze.

Her movements were hurried and clumsy as she tried to regain composure under the watchful eyes of the gathered nobles. Speculative glances trailed her like shadows, and their whispers filled the air. "Is she with Edward Saint-Clair?" one nobleman murmured. "Nay, she's surely from a southern house," countered a lady, nodding as if she'd unraveled a great mystery. Others imagined her as an exotic princess or dismissed her as the bastard of some obscure lord.

As they passed through the murmuring crowd, Mary's unease grew. Each step felt heavier under the weight of their stares, their silent judgments cutting sharper than any insult. Not one of them could have guessed the truth: that she was no noble, no princess, but a simple peasant girl.

Prince Charles guided her past the imposing figure of the Marshal, who stood steadfast by King John's side, his sharp gaze scanning the hall with unrelenting precision. Beside the king, a knight clad in polished armour—his personal guard—stood quietly, his hand resting on the hilt of his sword. Though his presence was understated, his watchfulness was unmistakable, a silent assurance of the king's safety.

The ballroom buzzed with music and conversation as Charles approached the king, who stood in discussion with a prominent lord. Subtly, Charles cleared his throat, the sound cutting through the noise and drawing a few curious glances. King John turned briefly, his deep purple robes and golden crown glinting in the flickering light.

The king's gaze swept over his brother before settling on Mary. His brow furrowed as he studied her, realisation slowly dawning. Mary? Her name floated to the surface of his thoughts as he pieced it together. His expression softened, surprise flickering across his face as he took in her attire and bearing—so unlike the chambermaid he had once known.

A rare light flickered in King John's eyes as he beheld Mary, warmth breaking through his usual stoicism and tugging a gentle smile to his lips. Despite his position, the weight of his crown had not hardened his heart entirely. Kindness, though often restrained, was not foreign to him. Had he misjudged Charles? Disbelief coursed through him as he struggled to reconcile why his brother had brought Mary here, adorned in fine garments and presented at a royal ball—far beyond the simple respect he had commanded.

Charles, dressed in a deep purple velvet tunic embroidered with their family's lion crest, stood at Mary's side with the air of someone enjoying a private jest. His hand rested lightly on her arm, both guiding her and, perhaps, staking a claim. The faint smirk tugging at his lips suggested he was waiting for his brother's reaction with barely concealed amusement.

King John's gaze flicked to Charles, his expression remaining neutral, though the smallest crease in his brow betrayed his thoughts. "Thou hast outdone thyself, Charles," he said dryly. "This was not the form of respect I envisioned when I commanded thee."

Charles inclined his head, his smirk sharpening. "I merely took thy royal decree to heart, brother. Respect, after all, is owed to those who deserve it. Surely thou dost approve of my efforts to ensure Mary's worth is seen."

The king's attention returned to Mary, his gaze lingering on her transformation. The candlelight illuminated the rich fabric of her gown and her delicate features, an image so incongruous with the maid he had once known. "Mary Winterbourne, 'tis a delight to lay mine eyes upon thee," King John breathed, his voice low, but a hint of wonder softened the usual gravity of his tone. For a moment, the tension between them faded, replaced by admiration and perhaps a touch of pride.

Mary fidgeted with the fabric of her gown, stealing a glance at the king as her knees trembled slightly under the weight of so many watchful eyes. Her cheeks burned, though whether from the attention of the crowd or the king's lingering gaze, she could not say. When she spoke, her voice quavered, scarcely rising above a whisper. "Y-Y-Your Majesty."

Charles's grip on her arm tightened briefly, his expression unreadable. "Steady thyself, Mary," he murmured softly, though the glint in his eyes suggested he relished her discomfort as much as he sought to ease it.

The king's brows drew together briefly, yet his expression softened as he watched her steady herself. "I am bereft of words," he admitted, his tone warm yet deliberate. His gaze rested on her once more, catching the flicker of her eyes meeting his before she looked away, the candlelight softly highlighting the fabric of her gown.

"By my troth, I cannot deny, thou art fairer than all the ladies gathered here," he said softly, his words carrying a sincerity that banished all pretense. "Yet with thy beauty, thou needst not adorn thyself so. Even unadorned, thou wouldst still outshine these folk."

Mary's breath caught, her fingers tightening on her gown as the sincerity in his tone struck her deeply. For a fleeting moment, she dared to meet his eyes again, the weight of his admiration hanging between them like a fragile thread, waiting for the slightest breath to snap it.

Charles cleared his throat pointedly, his smirk returning. "A most radiant compliment from our noble king, and rare it is, to light upon one such as Mary. Mayhap thou dost soften with thy years, brother."

The king turned his attention to Charles, his tone cooling as he responded. "Or mayhap I am more keen of eye than thee, Charles. A rare marvel, I confess, to perceive worth where thou dost see naught."

Charles inclined his head mockingly. "Thy wisdom is, as ever, unparalleled, my liege," he said, his words honeyed but laced with sarcasm.

Before either could press further, a loud voice boomed through the grand hall, accompanied by the resonant tolling of a bell.

"Presenting Her Royal Highness, the Queen Mother," the herald announced, commanding the attention of all in attendance. The atmosphere shifted with haste, anticipation mingling with deference as the guests turned their gaze toward the entrance. There, accompanied by the Queen Mother, stood Princess Sophia.

Sophia entered with elegant bearing, though the downturn of her lips hinted at a sadness she could not fully conceal. As the herald's voice proclaimed her arrival, a ripple of acknowledgment spread through the hall, a quiet murmur of recognition for the next members of the royal family.

Accompanying the royal figures were their personal knights, a detail that immediately caught Mary's eye. The torchlight flickered across their armour, polished to a blinding sheen. Gold accents traced the edges and joints, catching the light like the glint of sunlight on a blade. Embossed lions stood proudly on their chest plates, their intricate details hinting at valor and loyalty. These were not just any protectors; their poise and precision marked them as bound to the Queen Mother and Princess Sophia.

Mary's eyes darted to Sir Hector, his cloak swaying with his steps. The rich fabric, dyed to match Princess Sophia's gown, shimmered faintly with golden embroidery. Beside him, the Queen Mother's knight stood equally composed, his cloak echoing her deep royal hues. The delicate embroidery along its edges sparkled like dew kissed by sunlight, a testament to his station and the unspoken bond with his charge.

As the knights flanked the Queen Mother and Princess Sophia, the hall seemed to hold its breath. A ripple of motion broke the silence as the assembled nobles sank into bows and curtsies, the rustle of silk and velvet filling the air. Men bent low, their movements crisp and deliberate, while women descended with practiced grace, their skirts swept the floor in graceful arcs, the fabric rippling like a river with every curtsy. Only King John stood upright, his gaze sharp as it briefly met the Queen Mother's across the expanse of the hall.

The Queen Mother inclined her head, her chin lifting just enough to signal the nobles to rise. A subtle but commanding gesture. The guests obeyed as one, their movements smooth as a tide retreating, parting instinctively to form a path. The royals advanced with measured steps, their knights moving in perfect synchrony beside them. Sophia's smile, though precise and polished, faltered briefly at the corners, a fleeting crack in her otherwise flawless facade. Mary felt her pulse quicken as the procession drew closer. *Cast thine eyes downward. Meet not her gaze,* she thought, lowering her eyes to the floor.

Queen Mother Victoria Beaumont descended into a curtsy so fluid it seemed as though her gown poured around her like water. Her every movement was measured and graceful, a quiet reflection of her years as queen consort. When Princess Sophia followed, her knees buckled ever so slightly, a sharp jolt running through her leg. Every muscle tense, she eased herself down, her eyes flashing with an unyielding resolve that would not be swayed. Though her rise was slower, each deliberate motion carried the weight of royal training, concealing the ache in her limbs.

The knights behind them mirrored their charges with solemn bows, their heads dipping in perfect unison. Sir Hector's hand briefly brushed the hilt of his sword, his fingers tightening, a silent reassurance in his disciplined demeanor. Sophia's focus stayed rooted on the floor, her jaw clenched as though willing her pain into submission.

Mary's gaze flitted between the royals, lingering on King John as he stepped forward. His outstretched hand was steady, his smile measured and practiced, but a flicker of warmth crossed his face as his eyes met Sophia's. Relief softened his expression for a fleeting moment before the mask of formality returned. "Art thou well, sister?" His voice carried the practiced cadence of courtly decorum, concern faintly woven into its edges. "Thou dost appear rested."

Sophia nodded, her smile not quite reaching her eyes. "I thank thee, brother," she replied, her voice light yet carefully controlled. The words hung in the air, polite but distant, like the faint toll of a distant bell.

Mary's chest tightened as she watched them, her mind flickering to Mudlark Alley. There, reunions after hardship were raw and unbridled—siblings rushing into each other's arms, tears flowing freely, laughter breaking through sobs. Here, kinship was dulled by duty, emotions bound by rigid threads of royal expectation. The gulf between her world and theirs yawned wide, stark and cold.

Sophia moved forward with deliberate steps, her limp faint but noticeable. A fine sheen of sweat glistened on her brow, though she held her chin high. The light from the chandeliers burned too brightly, casting jagged shards into her pounding head. Her hand hovered over the vial hidden in her gown, the faint herbal scent of its contents still lingering in her mind. A faint quiver ran through her fingers as they gripped it tightly, her whole hand now a tight, tense ball. Whatever relief it promised, it could not mask the turmoil simmering beneath her composed exterior.

A pang of weariness tugged at Sophia's heart as she lowered herself into the chair, the weight of her burdens heavy upon her shoulders. Oblivious to Mary's presence, she murmured, "I fare well, Your Majesty, and do humbly thank thee." her voice steady but soft, the words rehearsed yet lacking conviction. The lie settled around her like a heavy cloak, suffocating and oppressive, one she wore with a desperate grace.

Had Sophia noticed Mary among the onlookers, that familiar face might have shattered her composure. The sight could have brought the tears she was staunchly holding back brimming to the surface; her façade would have crumbled. "Glad am I to be in mine rightful place, amongst those whom I hold dear."

"Mine rightful place?" Mary thought, a hint of scorn curling the edge of her lips, unseen by those around her. As she watched Princess Sophia standing there, draped in the clothing of royalty, a surge of incredulity washed over her. If this was truly her highness's rightful place, ensconced in luxury and formalities, what business did she have meddling in the lives of Mary and her family?

The king's smile broadened, a glimmer of approval lighting up his features as he nodded in satisfaction, unsure what else to say. "Good, 'tis well to hear," he proclaimed, his voice carrying the weight of authority.

He looked around the hall, his gaze sharp and commanding. With a swift, authoritative snap of his fingers, he signaled the waiting servants. "The guest of honour is here; let the feast begin!" he announced, his proclamation echoing off the high vaulted ceilings, stirring the assembled guests into excited murmurs. Servants sprang into action, their movements swift and fluid, as the hall burst into a flurry of activity, the rustling of fine tableware and the clatter of utensils setting the stage for the evening's festivities.

Mary observed the dynamics of the hall shift as the king's command resonated. She felt the weight of an unspoken tradition pressing down upon her, a reminder that this was not merely a gathering of family but a performance dictated by the expectations of nobility. The king's arm extended in a graceful sweep, a silent command for the guests to take their seats.

The princess, as the guest of honour, was granted the privilege of being the first to sit. Sophia, her movements slow and careful, almost limped to her seat, her attention still consumed by her own thoughts. A pang of weariness tugged at her heart as she lowered herself into the chair, the weight of her burdens heavy upon her shoulders, leaving her oblivious to Mary's presence.

Mary had never before attended a royal ball and knew little of how such affairs unfolded. Her stomach twisted with nerves as she watched the princess take her seat, the faint scrape of the chair against the stone floor echoing in the grand hall, marking the start of the feast. The assembled nobility settled into their places, an ocean of silk and velvet, their eyes gleaming with curiosity and expectation as the festivities commenced.

Mary's head spun as she sought Baldwin among the crowd, her heart racing with uncertainty. *What wouldst thou have me do? Whither should I turn?* Alas, he was nowhere to be seen. She sensed the weight of curious glances from the servants, their furtive whispers and knowing smirks revealing their awareness of her less than humble origins, while the noble guests around her maintained their polished composure.

Panic gripped her, each breath sharp and shallow. May I depart? Her eyes darted towards the grand wooden doors, their inviting presence calling to her.

The musicians played a soft tune on their lutes, each note rising and falling like the breaths of the crowd. As more guests found their seats, a wave of anxiety crashed over Mary, tightening around her like a noose.

Standing near the royal table, she felt the weight of every gaze upon her, each stare sharpening her awareness of her outsider status. Despite the fine fabric of her dress and the care taken with her hair, she feared that beneath the surface, they could see the truth of her commonness.

The flickering torchlight cast dancing shadows upon the stone walls, illuminating the subtle tremor in Mary's hands and the way her breath quickened. The murmurs of the nobility rippled through the air, a low buzz that seemed to swirl around her like a tempest. Each gaze felt like a dagger, their scrutiny slicing through her composure and leaving her heart racing, as though she stood on the edge of a precipice.

With a nervous glance towards the towering figures behind her, Mary moved cautiously, her heart racing as she sought a way to escape the oppressive atmosphere.

Could she slip away unnoticed before Charles could utter a word? Her heart pounded as she edged backward, her movements deliberate yet anxious.

As she hurried past the tables, her steps quickened, nearly causing her to bump into a guest. The woman's expression shifted to annoyance, brows furrowing as Mary's sudden movement startled her. "Forgive me, milady," Mary stammered, flustered, her voice barely above a whisper. Yet, without awaiting the woman's reply, she pressed onward, eager to leave the awkward encounter behind.

Mary weaved deftly between the last few guests, her movements fluid as she sidestepped those who blocked her path, her body swaying with the grace of a dancer to avoid any collisions.

With each determined stride, the door drew nearer, hope blossoming within her chest. But just as relief surged through her, a sudden disturbance shattered the air, halting her in her tracks.

With a resounding scrape, the king's chair slid back as he rose, his towering figure casting a commanding shadow over the hall. His voice, a thunderous boom, pierced through the din, calling out her name.

"Mary?" The word echoed off the stone walls, reverberating through her very soul. It felt as if her spirit had been torn from her chest, leaving her breathless and exposed in the hushed silence that followed. Even the musicians faltered, their melodies crumbling into disarray as all eyes turned towards her, their gazes piercing like a thousand daggers.

Caught in the spotlight, Mary's heart plummeted, as though she had been caught red-handed in an unforgivable transgression. Embarrassment washed over her, her face contorting into a grimace of shame.

With every eye in the hall fixed upon her, she turned slowly, each movement weighed down by the burden of humiliation, to face the imposing royal table.

The king's eyes had followed Mary as she made her way towards the door, confusion etched upon his face. He realized that she must not know where to sit, deciding instead to leave. After all the effort his brother had put into bringing her here, it felt a shame for her to depart ere the feast had even begun.

Whispers rippled through the hall as every single gaze flickered between the king and Mary. What title did this maiden bear, and from what household? She had arrived with the prince and now was being summoned by the king by name.

His Majesty stood at the central table, ensuring all knew his prominent position. To his right, the queen mother sat regally, her face more confused than anyone else in the hall. On his left, the guest of honour, his sister, sat in an elevated position marking her significance for the night. She blinked rapidly, fighting back tears that threatened to spill, and took a deep breath to steady herself. Gradually, she forced herself to focus on the scene unfolding before her.

With a sweeping gesture, the king directed her to the royal table. "Thou art to sit beside mine brother," he announced, his tone brooking no argument. It was clear he intended for his words to be followed. Beneath his authoritative exterior, a flicker of concern danced in his eyes, a testament to the fondness he held for her—more than propriety might allow.

Charles, positioned on the other side of their mother, watched, taken aback that his brother would make such a scene, especially as Mary was secretly just a maid. Charles's lips thinned as he watched Mary, his brow furrowing deeply. A fleeting glance, sharp and dismissive, flickered in his eyes, as if he regretted the decision to bring her, viewing her now as an unwelcome spectre at a grand celebration.

Heads turned sharply, and courtiers exchanged wide-eyed looks, their expressions a silent testament to their collective astonishment. Never before had the king so publicly dictated the seating.

The guests might not know that Mary was but a maid dressed fine, yet the servants recognised her and were visibly shocked. The queen mother's confusion deepened, her regal composure slipping just a fraction. The king's sister, finally recognizing Mary, looked equally bewildered, her shock evident as she took in the sight of the familiar face at such a prestigious gathering.

The prince's eyes narrowed at Mary, his lips pressing into a thin line and his brow furrowing deeply. His clenched jaw and the flicker of irritation in his eyes seemed to say, *Why dost thou still stand there?* He pointed sharply to the seat next to him, his nostrils flaring slightly as he barked, "Take thy seat!"

Mary's cheeks flushed crimson as she mumbled, "Of course, your Majesty," her voice barely above a whisper. She kept her gaze fixed upon the floor, avoiding the piercing eyes of the king, prince, and every guest. With her head bowed, she hurried past the tables, her steps quick and uneven, the whispers and stares burning into her back like hot coals.

Mary quickened her pace as she approached the royal table, the silence growing more oppressive with each step. Surely the musicians could resume playing; perhaps then the guests would return to their conversations, she thought to herself, a surge of embarrassment flooding her senses. She felt the weight of their scrutiny intensify, her heart thudding loudly in her chest. Her hands trembled as she fumbled with the chair, her movements jerky and hesitant as the wood scraped against the stone. Her breath hitched as she finally sat down, smoothing her dress with nervous fingers. She dared a fleeting glance at the king, who offered her a supportive smile, before dropping her eyes again, her cheeks burning as she clenched her hands in her lap, trying to steady their shaking.

The king cleared his throat. "Mine most esteemed guests, honoured lords and ladies of the court, and cherished companions," he began, his gaze sweeping across the hall. Upon this night, we are met to celebrate the blessed return of our dearly beloved Princess Sophia. " He paused, his eyes softening as he directed a warm smile at his sister. She quickly forced a smile, her lips trembling slightly, her eyes betraying her desire to be anywhere but here. "Ere we partake in this feast, let us take a moment to offer a blessing. May we give thanks for the abundance that shall be served." He reached for his chalice, lifting it high. "I extend mine gratitude to mine brother, Prince Charles, acting host at Thorncrest Castle. His hospitality hath made this evening possible." An awkward ripple of appreciative nods moved through the hall, with some guests exchanging unsure glances.

"Raise thy drink with me," the king's voice rang out, commanding attention. Without hesitation, the guests lifted their chalices in unison. "To the gods of the heavens, for their hand in guiding the princess home in safety." he said, placing the chalice to his lips. The entire gathering hesitated, confusion flickering across their faces. Still, they lifted their chalices and took a sip, the awkwardness palpable as they honoured the toast with uncertain glances exchanged around the hall.

With a satisfied nod, the king signaled for the feast to commence. Servants, who had been waiting by the oak doors, sprang into action. The head servant knocked twice on the door, a signal that set a chain of events into motion. As the hall waited, the king gestured to the musicians.

The musicians, poised with their instruments, immediately began to play. The gentle strains of a lute filled the air, soon joined by the soft, resonant chords of a harp and the deep, rich notes of a viol.

Mary could still feel the eyes upon her, each gaze like a weight pressing down on her shoulders. Her heart burned with resentment toward the prince beside her. She clenched her jaw, refusing to meet the gaze of the princess across the table, a person she had no interest in speaking to whatsoever. The queen mother's cold, assessing eyes only added to her discomfort.

She wondered, her mind racing, *Wherefore hath the king wrought such an unseemly spectacle?* Her thoughts spiraled, imagining the whispers and gossip among her fellow servants. They were surely talking about her now, if they weren't already. Mary's stomach twisted into knots as she shifted uncomfortably in her seat, her eyes darting around for an escape. The urge to vanish, to be anywhere but here, gnawed at her—but she straightened her shoulders, unwilling to crumble before their gaze.

The Queen Mother's eyes narrowed as she observed Mary, her mind racing. For the king to make such a scene and seat this girl at their table, she must be of great importance. "And prithee, Your Majesty, who might this noble maiden be?" she inquired, her voice dripping with curiosity and thinly veiled suspicion.

The hum of conversation resumed around the hall, but Mary could still feel curious glances and hear whispers speculating about her identity. The king, with a playful gleam in his eye, turned to his mother. He gasped theatrically, a playful smile spreading across his face. "Mother, how canst thou fail to know Charles's most cherished guest?"

The Queen Mother's cheeks flushed faintly at his jest, her usual composure faltering. A servant approached the king's side, pouring wine into his chalice. Prince Charles rolled his eyes, letting out a heavy sigh as he sneered, his disdain for the whole table clear as day. "Aye, Mother, 'tis none other than the illustrious Lady of Thornbriar herself," he drawled, his voice dripping with venomous mockery.

Mary's stomach churned at the prince's words. Thornbriar Cottage, the place she had been forced to live in by him, was the last place she wanted to be. Being mocked as the lady of that wretched household was a cruel twist of the knife, and the pain in her expression was unmistakable.

The Queen Mother's faltering composure was brief, replaced by a warm smile that masked her embarrassment. "Ah, yes, Lady of Thornbriar," she said, nodding as though she had known all along. "Such a pleasure to have thee with us," she added, her voice smooth and practiced despite the initial stumble.

The king suppressed a laugh, his shoulders shaking slightly at his mother's pretense. As the servant finished pouring the wine, the king picked up his chalice and took a sip, a hint of a smile playing on his lips.

The servant moved gracefully to the guest of honour, Princess Sophia, and began pouring wine into her chalice. Sophia's eyes, filled with sorrow, found Mary's. She paused, weighed down by the burden of words unsaid, her thoughts lingering on Mary's sister. *How farest they, I wonder? Surely she and Robert doth fret o'er Noor's fate.* Sophia's throat tightened, but she finally managed to choke out, "Mary." The single word hung in the air, drawing all eyes on the table to look up.

The king, his chalice still at his lips, tilted his head, curiosity flickering across his face at Princess Sophia's tone. The Queen Mother mirrored his movement, her eyes narrowing in confusion. Charles, however, shot Sophia a sinister glare, a silent warning not to say anything that might cast him in a bad light.

Mary slowly looked up, her eyes blazing with disdain, shooting daggers at Sophia. All she could think was, *I am forced to be here because of thee!* Yet, she dared not speak, for whatever Sophia might say could anger the prince—and risk far more than her pride.

Sophia's throat tightened at the sight of both the prince's sinister glare and Mary's dagger-like gaze. Forcing a smile despite her racing heart, she quickly said, "Thy gown is lovely, and thy hair is wonderful." She reminded herself that she had to hide the fact that she knew Mary, the stakes far too high. *For Robert's sake,* she thought, *I must pretend.*

The servant continued to fill the other chalices, moving methodically down the line of important guests. The king placed his chalice on the table, his eyes flicking between Mary and Sophia, a look of shock etched on his face. "Verily, thou art in the right, sister. 'Tis rare that I find myself so aligned," he said, shooting Mary a quick smile.

With an intimate tone, he brought his mouth close to Sophia's ear, taking a moment to collect his thoughts before speaking. "Art thou well?" he asked, his concern evident. Her tone when saying Mary's name had unnerved him. After all that she had been through, he wondered if this ball was happening too quickly. It seemed the court demanded its desires without regard for personal feelings.

Sophia forced a smile, her lips trembling slightly. "By all means, Your Majesty," she replied, the effort clear in her voice. Desperate to shift the focus, she turned to Victoria. "And Mother, might I say, how wondrous thou appearest, as ever," she added, her voice wavering just a bit.

Victoria's fingers fluttered gracefully over the lace of her gown, her cheeks glowing as she tilted her head. "Thou art too kind, dear," she purred, her fingers resting on the diamond of her necklace, its flawless surface catching the candlelight.

Charles let out a snort, his eyes rolling dramatically. He leaned back in his chair, looking utterly uninterested. "Aye, Mother, thy gem doth shine with a blinding light," he drawled sarcastically before taking a sip from his chalice.

Mary's eyes widened ever so slightly as she took in the diamond, its brilliance unlike anything she had ever seen. She felt a pang of discomfort, thinking of the poor souls who might have suffered for such a treasure. Horrible tales of diamond harvesting flickered through her mind. Pushing aside her unease, she forced a smile and whispered in a weak voice, "It is exquisite."

Victoria's smile remained poised, but before she could respond, the oak doors swung open. A flood of servants poured into the hall, balancing trays made of polished wood. The trays were laden with gleaming silver plates, each intricately engraved and bearing the royal crest. The plates, heavy and ornate, reflected the warm glow of the candles as the servants moved swiftly and with practiced precision, heading straight for the royal table to serve the family first, as was customary.

For the likes of Mary, this should have felt like a dream that would never come true. She was accustomed to either starving or eating stolen scraps and burnt meat from Noor and Robert's forbidden hunts. The lavish plates being placed before her, each dish meticulously prepared and beautifully presented, were a glaring reminder of how out of place she was.

Mary looked at her plate, her eyes widening at the mouthwatering feast before her. Slices of roast venison glistened, their savory juices pooling beside a delicate piece of salmon draped in an exquisite, aromatic sauce. A loaf of freshly baked bread emitted a warm, inviting scent, while vibrant carrots and tender leeks swam in a rich, velvety cream sauce. Her stomach growled in anticipation, but her eyes kept drifting toward the grand hall's exit. How could she indulge herself when she should be at Thornbriar Cottage, checking to see if Noor had finally returned?

Her fingers trembled slightly as she lifted the goblet of wine to her lips, hoping for solace in its bittersweet taste. The wine seared as it coursed down her throat. She took another gulp, yearning for its numbing embrace to shield her from the tumult of emotions that threatened to engulf her.

Mary's fingers trembled as she lifted the goblet of wine to her lips. The bittersweet taste hit her tongue, the liquid burning her throat. She took another swig, desperate for the numbing effect to drown the emotions threatening to overwhelm her. She tuned out the music and the conversation around her, focusing solely on the wine and trying to find some semblance of calm.

Mary's thoughts clashed, a battle raging in her mind. *Even if thou wishest to leave,* she reminded herself, *the king hath made such a fuss that more questions would be asked.* The prince himself wanted her here for a reason, and his threats had always been clear—she had to do as he said. Mary's chest tightened as she struggled with the urge to flee. She took a deep breath, resigning herself to the circumstances. She may as well enjoy the food, knowing she was not going back anytime soon.

Mary's fingers hesitated as she picked up the fork beside her. Though she had used cutlery in the servants' quarters, this fork—silver, ornate, and heavy with intricate engravings—felt foreign in her hand. She had polished such utensils countless times, handed them to the prince, yet she had never imagined using one herself at a noble's table. If her family ate, they would have no choice but to use their hands.

With a deep breath, she stabbed a piece of meat on her plate with the fork. Her inexperience with such formal dining was evident; the clink of the fork against the plate was louder than she expected. Heads turned, eyes briefly on her, the sound drawing unwanted attention. The prince's voice reached her ear in a hushed, moody whisper. "Strive not to conduct thyself as a savage brute."

Mary shot a sideways glance at the prince, her frustration simmering beneath the surface. She wanted naught more than to scoop up the fish and slap it in his face, but she just about restrained herself. Her fingers trembled slightly as she lifted the fork to her lips, the elegant utensil feeling awkward in her hand. Carefully, she used her teeth to take the venison into her mouth.

Her taste buds lit up at once—it was venison, something she had eaten before when Noor brought it back from a hunt. But this was different. The rich seasoning of garlic and rosemary, paired with the tender, perfectly cooked meat, was unlike anything she'd ever tasted. Surprise flickered across her face as the flavors overwhelmed her senses, a far cry from the charred scraps she was accustomed to.

Mary's restraint frayed like a thread on the verge of snapping. She cast a furtive glance around the table; the nobles were engrossed in debating Princess Sophia's suitors, their laughter and clipped words filling the air. Seizing the moment, Mary alternated between slicing pieces of venison and flaking bites of the delicately prepared fish. Hunger gnawed at her like a ravenous beast. She loaded the fork with as much as it could bear, shoving each bite into her mouth, the juices spilling onto her tongue like a forbidden indulgence.

Her fork moved with purpose, each motion faster than the last, until her plate was nearly empty. She reached for her chalice, taking a long sip of wine to quell the ache of her hunger. The chalice's cool metal brushed her lips, the wine's bitter tang cutting through the richness of the meal. She was too consumed by her feast to notice the princess's curious glances.

Across the table, Sophia watched Mary with quiet intensity. Once, such a display might have filled her with disgust. But now, her time among the poor had taught her the weight of hunger, and she felt a pang of understanding—and guilt—for the wealth spread before them. Her own stomach growled softly in sympathy, and she found herself eating with more haste, trying to mask her unease.

The conversation swirled around them like smoke, Sophia's family oblivious to the growing tension. To them, Mary was little more than furniture in the room, another object to be ignored. Servants swept past her with practiced indifference, yet several deliberately jostled her chair, their disdain for a maid seated among nobles written in every gesture. Mary swallowed her pride along with the wine, its heat spreading through her, softening the sharp edges of the hall around her.

Time stretched unbearably as the meal dragged on, each passing moment testing Mary's patience. She clutched her goblet tightly, the wine her only solace, and took another sip, its sharp tang burning her throat. The drink had loosened her limbs, yet dulled her wits, leaving her swaying slightly in her chair. Around her, nobles prattled on about matters of no consequence, their laughter hollow in her ears.

When the last plates were cleared and the ball began, Mary's pulse quickened. The king and prince had left their seats, mingling with the lords, and the queen mother had joined the dancers, her gown trailing like a shadow. Across the hall, Edward Saint-Clair led Princess Sophia onto the floor, their movements stiff with formality. The time to slip away had come.

Sliding her chair back carefully, Mary tried to stand, but her legs felt leaden, her body betraying her. She clung to the table's edge, her fingers curling around the worn wood as if it might anchor her swaying form. A wave of dizziness swept over her as she swayed unsteadily, blinking rapidly to clear her blurred vision. Each breath came shallow, her heart hammering in her chest. Finally, she managed a shaky step, then another, her movements awkward and halting.

The crowd blurred around her as she stumbled toward the exit, weaving through clusters of finely dressed guests. The laughter and music swirled together, a muddled hum that seemed to echo in her wineclouded mind. Her breath quickened, each step a struggle as she clung to the shadows, desperate to remain unseen. The oak doors loomed ahead, her salvation near.

But just as she reached for the handle, a firm hand closed around her arm, pulling her back. She froze, her breath catching in her throat, and turned sharply. Her vision swam as she tried to focus, only to find the king standing before her.

"Is this event truly so burdensome for thee?" he asked, his voice calm yet tinged with curiosity. His gaze rested upon her, calm yet questioning, as though he sought to read the truth in her unsteady stance. "What troubles thy heart this night?"

Her lips parted, but no words came. Her head spun, and the hall seemed to tilt. "Your... your majesty," she stammered, her voice thick and clumsy. The words faltered upon her tongue, her cheeks prickling with the heat of shame.

"I—" She faltered, blinking rapidly, the weight of his gaze unsettling her further. "I had not... I mean... why didst thou not say thou wert the king?"

Her words tumbled out in a jumbled rush, her tone slurred with frustration and confusion. She swayed slightly, her fingers twitching as she tried to steady herself. "We... we spoke of thy family afore... why... why wouldst thou not tell me?"

The king's brow arched, and the faintest smile touched his lips. "Didst thou not recognise me?" he asked, his tone light and almost teasing.

Mary's heart sank at the question, the wine dulling her sharpness. "I knew thee not; I mistook thee for one of the king's guards, and not the king himself!" she muttered, her words thick and uneven. "Foolish of me, truly..." Her voice trailed off as she averted her gaze, unable to meet his eyes. Her stomach churned, though whether from the wine or her own embarrassment, she could not tell.

The king stepped closer, his tone softening. "Dost thou wish to leave?" he asked, his voice a quiet murmur. "Thou art welcome here, Lady Mary. Yet if this gathering vexes thee, say so, and I shall see to thy comfort."

Mary blinked, her mind struggling to grasp his words. "I—I dost not belong here, Your Majesty," she blurted, her voice breaking. "I am no fit guest for a royal ball, nor for any noble gathering. I have dwelt in Mudlark Alley, the poorest wretch of Ravenswood. If but these fine folk knew the truth of me." The admission felt raw, the truth slipping out before she could stop it.

She swayed, reaching for the doorway, her fingers gripping the frame as if to anchor herself.

The king watched her closely, his head tilting just so, his face revealing little. "Thou art as much a part of this hall as anyone here," he said simply. "If thou wouldst stay, stay. If thou wouldst leave, thou hast but to ask."

A sheepish look crossed the king's features as he wondered if revealing his identity earlier would have changed anything. Would she have spoken with such candour, or would her words have been veiled in artifice? Would their conversations have been genuine? "In sooth, I beseech thee to grant me but a moment of thy time ere thou takest thy leave."

The king gently placed his hand on her arm, sending a rush of warmth through Mary that made her breath catch. Her heart skipped a beat, and for a moment, it felt as though the hall had stopped. His eyes were sincere and kind as he said softly, "I swear, I intended to tell thee whilst we were in the garden, but my brother delivered the news before me."

"At first, I thought thou knewest and wert merely playing coy," he admitted, his voice gentle. "But when I realized thou might not know who I was..." He hesitated, searching for the right words. "People treat me differently. Most of the folk I deal with never show me their true selves." His smile turned wistful, almost dreamlike. "From what I could tell, even in the short time we've spoken, thou felt real."

Mary's eyes widened in shock. *Real?* If she had shown her real self, he might think her mad. Emotions churned within her, threatening to spill over. She had made it clear that she did not favour the royal family, but had she spoken her truest feelings, she might have condemned both the prince and princess outright.

While Mary was lost in thought, the king noticed her expression change at the word "*real.*" He felt the need to explain. Clearing his throat, he subtly directed her gaze to a nearby couple. "The Baron and the Baroness FitzWalter," he said, nodding toward them.

Mary followed his gaze, turning slowly to look at the couple he had pointed out. The Baron wore an embroidered velvet doublet that shimmered under the candlelight. The elegant emerald silk of the Baroness's gown was beautifully decorated with golden threads and dazzling stones. Their clothes practically shouted, "We art wealthy and of great import!"

The king leaned in closer, a playful glint in his eye. "Advisors, thou sayest, close to my late father?" he said, his tone light but dripping with jest. "They be naught but mangy hounds, sniffing 'bout for power like scraps tossed to the floor." His words made Mary stifle a laugh, the unexpected humour breaking through her tension. She couldn't help but crack a genuine smile at the bizarre scene before her—the refined couple now seemed like wild creatures masquerading in elegant clothing. It was laughable, and for a moment, she felt a sense of camaraderie with the king.

Mary looked at him and asked, "Who else, pray tell, is not as they seem?" The king chuckled, a genuine, hearty sound that made his eyes crinkle at the corners. He leaned in closer and nodded subtly toward a large lady whose nose almost resembled a snout. "Yon hoggish dame o'er yonder," he said with a mischievous grin.

Feeling a surge of boldness from the wine, Mary leaned in as well, her eyes sparkling with mischief. "Someone thou art courting, Your Majesty?" she teased, her voice light and playful.

The king threw his head back, his laughter rolling through the hall like the toll of a deep bell. Nearby guests turned, their curious glances lingering before returning to their conversations. Mary couldn't help but join in, her laughter bubbling up uncontrollably. They both doubled over, the formal atmosphere of the grand hall momentarily forgotten as they shared this unexpected moment of joy.

As the king struggled to control his laughter, his shoulders shaking, he managed to speak between chuckles. "Thou dost jest, yet those two young men to her left… verily, they be her lovers, bought with coin." He gestured discreetly toward two strikingly handsome young men clad in fine clothing.

He continued, still chuckling, "They do serve but a few others within the hall." His gaze flitted toward a handful of other women, their strikingly unappealing appearances incongruous with their expensive attire.

Mary raised an eyebrow, amusement flickering across her face as if silently suggesting the king himself might have courted such women. "Have they offered thee coin for thy time, or hast thou given it freely?"

Mary rarely mocked another's appearance, yet the wine dulled her restraint, and she found herself unable to suppress a laugh. The absurdity of the scene fed their mirth, and their laughter grew uncontrollably. Tears streamed down their faces as they gasped for breath, the king's body shaking with unrestrained amusement. Mary clung to his arm for support, leaning into him as they both fought to steady themselves amidst their shared hilarity.

The King's lips curled into a grin as he shook his head, his laugh escaping in a low, amused chuckle. "There is not coin enough in all the realms,

Their unbridled laughter soon drew attention. A striking maiden approached, her eyes gleaming with jealousy and her noble lineage evident in her graceful bearing. Her gaze lingered on Mary with thinly veiled disdain, as though questioning her right to exist in such company.

Surprise flickered across the king's face at her sudden arrival. He quickly tempered his mirth, his demeanor shifting to one of composed respect. "Madame Élisabeth, quelle surprise délicieuse," he greeted her warmly, his tone resonating with genuine delight.

Duchess de Valois, known as Madame Élisabeth, sank into a low curtsy, her movements deliberate, as though each gesture demanded attention. When she rose, her lips curved into a polished smile, though her sharp eyes cut briefly to Mary, her disdain flickering like a blade. "'Espoir que vostre Majesté me sauvera une danse, s'il vous plaît," she requested a dance with the king, her voice rich and honeyed, each word dripping with expectation. The lilt of her Franican accent lent her request a seductive charm, though the steel in her tone left no doubt—it was less a plea and more a command.

Her gaze lingered on Mary once more, a dismissive flicker that barely hid her contempt, before returning to the king, her smile softening into something almost predatory.

The king's eyes briefly betrayed a flicker of irritation at the interruption. Yet, out of duty, he straightened his posture, adopting a regal demeanor. "Certes, Madame Élisabeth, I shall right gladly save a dance for thee," he replied, his tone courteous yet firm, though a trace of reluctance lingered.

Then, with a softer tone, he turned to Mary. "Ah, but allow me to introduce thee to Madame Élisabeth, Duchess de Valois, of the House of de Valois!" His voice carried the warmth of sharing a treasured secret. "Thou shalt find her company most entertaining."

As he spoke, a servant maid, Elowen, approached and offered him a drink. Though he accepted it with practiced calm, Élisabeth's narrowed eyes betrayed her displeasure. Her gaze snapped to Mary, the sharp glint in her eyes like the unsheathing of a dagger. Her lips tightened, a silent yet unmistakable declaration of animosity. Mary, feeling the weight of her stare, stiffened. Her stomach churned, a cold dread settling over her. Could this be the very woman Baldwin had warned her of?

The king turned back to the women, his voice steady yet commanding. "Madame Élisabeth, voici Mary de Winterborne." His words hung in the air as he allowed a moment for the introduction. The air between them grew taut, like a drawn bowstring, each glance and unspoken word heavy with meaning.

Élisabeth inclined her head with a polished grace, her smile carefully crafted but devoid of warmth. "Mary de Winterborne," she said, her voice honeyed, each syllable deliberate. "Pourquoy le roy ne salue point vostre titre ou maison? Que signifie cela?" *Pray, why doth the king not give thy title nor thy house so much as a passing nod?* The question dripped with saccharine courtesy, its edge as sharp as a finely honed blade hidden beneath velvet.

Mary's brow furrowed, her pulse quickening. The foreign phrases fell upon her ears, their meaning lost, but the disdain in Élisabeth's tone was unmistakable. Unease settled in Mary's chest like a stone.

Though the meaning eluded her, the contempt curling beneath Élisabeth's tone was unmistakable. As dread gnawed at her chest, Mary fought to steady herself, feeling trapped within the unseen battle waged around her.

The king, noting the flicker of confusion in Mary's eyes, shifted his attention back to Élisabeth. His expression was firm yet composed as he addressed her in a calm, measured tone. "Madame Élisabeth, si vous nous excusez, je vous retrouverai plus tard." *Madame Élisabeth, If thou wouldst pardon us, I shall seek thee anon.* His words carried the weight of quiet authority, a gentle but unmistakable command for her to relinquish the moment.

Élisabeth's demeanor darkened at his dismissal, her smile faltering into a brittle facade, the ire beneath thinly concealed. "As tu le désires, votre Majesté," *As thou dost desire, Your Majesty.* she replied, her words edged with the faintest hint of a threat. Her eyes flicked toward Mary, sharp and appraising, as if trying to place her—wondering who this girl could possibly be to warrant such attention. The absence of jewelry, the lack of a title to speak of, all hinted that she was not of the same station as the others around them. There was a flicker of indignation in the Duchess's gaze, as though the King's choice to spend time with someone so unadorned and seemingly out of place was a slight to her sensibilities. The Duchess's stare lingered a moment too long, her silent judgment cutting deeper than words could convey.

Mary felt the weight of Élisabeth's scrutiny like a chill on her skin, each passing second tightening the knot of unease in her chest. The noblewoman's disdain seeped into the air, thickening the silence between them, leaving Mary acutely aware of the precarious boundary separating her humble station from the grandeur of the court. Her pulse quickened, her hands trembling slightly as she tried to steady herself, her breaths shallow and uncertain.

Shock rippled across Élisabeth's face as her smile vanished. Mary's heart leapt as the King turned to her, his hand extended with regal grace. "Wouldst thou honour me with this dance, Milady?" he asked, his voice imbued with warmth that seemed to cut through the tension like sunlight through storm clouds.

Mary froze, her lips parting in stunned silence. Such an honor was beyond her imagining. As the music swelled, her thoughts scattered, and her breath caught in her throat. Yet she knew better than to keep him waiting. With trembling fingers, she placed her hand in his, the contact sending a rush of breathlessness through her frame.

The King's presence enveloped her as he led her to the floor, his voice a low murmur as they moved through the crowd. "The Duchess De Valois, Madame Élisabeth," he began, his tone smooth and measured, "She is of Franican blood, her kin holding an estate in Stowshire. Its lands stretch wide, and its coffers run deep. Her lineage is as old as the stones that shape her manor."

Mary, emboldened by wine and numbed to the gaze of the gathered lords and ladies, leaned in closer, her voice dropping to a hushed murmur. "What spake Madame Élisabeth?"

The King's eyes swept across the room, his posture straight as he took in the scene, his fingers absently brushing the fabric of his sleeve. He sighed, the breath slow, as if carrying a weight too heavy to speak. "'Tis of no import," he replied, his tone distant, as if the words were weighed down by the years. "Madame Élisabeth is a woman skilled in securing her desires. She wields her tongue as deftly as any knight doth his sword. Noble women are raised thus—to chase after title, land, and favour above all."

He shifted slightly, his gaze flicking toward Lady Beatrice Eldridge, who danced in her green gown, her eyes never leaving them as she moved. The King's lips curled with a knowing smile, his voice rich with mockery. "Lady Beatrice, in that green gown, is said to be the companion of Lady Eleanor Granthorne. Whispers follow Eleanor's flight from these lands, though none agree on why she did so. Yet, scarce a week later, Lady Beatrice seeks the company of Lady Eleanor's betrothed, Lord Dorian Ashford."

Stepping closer to Mary, the King's voice dropped lower, his words tinged with dangerous amusement. A slight lean of his shoulder and the subtle raise of his brow made the words sting. "She hath yet to win Lord Dorian Ashford, yet scarce a week gone by, and she doth fix her sights on her friend's betrothed? The court may murmur, but if she were to wed him, would it matter that Eleanor's heart be bruised?"

Mary's breath faltered as her eyes flickered to Lady Beatrice, still dancing with a smooth, practiced grace, but her gaze never straying far from them. The King's words settled in her chest like cold stone. The hall seemed to hum with a quiet tension, whispers fluttering like moths. Struggling to swallow, Mary met his gaze, a flash of defiance sparking beneath the unease that twisted in her stomach.

The King turned, his hand settling lightly on her arm, pulling her a fraction closer as though the motion itself were the command. "Even the House of Valefort sought Lord Edward Saint-Clair for Princess Shorwynne, for he was favoured to court his own princess, the two being close companions. Yet, that mattered not."

His movements were fluid, each step a calculated part of the court's intricate dance. Mary's pulse quickened, the weight of his words wrapping around her like a noose. There was no safe space here—only the game, and she was just another piece on the board.

"I would scarce call them companions if they do pursue each other's betrothed." She paused, swaying slightly as she glanced at him, her words thick and slow, her brow furrowing in confusion. "Do... Do... Duchess De Valois... M-Madame Élisabeth... seek t'court ye, yer grace?" The thought of someone as cold and polished as Madame Élisabeth wanting to wed the King unsettled Mary, stirring something deep inside her. She blinked rapidly, as if trying to shake the image from her mind.

The King's lips quirked into a half-smile, but his eyes held a certain amusement. He regarded Mary for a moment before his gaze shifted to the dance floor, his posture relaxed, but there was a subtle tension around his jaw. "It would seem so," he said, his tone playful yet guarded, "though I deem she and mine brother would fare better together."

Mary hiccupped as she swayed, her movements loose and unsteady as they danced. Her words came out thick, her voice a little too loud for the moment. "Whom in the hall... dost thou fancy, then? Courtin', I mean... Who might thee think to be... courtin'?" Her eyes locked with his, as if she were bracing for a punch to the stomach.

The King's face flickered, amusement dancing across his features before he masked it with a halfgrin. He leaned in slightly, his voice full of mock seriousness. "I thought ye knew, ye hoggish wench o'er yonder!" He gestured back toward the large lady whose nose almost resembled a snout.

The sound of their laughter filled the space, unrestrained and warm. Mary's giggles bubbled up, breathy and carefree, while the King's laughter was a deep, rumbling sound that vibrated in his chest.

The King, still grinning, leaned closer, his voice playful but sharp. "Who wouldst thou be thinkin' of courtin' in this hall, eh?" His eyes gleamed with mischief, clearly enjoying the moment and the game they were playing.

Mary smirked, her lips curling up with mischief. "Whot troublesome questions, eh? Half th' men here, their bellies be spillin' over th' belts, an' some look as though they've been whacked 'bout th' face, they do!" She gestured with a tilt of her head, her eyes narrowing as she looked toward a man to the left of them, his face scrunched in a way that made him appear less regal than he might've hoped. "Mayhaps the man yonder," she said, her words slurring just enough to show her tipsiness, her finger pointing lazily toward him.

The King's grin broadened, his voice lighthearted as he jested, "Ah, but mayhap thou findest the King to be fair of face, dost thou not?" Without waiting for her reply, he spun Mary into a graceful twirl.

As the twirl ended, Mary found herself back in his arms, her breath quickening. The soft press of his hand on her back sent a shiver through her as pride and nervousness mingled when she noticed the curious glances of the gathered guests. Maidens danced with noblemen, but their eyes drifted to her and the King, their envy almost palpable. "Methinks, Your Majesty," she teased, her voice trembling slightly with delight, "that thou hast quite the audience. Surely it must be thy charm—or perchance our less-thangraceful steps that doth draw them in?"

The King turned his head briefly, his gaze sweeping across the maidens of Clervaux, Dunstan, and Eldridge. A knowing smile curled his lips as he turned back to her. "Maidens of fine lineage," he murmured, his voice low and warm. "Yet His Majesty's gaze is fixed upon one alone, and with her he doth dance with the utmost grace and skill."

Mary laughed softly, her eyes alight with mischief. "Grace and skill, sayest thou? Hath His Majesty partaken of spirits to dream such fancies?" Her tone turned playful. "Dost thou always speak of thyself in the third person?"

He spun her again, this time drawing her closer. His chest brushed hers, the improper closeness sending a shiver down her spine. His lips hovered near her ear, his breath grazing her neck as he murmured, "Only when he findeth himself nervous around a fair maiden."

Mary's cheeks burned at his words, her composure faltering. Around them, gasps and widened eyes betrayed the crowd's disbelief. The closeness was scandalous, yet the King seemed unbothered, his steady hand keeping her grounded even as whispers rippled through the hall like wildfire.

As if to stir the gossip further, the King placed his hand upon her waist for the briefest of moments. Beatrice Eldridge, indignant, whispered furiously to another guest, her gestures sharp and accusatory. Though Mary could not hear the words, the weight of the stares pressed heavily upon her. She turned to face the King, her voice trembling. "Your Majesty, they do watch."

The King's eyes twinkled with mischief, his tone both playful and firm. "Wouldst thou have me dismiss them, Lady of Thornbriar?"

Mary inwardly cursed the absurd title. She loathed Thornbriar Cottage and the Windhaven family. Though Windhaven held no noble rank, she found herself wishing she truly were the Lady of Thornbriar. Were she such a lady, perhaps she might hold a real chance with King John.

Her thoughts filled with doubt, insecurities gnawing at her as she longed for what she knew she could not have. His Majesty could have any lady in all the realms—why then had he chosen to dance with her? Was she merely a passing amusement, a fleeting companion for the evening's revels? Was his attention no more than an act of drunken hospitality? Her heart raced, her confusion tightening its grip upon her chest. She feared she meant nothing to him and that once he tired of her, she would be but a forgotten memory.

The King's brows knit together as his lips pressed into a thin line. He leaned in slightly, his usual ease replaced by a quiet intensity, watching her face as though trying to read the thoughts hidden beneath her troubled expression. "Is there aught troubling thee?" he asked, his voice softening with care. He paused briefly, scanning the hall before returning his gaze to her. His brow furrowed with determination, his tone resolute. "If 'tis one or more guests that doth vex thee, thou must not heed them. I shall see them removed at once."

Mary's eyes filled with sadness, her shoulders slumping slightly. She looked down, unable to meet his gaze. "'Tis I who should leave, Your Majesty," she murmured, her voice trembling. "As I have spoken, I do not belong."

His fingers lingered just below her chin, the warmth of his touch both hesitant and gentle. Slowly, her head tilted upward as though responding to a quiet command unspoken. Her gaze, reluctant at first, met his. The quiet intensity in his eyes seemed to pull her in, urging her to see the sincerity he held there. His eyes, soft yet commanding, searched hers as if urging her to believe his words. "Thou art here by the invitation of the prince himself," he said softly, his voice filled with conviction. "And I, the king, would have thee here. Therefore, thou dost belong."

Mary's heart fluttered. Though the feeling of belonging escaped her, the warmth in his eyes and the kindness in his words wrapped around her like a protective cloak. For a moment, her doubts and insecurities melted beneath the weight of his smile.

Out of the corner of her eye, Mary glimpsed Princess Sophia twirling gracefully in the centre of the hall, her gown sweeping the ground as she moved with the same nobleman she had often seen her with. A knot of unease coiled in her chest, and her brow furrowed as she turned to the King. "Your Majesty," she asked, her voice wavering slightly, "with whom doth Princess Sophia dance?"

The King followed her gaze, his face brightening as he spotted his sister. "Edward Saint-Clair of Ironwood, son of Lord Geoffrey Saint-Clair," he answered, his voice touched with pride. "A nobleman of great charm and influence. 'Twould seem my sister hath taken a great liking unto him since her return."

Mary's stomach churned at the name. She could almost see Robert's face in her mind, his eyes darkening with heartache. Her pulse quickened as the image of his sorrow seized her thoughts.

The King's gaze lingered on hers, narrowing ever so slightly, as though weighing the depth of her understanding. His eyes seemed to probe quietly, seeking hidden knowledge or recognition within her, as if testing how much of the courtly world she truly grasped. He knew well the chasm between the upbringing of noble children and that of common folk. Where he had been blessed with the best tutors, lessons in governance, and the wisdom of senior courtiers, he could only guess at the scraps of learning a maiden of Mary's station might possess. Without parents and only recently serving within the castle walls, how could she fully comprehend the importance of royal unions?

As they swayed across the floor, the King's movements were deliberate and steady, guiding her with ease. He spun her gently, drawing her back with swift grace, his eyes locking onto hers the moment she turned toward him. "Royal duty oft doth feel as a chain," he said, his voice low but firm. "When it cometh to alliances, 'tis of great import to choose wisely. Briarwood hath grown strong through such unions. I do hope, whosoever taketh my sister's hand, he shall be kind."

His words hung in the air as they continued to move, her dress swirling around her. A fleeting shadow passed across his features, and his grip on her hand tightened ever so slightly. The burden of marrying for duty instead of love was etched into his expression. "Edward Saint-Clair is numbered 'mong the suitors deemed for Sophia's hand," he added. "He is not of royal blood himself, yet the House of Saint-Clair hath many ties to royalty. His brother's cousin, and others of his kin, have wedded royals from far-off realms in days of yore. A union with him would yet bring favour to our lands."

The King's movements remained poised, yet a subtle tension in his stance betrayed the weight of these considerations. His steps, though graceful, held an edge of restraint, as though he too was bound by the very chains of duty he spoke of.

"Moreover," the King continued, "the Saint-Clairs have their hands in many a trade—wine, weapons, fine raiment, and lands for tilling. Their estates stretch wide o'er the realms, with holdings in great abundance. Such wealth and power maketh them most precious allies."

Mary's heart sank as his words took root. Her breath hitched. Would the King himself marry for Briarwood's gain rather than for love? Was this why Princess Sophia danced with Edward Saint-Clair? Had she always known her fate was sealed? The thought that Sophia had toyed with Robert's affections, knowing full well she was destined for another, struck Mary like a cruel betrayal.

Her throat constricted, and her eyes burned as sorrow twisted with anger, each vying for control over her composure. She fought to appear calm, though the weight of the truth bore down upon her. The thought of Robert's heartbreak, compounded by the cold reality of royal duty, felt unbearable.

Struggling to find her voice, Mary swallowed hard and cleared her throat. "He is handsome as well, and with all thou hast spoken, it seemeth he be a fine match for our princess," she said, her words shaky and uncertain as she gently pulled away from the King's grasp. "Your Majesty, 'tis been an honour, yet I must now take my leave."

As she pulled away from the king, something held her rooted to the spot, a sense of dread creeping over her as she spotted movement out of the corner of her eye.

Through the lively swirl of gowns and the boisterous laughter of the nobles, Princess Sophia and Lord Edward Saint-Clair were making their way toward the king and Mary, navigating through the bustling throng with practiced ease. The music and chatter filled the grand hall, but Mary felt a tightening in her chest as the distance between them closed.

The sight of Sophia nearing sent a jolt through Mary, her hands curling into tight fists, knuckles paling as tension rippled through her. *Flee! Hie thee hence at once!* Mary hissed at herself.

Sophia leaned heavily on Edward's arm, her once effortless grace now replaced by unsteady, faltering steps. Each stride betrayed the weight of her injury, the slight limp in her gait masked poorly beneath her flowing gown. Edward's firm hand held her side, guiding her through the throng of nobles, his face betraying neither frustration nor sympathy, only the duty of the moment.

As they neared Mary and the king, Sophia's lips pressed into a tight smile, though the strain in her eyes revealed the pain she fought to hide. The flicker of candlelight from the chandeliers above danced over her pale complexion, making the sweat beading along her brow gleam faintly. Her leg, though concealed beneath layers of fine fabric, clearly hindered her, causing her to lean more heavily into Edward with each passing step.

Mary watched as they approached, her gaze narrowing at the sight of the princess's struggle. The subtle tremble in Sophia's shoulders, the stiff movements that no amount of noble bearing could conceal, only deepened the chasm between them. The princess was in pain, vulnerable—but even now, her pride and position held her aloft, as if mere willpower kept her from collapsing.

Edward's expression remained cold, his grip tightening as they finally stopped before the king and Mary. The contrast between his rigid control and Sophia's strained posture was stark. Sophia threw a quick glance at Mary, her eyes sharp yet clouded with something else—perhaps weariness, perhaps defiance.

Sophia curtsied to her brother, though the motion was unsteady, her legs trembling beneath the weight of both injury and weariness. Edward bowed beside her, his movements precise, though his hand never left Sophia's arm, subtly bracing her in a display of duty. His face remained a mask of polite indifference, showing no sign of the effort it took to keep her upright.

"Your Majesty," Sophia greeted, her voice soft, laced with a forced lightness that trembled at the edges, betraying the discomfort she tried so hard to conceal.

Edward, rising from his bow, glanced briefly at the king, his expression carefully controlled. "Thy Majesty." he added, his tone clipped and formal, as though this display of propriety was merely a formality to be endured. His arm remained steady, offering Sophia the support she needed but could not openly acknowledge.

Mary's knuckles whitened as she clenched her fists tighter, the tension between them now palpable.

Her words were sweet, but there was no mistaking the calculated glance Sophia threw in Mary's direction—a brief, piercing look, as if she could read the turmoil Mary was struggling to conceal. She didn't linger, though, her gaze quickly turning back to her brother, as if Mary were of no importance.

A subtle warmth flickered in the king's eyes as he extended his hand toward his sister, the gesture full of familiarity and affection. His fingers, steady yet soft, seemed to reach out as though offering not just a dance, but a sense of comfort and connection. There was no need for words; the silent exchange between them carried the depth of their bond, drawing her into the moment with ease. "'Tis my honor, dear sister," he said, his voice filled with relief as he looked at her, as though her presence alone had eased some long-held burden from his heart.

Mary dipped into a shallow curtsy as the king acknowledged her one last time before turning away with the princess. "Thank thee for thy company," he said softly, though there was a lingering weight in his words, as though he regretted their parting.

Before Mary could gather herself to leave, her path was blocked by Lord Edward Saint-Clair. Disdain radiated from him, his posture rigid and unyielding, his gaze sharp and calculating. It was as if, in a single glance, he had summed her up and deemed her unworthy. Broad shoulders stretched beneath the rich brown fabric of his tunic, adorned with golden embroidery that sparkled like tiny stars as he shifted his weight. Emblazoned on his chest was the Saint-Clair crest: an iron tree entwined with crossed swords, a silent proclamation of power and heritage that spoke louder than any words.

His hand cut through the space between them, its meaning unmistakable. This was no courteous request. "Pray, I would have thee dance with me," he said, his voice low and commanding, carrying a weight that brooked no refusal.

Mary's stomach churned. She had no desire to entertain him, nor to draw the gaze of the room to her lowly presence. "My lord," she began, her voice measured despite the knot in her throat, "I had meant to take mine leave. I—"

"Thou shalt not depart 'ere I have spoken." His words, sharp and cold, left no room for protest. His grip on her arm was firm as he drew her toward the whirling throng of dancers, his authority a tether she could not escape. "The princess hath instructed me to speak with thee, and I shall not disobey her will."

Her heart hammered as he guided her into the midst of the swirling nobles, the vibrant gowns and polished armour glittering under the chandeliers. *Did the princess impart all unto him?* The thought sent a shiver down her spine. She glanced around, searching for an escape, but the room's gilded laughter and spinning dancers offered no reprieve. "Why doth the princess not speak to me herself?" Mary murmured, her voice trembling as she dared to question.

Edward's lip curled into a thin, cutting smile. "The princess doth not soil her hands by speaking with the likes of thee," he said, his tone laced with quiet cruelty. "In sooth, I should not be troubled to deal with thee either. Had my servant Wynn been in Briarwood, and had the princess permitted it, 'twould be he who would handle this matter in mine stead."

Humiliation burned under her skin, but she forced herself to keep her voice steady. "What doth the princess wish of me, then?"

Edward leaned closer, his breath warm against her ear, though his tone was frigid. "Thou art to know that ill fate hath befallen thy sister, Noor Winterbourne," he said. The words struck like the clang of iron. "None know whether she liveth or hath perished. I hath been tasked with delivering this news, and believe me, I take no pleasure in it."

Noor. Her sister. The name echoed in Mary's mind, shattering her composure. Her breath caught, the lively hum of the hall fading to a distant murmur. A thousand images of Noor—her sharp tongue, her defiance, her cleverness—flashed through her thoughts. "Liveth she still?" Mary whispered, her voice faltering. "Or hath she perished?"

Edward's gaze softened briefly, though the mask of duty returned almost at once. "Thy sister is gone, of that much thou canst be certain, which I assume thou knowest. I know naught of her fate. For days have I sought her, yet the trail groweth cold."

The weight of his words pressed upon her chest, threatening to crush her. "What hath happened?" she managed, though her voice was weak.

"The princess and thy sister were set upon in the forest," Edward replied, his tone even but tinged with weariness. "The princess escaped. Noor… did not. I have walked the woods, questioned villagers, searched places no lord would normally tread. Yet, she remains elusive."

Mary's thoughts churned, fear gnawing at the edges of her reason. The princess had escaped—of course she had. But Noor, left behind? Edward's composure, his fatigue—were they signs of truth or veils for darker motives? "Your Grace," she said, her voice rising despite herself. "What part didst thou have in this?"

His jaw tightened, his gaze hardening. "Mind thy station, peasant, and hold thy tongue if thou wouldst not provoke my ire."

Edward's brow furrowed, his irritation clear. Yet, there was no malice in his reply, only the frustration of a man unaccustomed to such scrutiny. "I have no hand in thy sister's fate," he said flatly. "Were any to speak ill of mine own kin, I too would ask as thou hast. But dost thou truly think a SaintClair would stoop so low?"

His words were meant to reassure, but they did nothing to quiet the storm in her mind. Her thoughts turned to a name she had not dared to utter before. "The man with the silver locks…" she whispered. "He doth surely know something."

Edward's steps slowed, his expression sharpening. "The man with silver locks?" he echoed, his voice edged with confusion. "That helpeth me not."

Mary nodded, desperation tightening her throat. "The maid sang of him. None doth wish to speak of him, but I know he hath knowledge of Noor."

Edward sighed, the lines of his face deepening. "I shall gather what knowledge I can," he said curtly. "I gave the princess mine own word. Be content with that."

The music swelled, its final notes drawing the dance to a close. Edward released her hand, his grip steady to the last. "If thy sister yet liveth," he said quietly, "she is a hard maiden to find."

Mary bowed stiffly, her hands trembling. "I thank thee, my lord," she said, her voice hollow. Without waiting for a reply, she turned and moved swiftly toward the exit.

The weight of unseen gazes burned on her back as she crossed the hall, her every step shadowed by the guards' unrelenting eyes. Mary ducked her head, weaving through the twirling nobles, their laughter and swirling gowns an oppressive blur around her. A stray elbow brushed her arm, a pointed heel narrowly missed her foot, but she pressed on, shoulders hunched to avoid notice. The gilded hall seemed to stretch endlessly before her, the glint of polished armour and the muted glow of candelabras making her feel all the more exposed.

She hesitated as she neared the door, her breath quickening. For the briefest of moments, her gaze flicked toward the king. He stood with Madame Élisabeth, his head thrown back in laughter, his ease and grandeur a cruel contrast to her turmoil. The sight struck her like a dagger to the chest—the grief of memory mingling with the sharp sting of deprivation. This world, so vibrant and rich, was not hers. It never would be.

Her pulse quickened as she forced her gaze away, slipping past the threshold with a haste she dared not show. The air shifted, cooler and darker, as the corridor enveloped her. Shadows danced on the walls, the flicker of torches casting jagged shapes that seemed to mock her every move. Mary's footsteps echoed faintly against the stone, the sound magnified in the suffocating stillness.

Her pulse roared in her ears as she quickened her pace, the laughter and music of the hall fading behind her. She couldn't shake the feeling of being followed, of unseen eyes lurking just beyond the torchlight. Every shadow felt alive, every corner a potential threat. Yet, she dared not look back. She couldn't risk it—not now, not when the fragile mask of composure she'd worn so carefully was moments from shattering.

The corridor stretched endlessly before her, the distant curve promising neither comfort nor escape. Mary pressed on, her breath shallow, her fingers brushing the rough stone wall for grounding. She had to keep moving. She had to find Noor—or at least the truth of what had become of her.

Each step grew heavier as Mary rushed through the winding corridors, the weight of the night's revelations pressing down on her. *Noor—attacked and left for dead? By heavens, what wickedness hath befallen her?* The words beat in her mind like a drum, relentless and unyielding. The memory of Charles's words lingered, dark and foreboding, a promise of wrath yet unfulfilled. *Had he not sworn to make her suffer? Doth his mark lie upon this tangled mess? What logic be at work here, pray tell? Noor hath done naught to offend him, save exist under his contemptuous gaze.* Her breath quickened, and the bitter tang of wine clung to her tongue, her chest tightening with fear.

The echoes of the grand hall's music faded behind her, devoured by the stone silence of the passageways. Her steps rang unevenly against the cold floor, each strike loud and sharp, her balance wavering with every hurried pace. The torchlight flickered weakly along the walls, casting jagged shadows that seemed to claw at her from every corner. Her vision blurred slightly, the dancing light distorting the stones around her. Her pulse roared in her ears, drowning the faint whispers of distant voices.

Ahead rose the spiral staircase, its steps hollowed and slick from countless years of passing feet. Mary paused at the top, her breath catching as the stairway seemed to twist beneath her. She pressed her hand against the rough wall for balance, its surface gritty beneath her palm. Her foot slipped slightly as she began to descend, the weight of her gown pulling heavily against her legs. She stumbled, catching herself with a gasp, her scraped fingers stinging as she gripped the jagged stone. *Hath the prince cast her unto death's door?* The thought clung to her like a shadow, heavy and cold.

    The guards stood silent at the base of the stairs, their figures rigid in the dim light. Aldric and Gareth, Charles's sentinels, flanked the door to his chambers, their expressions carved in stone. Their eyes moved to her as she approached, their gazes sharp and unrelenting, but they made no sound. Mary's legs wavered as she neared, but she lowered her head, her steps quickening as though she might slip past their scrutiny unnoticed. Her trembling hand pushed at the heavy door, its low groan echoing into the chamber beyond.

    Inside, the heat from the hearth hit her in a suffocating wave. Flames whispered to the darkness, spreading shadows across the walls like outstretched fingers. She staggered slightly, the weight of the air pressing against her chest, each breath an effort. She reached for the bedpost, her fingers curling tightly around the wood to keep herself upright. Her soiled dress lay crumpled nearby, forgotten in the chaos of the evening—a grim reminder of how far this night had turned.

    The gown she wore now felt stifling, the fabric clinging to her clammy skin like a silken noose. Her fingers fumbled at the laces, struggling to free herself from its grip. She pulled harder, her hands unsteady, her breath uneven as the fabric slid from her shoulders and pooled at her feet. She stood for a moment, her figure lit by the flickering firelight, before her eyes caught on the polished metal mirror hung on the far wall. Its surface warped her reflection, the pale face and trembling form staring back twisted and unfamiliar. A fleeting steeliness in her gaze marked her retreat, mouth compressed in a firm, unyielding silence. *Noor would not falter. Noor would meet such trials with fire in her veins.*

    Her old dress lay within reach, its coarse fabric a stark contrast to the finery she had cast aside. She seized it, pulling it over her head with shaking hands. The rough weave scratched against her skin, grounding her for the barest of moments. *She cannot be gone. She is too strong for such an end.* Yet the image came unbidden—a shadowed forest, Noor lying broken upon the earth, her wide eyes fixed on the heavens, her hand outstretched in eternal silence. Mary froze, her chest constricting as her breath caught painfully. *Nay, I must not think it. I cannot! But... what if it be so?*

    Her fists clenched as she forced the thought aside, her trembling hands finishing the laces of her old dress. *If Charles hath laid his hand upon her, I shall see him pay dearly. His crown, his title—naught shall shield him. If she yet liveth, I shall find her. And if she doth not...* Her breath steadied, her resolve hardening. *I shall know the truth. For love of her, I shall see it done.*

    Just as Mary moved to leave, a low creak filled the chamber. The door swung open behind her, and she froze, her heart hammering as though it might burst. Slowly, she turned, dread tightening her chest.

    Charles stood in the doorway, his silhouette swaying slightly in the flickering firelight. His unsteady hand gripped the doorframe, though his dark eyes locked on hers with unnerving focus. Her breath hitched, her chest tightening further as he took a step forward. The space seemed to shrink, the air thickening with his looming presence.

"And where…" he began, his words slurred, his voice roughened by wine, "dost thou think thou art going?" He shut the door behind him with a heavy thud that reverberated through the chamber. His gaze locked onto hers, his hand trembling slightly, a telltale sign of drink—or perhaps something darker.

Mary's pulse quickened as panic set in. "I… I sought naught but a breath of air, your highness." She stammered, her voice trembling. She gripped the bedpost for balance, her legs feeling like water beneath her.

Charles scoffed, his sneer twisting his lips. "Fresh air?" he repeated, his tone dripping with mockery. "Dost thou take me for a fool?" His eyes dropped to the discarded gown on the floor, and a cruel laugh escaped him. "Fresh air in rags, no less? Thinkest thou to leave the castle unnoticed, dressed so?"

Her breath came in shallow bursts, fear warring with the hot surge of anger that the wine emboldened. "Didst thou harm my sister?" she demanded, the words spilling out before she could stop them. "Tell me at once! Hath Noor returned to the wretched cottage thou hast forced us into? Speak, is she safe, or…" Her voice broke, tears brimming in her eyes. "Hath thou done her harm?"

Charles's sneer deepened, and he swayed as he took another step closer. A slight curl touched his lips, and it chilled her to the bone. "Harm?" he murmured, his words thick with false innocence. "'Twas not I who brought ruin upon her. Thy sister…" He leaned in, the sickly stench of wine and bile filling the space between them, "hath a sharp tongue and sharper hands. 'Tis no surprise she met her match."

Mary's legs threatened to give way as his words sank in. "Noor… what dost thou mean?" she whispered, the slur of wine thick in her voice. Her knees buckled slightly, and she gripped the bedpost tighter. "Tell me plainly! Hath she survived?"

Charles tilted his head, his smile chilling. He stepped closer, his shadow swallowing hers in the dim light. "She attacked the princess," he lied, his voice low and deliberate, each word sharpened to cut deep. "Ne'er did I have choice but to halt her." His breath brushed her cheek, the sour stench of wine curling in the air between them, and Mary's stomach churned at his nearness. He leaned in further, his lips curling with almost gleeful malice as he added, "A warning, sweet Mary. Pray, thou dost heed it."

Inwardly, Charles's mind flickered to the memory of that night—the blood-soaked forest floor, Noor's body crumpled in the dirt, her eyes blazing with unbroken defiance even as her life slipped from her grasp. She had spat her vow then, a venomous promise: I shall haunt thee 'til thy dying breath, Charles. Thy lies, thy wickedness, they shall consume thee in the end.

At first, he had believed her. How could he not? Those mocking words, uttered with her final, ragged breaths, echoed in his mind like a curse: *"Fear not, my liege; this is not the finality of our tale. I shall return in spirit, lingering with thee in every moment of thine affection. Those whom thou dost*

cherish shall be mine to claim, for whatever thou dost desire, know that my spirit shall seize it as well."
Even as her blood soaked the forest floor, her eyes burned with a venomous clarity that refused to dim. That promise—so vile, so deliberate—clung to him like the stench of death. Surely, if any soul could defy the grave and claw its way back to haunt him, it would be hers.

The hours after the attack had been a torment. Every shadow seemed alive, each flicker of a flame a cruel reminder of her vow. Charles imagined her spirit lurking just beyond his reach, ready to strip him of all he held dear. Sleep eluded him; even the stillness of the castle offered no reprieve. The promise she had made felt as real as the blood on his hands.

Unable to bear the thought of her spectral vengeance, Charles had summoned the Shadow Serpents. Arrangements were made swiftly for the witch Agathe, for Charles could not suffer a moment longer than necessary. Her assurance was a relief Charles could not name, though it did little to erase the unease lingering in his chest. Noor's dying words still echoed in his mind, a sinister melody that refused to fade. But if the witch had spoken true, her spirit would be bound, silenced forever. Whatever else haunted him, it would not be Noor.

Yet, the lie he had spun that night still served him well. Saying Noor had attacked the princess served as his excuse, silencing any who might question him. The truth—that he had struck out in a moment of wrath, believing a slight where there was none—would serve him poorly. Better to let the lie linger, to let Noor's name bear the weight of treason, even in death.

Mary's vision swam, tears spilling freely as her mind reeled. "Thou liest!" she choked, her words stumbling over her tears. "Noor would ne'er harm the princess! She… she could not!" Her voice rose, trembling with desperation. "Speak no riddles! Dost she live?"

Charles shrugged lazily, the motion exaggerated by drink. "'Tis not my concern whether she draws breath or lies still in the dirt," he said, his tone cold. "What matters is what tale I tell. Would they believe thee, a trembling maid reeking of wine, over a prince?"

Mary's fury flared, burning away her fear. She stumbled forward, her tears hot on her cheeks as she hissed, "May the gods show no mercy to thy soul, Charles. May thou know naught but torment 'til thy final breath." Her voice broke, but the venom in her words rang clear.

Charles laughed, a harsh, hollow sound. "Threaten me, wilt thou?" He leaned closer, his balance wavering as he whispered, "Be sure to tell the gods thy tale when next thou prayest… if they still listen to the likes of thee."

Fury burned hot in Mary's chest, a storm she could neither contain nor unleash. She drew in a ragged breath, the weight of Charles's presence pressing down on her like an iron chain. The heavy oak door loomed beyond him, her only escape, but he stood in her way, his shadow long and menacing in the flickering firelight.

Her trembling hand lifted, brushing her skirts as she tried to summon courage. "Your highness," she stammered, her voice breaking as tears welled in her eyes, "I beg thee, let me pass."

Charles tilted his head, amusement flickering across his features. He did not move, his body a deliberate barrier, his eyes gleaming with cruel satisfaction.

The air between them felt suffocating, his presence like a wall she could not breach. Mary's pulse quickened, her legs shaking beneath her, but she forced herself to step forward, her chin lifting slightly despite the tears streaking her cheeks. "Pray, allow me passage." She repeated, her voice firmer this time, though it quivered with emotion.

For a moment, he did nothing, simply watching her with a faint, mocking grin. Then, with exaggerated care, he shifted to the side, his hand brushing the edge of the doorframe. "As thou wishest," he murmured, his tone heavy with derision. "But take thy time, sweet Mary. I do so enjoy watching thee scurry."

Her stomach churned at the words, but she refused to look at him as she moved past, her shoulder brushing the rough fabric of his tunic. She fought the urge to flinch, her focus fixed on the door. Her hand found the iron handle, its cold bite grounding her as she pulled. The door was heavier than she'd expected, and it groaned in protest as she wrenched it open with all the strength she could muster.

Her tears blurred the torchlight into hazy smudges, her vision swimming as she pushed forward. The guards outside Charles's chambers exchanged glances but made no move to stop her. Their presence was a distant blur, their polished armour glinting like shards of ice in the dim light. Her pulse roared in her ears, louder than their murmurs, louder than the lingering echo of Charles's cruelty.

Leofric Oswinbrook

Ye Olde Thistle & Thorn Chapter Twenty

Leofric Oswinbrook pressed on through the winding streets of Ravenwood Town, his boots splashing into puddles that seemed colder than ice itself. The wind howled down the narrow lanes, sharp as a blade, tugging at his sodden cloak and forcing him to hunch against its fury. The rain had turned relentless, each drop striking his face like a lash. His soaked clothing clung to his frame, heavy and wretched, as though the storm sought to drag him into the earth.

Through the haze of rain and darkness, the back of Ye Olde Thistle & Thorn finally emerged, its faint glow slipping through cracks in the shutters. Relief flickered in his chest, though the storm's fury drove him onward, pushing him toward the server's entrance nestled near the storeroom. The barrels and crates stacked against the wall glistened with rain, their surfaces slick under the dim light spilling from the tavern windows. Leofric reached for the latch, his fingers stiff and uncooperative, and after a moment of struggle, shoved the door open with his shoulder.

The heavy oak door groaned as it gave way, and Leofric stumbled inside, letting it shut behind him with a dull thud. The unwelcoming cold of the storeroom greeted him at once, though it could do little to chase away the lingering chill in his bones. The air smelled of aged wood, dried herbs hanging from the low beams, and the faint tang of spilled cider. Barrels and sacks were stacked in neat rows along the walls, though a few crates sat open, their contents half-sorted.

Leofric shrugged off his drenched cloak, the sodden fabric landing with a wet slap on the floorboards before he hung it on a peg by the door.

Leofric straightened, his boots squelching softly against the floorboards as he stepped into the narrow corridor. The faint light of the cooking quarters spilled into the passage, flickering against the stone walls. With each step, the warmth grew thicker, carrying with it the savory aroma of bubbling stew.

The door to the cooking quarters stood slightly ajar, a thin band of golden light spilling into the corridor, the fire roaring with enough heat to banish even the memory of the storm outside. Inside, the kitchen was a frenzy of motion, with the steady clink of iron ladles stirring stews, the sharp crackle of wood in the fire, and the low hiss of boiling pots. Wooden spoons scraped against the sides of cauldrons, and the metallic clang of an iron kettle being set aside echoed in the bustle.

Henry and Walter worked at the far end of the table, Henry chopping vegetables with quick, efficient strokes of his knife. His broad shoulders rose and fell with each movement, while his eyes stayed focused on the task at hand. The rich aroma of simmering stew mixed with the savory scent of meat crackling on the fire. Walter, standing nearby, ladled cider into a pot, wiping his brow as he quickly moved from one task to the next.

Leofric stepped into the room, the warmth from the fire almost overwhelming after the cold night outside. His boots squelched softly against the stone floor as he moved closer to the hearth. He held his hands toward the heat, wincing slightly as the cold in his bones slowly began to thaw.

"Leofric?" Henry's voice called out, though Leofric barely heard him at first, still lost in the sensation of warmth flooding his body. Walter turned then, looking over his shoulder at Leofric with a raised brow. "Is it not thy evening off?"

Leofric nodded, a faint smile playing at his lips, though his mind was still half in the icy streets. His fingers, now tingling with life again, continued to stretch toward the flames, as though they could absorb more of the fire's heat. But even as the warmth spread, there was a part of him that still felt the cold, clinging to him like an unwelcome guest, reminding him that the frost was never far away.

"Aye," he replied, his voice low, as if the cold had stolen some of his strength. "It is meant to be mine night off, but the princess's return hath made it a busy night indeed."

At the sound of his voice, Henry slowly turned his head toward Leofric, his brows furrowing slightly in surprise. As Leofric spoke, the movement caught Walter's attention. The other man glanced up from his work, meeting Leofric's gaze as he continued his task of boiling the cider, his eyes narrowing in curiosity.

Leofric moved even closer to the hearth, his hands now nearly touching the flames. The heat was so intense it almost stung, but still, the cold seemed to cling to him, like an unwelcome ghost that refused to be banished.

Still, each time Leofric glanced back at the door, he swore he could feel the icy breath of the storm lingering behind him, waiting to claim him once more.

Henry rolled his eyes at Leofric's dedication. If he were in Leofric's position and had his coin, he'd be drinking until the early hours. "That it be, old friend, yet why dost thou not join in the revels thyself?" he asked, setting down the pot he had been cleaning.

The other lad, Walter, who was boiling more Spiced Thorn Cider for the tavern, grinned as he chimed in. "Wert thou not meant to court a certain maiden this eve? The one thou hast spoken of so oft? I thought this to be the night thou hast longed for."

Leofric shifted closer to the hearth, the fire's warmth slowly thawing his chilled fingers. Though the heat eased the stiffness in his body, the weight of his unspoken questions kept his shoulders tense. The flickering firelight played across his face, highlighting the furrow in his brow as the flames crackled quietly.

He cast a glance at his companions, the weight of his unease thick in the air. "I didst venture to Thornbriar Cottage," he muttered, his voice low, yet carrying the burden of his concern. "None answered my call."

Leofric had already told Henry and Walter about Noor's supposed nervousness, convinced by her words that someone had been following her. He couldn't shake the memory of what he thought was anxiety on her face, though in truth, it had likely been another of her carefully crafted expressions. As he recalled it, a gentle heat began to flow through his hands, unaware that he had misread her calculated demeanor.

Henry and Walter exchanged uneasy glances, their discomfort clear. Henry's eyes widened slightly, his brow knitting together in confusion as he turned back to Leofric. "Thornbriar Cottage?" he asked, his voice tinged with surprise. "Dost thou mean the household of Windhaven?"

Before Leofric could respond, Walter jumped in, unable to contain himself. "I've heard some grievous tales." he said, his voice dropping to a hushed tone. "They treat not their maidservants with kindness. In sooth..." He hesitated, his lip trembling. "Margery, the maiden I courted... I believe she hath taken her own life after whatever ill fate hath befallen her whilst in their service."

Leofric's grip tightened on the edge of the hearth as the weight of Walter's words hit him, a cold knot forming in his gut. The sound of the pot clattering to the floor pulled him back to the present as Henry, too shaken by the news, had dropped his rag.

"Oh, Walter!" Henry exclaimed, his voice thick with sorrow. "I do recall Margery, yet the cause of her tragic end hath ever eluded me. I grieve for thy loss." His words stumbled out, heavy with sympathy as he reached out, his face etched with regret.

Leofric's throat tightened, his mind reeling at the news. "As do I! I grieve for thy loss." His voice cracked with shared sorrow. He, too, had known Margery, though he had believed she had simply left Walter for another. "I cannot fathom the heartache thou must feel," he added quietly, his voice thick with empathy.

Walter reached for some cinnamon and dropped it into the boiling pot, his movements deliberate and slow. His voice, though somewhat cold, betrayed the pain he tried to conceal. "I did not share this tale for thy pity," he said, his eyes fixed upon the pot. "Nay, I speak more to tell thee that the Windhavens vanished. Their bodies were never found, though there was blood all over Thornbriar Cottage. It would not surprise me if someone had sought their vengeance."

The warmth of the chamber seemed to fade as Walter spoke. Henry's mouth opened and closed as he fumbled for words. "Well, all the same, thou hast our sorrows," he finally managed, his voice heavy with sympathy. He cleared his throat, attempting to shift the mood. "I have heard a few different tales about the Windhavens," he began, lowering his voice to a conspiratorial whisper. "Some say a ghost did hang them in the dead of night."

He paused, casting a wary glance around, as though expecting to see a spectre himself. "And others speak of dark witches," he continued, his tone growing more ominous, "who took their souls and damned them to fiery pits in the afterlife." His eyes flitted about the cooking quarters, the shadows seeming to deepen with each word.

Leofric stood unmoving, his hand still gripping the edge. The weight of the dark tales pressed down on him, the image of Noor enduring their cruelty twisting like a blade in his chest. The warmth of the fire could not banish the cold dread that settled deep within him.

He froze, the importance of the confession sinking in, forcing him to re-swallow his words. "Walter," he began, his voice thick with emotion, "I am deeply sorry for what hath befallen thee and Margery." Each word felt heavy, the sorrow palpable in the air.

His mind drifted back to the days when Noor and Mary had served the Windhavens, memories now shadowed by suspicion. For an instant, his expression faltered, the weight of the past colliding with the present. "Robert did confide in me, sharing his concerns about Noor and kin suffering at the hands of the Windhavens," he continued, the memories gnawing at him. "It troubles him deeply. But Noor—she has always been strong-willed. I get the sense that the abuse did not break her."

He paused, recalling the defiance in Noor's eyes even in the darkest moments. A flicker of admiration mixed with concern crossed his features. "If anything, their cruelty hath only sharpened her, like steel forged in fire."

Henry's brow furrowed, the knife in his hand pausing mid-slice. "I thought Robert's sister was named Mary?" His voice trailed off, a slight pause in his words as if he were trying to make sense of it himself.

Leofric's chest tightened, his breath catching as a rush of memories rose to the surface. He forced his voice steady, though a shadow crossed his face as he spoke. "He hath two kins, Mary being their eldest sister, and Noor, the twin of Robert." The name left his lips with an air of longing, his gaze drifting, lost for a moment in the memory of her. A quiet ache gnawed at him—where was Noor? What had become of her?

Behind them, the sharp crack of wood on wood rang out, breaking the moment. "Chatter not on thy rest, for work awaits!" The cook's voice rose above the clatter, a harsh note of impatience cutting through the room. His eyes flashed toward the three of them, his stance stiff with barely concealed frustration, as his hands flew through the preparation of the meal.

Leofric rolled his eyes, though his expression quickly returned to its neutral state as he turned toward the door. "I must take my leave to aid Adom, for it seems the folk of Ravenstone doth wish to drink to the return of her Highness." His voice was tinged with a weariness that wasn't quite from the work ahead, but from the weight of his thoughts.

He gave Henry a brief nod, his eyes lingering on the other man's face for a moment longer than necessary, as if to offer some silent apology. Then, with a soft sigh, Leofric turned away. His boots scraped against the stone floor, each step echoing in the silence that followed.

As he passed through the doorway, the warmth of the kitchen receded, the coolness of the hall sweeping over him, as though the air itself was pressing in. Flickering torches along the walls cast erratic shadows, their flames dancing and leaping against the stone like fleeting moments of clarity in a storm of confusion. Leofric's mind remained fixated on Noor, the uncertainty gnawing at him, his thoughts as erratic as the shadows around him. Where was she? What had happened? Each step seemed to draw him further away from answers, and the weight of Walter's worried words seemed to cling to him like an unwanted shroud. As Leofric drew closer to the bar, laughter burst from nearby tables, the clatter of tankards against wood echoing through the air. Voices rose in spirited conversation, blending with the sharp notes of a fiddle and the shuffle of feet across the floor. The tavern seemed to swell around him, each sound growing louder with every step. Clinking chalices, raucous laughter, and the scraping of chairs filled the air. The smell of ale, sweat, and smoke hung thick, mixing with the scent of spilled drink. The tavern bustled with activity; drunks staggered between tables, maidens served trays laden with ale, and a storyteller stood on a small platform near the hearth, captivating the crowd with his tale. The air was alive with the hum of voices, clashing together in a rowdy symphony of merriment.

Behind the bar, Adom poured Thistle Ale into a chalice, his hands moving deftly between the kegs. He glanced up with a grin as Leofric approached, his voice booming over the noise.

"What brings ye here on your eve of respite, Leofric?" Adom called out over the hum of the tavern, his voice rising above the din. The Ye Olde Thistle & Thorn was as busy as ever, its lively warmth spilling out into the cold night. The tavern was filled with loyal regulars, their mugs of Spiced Thorn Cider and Thistle Ale raised in celebration. With news of the princess's arrival in Briarwood, the town was caught up in revelry, and the tavern was no exception.

Leofric's father had insisted on longer hours for the staff tonight, seeing the bustling crowd as an opportunity to earn a bit more coin. The air was thick with the smell of stew and the sharp tang of ale, and the clatter of mugs and conversation filled every corner of the room. The tavern was overflowing with the merry chatter of patrons, each voice raised in song or laughter, the mood light but charged with excitement.

Adom, standing behind the counter, caught sight of Leofric and flashed a mischievous grin. "Looking to earn your father's favour, are ye?" he teased, leaning toward him with a knowing look.

Leofric shot him a wry smile, but his gaze wandered to the room, distracted by the frenzy of the evening. His father's expectations were a heavy cloak around his shoulders, but for now, he chose to remain silent, his thoughts elsewhere.

Leofric began to speak, "My father did bid me..." but his words faltered as his gaze fell upon a familiar visage, seated at one of the tables—Robert Winterbourne. His heart quickened, a surge of hope flickering to life. Leofric's pulse quickened, his heart drumming louder in his chest as his eyes locked onto Robert. His breath caught for a moment, the noise of the tavern fading around him. Without a word to Adom, he ducked under the bar, eyes fixed on Robert, and pushed through the crowd of swaying patrons.

Adom, wiping his brow with the back of his hand, quickly turned to another tankard and began filling it with Spiced Thorn Cider, his motions practiced but distracted. As he worked, his gaze flicked toward Leofric's sudden departure, confusion flickering across his face. "Whither dost thou go?" he called, his voice raised but lost in the clatter of mugs and rowdy patrons. His head stretched to follow

Leofric, but his hands never stopped, pouring another drink with an almost absent focus, the amber liquid spilling into the chalice.

Robert sat hunched low over a chalice, his shoulders sagging as though the weight of the entire tavern rested upon them. Leofric paused mid-step, his stomach tightening at the sight. Robert—ever the charmer, ever surrounded by mirth and stolen glances—now sat in a silence so strange it almost felt unnatural. Around him, maidens perched like restless birds, their flirtations wasted on a man who seemed oblivious to their presence.

Leofric pushed forward, weaving through the throng of patrons with practiced ease. Familiar faces turned to greet him as he passed. A burly man raised a mug in his direction, and Leofric managed a curt nod. A pair of women, their cheeks flushed from drink, called out Leofric's name, and he forced a faint smile. His hand clapped a shoulder here, brushed past an arm there, but his steps did not falter. His attention stayed fixed on Robert, even as the press of bodies, the laughter, and the clamor of raised tankards made the short distance feel like an eternity.

As he neared the table, the scene before him sharpened. Two maidens sat close to Robert, one on each side. To his right, a petite lass with golden hair cascading in loose waves leaned in, her lips brushing dangerously close to his ear. She whispered something meant to tease, her fingers grazing his sleeve with deliberate softness. Her pale blue gown dipped just enough at the neckline to hint at her figure, shifting as she adjusted her posture to stay firmly in his line of sight.

On Robert's left, a taller maiden with fiery curls spilling over her shoulders rested a hand on his forearm. Her gown, a rich green, was tightly laced, accentuating every curve. One hand toyed idly with the edge of her tankards, her bright eyes fixed on Robert's face.

Her lips curved into a polished smile, but the longer the silence dragged on, the more her composure faltered.

Neither woman acknowledged the other, their rivalry muted by the fact that Robert's gaze remained stubbornly fixed on the chalice before him, as though it might offer answers to questions too heavy to speak aloud.

Leofric straightened his back as he approached, his shoulders squared. He paused at the edge of the table, his commanding presence enough to draw the maidens' attention. They glanced up, their coquettish expressions faltering slightly beneath his gaze. Clearing his throat, he spoke, his voice steady and calm but leaving no room for protest.

"Good e'en, fair maidens," he said with a nod, his tone courteous but firm. "Pray pardon me, but might I borrow Robert but for a moment? Adom shall gladly see ye both served a fine chalice of Thistle Ale, and that at no cost to thee."

The blonde hesitated, glancing toward the ginger as if gauging her reaction before reluctantly rising from her seat. The ginger arched a brow, her lips pressing into a pout. For a moment, it seemed they might refuse. Then reluctantly, they rose from their seats, their dresses brushing against the benches. The blonde tugged at her neckline with one last attempt at subtlety before turning toward the bar. The ginger lingered, her bright eyes darting back to Robert one final time, but his unchanging expression gave her no reason to stay. She followed her companion with a frustrated flick of her curls.

Leofric slid into the chair across from Robert, his movements measured. Robert didn't stir, didn't so much as glance up to acknowledge the maidens' departure. He simply took another slow, absent sip from his chalice, his shoulders sagging further, as though the drink weighed as heavily as the room itself.

Leofric leaned forward slightly, his voice low but edged with firmness. "All is not well with thee," he said, watching Robert closely. The thought of Noor pressed against his mind, sharp and insistent, but he held back from mentioning her name just yet.

The silence between them stretched, thick and heavy. Leofric waited, unmoving, his steady gaze refusing to yield. Robert remained fixed in place, his hand gripping the chalice as though it were the only thing keeping him tethered to the room. At last, Robert stirred, his lips moving as though the words themselves were too great a burden to shape.

"Leo…fric…" he murmured, his voice hoarse and sluggish. His head remained bowed, his gaze fixed downward as though even meeting Leofric's eyes were too much. "Mine good…friend…all is perfectly…well."

The lie clung to the air, weak and transparent. Robert's tone betrayed him, the words crumbling under the weight of their falsehood. Leofric sat back, his jaw tightening. Whatever had broken Robert, it ran deep, and Leofric wasn't leaving until he understood it.

Leofric narrowed his eyes, his gaze fixed upon Robert's haggard form. "Thou dost look as one who hath drowned a kitten, despite the fair maidens who drape themselves o'er thee," he said, his tone light but his concern evident. Yet Robert's slouched figure, the dark hollows beneath his eyes, told a tale that no jest could mask. His earlier assurance was as feeble as the man who uttered it.

At the far side of the tavern, the storyteller struck his final chord, the last notes hanging in the air before fading into an expectant hush. For a heartbeat, silence reigned, broken swiftly by the scrape of chairs, fists pounding on tables, and a thunderous wave of applause that surged through the travern. Laughter mingled with cheers as mugs clinked together, the crowd's excitement swelling like a tide.

The storyteller raised his voice above the din, a showman's grin spreading across his face. "Good folk, this eve I shall sing of the fair princess's return and the beast that held her captive!" The lilting melody of his vielle followed, filling the tavern with a richness that seemed to wrap around the patrons, drawing them into the tale.

Leofric waited, his stomach knotting. He needed the music to mask the weight of his words. The melody rose, mingling with the lively chatter, and Leofric took a steadying breath before speaking. His voice was low, urgent. "What burdens thee? Hath something befallen Noor?"

Robert's hand faltered on the chalice, his eyes widening at the mention of her name. He raised his gaze for the first time, the dullness in his expression replaced by a flicker of alarm. His thoughts raced. *What mischief hath Noor wrought now? She, ever blind to the price of her deeds, daring to defy the very fates themselves, flouting the law as though 'twere naught but a trifle.* Yet Robert also knew that Leofric's question was not without motive—he had long suspected his friend harboured feelings for his sister.

"Why dost thou fret for Noor?" Robert asked, his voice tinged with bitterness. He set the chalice down, though his grip lingered. "Perchance thou thinkest me mad, yet I dost wonder oft if Noor be of sound mind. Mayhap 'tis better so—nay to feel aught at all. Not once have I seen her reduced to weeping as I am now. Nay, she shows neither guilt nor remorse—scarce any feeling whatsoever. I am a man; I ought to be stronger than she." He paused, his voice softening, tinged with doubt. "But I suspect she hath not lingered at Thornbriar Cottage. Most like, she seeks solace in Mudlark Alley instead." He raised his eyes to Leofric, the faintest glint of curiosity shining through. "Yet I wonder—what is thy concern truly? Noor's fate, or thine own heart?"

Leofric stiffened at the accusation but pushed it aside. His unease only deepened. "She were here, at Ye Olde Thistle & Thorn, but a few days past," Leofric said, leaning closer. His voice dropped lower, heavy with meaning. "She did speak to me, saying she felt a shadow upon her, as though she were followed."

Robert's hand faltered on the chalice, his drunken haze wavering as Leofric's words struck him like a blow. He tried to focus on Noor—her defiant smirk, the way she brushed off danger as though it were naught but a passing breeze—but the image faded, replaced by another. Sophia. Her face came unbidden to his mind, framed by the golden light of memory, soft and vulnerable in a way Noor never was. The thought of her slipping into darkness, lost and alone, gnawed at him.

The conversation blurred in his drunken state, and he could no longer separate Leofric's words from his own fears. Sophia... Panic surged, sharp and urgent, his heart thundering as though chasing a shadow of its own. He leaned forward, unsteady, his voice cracking with desperation. "What? Who followeth her? Why?"

The sudden desperation in Robert's tone startled Leofric, sending a chill down his spine. The wildness in his friend's gaze was unnerving. "I know not," Leofric admitted, his voice faltering.

Robert's fear was unmistakable, pressing upon Leofric like a weight. "She spoke no name nor gave me aught to follow," Leofric said, his tone cautious.

Robert's hands slammed against the table as he lurched forward, gripping Leofric by the shoulders. His breath was hot with the stench of ale, his voice raw with urgency. "Pray, tell me what thou knowest!" he demanded, his eyes wide with alarm.

Leofric inhaled sharply, his mind racing for clarity. He steadied himself, prying Robert's grip loose as he spoke. "She entered here that night and partook of an ale. I gave unto her a dagger, for she bore no weapon to protect herself," he said, his voice grim. "But she said naught of who might follow her or where she intended to go. She vanished as swiftly as she came."

The tavern roared with life, a throng of voices rising in drunken song, the lilting notes of a vielle rose above the din, weaving through the lively chatter and song that filled the tavern. Patrons clapped in rhythm, the thud of tankards slamming against wooden tables punctuating the storyteller's ballad. The verses tumbled over one another as revelers grew louder, their words stumbling, laughter breaking through like cracks in a dam. The air was thick with the tang of spilled ale and the warm haze of firelight.

But Robert, though seated before Leofric, drifted far from the merriment that surged around him. The tavern blurred, the music and laughter fading into a meaningless hum. His thoughts reeled, unsteady as his grip on the table. Did she flee of her own will? A flicker of hope stirred, faint and fleeting. Or was she taken?

Then, through the ale-drenched fog in his mind, Leofric's words struck him anew. *She entered here that night… she vanished as swiftly as she came.*

Robert blinked, his drunken mind twisting the meaning before he even realized it. His breath hitched, and in a sudden, muddled certainty, he latched onto the only answer that made sense. *Sophia. Surely, he speaks of none other than Sophia.* His pulse hammered in his ears. *Her kin must have found her. They must have dragged her back. They took her before I could stop them.*

His chest grew taut, each unanswered question pressing heavier upon him. *Her household—who are they? I know naught of her past, nor where she might seek refuge. She vanished, leaving behind only confusion.*

The emptiness of The Sleeping Dragon Inn clawed at his thoughts—her chamber stripped bare, her belongings gone as though she had never been. *Did she find another inn? A friend's hearth? Rosalind, aye, she did speak that name, yet gave no clue where such a friend might dwell.* He pressed a hand to his temple, the pressure doing little to calm the rising tide of dread. *Shorwynne… a name distant as the realm she resides in, Eldoria—a place across the seas, far beyond my reach.*

"Ashbourne," he muttered, the name slipping unbidden from his lips. A thread of memory pulled taut, stubborn and unyielding. Did she not speak of the Ashbournes once? His eyes narrowed, the thought stirring more clearly now. "Stowshire," he whispered, his voice trembling as clarity began to pierce the drunken fog. His hands gripped the edge of the table, knuckles pale. "Stowshire!" he said, his voice cutting through the din, sudden and sharp. "A servant might yet bring us tidings!"

Leofric leaned back, startled by the outburst. He knit his brow, his gaze fixed on Robert's face. "Stowshire?" he echoed, confusion lacing his voice. "Didst thou not say she might linger in Mudlark Alley? What cause would she have to be in Stowshire?"

Robert faltered, his thoughts twisting upon themselves. Noor's defiant glare blurred with Sophia's soft smile until their faces seemed one. He shook his head as if to clear it, his lips moving before he could stop them. "The Ashbournes," he muttered again, as though speaking the name would untangle the confusion in his mind.

Leofric watched him carefully, the unease clear in his eyes. "Thou art certain?" he pressed, though doubt lingered in his tone. "Did she not confide that she believed herself followed?"

Robert lurched to his feet, unsteady but clinging to the thought of Stowshire as though it were a lifeline. "Aye, Stowshire," he said, his words slurred yet insistent. His hand braced against the table as he staggered, his conviction fragile but unyielding.

Leofric rose beside him, his tone firming with resolve. "Then we shall take one of my father's steeds," he said, shoving his chair back with a scrape that turned heads. Several patrons paused mid-drink, their gazes following him, but Leofric paid them no heed. He steadied Robert with a hand on his arm as they began to make their way through the press of bodies.

The tavern surged around them, laughter and song spilling into every corner. Robert leaned heavily on Leofric, nearly dragging him off balance, yet they pressed on toward the door. The crowd swayed, drunken revelers cheering and shouting, their voices blurring into a single, chaotic hum.

"Robert! Where goest thou?" called the blonde maiden from the bar, her golden hair gleaming in the firelight. She hesitated, leaning forward slightly, her eyes filled with curiosity.

Nearby, the taller maiden with fiery curls spun around, nearly spilling her drink. Her cheeks burned red as her eyes narrowed in annoyance. "Robert! Thou didst swear thou wouldst dance with me this eve!" she snapped, her voice rising above the din, her glare sharp enough to cut.

Leofric turned, a wry smile tugging at his lips, though it did little to mask the tension knotted within his chest. Raising his voice above the din of the tavern, he called, "Fear not, fair lasses! We shall return ere long, full of tales to gladden thy hearts." His words carried across the room, cutting through the steady melody of the singer by the hearth. A few curious glances turned their way, but the singer's voice quickly reclaimed the crowd's attention. With a small wave, Leofric turned back, gripping Robert firmly as they began to navigate the crowded floor.

The tavern swayed with life, voices rising in time with the singer's refrain as Leofric and Robert ducked and wove their way toward the door. A pair of drunken men stumbled across their path, sloshing ale from their mugs as they bellowed a crude harmony, forcing Leofric to pull Robert aside to avoid a collision. "Careful, Robert," Leofric said with a quick grin, his tone teasing despite the urgency. "We would not wish to disappoint the maidens with thy face battered ere thou art gone."

Nearby, a trio of revelers shouted along with the singer, their arms flung around each other in a rowdy display. They blocked the way, swaying precariously with each verse. Leofric muttered under his breath before squeezing through, his grip firm on Robert's shoulder. Glancing back toward the bar, his grin widened. "The ginger hath the eyes of a hawk. No doubt she will track us down should we tarry too long."

Robert, his head low and his steps unsteady, gave no reply, his gaze fixed somewhere distant. The singer's voice swelled behind them, the lilting notes chasing them through the throng. Leofric pressed onward, the weight of his friend leaning heavier against him with each step.

At last, they reached the door, shoving it open as the cold night air rushed to meet them.

The chill struck sharply, bracing and unforgiving, cutting through the lingering warmth of the tavern. Behind them, the muffled hum of laughter and song spilled faintly into the street, blending with the sound of the storm.

The cold jolted Robert briefly from his stupor, the fog of drink lifting just enough for him to mutter, "Stowshire..." The word barely passed his lips, little more than a breath lost to the night.

Leofric's grip on his arm tightened. He guided Robert toward the stables, the rain lashing against their faces as the cobblestones beneath their boots turned slick with mud.

The rain pooled in shallow hollows along the uneven streets, the stones treacherous beneath their hurried steps.

Overhead, the clouds hung low and restless, the air thick and heavy as if burdened by some unspoken warning. *Noor... where art thou?* The thought pressed heavily on Leofric, his unease growing with every step.

They reached the stables and mounted one of Leofric's father's horses, urgency brooking no delay. With a sharp nudge, the steed bolted forward, its hooves striking the cobblestones in a rhythm soon lost to the relentless drumming of the rain.

Robert swayed in the saddle, his grip slack and his head bowed. His thoughts drifted, untethered, slipping between fragments of Stowshire and the memory of Sophia's face. *Where hast thou gone, Sophia?* Her image came to him unbidden, soft and distant, stirring a deep ache in his chest. She felt close enough to touch, yet impossibly far.

Leofric, his jaw set, pressed the horse onward. The rain stung his face, his cloak sodden and clinging to his shoulders. Noor's name echoed in his mind, insistent and unyielding. *She must be found.*

The wind howled louder as they rode, each gust cutting through their soaked cloaks. Behind them, the lights of Thorncrest Castle grew faint, swallowed by the storm. The darkness pressed in, heavy and unrelenting, as though the night itself sought to bar their passage.

<u>The Nightmare of Vengeance</u> <u>Mary's dream</u>

Chapter Twenty-Two

As if time itself had leapt forward, wine and dreamland gripped Mary in an unyielding embrace. Her thoughts spun and blurred, a muddled storm of confusion and something deeper—anger, grief, or perhaps both. She drifted through the castle's familiar halls, her feet faltering as though the stones shifted beneath her. The walls seemed to ripple in her vision, their sturdy frames bending like reflections on disturbed water.

The guards outside the prince's chambers—Aldric and Gareth—were distorted, their faces warped into grotesque caricatures. Aldric's snores echoed unnaturally, a guttural rhythm reverberating in her ears. Yet it was Gareth's wide, glassy-eyed stare that gripped her most. Though his gaze never moved, it pierced her, hollow and accusing. Her stomach churned, but she swallowed the rising bile, her hand tightening on the dagger at her side—a lone tether to reality.

She didn't recall the walk to Charles's chamber. Suddenly, the door loomed before her, unnervingly large and unfamiliar despite the countless times she had passed through it. Her fingers fumbled on the handle, slick with sweat. The cold metal seemed to dissolve and reform beneath her grasp. With a shove, the door groaned open, and she stumbled inside.

Shadows writhed unnaturally across the chamber, long fingers stretching across the stone walls. She blinked, but the shapes only twisted further, refusing to take form. The room swayed—or perhaps she did—each step pulling her closer to the bed. Charles lay still beneath the dim flicker of candlelight, halfhidden by the folds of the linen. Her breath hitched, anger rising hot and swift, choking her.

The dagger felt heavy now, dragging her hand forward as though it had a will of its own. A voice, serpentine and foreign, whispered in her mind: Fear thou not. Bring an end to his wretched life. Her grip tightened. The steel caught the dim light, cold and unyielding, heavy with the weight of what must be done. Yet as anger surged, so too did doubt. Grief, raw and choking, struck like a blow, a broken sob escaping her lips.

She hated him. That much was clear. Hatred festered within her, a sickness she could not purge. Every shard of her pain pointed back to him. The dagger shook in her hand as she fought the urge to rouse him, to force him to face what he had made of her. Yet she could not act. Not yet. A haze clouded her vision, and when she blinked, it shifted.

The bed was empty. Blood soaked the linens, seeping thick and dark into the stone floor. Panic crushed her chest, her breath shallow and sharp. She wiped at her hands, but the blood clung to her skin, warm and wet, smearing further with each frantic motion. The chamber tilted, shadows closing in, wrapping her in their suffocating embrace.

A voice, cold and venomous, curled through her mind: This is what thou hast desired. He deserveth death.

Then the world shifted again. She was in the corridor, her bare feet striking cold stone as she ran. The air was sharp, biting her skin, her breaths ragged and uneven. The dagger was still in her hand, slick with blood—whose, she could not say. Her thoughts splintered, fragments of reason and chaos colliding. Cease thy course! Spare him! End his life! Blood doth cry out!

She stumbled to a narrow archway, its frame dark and unyielding, torchlight faintly flickering beyond. Her reflection did not meet her in the polished iron nearby, but her mind conjured it regardless: hollow eyes, sunken cheeks, her face a spectre of herself. Behind her, shadows twisted into shapes, formless figures leering from the dark. She spun around, but the corridor was empty.

Another blink, and she was somewhere else entirely. The floor beneath her was soft—too soft, like sinking into damp earth. Blood slicked the ground, spreading in viscous pools. It stuck to her hands, seeped into her clothes, and tainted every breath with the bite of iron. The sharp tang of iron filled her lungs, nausea rolling through her. She gagged, but no sound escaped.

Her legs carried her forward, though each step felt heavier, the weight of grief and fury dragging her down. The dagger pulled at her, its burden no longer steel but the unbearable weight of her wronged hopes. Her mind screamed, the words incoherent fragments spinning through her thoughts. Flee. End it. Stay thy hand. He deserveth this. The voices clashed, a storm that offered no solace.

Darkness claimed her again, a blackout dragging her into oblivion. When she awoke—if waking it could be called—the world was no longer solid. The stone walls seemed to waver, and the shadows crowded close, tightening around her like unseen hands. Bare feet scraped across uneven stone, and the dagger in her hand gleamed faintly in the flickering light. Its weight carried the ache of past hurts and the searing anger of the present. The chamber spun once more, and from her lips escaped a single cry—a sound neither victory nor defeat, but a keening wail for a justice that would never be hers.

Awaking up

Mary jolted awake, her heart pounding against her ribs as though still fleeing from some wicked spectre. A sharp, searing pain pierced her skull, like the relentless strike of a blacksmith's hammer upon iron. A low, guttural groan escaped her parched throat, her trembling hands flying to her head as if she might still the torment, yet the agony persisted.

She had never known such anguish. Though drink was no stranger to the common folk, she had seldom partaken, her days filled with toil and nights offering little chance for indulgence. Yet now, the vile weight of the wine clung to her like a curse, a bitter remnant of a night steeped in chaos.

The chamber swirled around her as panic surged in her chest. Her eyes fluttered open, revealing a grand and unfamiliar room—far removed from the rough pallet of straw she called her own. Thick fur blankets tangled about her legs, their warmth at odds with her humble standing. The bed beneath her was vast and canopied, its curtains of rich silk drawn close, their folds heavy with embroidery, enclosing her in a world of warmth and secrecy. The posts, hewn of dark wood, did rise as solemn towers, their presence casting a shadow of might over the bed.

"Have I done it?" The thought struck her like a hammer blow. "By God's mercy, have I taken his life? Does the prince lie slain by mine own hand, or was it but a cursed dream?" Her head throbbed, her mouth dry as dust, and her stomach churned with uncertainty.

Her eyes did roam the chamber, and each token of splendor did whisper of how far she had wandered from her humble life. Heavy tapestries covered the stone walls, their vivid scenes of hunts and battles staving off the winter chill. Iron sconces held candles burned low, their wax pooled and hardened below. The faint scent of burned tallow and damp wool lingered in the air, fitting for a chamber of such station.

"Wherefore am I?" The question burned in her mind. This place was no fit lodging for the likes of her. Every detail bespoke wealth and privilege, whispering of a world she had no place in.

Her eyes did waver ere they fell upon the motionless form at her side. Silent. Regal. Her breath hitched. *The king?!* Cold realisation swept over her, but with it came an unexpected warmth in her chest. How camest I to lie at his side?

Her thoughts scrambled, fear gripping her like iron shackles. If the prince yet draws breath... and he finds me here, at his brother's side... what fate shall befall me? Her blood turned to ice, yet a traitorous flicker of something else—curiosity, or perhaps desire—made her pulse quicken.

She tried to push herself up, but the moment she moved, sharp agony flared behind her eyes, sending her sprawling back onto the bed, breathless. She gasped, the ache in her head blinding her, the king's nearness only heightening the confusion spinning through her mind.

The king stirred beside her. The bed shifted as he moved, the warmth of his presence growing more oppressive with each breath he drew. Yet a part of her longed to lean into it. His breath lingered near, each exhalation drawing her unwelcome awareness to his presence. His eyes opened slowly, catching the dim light, and in them flickered a glint that sent her pulse racing—half with fear, half with something she dared not name.

"Good morrow," he whispered, his voice low and commanding, each word stirring a flutter within her chest.

His arm slipped around her slowly, his touch soft yet firm, drawing her close before she could resist.

It felt wrong, improper—yet his nearness wrapped around her like a forbidden comfort.

Mary's heart raced, her pulse quickening. *What folly is this? How is it I have been brought to such peril?* Yet even as the thoughts churned in her mind, she could not ignore the pull, the way her body responded despite her warring thoughts. I have fallen far—deeper than ever I could have dreamt.

Her memories of the previous night were a dark void, unreachable no matter how hard she tried. Her heart pounded, each beat echoing like a drum in her ears. What had happened? She sat frozen, wondering what peril she had stumbled into. "Your Majesty," she began, her voice trembling, "I recall naught of what did transpire yesternight. My memories are lost unto me."

The king's groggy voice cut through the haze, his tone slurred but clear. "Thou wert in Thorncrest Castle," he said, concern edging his words. "Curse mine own brother's name. I know not what offense he hath given thee to kindle such ire, but blame thee I shall not, for oft do I curse his name as well."

Fragments of the night rushed back. She could almost taste the bitterness of the words she had shouted, fueled by anger and desperation. Was the prince truly a victim of her doing? Surely the king would have mentioned if his brother were dead.

"Thou wert waving a small dagger," the king continued, a shadow passing over his face. "Thou didst take a swing at me with it." His jaw tightened briefly, his expression darkening. "The guards hath slain men for far less."

He paused, his gaze hardening. "Sir Eadric, mine own knight, was upon thee before thou couldst draw nigh. His blade rested against thy throat, yet still, thou didst not flinch." He leaned forward, his voice quieter now, laden with gravity. "Thou didst demand a moment alone with mine brother, that thou might slay him."

A chill ran down Mary's spine. She trembled, the king's warning sinking in. The weight of her actions, the danger she had placed herself in, pressed down on her, suffocating her with dread.

Mary's face turned pale, her eyes wide with terror. Her lips trembled as the words caught in her throat. "Your Ma---jesty," she stammered, her voice barely a whisper. "I do beseech thee for forgiveness. I was not mine own self." Tears welled in her eyes, threatening to spill as she pleaded, her whole body trembling with fear and remorse.

The king let out a low sigh and rolled over, reaching for the nearby stand. His fingers wrapped around the ornate handle of a gold pitcher, lifting it with ease. The matching golden goblet gleamed in the soft interplay of morning light streaming through the window slits and the steady glow of the hearthfire as he tilted the pitcher, rich red wine spilling smoothly into the goblet.

He raised the goblet to his lips, taking a long, deliberate sip. As the liquid touched his lips, the tension in his face eased, replaced by a quiet satisfaction. Once content, he set the goblet down with a soft clink. "No harm hath been done," he declared, his voice steady.

Pouring more wine into the chalice, he extended it toward Mary, his eyes meeting hers with calm assurance. His gaze lingered for but a heartbeat longer, and warmth unfurled within her chest. Her pulse quickened, each thrum resounding in her ears. Her hands quivered, startled by the unexpected offer that hung in the air like an unspoken challenge. Sharing a drink with the king was far from customary, but her parched throat urged her forward. She reached out, fingers trembling, and accepted the goblet.

Mary's eyes darted to the door, her pulse racing at the thought of being caught in such an intimate setting with the king. The warmth of his nearness, the way his presence filled the royal chamber, made her heart flutter with an unfamiliar thrill. Her gaze shifted back to him, then quickly to the flickering shadows cast by the fire burning steadily in the hearth.

As she brought the goblet to her lips, her eyes flicked nervously around the chamber. The king's laughter, low and warm, broke the silence. "Fear not," he said, his voice smooth and reassuring. "Mine chambermaids have come and gone this morn. They have already seen thee."

Her breath hitched, his words sinking in. As he spoke, a shard of unease worked its way into her mind, her chest tight with sudden worry. His voice softened, pulling her thoughts to the space that lay between them, now near vanished. She took a hurried sip, the wine burning down her throat, yet the tension between them only seemed to grow.

The corners of his mouth lifted, his eyes still locked on hers, the smile lingering as though it was meant only for her. "I treat mine household servants well. Rare is it that gossip escapeth mine halls." His tone was soothing, but there was a glint in his eyes—something deeper, unspoken.

Mary's trembling hands returned the goblet to the king. Her wide, glistening eyes met his. "I thank thee, Your Majesty," she murmured, her voice barely above a whisper. She hesitated, her heart pounding, before daring to ask, "Might I inquire, how came I to be here, in the king's bedchamber?"

The king chuckled, his gaze softening as he looked upon her. "I tried to have mine men escort thee home, but thou didst refuse. Thou didst insist that thou couldst not return and that thou must stay with me." He paused, the memory clearly amusing him. "Such boldness, indeed, most rare for one of thy standing. To demand to stay with me—aye, even maidens of noble title would scarce make such a demand."

He leaned back, his laughter rumbling low and warm. "I was agreeable to thy staying here. I offered thee a guest chamber, but thou didst refuse," he said with a shake of his head. "Thou wast most insistent upon staying in mine own chamber, and I must confess, 'twas most beguiling."

Mary's face twisted in disbelief. "Here, Your Majesty? As in thine home?" Mary's voice wavered, her words tumbling out in a rush before she could stop them. Her cheeks flushed, and she glanced down, unable to meet his gaze, as the weight of her boldness from the night before settled heavily upon her.

The king picked up the goblet again, a knowing smile playing on his lips. "Here, in sooth, is Ravenstone Castle," he replied, taking another much-needed sip of wine. As he lowered the goblet, their eyes met, and the air between them grew heavier, charged with something unspoken. His smile hinted at more than just amusement, and Mary's heart fluttered, wondering at the depth of it.

They lay together, propped up on the bed, the finest fur blanket she had ever felt draped over them. The luxurious fur contrasted sharply with the throbbing in her head and the churning in her stomach. Mary's face flushed with embarrassment as she realised she was wearing what she assumed was the king's white tunic and nothing else. Had she been standing, it would have barely reached above her knees. Such behaviour was unfitting for a noble lady, but even as a commoner, she had hoped to save herself for marriage.

"Am I... am I to assume that we art to..." She paused, her voice trembling as tears threatened to spill from her eyes. "Didst... we...?" The words faltered on her lips, heavy with the weight of her uncertainty. "Did I bestow upon thee mine innocence?" The thought hung in the air, a dagger twisting in her chest, the ache of not remembering deepening her sorrow.

She could barely bring herself to look at the king, her heart pounding as she awaited his response.

The king's eyes softened as he caught her unspoken question. "Thou needst not worry," he said gently. "We did naught untoward, thou hast my word." His tone was earnest, but his gaze lingered on her, his voice dipping lower. "Unless, of course, thou dost count thy relentless need to hold me and thy rather robust snoring as untoward."

Mary's cheeks turned an even deeper shade of red, her embarrassment mingling with a reluctant smile. She was mortified but found herself unable to suppress a giggle. "I did no such thing, Your Majesty!" she protested, her voice a mix of horror and flirtation.

The king laughed heartily, his eyes bright with mischief as he watched her. "Oh, but thou didst, fair maiden," he said, taking another swig of wine. "Thou didst practically chase me around the bed."

Her mortification deepened, but so did her laughter. There was a light in the king's eyes, something teasing and tender, and as he looked at her, Mary felt her heart flutter again, wondering if perhaps the pull she felt was not hers alone.

Mary threw her hand on her forehead, torn between laughter and mortification. Her heart raced with embarrassment. "Forgive me, Your Majesty, I pray thee," she said, her voice muffled through her shame and amusement.

Despite her initial horror, his jesting tone and twinkling eyes began to soothe her nerves. A hesitant, genuine smile crept onto her lips. "I suppose there be fouler things for which one might be remembered," she said softly.

In a sweet and laughable tone, the king replied, "I reckon that be true, aye." He lifted the fur blanket slightly to adjust himself, and as he did so, Mary caught a glimpse of his nearly naked form. Her breath caught in her throat, her cheeks flushing as she quickly averted her eyes, heart pounding with a mix of shock and unexpected desire.

Mary pushed aside any untoward feelings, her countenance turning solemn. "Your Grace... Did the prince glimpse me with the dagger?" She paused, her voice barely more than a whisper. "Did he hear?" Her eyes searched the king's face, anxiety casting shadows upon her gaze. "Did he hear what I didst say? Doth he know I came seeking him, dagger in hand?" she asked with fear in her voice.

The king's smile faltered momentarily. "Thou needst not worry," he said, his tone attempting to soothe. He had seen her, as had Sir Eadric and the guards; no one else had witnessed or heard anything. But if any of them had glimpsed the scene, he would simply pardon her should they wish to step forward. "Thou needst not fret; Charles shall hear naught of this, upon mine honour."

His smile returned, a facade of reassurance that did little to alleviate the unease gnawing at Mary's conscience. "Whilst I shall shield thee this time, know thou well that 'tis treason to lay a hand against one of royal blood, punishable by death most cruel. I swear, there are days when I would love naught more than to see mine own brother's end. Yet even if thou couldst succeed in taking his life, I do not reckon thou wouldst bear well the burden of guilt for taking a human soul."

Mary's heart pounded fiercely as the king's words lingered in the air. The warmth of his breath mingled with hers, stirring a forbidden desire she could scarcely admit to herself. Her pulse quickened, each beat echoing like a war drum in her ears, as though her very soul were about to burst from within her chest. "I know not what came over me."

For a heartbeat, their gazes intertwined, his steely focus holding hers captive. A shiver coursed through her as his strong yet refined hand brushed her cheek. The touch was like the softest whisper, sending a tremor through her entire being. His hand trailed the subtle contours of her face, hesitating for a moment on her cheekbone before drifting down to the slope of her chin. With a tender yet commanding touch, he tilted her face upwards, drawing her lips perilously close to his. "We knoweth not each other well, yet 'twould haunt mine soul to have thee charged with the murder of mine brother, or any folk. I beseech thee, prithee, try not again."

Mary's heart raced, a whirlwind of fear and longing. *Had the king not laid eyes upon me in such a state, I would have been willing to end the prince,* she thought, the weight of that admission sending a fresh wave of shame through her. "I do swear, mine intent was but to frighten the prince. Thou speakest true; I could ne'er bear the weight upon mine own soul had I spilled his blood." Her voice trembled slightly, yet she forced herself to hold his gaze, desperate to convey her sincerity.

Her breath caught, eyes wide with both fear and longing. The scant distance between their lips felt charged with unspoken tension. She could feel his desire mirrored in her own racing heartbeat, each pulse echoing the uncharted emotions swirling within her. The world around them faded into the shadows of the chamber, leaving only the tantalizing space between them—a whisper away from a forbidden kiss. Her body trembled, a mixture of yearning and apprehension flooding her senses, her heart aching to close the gap, to feel the king's lips against hers in a moment of stolen passion.

She knew all too well the peril of letting her guard down, even for a fleeting moment. Drawing a steadying breath, she summoned the strength to voice her decision. "I must take my leave," Mary declared, pulling away from him. Her voice, filled with resolute determination, brooked no argument.

The king's eyes widened briefly in shock at her abruptness, his breath catching in surprise. He watched her, astonishment mingled with a playful inquiry in his gaze. "How dost thou possess the vigor to rise from thy bed?" he asked, rubbing his temples—a gesture of weariness and contemplation. "Thou wast more drunken than I yestere'en."

Mary's eyes flickered with a brief flash of annoyance, her lips pressing into a tight line. She quickly smoothed her expression, bowing her head slightly as though to hide the momentary lapse, mindful of the respect owed to the king. The weight of the heavy fur blanket draped over her shoulders was both a comfort and a burden, grounding her in the moment. For a fleeting second, she longed to stay in its warmth, to remain in the safety of his presence. But her fingers curled into the thick folds of the fur, her grip tightening as her thoughts turned to her quest.

Her voice wavered as she spoke, low but insistent. "Your Majesty, dost thou know of the man with the silver locks?" She dared a glance at him, her eyes betraying the vulnerability she fought to conceal. The thick fur shifted in her grasp as doubt crept in—memories of cold shoulders and indifferent stares weighing on her mind. She gripped the thick fur blanket tightly, the coarse yet soft texture pressing against her palms as she braced herself for his reply.

Confusion creased the king's face, his brow furrowing as he echoed her words, his tone questioning. "The man with silver locks?" he repeated, seeking clarification. A flicker of curiosity sparkled in his eyes, like a shy smile on a sunny day. "That could be any soul, forsooth."

Mary bit her lip, her mind racing to recall any distinguishing details about the man she sought. The weight of her desperation settled upon her as she struggled to articulate the description. "I believe he is some sort of sword hire," she managed, her words cautious yet tinged with a flicker of hope. "He's served thy brother, His Highness."

At the mention of his brother, the king's jaw tightened, and a flicker of something sharp passed through his eyes. His hand paused mid-motion, fingers curling around the goblet as though steadying himself. A faint sigh escaped his lips, his brow creasing with a weight he did not bother to hide. "What hath my brother gotten himself into now?" he muttered under his breath, the burden of his sibling's actions bearing down upon him. His gaze shifted back to Mary, a glimmer of recognition in his eyes. "Mayhaps I know of the man thou seekest. Hath he aught to do with why thou didst attempt to slay the prince?"

Mary's breath quickened at his words, her heart pounding in her chest as a knot of dread twisted within her. She averted her gaze, her fingers twisting nervously, a tide of shame surging through her. "I do swear, I meant only to frighten the prince," she replied, her voice steadying as she summoned the courage to meet his gaze again. "The man whom I seek hath naught to do with my wretched ill conduct yestereve."

King John regarded her intently. "But thou must tell me more of thy purpose in seeking him." His expression shifted, suspicion mingling with concern.

Mary's heart fluttered with a surge of both relief and anticipation at the possibility of finding the man she sought. She cautiously chose her words, acutely aware of the potential consequences if her intentions were misconstrued. She treaded delicately, her voice betraying a sense of urgency mingled with caution. "Ah, Your Majesty, 'tis naught to do with thy brother," she hastily clarified. "I believeth the silver-haired man may hold knowledge of mine sister's fate. Rumours spoke of some mishap, and I thought perchance he might know whither she hath gone."

The king's brows knitting together as a sense of foreboding settled in. He could not afford to blindly trust those around him, especially someone he had grown fond of, now lying beside him in his bed. "Swear thee once more that thou dost seek only thine own sister, and not a means to end my brother's life," he began, his voice low and steady, each word weighed with concern. "Mark thee well: the slaying of the prince is a most grievous crime against the crown, and should he fall to any suspicious harm, I shall be left with no choice but to question thee."

As he spoke, his gaze remained locked on hers, searching for the smallest giveaway—a twitch, a flutter, a glimmer of deception. Though he doubted Mary was truly capable of taking a life, the weight of misplaced trust pressed heavily on his heart, and his feelings for her only deepened the complexity of the moment.

It was true; she wanted the prince dead. A dagger to the heart seemed too merciful for such evil. But even if it came to that, could she truly do the deed? "A regrettable action on my behalf," she began, her voice steady despite the turmoil within. "I simply drank far more wine than I could handle." That part was true. The next part was not. "I would never truly wish ill fate upon his highness." Her breath hitched as she frantically searched for a safe phrase, her mind racing to protect her loved ones.

The king lifted his goblet once more, pausing before taking a sip. "To seek a hire costeth a considerable sum of coin, most especially if the man thou speakest of is the one I believeth it to be," he said, his voice heavy with warning. "As a rule, one must ever be wary of those who slay for coin." His eyes bore into hers, the weight of his words hanging in the air. He then took a large swig of the wine, the liquid disappearing quickly from the goblet. "What doth bind thy sister to a man whom my brother perchance hath hired aforetime?"

The air in the chamber grew thick, coiling around Mary like a serpent as his questioning gaze pierced through her. She clutched the goblet, its cool surface barely calming the rapid beat of her heart. Words danced on the tip of her tongue, but the weight of his scrutiny made them falter. An overwhelming urge to draw closer, to find solace in his presence, tugged at her. Yet the gravity of the moment held her in place, as if invisible chains bound her to the spot. This felt more like an interrogation than a conversation, and the thought of uttering a single wrong word sent a chill down her spine.

"And what manner of accident dost thou speak of?" he asked, his voice steady yet laced with curiosity.

"Mine sister was ensnared in the midst of a quarrel, yet the matter hath since been settled," she offered, her voice measured and purposefully vague. Quickly, she brought the goblet to her lips and drank, hoping to hide any betraying expressions.

The king's brows furrowed, suspicion deepening the lines on his forehead as he scrutinized Mary's words. "In sooth, the man of whom thou dost speak must be Lucian Blackthord, a knave with locks of silver. With skills this sharp, he's the one everyone looks up to—and also fears. He demandeth much coin for his services, near running the Shadow Serpents as if they were his own. A man such as he holdeth but little loyalty to any."

A flicker of uncertainty crossed the king's face, a fleeting glimpse of self-doubt that stole his regal composure. These were the types of people who killed for coin without a second thought. He imagined Mary hiring them for details about her sister but falling short of the fee, causing them to take her life as payment. A sense of guardianship welled up inside him, threatening to overflow. "Medle not with him, nor with shadow serpents, for should they wish thee dead, they shall not think twice upon it," he said slowly, his voice heavy with resignation. "I doth hope thy sister fareth well, yet the fee for knowledge from the Shadow Serpent is no trifling sum."

Mary's heart raced as shock coursed through her. Lucian had shown her kindness in sorts, even if it was for his own gain. He had a maid bathe her, showed her forms of self-defense, and had a dagger made for her. While he was intimidating, and she was very fearful of him, it felt strange to hear the king speak of him so. She had not thought of coin. "What thinkest thou he might say, should I offer him aught other than coin? Serveth he perchance in the Shadow Serpents?"

The king straightened slightly in the bed, his brow furrowing as his gaze sharpened, fixing upon her with an intensity that seemed to draw the very breath from the air. "Thou shalt not lie with the Shadow Serpent, nor consort with Lucian! Heed mine warning, for there is naught but peril in their company!" His voice resounded with authority, yet beneath it lingered a tremor of fear for her safety, a glimmer of protectiveness that betrayed his deeper feelings.

Mary could see the conflict in his eyes—she was but a maiden of no wealth, yet he understood her desperation. If he were in her situation, he would do the same for his own sister. The weight of his obligations clashed with his emotions.

"Wouldst thou prefer I send one of mine men to gather knowledge?" he offered, his tone softening slightly as he searched her face for understanding. "Thou may remain abed." He halted, the weight of his words dawning upon him, realising how they might sound. "To be clear, thy remaining abed is no condition of mine offer."

Mary's eyes widened, taken aback by the king's unexpected offer. She felt a rush of warmth, a mix of genuine surprise and the sweetness of his concern. "Thy Majesty, 'tis most gracious of thee," she stammered, her voice tinged with a blend of gratitude and uncertainty, "Yet I do assure thee, I am more than capable."

Her heart raced, not just from the closeness of the king but from the lurking fear of what could happen if the prince discovered that she was seeking the advice of the Shadow Serpents. Accepting the king's help might draw unwanted attention, placing both her and her kins in even greater peril.

Mary passed the goblet back to the king, their hands brushing, sending a thrill down her spine. He took the goblet, their fingers lingering for a heartbeat, before he placed it back on the stand. The natural light from the window cast soft shadows across his bare chest, now fully visible.

He turned to her with a swift motion, his gaze intense. "Very well," he said once again, making no effort to cover himself. "Go thou to The Rusty Sword Inn upon Cutthroat Row. Seek out the barkeep, and say thou art in search of an old-fashioned blade. He shall guide thee further. Find thy place at a table in the corner, and there shalt thou wait."

Her pulse quickened at his words. The very mention of Cutthroat Row made her skin crawl. The Rusty Sword was infamous—a place where the roughest men gathered. People talked about the savage brawls and how some folks walked in but never walked out.

The king could no longer restrain himself. With a sudden, urgent motion, he reached for her, his hand encircling her waist and drawing her across the bed until she lay almost beneath him. Time seemed to slow, each heartbeat echoing in the silence. Mary's breath hitched as his lips hovered inches from hers, their breaths mingling in the intimate space between them.

It was a fleeting glance, a hair's breadth of contact, yet the spark that flew between them ignited a fire that still lingered. Her eyes, wide and sparkling with emotion, locked onto his, everything else fading into oblivion. Then, with a tender yet fervent movement, his lips met hers.

In that instant, the chamber melted away, leaving only the wild urgency of his touch and the gentle reverence in his eyes—a contradiction that razed her defenses and left her trembling. Lips caressed lips, a fleeting tremor of intimacy shaking her very foundation, laying bare the vulnerability of her heart. Mary melted into him, her heart pounding as she clung to the intensity of the moment.

Time stood still as their lips met, each moment swelling with unspoken emotion and desperate longing. Every contour of her face became familiar terrain as his hand coasted along the landscape of her skin, pausing on the tender arc of her cheekbone. In the silence, their bond crackled to life, fueled by the thrum of emotion that lay beneath the surface, waiting to erupt.

When he finally pulled away, it was with palpable reluctance, his eyes still burning with desire and unvoiced promises. The air caught in his throat as his gaze held hers, transmitting the unspoken turmoil that knotted his insides and tore at his grip on control.

"Whilst thou art at The Rusty Sword," he murmured, his voice still gravelly with the remnants of last night's indulgence, "thou mayst wish to sample the pottage. They do mix in herbs and vegetables, though 'tis more a remedy for a sore head than a feast for the belly."

She stared at him, scarcely believing her ears—the king, of all people, sprawled next to her in his bed, speaking of Cutthroat Row as if he knew its dark alleys by heart. The notion that he could suggest a dish from Briarwood's most infamous tavern sent a shiver through her, as though the shadows of that wretched place had seeped into the king's chamber.

A grim shadow flitted across Mary's mind. Her thoughts strayed to the red lanterns that hung ominously above the doorways of Cutthroat Row, marking the brothels. The image of the rain-soaked maiden flashed before her eyes, leaning out of a window, her wet shift clinging to her form as she beckoned with promises for ten coins. Mary's heart pounded with a mix of curiosity and dread.

Had the king seen that very maiden? Had he, with a casual toss of ten coins, indulged in the same dark corners of Cutthroat Row? The thought clawed at her mind, unbidden. His knowing mention of the pottage at The Rusty Sword took on a new, unsettling light. Could his familiarity with such a place be borne of more than mere hearsay?

Mary's thoughts drifted back to the faces she had glimpsed as she walked through Cutthroat Row, past brothels that seemed to blend into the squalid chaos of the place. Some windows were little more than crude openings, covered with stretched parchment or oiled cloth, translucent and brittle, barely holding back the wind and rain. Outside these poorer establishments, red lanterns flickered weakly, their light casting uneven shadows on sagging wooden frames. The women who leaned out from these places had hollow eyes and distant gazes, their faces framed by the rough, weathered edges of the buildings, as though life itself had begun to wear them down.

Yet, just a few steps further, the scene would change. Wealthier brothels stood amidst the decay, their barred windows draped with dyed wool or heavy leather hangings. Red lanterns burned brighter here, their glow illuminating intricately carved doorframes or entrances framed by faded yet elaborate tapestries. The women within these establishments leaned out with painted faces and bold defiance, their eyes gleaming with a pride that seemed to challenge the lawlessness around them. They wore their roles like armour, claiming power in their place among the chaos of Cutthroat Row.

Mary shivered at the memory of it all. The contrast unsettled her: the hollow-eyed despair of some and the bold defiance of others, all jumbled together in the Row's tangled web of wealth and poverty. What strength, she wondered, did it take to wear such pride, or to endure such despair? She frowned slightly, but the faces lingered, etched in her thoughts like shadows refusing to fade.

Lost in her musings, Mary barely noticed the king's movements beside her. He shifted on the bed, his arm disappearing into the shadows by the bedside, groping around for something unseen. Moments later, his hand reemerged, gripping her dagger. The sunlight filtering through the narrow window caught the blade, causing it to gleam in the flickering light of the fire and candles.

Mary's eyes widened, her breath catching as the king held her dagger aloft, the blade reflecting eerie patterns on the walls. Images of the night before flooded her mind: her stealthy steps through the darkened corridors, heart pounding with each echo, the dagger in her hand a cold promise of death.

The king could have cast her into the dungeon, subjected her to the tortures reserved for traitors. Yet, instead of shackles, he had brought her to his chamber, offering her shelter. A riot of emotions battled for dominance in her head, leaving her face scorching hot and her lip trembling as she fought to keep her thoughts from spilling out.

"Verily, this be the dagger thou didst clutch so tightly yestereve," he murmured, turning it in his hand, the edge catching the light again. His brow furrowed slightly, the question hanging in the air: How had she carried such a weapon into the heart of the castle, past the guards? As their gazes locked, a flicker of curiosity danced across his features, raw and unrestrained.

He hesitated briefly, the dagger's silver blade flashing in the light as he extended it toward her. "Keep this well hidden at The Rusty Sword, I prithee," he cautioned, his voice laced with concern.

Mary's fingers trembled as they brushed against his while taking the dagger. She could feel the chill of the steel seep into her hand, a cold contrast to the warmth of her touch. Her mouth went dry, and she swallowed hard, her gaze shifting briefly to the floor. She clutched the hilt tightly, the weight of the weapon anchoring her in the moment. She glanced up at the king, her eyes reflecting a flicker of fear, and nodded, her voice a mere whisper. "Aye, I shall, Your Majesty."

The king's voice dropped to a grave whisper, each word laden with a weight of warning. "Take heed at The Rusty Sword and upon Cutthroat Row. That tavern and street doth teem with rogues and knaves."

Mary's eyes narrowed slightly as she looked at him, still grappling with the idea that he, of all people, had traversed the treacherous alleys of Cutthroat Row. The knowledge that the king had walked among such danger—and more than once by the sound of it—intrigued her. Despite the fear twisting in her gut at the thought of stepping into that den of iniquity, a spark of mischief flared within her. "Art thou truly afeard of every place beyond Stowshire and thy grand castle?" she teased, her voice carrying a mock defiance as she arched an eyebrow at him. She spoke with a teasing lilt, trying to conceal the anxiety knotting in her chest.

A knowing smile spread across the king's lips. He let out a deep, hearty chuckle that resonated throughout the chamber. "Thou dost jest, fair maiden, yet these scars were not earned within the safety of stone walls." He pulled the fur blanket away from his body, revealing a landscape of discoloured skin and jagged scars, remnants of battles long past. "I hath fought in many battles for the safety of the kingdom."

The scars varied in hue from angry red to faded white, some still raised and puckered, others smooth and silvery with age, clearly long healed. Each scar bore witness to narrow escapes and hardfought triumphs. "Granteth that me merit to pass judgment upon Cutthroat Row?" he asked, his eyes locking onto hers, challenging yet amused.

A gasp escaped Mary's lips as she lifted her fingers, hovering them just above one of the scars. She pulled her hand back, hesitating since the king had not directly invited her to touch. "I knew not, Your Majesty."

The king's eyes softened, and he slowly took her hand, guiding it gently toward one of the scars. His touch was firm yet reassuring, as if to say it was alright to explore the marks of his past. "A great king may not cower in his castle whilst knights and valiant defenders fight," he said, his voice resolute and filled with the weight of experience.

Mary's fingers grazed one of the scars that marred his skin, her touch gentle and fleeting. For a moment, a blend of sorrow and pride softened her features. She could scarcely imagine Prince Charles leading an army into battle; if he had been crowned king, he would have orchestrated countless bloody wars from the safety of his gilded throne. Briarwood had been blessed with John as its sovereign; his presence was a stroke of fortune that had spared the land much turmoil.

Each scar on the king's skin told a tale of fierce battles once fought. The thought of him enduring such brutal encounters sent a shiver down Mary's spine; he was both brave and noble. Not only could those wretched blades cut deep enough to be fatal, but the looming threat of infection was even more terrifying. Unlike the sword, which delivered immediate and visible danger, infection crept in silently, turning a survivable wound into a deadly affliction. She imagined the weight he carried, having witnessed the deaths of bold defenders and, even worse, bearing the burden of having taken lives. Sorrow welled in her heart as she finally withdrew her hand. "I trust thou wilt not take offense at mine departure," she murmured, her voice laced with regret. "I pray thou dost understand; I must away... for mine sister."

Mary turned slowly to the edge of the bed, her limbs heavy with exhaustion, and sat up. The warmth of the king's chambers, the soft embrace of the fur blanket, tempted her to stay. The blanket's luxurious softness brushed against her skin, a siren's call promising respite from the relentless worry gnawing at her heart. Yet, the urgency of finding her sister, the gnawing fear, demanded her attention, overpowering her yearning for rest.

With a steadying breath, she forced herself to rise, each movement a battle against her own aching body. She gripped the edge of the bed, her fingers sinking into the plush fur, fighting to stay upright. The blanket slid off her shoulders like a comforting whisper, reluctantly letting her go. Her legs trembled, as if made of fragile reeds, barely able to bear her weight.

The morning light, harsh and unforgiving, pierced her skull like a hangman's noose, tightening around her head with every breath. She stood, swaying slightly, her face pale and clammy, battling the waves of dizziness that threatened to drag her back into the bed's comforting embrace.

Each step toward the door felt like a test of will, her vision blurred, and her body screaming for the solace of rest. The hangover's brutal grip was like a punishment, a grim reminder of the night's excesses, but she pressed on, driven by the burning need to find her sister. The softness of the fur blanket clung to her thoughts, a distant echo of the comfort she was leaving behind, but she steeled herself, knowing she could not succumb to its allure.

A surge of self-consciousness hit Mary, her cheeks warming as she glanced down at the borrowed tunic she wore. A flush crept up her neck, and she dared a glance at the king. Her voice barely above a whisper, she asked, "Thy Majesty, wherefore might mine garments be found?"

The king's gaze softened, noticing her discomfort. He nodded towards the large, ornately carved chest at the foot of the bed. "The chest," he said gently. "Thy garments were drenched, so I did bid mine chamberlain take them away. Fresh raiments, and aught else that a maiden might require, hath been placed within."

A nervous laugh bubbled up as she moved to the chest, cheeks still tinged with pink. "Your Majesty, thou art most gracious; 'tis an honor that thou shouldst not have considered," she murmured, her fingers trembling as she lifted the lid. Inside, she found two distinct outfits, each carefully arranged.

The first was an elegant gown, fit for a noblewoman, crafted from rich velvet in deep emerald hues. The bodice was intricately embroidered with gold thread, and the long, flowing sleeves cascaded beside a skirt that fell in soft, luxurious folds. A matching cloak, lined with silk and trimmed with ermine fur, lay beneath, promising warmth and grandeur.T

he second set was simpler, the attire of a chambermaid. A plain linen dress in a soft brown, its fabric coarse yet sturdy, was folded neatly beside a rough woolen cloak. The cloak's edge bore the royal crest: a lion, stitched in deep purple thread, its fierce gaze unmistakable even in the dim light. The thread caught a faint shimmer as Mary traced the embroidery with hesitant fingers, her breath catching. The weight of the crest, small yet laden with meaning, pressed on her like an invisible hand.

Humble as it seemed, the attire carried a presence—a quiet proclamation of her connection to the king, intentional or not. The sturdy apron, laid out beside it, hinted at the daily labour expected of its wearer, though the lion's silent roar on the cloak spoke of a realm far removed from Cutthroat Row.

Mary's lips parted slightly, a mix of unease and wonder crossing her face. Her fingers lingered for a moment longer before she drew the cloak closer, the rough wool brushing her palms as her gaze flicked toward the king.

The king shifted slightly, his gaze earnest yet hesitant. "Know this, thou art worth more than any gift a man might offer thee. If a star were thy desire, I wouldst labour to pluck it from the heavens for thee. Shouldst thou wish for a wild bear or a wolf, I would wrestle the beast without a moment's doubt." His lips curled, eyes glinting with jest. "Though, pray, let us hope thou dost not make such demands of me—at least, not in these early days." He paused before continuing, a softness in his voice, "Yet I would not presume, nor bring thee any discomfort. I knew not whither thou wouldst wander, nor whether a noble gown would suit all corners of the town. Shouldst thou find thyself in less savory places, such attire might draw unseemly eyes. Though I know not thy circumstances well, I wished only to grant thee the choice."

The king glanced at the gown. "The emerald gown is but a modest token of mine affection," he said, his voice tender. "I had hoped it might bring thee comfort and warmth."

His eyes held a mix of hope and uncertainty, revealing his desire to please without overstepping. There was a gentle vulnerability in his demeanor, a quiet hope that she would see his gesture as sincere, not presumptuous.

Mary's heart fluttered as she considered the two outfits, her fingers brushing against the rough fabric of the simpler dress. She felt the subtle tension between them, an unspoken question lingering in the air. She noticed his gaze linger for a moment before he turned away, giving her the space to change. What struck her was the simple yet powerful way he showed his respect.

With gentle reverence, she spoke, her tone a delicate balance of respect and regret, a vulnerable façade she dared not let slip. "I am honoured that thou dost deem me worthy of such a beautiful gown. Yet, I must tread the streets of Cutthroat Row," she reminded him, a subtle warning of the danger a dress like this could attract in such a place. "Even upon my return home, I lack the means and occasion for events where such a dress might be fitting." She placed the elegant gown back into the chest with care, opting for the more practical attire. The king, still facing away, his posture stiff with understanding, responded quietly, "Mayhap thou couldst save it for another occasion, a more fitting one—such as a private feast with the king." His voice held a tentative hope, a soft undertone of something more personal.

Mary's fingers brushed the rough fabric of the simpler dress as she glanced at the elegant gown once more. The king's words echoed in her mind, leaving her momentarily stunned. Her heart skipped a beat at the suggestion, and she felt a warmth creeping up her neck, her cheeks flushing with the unexpectedness of it all. She took a deep, steadying breath, trying to calm the rapid fluttering in her chest. The reality of a chambermaid being invited to a private feast with the king seemed surreal, almost like a dream she dared not believe.

The idea of a king dining privately with a chambermaid was unheard of and carried implications that made her pulse quicken. "Surely, the king is far too burdened with matters of state to sup with a mere chambermaid. What, pray, would the court utter of such folly?"

Her cheeks warmed as she began to disrobe, her movements hesitant. The tunic slipped from her shoulders, the fabric whispering against her skin before pooling at her feet. She hesitated, the cool air brushing her bare arms and raising gooseflesh. Her fingers trembled as she reached for the plain linen dress, its rough texture grounding her as she hurried to pull it over her head.

She stole a glance toward the bed, her face flushing deeper. The king lay propped against the pillows, his head tilted slightly, his gaze distant. The faintest twitch of a smile curved his lips as he spoke. "What care I for the prattle of the court? Eating is no burden, I say; indeed, we all partake, do we not?" His tone was light, teasing, though his eyes drifted toward the narrow window. Pale light filtered through its small opening, softened by the faint sheen of oiled cloth stretched taut to block the chill.

Mary's hands fumbled with the apron strings, her fingers clumsy as she tied them around her waist. The familiar task did little to steady her racing heart. She risked another glance at him, her cheeks warming further at the subtle amusement still dancing on his lips. "I did think thou noble folk cared not for scandal?" she said, her voice a delicate blend of jest and genuine curiosity.

With a gentle tug, the dress slipped over her head, its rough fabric scratching comfortably against her skin, momentarily calming the storm within her. The weight of the situation pressed down, much like the dress itself—a steady, familiar presence in an otherwise confusing moment.

Mary's cheeks flushed with warmth as she awkwardly adjusted the dress, her heart pounded at the thought of his attention, a mixture of surprise and shy excitement.

As she finished dressing, she turned to face him fully, her hands smoothing down the front of her dress with nervous precision. The king's gesture of looking away, allowing her privacy, touched her deeply. The thought of being noticed and valued by him, despite her humble station, sent a shiver through her—a thrilling rush of emotions that hinted at a gentle, budding affection.

The king lay on the bed, his gaze fixed on the distant wall, his posture relaxed yet respectful, a hint of playfulness in his tone. "What sayest thou?" he asked, his voice low and teasing. "Wouldst thou dare to be embroiled in a scandal with the king?" The question lingered in the air, a challenge wrapped in jest. Mary's fingers nervously traced the rough fabric of her dress, her thoughts racing like the wind in a storm. She drew in a shaky breath, her heart pounding in her chest like a trapped bird.

"I am dressed, Your Majesty," she said softly, her voice quavering with a blend of gratitude and uncertainty. "Verily, I owe thee more than I can ever hope to repay for thy kindness. Mine drunkenness left me lost in a world of madness, and in that world, waking beside thee—though it may be wrong—hath brought much-needed light to mine life. And the news of the Shadow Serpents hath granted me hope in finding mine sister. It is a debt I cannot repay." She shyly faced away as she spoke.

The king's brow furrowed slightly, surprise flickering in his eyes as he absorbed her words. He shifted beneath the luxurious fur blankets, the warmth of their fabric contrasting with the cool air of the chamber. His upper body lay exposed, the definition of his muscles evident, a silent testament to the life of a warrior and ruler. A hint of kindness creased his face, hinting at a ruler whose crown hadn't completely hardened his heart. "Waking with me ought not be wrong; in sooth, I desire thee to wake with me again."

Mary's heart fluttered at his words, warmth blooming within her that she could hardly suppress. As the weight of reality bore down on her, her words tangled in her throat, refusing to emerge. "Pray, take no offense, Your Majesty," she murmured, her eyes lowering to the floor as she fought to quell the tumult of emotions swirling within. "Your Majesty, it bringeth me much joy to share thy time, and 'tis an honour beyond measure to speak with thee. Yet, I desire not to be part of any scandal, neither with thee nor with any other. Even were I had noble title, our sharing a bed would be cause for scandal upon us both. Let us accept that we have enjoyed this fleeting moment, and now must part ways."

The king sighed softly, rubbing his temple as if to ease the ache that lingered there. "Verily, this headache doth serve as a cruel reminder of last night's excesses," he muttered, a rueful smile flickering at the corners of his lips.

For an instant, his gaze wavered, eyes widening as her words settled in the air between them. A subtle tension gripped his brow, and his lips parted slightly, as if he were about to speak but found himself momentarily at a loss. The warmth in his expression dimmed, replaced by a flicker of uncertainty, revealing the struggle within him to reconcile her sentiments with the reality of their situation.

A silence hung between them, thick with unspoken thoughts, a moment of clarity that needed no verbal affirmation. "There doth lie a small sack of coins within the chest," he said, his tone shifting to one of practicality. "It shall provide thee with the information thou needest." He paused, ensuring she absorbed his words, the weight of his concern evident in his eyes. "When thou takest thy leave from the castle doors, a carriage shall be waiting to convey thee. Inform the driver thou wishest to go to The Rusty Sword Inn," he instructed, a hint of worry threading through his voice. He hesitated, recognising that a royal carriage on Cutthroat Row would attract unwanted attention. "Perhaps have them drop thee off a few lanes away."

The thought of her walking alone troubled him deeply. "Art thou certain I cannot send someone to fetch the information for thee? Or at least have someone accompany thee?" he implored, his eyes searching hers for any sign of hesitation.

Mary's eyes widened in shock at his generosity. *He is kind, and I do hope he means no offense. Yet, am I better than the maiden in Cutthroat Row who doth offer herself for ten coins? He swears that naught untoward hath occurred, and I am not in a place to refuse his kindness. Yet in offering the coins, what dost he think of me?* "Your Majesty!" she exclaimed, her voice breaking with emotion. "Your Majesty, thou needst not pay me for mine time."

The king's expression shifted, a mix of surprise and earnestness crossing his features. He leaned slightly forward, concern etched in his brow, and for a fleeting moment, the gravity of her words weighed heavily upon him. "My fair maiden," he replied, his voice steady yet gentle, "I offer not payment for thy time." A soft smile touched his lips, reflecting his sincerity. "Verily, the coin was meant as a gift, yet now I perceive thou hast need of it to procure information, rather than offering thy service to Lucian Blackthorn or the serpents."

Her hands trembled as she reached into the chest, fingers delicately brushing against the small sack of coins. She lifted it gently, almost reverently, feeling the unexpected weight of his gift. Her breath caught, and she struggled to steady her racing heart. "I..." she started, then simply nodded, overwhelmed by his generosity.

Mary's hands did tremble as she clasped the sack of coins, her eyes brimming with unshed tears. "I am so very... beholden to thee!" she stammered, her voice laden with emotion. "I shall repay thee, I do swear it." The burden of debt weighed heavily upon her, even as she fought to make ends meet.

She glanced at the king, her heart pounding. "The ride to the inn shall be far too great a strain, and I require no company upon the journey," she added, her voice firm yet laced with a touch of anxiety.

Mary's heart thudded wildly as the king rose, wrapping the fur blanket around his bare shoulders. The morning's chill receded as he moved, his skin radiating warmth like a small sun through the thick fur. He advanced with a measured grace, his presence seeping into her like a slow burn, setting her pulse thrumming in time with his. Each step closer stoked the anticipation coursing through her veins.

As he reached for the door, the blanket shifted slightly, his arm sliding past hers, their bodies almost touching as he grasped the handle, his chest mere inches from her dress. Her breath hitched, her fingers clutching the rough fabric of her gown, seeking any semblance of poise. The simplest touch was all it took. When their arms brushed, a spark ran through her, leaving a tantalizing buzz on her skin. A fierce blush spread across her cheeks as the lingering touch sent her heart racing with an excitement she couldn't ignore.

Time stood still as their gazes locked, the surrounding noise fading into silence. In his eyes, a maelstrom of emotions churned beneath the surface, straining against the leash of control and threatening to consume her very breath. She found herself unable to look away, drawn into the depths of his gaze, feeling a longing she couldn't quite name or deny.

As his lips hovered inches from hers, the soft rustle of his breath sparked a chain reaction of feelings that left her quivering with anticipation. The proximity of his bare skin beneath the fur, vibrating with restrained power, quickened her heart's beat. A war raged within her as she grasped her gown, one part of her yearning to melt into his warmth, the other steeling herself against the temptation. "'Tis not debt, but a gift, yet if thou wouldst use the word 'debt' as some excuse to see me again, then let it be a debt indeed."

Through the narrow crack of the slightly ajar door, Mary caught a glimpse of a guard standing sentinel, the glint of his armour catching the faint light. She imagined another guard just out of view, a silent shadow at the door's side, vigilant and ready. The king, with the fur blanket securely draped around his body, leaned into the doorway, his voice firm yet weary as it carried a command through the quiet air. "Alaric, come forth."

Mary strained her ears, catching the distant patter of footsteps echoing softly down the stone corridor. The silence was broken only by the sure steps of someone approaching. She sensed the careful, practiced movements of the king's personal servant as he drew nearer. The whisper of fabric brushing against stone and the gentle thud of leather-soled shoes spoke of his swift, unassuming approach. Though she couldn't see him, she felt the urgency in the air, as if the very walls awaited his arrival.

Through the narrow gap, Mary caught a glimpse of Alaric Stonebrook leaning forward, bowing low, his form partially obscured by the doorframe. The morning light filtered through the castle windows, casting a soft glow on his deep purple doublet, which bore the royal crest—the lion rampant in Gold, standing proudly on one hind leg with claws outstretched. As a personal attendant, his workload was heavy, but the emblem on his chest reminded him that loyalty to the crown was his highest priority. A golden crown adorned with amethysts rested atop the lion's head, signifying the king's personal crest and the privilege of his service.

Over his shoulder, he bore a leather satchel, its contents likely filled with messages and provisions for the king, ready to fulfill any need that might arise.

Alaric's voice, low and steady, drifted into the chamber, "How might I serve thee, Your Majesty?" Alaric's demeanor was calm, yet there was an unmistakable alertness in his posture, his eyes sharp and attentive, ever prepared to respond to the king's desires or to shield him from potential disturbances.

The king shifted slightly, his gaze lingering on Mary with a touch of unspoken concern. He turned to Alaric, his voice steady despite the weariness that clung to him. "See that mine guest is escorted to the carriage," he instructed, his tone imbued with authority. "And ensure a knight doth accompany her to whither she may need go beyond these walls."

Mary's eyes widened, her breath catching at the king's unexpected order for a knight. Alaric, ever composed, responded with a practiced bow, his demeanor calm and professional. "As thou dost wish, Your Majesty," he said, his tone steady, ready to fulfill the command with the diligence expected of him.

The king stepped back, the blanket shifting slightly around him, gesturing for Mary to move past. As she did, he leaned in close, his breath warm against her ear, whispering softly. She could feel the intensity of his words without needing to fully hear them. With just a few hushed words, he set her heart careening out of control, like a landslide tumbling down a mountainside. The faint murmur of his message lingered: "When thou findest what thou dost seek and all is well, remember mine dining invitation." The proximity and quiet intensity of his words left her with a sense of excitement and a fleeting warmth that she carried as she moved towards the door.

*

Mary trailed Alaric down the winding spiral stairs, the grandeur of Ravenstone Castle closing in around her. Each step echoed within the narrow stone corridor, throbbing dully through her temples, a cruel reminder of the revelry. She pressed her palm to her forehead, willing the ache to subside, but it clung to her stubbornly, an unwelcome shadow of excess.

As they descended, the chill of the stone walls did seep through her thin raiment, biting at her flesh and sending shivers down her spine. She had anticipated warmth within such a magnificent castle, yet the cool air wrapped around her like a cloak of unease, amplifying her discomfort and underscoring her humble origins.

The stairs twisted downward, a sinuous path that unwound beneath their feet. The flickering torchlight dance upon the stone walls, casting light upon intricate tapestries and ornate carvings, as though to mock her plain attire. Each turn reveal'd more of the castle's grandness, deep'ning her sense of unworthiness.

Once they reached the bottom, the stairs opened into a long corridor lined with heavy oak doors leading to various chambers. Alaric led the way, his purposeful stride echoing in the silence. The air grew cooler as they approached the outer doors, the faint draft promising the freshness of the courtyard beyond.

Grateful for the quiet, Mary focused on the muted sounds around her, but even the soft echo of their footsteps felt jarring. Occasionally, Alaric gestured to a grand tapestry or a marble statue, his low and respectful voice offering brief anecdotes about their origins and worth, yet the words drifted past her like whispers on the wind. Each syllable only heightened the heaviness in her head, reminding her of the clarity she lacked.

As they approached the courtyard, a faint draft rushed in, carrying the crisp bite of morning air. Mary inhaled sharply, the coolness cutting through her like a blade, sharpening her senses but also intensifying her discomfort. Two guards, clad in shining armour, stood at attention beside the massive wooden doors, their presence a silent testament to the king's authority. A doorkeeper, dressed in livery, stepped forward, his hands ready to swing open the imposing barriers.

With a nod from Alaric, the doorkeeper heaved the doors open, the ancient hinges groaning under the weight. Light burst through the opening, flooding the dim corridor and forcing Mary to squint against the sudden brightness. She raised a hand to shield her eyes, feeling a momentary rush of dizziness as her vision adjusted.

Stepping into the courtyard, Mary blinked against the glaring morning sun, its harsh rays pounding against her temples and intensifying the ache in her head. The ancient stones beneath her feet were worn and cracked, the creeping ivy weaving itself into the rough surfaces like nature's embrace. Cobblestones, smoothed by countless footsteps over the years, stretched out before her in a patchwork of muted grays and browns.

At the centre of the courtyard stood a grand stone fountain, bubbling quietly, its water shimmering in the sunlight—a serene spectacle, yet one that felt almost unattainable.

Mary stepped further into the castle courtyard, her heart racing as she took in the bustling scene around her. Armour shone like diamonds in the sun as knights strode purposefully, their movements a study in precision. Amidst the chorus of calls and salutes, her senses reeled from the barely controlled tumult. This place was far grander than Thorncrest Castle, and she felt both exhilarated and out of place among the nobles and soldiers.

Each step toward the carriage felt heavy, her limbs moving sluggishly as she fought against the fatigue that wrapped around her like a shroud. The cold clung to her skin, yet the warmth of the sun beckoned, a tantalizing reminder of comfort that felt just out of reach.

Mary's eyes widened as she took in the carriage awaiting her, its dark wood polished to a deep shine. The horses hitched to it were magnificent beasts, their coats glossy and their muscles rippling with each movement. They snorted and pawed at the cobblestones, their breath forming misty clouds in the cool morning air, a stark contrast to the turmoil in her mind.

The doorkeeper, with a respectful bow, stepped aside to let her pass, signaling her transition from the shadowy confines of the castle to the vibrant, living heart of the courtyard.

"Sir Eadric," Alaric began, his voice embodying the weight of the king's command without assuming authority over the knights. A tall knight with a broad chest stepped forward, his hand resting casually on the hilt of his sword. Alaric met his gaze, the seriousness of his message clear.

"By the king's decree, this fair maiden shall be accompanied upon her journey." Alaric gestured toward Mary, his tone resolute. "His Majesty bid thee safeguard her beyond these castle walls and see to it that she arriveth at her next destination unharmed."

Sir Eadric nodded, understanding the gravity of the king's order. "Good morrow, Alaric. It shall be done," his voice steady and resolute. He signaled to another knight, who straightaway moved to ready his steed. "In one accord, the knights stood to attention, their steadfast bearing a true testament to the respect they held for the king's authority."

Alaric's expression remained composed as he addressed Mary with quiet professionalism. "Thou art in capable hands," he said firmly. "Sir Eadric shall see to it that thy journey be both safe and swift."

With that, Alaric turned to the carriage, opening the door with practiced efficiency. Mary took a deep breath, feeling a tumult of relief and frustration. The grandeur of the carriage and the presence of a knight might draw unwanted attention, potentially alerting Prince Charles to her whereabouts. With the king's wishes looming large, she felt her own convictions shrink in significance. The sooner she reached Cutthroat Row, the sooner she could dismiss both the carriage and the knight. "I thank thee."

As she settled into the carriage, the soft leather yielded to her touch, releasing a faint scent of polished wood. As the door closed behind her, she caught a final glimpse of Alaric standing tall beside the knights, a silent executor of the king's will.

Sir Eadric mounted his horse with practiced ease, his steed snorting softly as it prepared to lead the way. With a final nod to Alaric, Sir Eadric gave the signal, and the carriage began to move, its wheels crunching over the cobblestones as it set off into the morning light.

The Rusty Sword Inn

The coachman brought the carriage to a halt with a jarring lurch, its wheels settling unevenly on the cobbled road just outside of Cutthroat Row. With a furtive glance over his shoulder, he quickly helped Mary down, his expression tight with thinly veiled relief as he clambered back onto his perch, eager to leave the place behind. Sir Eadric remained mounted on his horse, a silent guardian, his presence drawing the wary stares of those lurking in the shadows.

Though the sun hung high in the mid-morning sky, Cutthroat Row was a world unto itself, where light seemed to falter and die before it could penetrate the gloom. Each step along the crooked, narrow street was fraught with peril, the air thick with the stench of refuse, unwashed bodies, and old smoke. Abandoned carts and broken barrels littered the path, a reminder of the neglect that festered here, while unseen eyes tracked their every movement from darkened windows and alleyways.

Mary kept her gaze down, her breath shallow as they moved further into the heart of the Row. The walk was longer than it seemed, each twist and turn a labyrinth of danger. Brothels with their painted façades stood silent, their red lanterns unlit for now, but the signs of indulgence and decay were everywhere. Gaunt figures huddled in corners, their whispers riding the wind like the hiss of snakes, and each step she took was a step deeper into their domain, where the law held no sway.

Sir Eadric's steady presence did little to ease the tension knotting in her chest. His hand rested on the hilt of his sword, and his armour glinted faintly in the patches of sunlight that managed to seep through the closing gaps of the street. Yet even a knight could not fully banish the creeping dread that gripped her.

As they pass a band of knaves, their tattered garb and marred visages did bear witness to the harsh lives they had led. One spat on the ground, his sneer a challenge that went unanswered. Dark eyes lingered on Mary's form as she clutched her cloak tighter around herself, her pulse quickening. Here, she was an outsider, and they knew it.

At last, the sign of The Rusty Sword swung into view, its crooked wood creaking on rusted chains. The tavern loomed ahead, its windows mostly shuttered, though faint wisps of smoke curled from within, and the glow of candles hinted at life inside. The door, aged and battered, seemed to bear the weight of countless grim tales, and Mary hesitated as they neared it.

"This is where I must leave thee," Sir Eadric said, his voice low and grave. "Thou wilt fare well within, though danger lurks about these streets."

As he spoke, the horse shifted under him, its muscles bunching in anticipation. Sir Eadric pressed his heels firmly, and the steed surged forward, hooves striking the cobblestones with a steady, resonant rhythm. The sharp clatter of iron shoes echoed as he turned sharply, guiding the horse down the narrow street. His figure, straight and sure, moved swiftly through the deepening shadows. Mary swallowed hard, her throat too tight for words, nodding in silence. She hath no choice but to proceed, though the fear did gnaw upon her very insides. With one last glance toward the ruffians who still watched her with cold, calculating eyes, she stepped forward, pushing the heavy door of the tavern open.

Sweat-drenched floors, spilt ale, and days of hard labour lingered in the air, creating a putrid stench that slapped you in the face. Though a fire crackled in the hearth and candles flickered on the tables, the tavern felt cloaked in shadow, as though the light could not reach every corner. The patrons—all rough, dangerous men and women—sat hunched over their drinks, their faces partially hidden beneath hoods or greasy locks of hair. Their eyes did trail her steps as she made her way further into the chamber. The weight of their stares pressed upon her, suspicion and an unspoken threat lurking behind each glance.

Mary's steps faltered, her heart pounding in her chest. She had been to Cutthroat Row once before but had never set foot in this tavern. The prickle of many eyes did press upon her, unseen yet keenly felt, as though every soul here did mark her out as a stranger to their midst. She was a maid from a place far removed from the lawless streets of Ravenswood Town, and the men and women here knew it. The air buzzed with unspoken danger, each breath she took laced with the awareness that a wrong word or misplaced step could seal her fate. At the nearest table, a grizzled man with a scar slicing down his cheek clutched his chalice with gnarled fingers, eyes narrow and suspicious as they tracked her every movement. Beside him, a woman with matted hair and a wicked grin, exposing a missing tooth, leaned back with a rusty dagger resting casually on the table, her gaze heavy with unspoken threats.

Mary's heart thundered in her chest, each beat resonating with the silent dread coiling within her like a serpent poised to strike. Moving as if in a trance, she pressed on, senses overwhelmed by the thick haze of smoke that curled lazily in the air, each step pulling her deeper into the lair of shadows and secrets.

To her left, a group of burly men with rough, weathered faces sat hunched over a game of dice, their eyes flicking toward her with barely concealed interest. The largest among them, a giant of a man with arms like tree trunks and a beard that reached his chest, glanced up from his game. His eyes glinted with a predatory gleam as he nudged his companion—a thin, wiry man with a twitching eye—who responded with a slow, knowing nod.

Further into the tavern, two hooded figures whispered in hushed tones, their faces obscured by the shadows of their cloaks. One lifted a hand, revealing long, twisted fingers that seemed to dance in the flickering candlelight. Their conversation halted as Mary passed, the silence wrapping around her like a dark veil, drawing her into their orbit of hidden intentions and whispered plots.

At another table, a man with a patch over one eye and a long scar trailing from his temple to his jaw leaned back in his chair. The razor-sharp focus in his eyes immobilized her, stalling her breath as an unspoken message seeped into her bones, frosty and unreadable. Across from him, a younger man with wild eyes and ink-stained hands scribbled furiously on a piece of parchment, the faint scratch of quill against the surface punctuating the silence. His attention momentarily diverted by Mary's presence, he paused, his brow furrowing as he took her in.

As she pressed deeper into the tavern, the air grew thick, the murmur of voices a tangled din of curses and low-spoken bargains. Her breath came in shallow gasps, fear tightening about her chest like an iron band. The weight of countless eyes bore down on her—some filled with hunger, others with warning.

Near the back of the tavern, a lone figure sat cloaked in shadows, his face obscured by a widebrimmed hat. He remained perfectly still, a dark silhouette against the flickering light, a sentinel watching her every move. The candlelight glinted off the edge of a blade resting on the table beside a half-empty tankard, the metal gleaming like a snake's eye in the gloom.

Mary's steps faltered, the realisation of her surroundings sinking in like cold water soaking into her bones. The air at The Rusty Sword hung heavy with peril, and a single careless whisper could be your death sentence. The fear that coiled within her tightened its grip, its silent hiss echoing in her mind as she navigated the treacherous path to the bar, each step a testament to her resolve in the face of the unknown.

As Mary approached the worn wooden bar, her heart thundered like a runaway steed, each hesitant step echoing the dread that clung to her like a shroud. The barkeep, a gruff man with a bushy beard, glanced at her briefly, his eyes narrowing in a quick assessment before returning to the rhythmic clinking of tankards and the steady pour of ale. His hands moved with practiced ease, calmly filling tankard and wiping down the counter, seemingly unfazed by the chaos that filled the tavern.

Mary's voice quivered, a fragile thread trying to weave itself into the chaotic din of the tavern. "May I trouble thee for some pottage?" Her hands fumbled in her pockets, fingers trembling as she pulled out a few tarnished coins given by the king. The metal clinked softly on the bar, a tiny beacon in the sea of noise and shadows. Her eyes flickered nervously around the tavern, catching fleeting glimpses of leering faces and shadowy figures hunched over their drinks, each gaze a silent accusation or unspoken threat. Leaning closer, her voice barely a whisper above the clamor, she added, "Verily, I seek an oldfashioned sword, good sir." Her words, hesitant and uncertain, were quickly swallowed by the surrounding cacophony.

The barkeep's eyebrow arched, a subtle signal of intrigue tempered by caution. His eyes flickered briefly to Mary's chambermaid uniform, noting the emblem embroidered near the hem—the lion rampant, crowned. Not only did she serve the royal family, but the king himself; it was a silent reminder of her connection to the royal household. Yet, suspicion dulled that spark as he quickly masked his interest. He had seen many folk from different places and ranks come here; in his mind, they were either stupid or desperate. Either way, he cared not for her troubles. "One shall bring it unto thee," he grunted, his tone gruff and detached, as if her request were as ordinary as asking for another chalice of ale.

Mary retreated to a dimly lit corner, her legs shaky as she sank onto a rough wooden bench. The shadows here seemed deeper, the murmur of conversations around her a distant hum, disconnected from the rising anxiety that gnawed at her insides. Every now and then, the folk in the tavern would cast glances her way, their eyes lingering on her a little too long, as if questioning why someone like her was seated in such a place. Each minute stretched into an eternity, every passing second amplifying the gnawing unease that twisted in her gut. Laughter and raucous chatter filled the air, the tavern's patrons seemingly indifferent—or at least feigning indifference—to the storm of fear raging within her secluded nook.

Her hand drifted to the hilt of her dagger, the cold metal a small, steady anchor in a turbulent sea of uncertainty. She curled her fingers around it, feeling the familiar weight pressing against her palm, a silent vow of readiness should the need arise. Though she lacked much skill in wielding it, she had taken the blade with her for this purpose alone—prepared to face whatever danger lurked in the shadows. The dagger offered but a modest weight, yet one most comforting. It reminded her that, despite the perilous company and dark corners, she was not entirely without means to defend herself.

Mary's gaze flitted across the dimly lit tavern, where shadows writhed like restless spirits in the flickering candlelight. The air felt thick, oppressive, pressing down upon her as if each second conspired against her. Her pulse pounded in her ears, faster and louder with every passing breath. The tavern's hum of conversation buzzed around her, but her attention narrowed to a distant table where a man's eyes had been fixed on her for far too long.

He leaned toward his companion, whispering something low and coarse. Both men exchanged a glance, their lips curling upward in wicked mirth, as if they shared some unspoken devilry. A dark gleam flashed in their eyes, and their quiet laughter slithered through the air, sharp and vile. Their grins stretched, slow and sinister, like predators savoring the hunt, each one ready to pounce the moment her guard faltered.

Draven, the first man, larger and meaner than the rest, pushed back his chair with a deliberate scrape that seemed to echo across the tavern. His smirk deepened, his steps slow, measured, each one a deliberate warning as he approached her. He moved like a predator, confident and savoring the tension that filled the air.

Mary's stomach twisted, a chill creeping up her spine. Any soul may be a Shadow Serpent, she thought. He could very well be one, might he not? Her fingers tensed on the edge of the table, nails pressing into the rough wood, her mind racing.

Draven's heavy boots thudded upon the floor, each step seeming to steal the very breath from her breast. Mary's eyes, though wide with unease, remained locked on him, refusing to waver. The candlelight sputtered, throwing twisted, jagged shapes across his weathered face, the deep scars cutting through the flickering light like cracks in stone.

His gaze lingered upon her, like unto a blade, slow and deliberate, marking each detail with a gleam that set her very skin to crawling. There was no curiosity there—just the cold calculation of a hunter sizing up his prey. She could feel the weight of his intention, the way he looked at her not as a person but as an opportunity. Vulnerability, isolation—he saw it all and cared for nothing more.

The faint smile never left his lips, though the malice behind it thickened with each step he took. It was a smile that promised nothing good, and the closer he drew, the more the space around her seemed to shrink, the walls of the tavern closing in like a trap.

He stopped just shy of her table, towering over her with the stench of ale and sweat clinging to his skin. His eyes, gleaming like a wolf's just before the kill, sent a cold jolt through her, freezing her to the spot.

The heat of his breath reached her, carrying with it a threat unspoken but clear. Her hand twitched toward her dagger, but the distance between them was suffocating, his shadow swallowing the flickering light that danced on her trembling hands.

Mary forced herself to breathe, but her chest felt tight, each inhale a battle against the rising dread clawing at her insides.

He dragged his tongue slowly across his lips, the motion deliberate, as if savoring the thought before he even spoke. "Well now," he rasped, his voice thick with mockery, "what business hath a pretty little thing like thee in a den such as this?" His eyes roamed over her, hungry and lingering, appraising her like a butcher eyeing fresh meat, each glance stripping away her defenses.

He leaned in closer, his breath foul as it brushed her skin. "Should I offer thee coin," he sneered, his voice low and taunting, "or dost thou wish me to follow thee into the alley and to seize what I desire by force?" The evil gleam in his eyes flickered with dark amusement, a twisted promise lurking beneath his words. The edges of his lips curled slowly, a grin creeping across his face, not out of humour but out of something far more vile—an unspoken promise of what he intended. It wasn't just a smile; it was the look of a wolf catching the scent of fear, lips parting in satisfaction as if already savoring the conquest.

"Mark my words," he whispered, leaning even closer, his tone chilling, "I shall have mine own way with thee." His eyes glinted like a predator cornering its prey. "Were I in thy stead, I would take the coin I do offer and accept thy fate. Should I be made to seize what I desire by force, thou shalt find it a more grievous affair, indeed." The weight of his threat hung in the air, the cruel intent behind it unmistakable, his gaze pinning her in place, daring her to defy him.

Mary's breath caught in her throat as a harried woman approached, her apron stained from countless meals, the fabric a patchwork of grime and wear. The woman bustled toward her, wooden bowl in hand, steam rising in lazy tendrils that curled into the air. With a swift motion, she set the bowl down with a sharp clatter, the sound echoing in the bustling tavern.

"There thou art, lass," the woman said, her gaze darting towards Draven standing across from Mary, eyes narrowing with warning. "The maiden hath business with THEM!" Her tone was firm, slicing through the ambient noise like a blade. "Even were it not so, take heed of the garments she doth bear!"

She leaned slightly closer, her voice dropping to a conspiratorial whisper as she continued, "Though thou art in Cutthroat Row and may not face the court's judgment here, should the royals take offence, they need but hire swords to see thee done away with."

Draven shifted, discomfort etched across his features as he met the woman's fierce gaze. He forced a smile that didn't quite reach his eyes, an attempt to mask the unease churning within him. "Two more ales, I prithee," he said, his tone casual, though it lacked any genuine warmth.

Yet, beneath the surface, annoyance flickered in his expression, a momentary flash of frustration that he quickly stifled. The very air seemed heavy, fraught with unspoken threats and the unyielding weight of power untamed. He could almost feel the watchful eyes of those more powerful than himself, lurking in the shadows of the tavern, their presence a constant reminder of the precarious position he occupied.

Even as a criminal himself, he understood the hierarchy that governed these streets. A single misstep could bring ruin, and the last thing he desired was to incur the wrath of those above him.

With a dismissive wave of his hand, Draven turned from the woman, his smile fading as he took a step back, the tension between them still crackling in the air. He pivoted on his heel, the scrape of his boots against the wooden floor echoing in the brief silence that followed.

As the weight of Draven's presence lifted, a breath Mary hadn't realized she was holding escaped her lips, a gentle sigh of relief. Mary turned her gaze to the waitress, her eyes wide with gratitude, as if the woman had plucked her from the jaws of a lurking danger.

"Thou hast my thanks," she said, her voice trembling slightly with the remnants of fear. "I knew not what to do." Her words came out in a rush, imbued with the raw emotion of someone who had narrowly escaped a perilous fate.

The maiden nobbed, "They would not take kindly to it, whether thou art a potential customer or one of their spies, for thee to come to harm whilst dealing with them would bring ill upon their name. They would slaughter him and his kin as a lesson." The woman said before moving swiftly from table to table, her arms full of tankards and plates, barely sparing a glance at the customers she served. Mary's heart pounded with uncertainty. Was this woman involved with the Shadow Serpents? The code had been spoken, but no sign of acknowledgment came. Her mind swirled with questions as she stared at the steaming pottage, feeling more adrift than ever in the noisy tavern.

Mary's hand trembled as she picked up the wooden spoon, eyeing the murky pottage with a mix of dread and determination. The surface was dotted with unidentifiable lumps, and a faint, sour odour wafted up, which made her curl her nose in revulsion. Grimacing, she dipped the spoon into the thick, unappetizing stew, lifting it cautiously to her lips. Her stomach churned at the sight, the grayish broth clinging to the spoon like mud.

With a resigned sigh, she braced herself and took a small mouthful, the taste as vile as the smell. The bitter flavor blasted her senses like a sudden storm. The dense liquid seemed to stick to the roof of her mouth, refusing to go down quietly, finally sliding down her throat with a faint grittiness. The aftertaste lingered, acrid and foul, making her gag. Yet she recalled the king's words about its curative powers and, with a deep breath, prepared for another bite, hoping the promised remedy for her hangover was worth the torment.

Mary forced down five reluctant spoonfuls of the pottage, each one a test of her resolve. The stew, thick and unappealing, left a sour tang on her tongue. Each swallow felt like penance, the warm, lumpy liquid settling uneasily in her stomach.

She steeled herself for another bite when movement caught her eye. She froze, spoon hovering mid-air, as a figure emerged from the shadows where daylight mingled with the flickering glow of candles and the hearth's fire. The tavern fell silent, a hush washing over the patrons as Roric Darkmane glided into view. His cloak billowed behind him, a garment most opulent, wrought of the finest fabric and trimmed with fur that whispered of ill-gotten wealth and a rogue's standing. A gold pin in the shape of a coiled snake gleamed at his collar, an emblem that commanded respect and fear in equal measure. She was sure it was the same pin that Lucian Blackthorn had worn that day; surely, this had to mean they were both part of the Shadow Serpents.

Roric slid into the seat across from her, his movements belying the grace that ill-matched his imposing stature. The interplay of daylight and firelight obscured his features, making him both present and hidden, but the air of authority that surrounded him was unmistakable.

An air of secrecy enveloped him, sending a prickle of unease along Mary's skin. She leaned back slightly, instinctively tightening her grip on the hilt of her hidden dagger. The heat radiating from Roric made her pulse quicken, each heartbeat echoing in her ears.

As his gaze didst wander o'er her, he took in how her pallid visage did betray her hangover, the remnants of yesternight's revelry still etched upon her countenance. The table obscured her lower half, but her upper garments, simple and modest, marked her as a maid.

"An old-fashioned sword, sayest thou?" he murmured, leaning closer, his breath warm and unwelcome. "All the old swords be in use," he continued in a low tone, a glimmer of mischief dancing in his eyes. "What sayest thou to a younger blade?" The implication hung in the air, suggesting a less experienced member of the Shadow Serpents—someone perhaps untested, yet still steeped dangerous.

Mary's fingers trembled as she set the spoon down, the clamor of the tavern swallowing the sound. "Ale for a youngling, sayest thou?" she retorted, striving to keep her voice steady. "Speak plain, art thou with the Shadow Serpents?!"

A shadow loomed over her, the flickering candlelight barely illuminating the hard lines of his face. His touch, firm and deliberate, pressed against her wrist, pinning it lightly to the rough wooden table. The grip was not forceful, but it carried a silent warning—a reminder of his control over the moment. The tavern seemed to close in around them, shadows lengthening as tension thickened the air.

Without breaking eye contact, she shifted slightly. Her hand moved under the table, fingers brushing against the dagger strapped to her leg. With deliberate calm, she drew it out and placed it on the table between them, the blade catching the interplay of sunlight filtering through the narrow windows and the flickering glow of the hearth. "With all due respect, I come not empty-handed. I pray thee, attempt not any mischief."

Roric's gaze flicked to the dagger, a faintly amused curl touching his lips as if acknowledging her boldness, however futile. He tilted his head slightly, a smirk tugging at his lips, as if the sight of the blade amused him more than it worried him. The blend of natural light and the tavern's flickering candle glow cast shifting shadows upon his visage, lending his countenance a ghostly and near unreadable quality.

Mary's heart raced, but she kept her face impassive, her fingers lightly resting near the blade. She forced herself to breathe evenly, the cold steel grounding her amidst the tension.

As their eyes locked, the stranger's lazy smile dared her to act, his gaze a blend of humour and disdain, belittling her defiance as mere bravado.

Mary met his gaze unflinchingly, determination etched in her eyes. The world around them faded, leaving only the two of them in a silent standoff.

Her heart thundered against her ribs, but she gripped the table's edge, drawing calm from the solid wood beneath her fingers.

The cacophony of noise in the tavern faded as he let out a laugh, a cruel edge cutting through the din. "Thy petty dagger shall avail thee naught here." His gaze swept over her, noting the chambermaid garments she wore, the faint crests of royalty almost hidden but not escaping his sharp eyes. She didn't belong to Cutthroat Row; her presence was too clean, too cautious. To him, she looked like a maidservant from some noble household, unaccustomed to wielding a blade.

Before Mary could react, his hand shot out like a striking serpent, clamping onto her wrist with the grip of a seasoned warrior. Pain shot up her arm, wrenching a cry from her lips. Her world narrowed to the burning agony radiating from his hold, the tavern's chaos fading into the background.

Her fingers instinctively released the dagger, the blade skidding across the table with a jarring screech that momentarily turned heads, before patrons returned to their drinks and hushed conversations, their indifference palpable.

His grip tightened, a silent command that did crush any flicker of defiance. Mary's heart raced, a cold dread spreading through her veins. "Mark this well, thou didst seek our aid," he hissed, his voice a cold whisper that sent shivers down her spine. "Show me disrespect once more, and thou shalt reckon with fewer fingers."

Slowly, his grip slackened, releasing her wrist with a disconcerting calm that starkly contrasted his aggression. "A younger sword," he said, his tone now disturbingly casual. "'Tis keen and well-proven, fit for any task thou dost require." His sudden shift in demeanor sent a chill down Mary's spine, her mind scrambling to keep up with his changing moods.

Mary yanked her hand back, cradling it close to her chest as the sharp ache pulsed through her wrist. Her fingers brushed over the reddened skin, the faint marks left by his grip stinging like a brand. For a moment, she held it there, close, as if protecting it from further harm. Slowly, she lowered her hand, resting it just above the table's edge, her other hand hovering near the dagger. Mary shifted uneasily upon her seat, the weight of his unwavering gaze pressing heavily upon her. Gathering what courage she could muster, she spoke, her voice quivering as she forced the words out. "I meant no disrespect, good sir. 'Twas before thine arrival that one of those men yonder approached me, and well, let us say his intentions were far from a friendly discourse."

Fear clipped her words short, so they came out staccato—a low, barely audible murmur that revealed the panic she struggled to hide. "I know this place to be naught but peril, and I do ken well thy reputation, which would strike fear into the heart of any." She searched for the right words, her brow furrowing as her mind struggled to recall the details that danced just out of reach.

"Yet I am in search of a man—one with hair of silver, who mayhap holds word of mine sister's recovery." Her heart pounded, the silence that followed amplifying her unease. "Forgive me, I have but only learnt of his name today, and even now as I strive to recall it, I cannot. Luthian Blackmoor? Nay, that is not it. Lucan Darkthorn? Nay, that doth not seem right. Cassian Blackshade?"

A smirk played upon his lips, a glint of calculation in his eyes, as he relished her discomfort. *Lucian Blackthorn?! By the saints, he be no mere blade for hire. Nay, he ranks high amongst the Shadow Serpents, though too flighty to lead them.* "Knowledge is power, and power doth come at a cost," he said, his eyes flicking to her face as if to remind her that nothing is freely given. The silence hung heavy between them, an unspoken demand for coin.

Mary's heart hammered as she fumbled in her pocket for the pouch of coins the king had given her. Her hands shook as she withdrew it and slid it across the table, the clink of metal breaking the tense silence. "I shall convey thy message," he said, his tone devoid of warmth. His promise, though given, felt like a transaction secured by coin, more bound by the clink of silver than by any earnest effort.

He paused, his gaze drifting to her simple chambermaid garments, incongruous with the small sack she had offered. The coins inside jingled softly as he poured them into his hand, their metallic glint starkly out of place for a servant.

Of all the Shadow Serpents she could have named, she asked for Lucian Blackthorn—the most dangerous and costly of them all. His name wasn't one bandied about by common folk. The Serpents were a shadowed secret, known only to nobles and the powerful, their existence veiled in whispers and sealed in blood.

How did a trembling maid, dressed in the garb of a servant, even know of them? And not just any of them—Lucian. It was unthinkable, absurd even, that she would dare utter his name, let alone seek him out.

As he counted the coins, his fingers deftly flipping each piece, he pondered their origin. The shine of the silver suggested wealth far beyond her earnings. Had she overheard her master in whispered conversation, or had someone deliberately provided her with these funds and the knowledge to come and ask for the shadow serpents?

He leaned closer, the shadows deepening about them, and spoke in a low, conspiratorial whisper, "Whom shouldst thou seek should he desire to answer thy request?" The warmth of his breath brushed against her skin, carrying a hint of danger that made her pulse quicken.

Mary hesitated, her heart quivering at the thought of revealing her identity. "Wouldst thou kindly inform him that 'tis the maiden from the fields, who now must dwell in the cottage of ill fate?" The words slipped from her lips, careful and calculated, but inside, dread coiled tighter around her heart.

Roric's brow knit together in thought, his mind swirling as he weighed her words. The prince would not have told her of them, nor would he send a maid to this tavern. The princess, perchance? After all, she hath been missing these many days and likely mingled with the peasants. 'Tis said the princess doth hold her handmaiden as her dearest friend. Yet the women of the royal family know but little of the Shadow Serpents... Perchance the king? "Should the man with silver locks thou speakest of know not thy cryptic message, perchance I may tell him to seek thee at Ravenstone Castle, in the presence of His Majesty, the King?" His voice was steady, but the undercurrent of intrigue sharpened his gaze as he studied her reaction.

Anxiety coursed through her veins like a trapped bird beating its wings, its tremors spilling into her trembling hands. Mary fought to steady her breath, each inhale shallow and shaky. The flickering candlelight cast long, wavering shadows, deepening the oppressive darkness that seemed to close in around her, breathing with a life of its own. She felt an invisible weight around her neck, as if it threatened to pull her under and drag her loved ones down with her.

"The king, say'st thou?" she replied, her voice steadier than she felt, but even she could hear the slight quiver beneath her words.

A glint crept into his eyes, sharp and calculating, as though he'd uncovered a game she wasn't aware she was playing. Leaning back in his chair, he let a smirk settle on his lips, slow and deliberate, like a hunter savoring a cornered prey. He leaned back, his smirk deepening as though the weight of the moment amused him. Every movement carried an unspoken assurance, a quiet claim of dominance that needed no words.

"The aged blade thou seekest is otherwise engaged," he said, rising with an unhurried grace. There was a trace of mockery in his words, though his tone stayed measured. "When he cometh to thy aid, I cannot say, but thy coin shall bear thy message."

He turned, his boots tapping a measured rhythm against the tavern floor, each step drawing more attention to the weight of his words. The noise around them resumed, though muffled, as if the room itself held its breath while he passed. Mary's fingers gripped the edge of the table, her knuckles pale, as the weight of his final words sank in. He hadn't denied her outright, but his answer carried its own warning: nothing in this place came without a price.

The Weary Return

Ye Olde Thistle & Thorn

Chapter Twenty-Three

As the sun climbed higher into the late morning sky, its warmth failed to reach the narrow, cobbled alley behind *Ye Olde Thistle & Thorn*. Shadows clung to the damp stone walls, and the air was thick with the mingling scents of sour ale, wet earth, and decay. The faint din of the marketplace felt distant, like a cruel reminder that life continued apace while they dragged themselves through the mire of regret.

Leofric's boots squelched against the mud-caked stones, each step a slog that sent a dull ache radiating up his legs. His shoulders slumped, and his cloak hung heavy, wet with the morning's chill. He cast a sidelong glance at Robert, who staggered beside him. Pale as death itself, Robert's face gleamed with a thin sheen of sweat, his hollow eyes bloodshot and darting. One hand pressed against his stomach, as though to quiet the storm that churned within.

"By the gods," Robert muttered, his voice ragged and low, "I do believe mine entrails prepare to stage a rebellion."

"Hold thy tongue, and pray they do not," Leofric grumbled. His own throat felt raw, as though the cold air had clawed at it since dawn. Reaching the tavern's service door—a warped and weather-beaten plank barely holding itself together—he gripped the iron handle, fingers stiff and unresponsive. He shoved the door open with a grunt. The hinges screeched loud enough to echo down the alley, a sound sharp enough to make both men wince.

The cold struck them like a blow. The storage room yawned before them, its air thick with dampness and mildew. Barrels and crates lined the wattle and daub walls, their surfaces slick with condensation. Somewhere in the shadows, water dripped in maddening rhythm. The wooden floor beneath their boots creaked faintly, its planks warped from years of damp, but still more forgiving than the unforgiving chill outside. The faint scent of rot clung to the air like a bitter ghost.

Leofric muttered a curse under his breath, the words lost in the oppressive silence. Robert lingered near the doorframe, his breath misting faintly in the frigid air. His grip on the wood seemed less for balance and more to steady himself against the churn of bile in his throat.

"Thou art as pale as a corpse," Leofric said, his tone lacking its usual sting. Exhaustion dulled even his wit.

Robert swallowed hard, his Adam's apple bobbing visibly. "And thou dost look the bearer of mine shovel," he murmured weakly, his lips curling into the ghost of a humourless smirk.

Ahead, the doorway to the hall beckoned, its narrow frame leading into deeper shadow. The faintest flicker of light spilled through, promising warmth that felt impossibly far away. Leofric trudged forward, his boots dragging against the wooden planks, each step echoing faintly in the silence. Robert followed, slower and unsteady.

When they reached the kitchen, the change in temperature was almost cruel. The hearth's low fire radiated a teasing warmth, but it stopped short of banishing the chill that clung to them like a second skin. The room smelled of simmering stew, its faint, savory aroma nearly lost amidst the damp scent of old wood and stale air. Herbs dangled from the beams above, brushing against Leofric's head as he passed.

Leofric dropped heavily onto a bench by the hearth, the worn wood creaking in protest. He hunched forward, elbows digging into his thighs, his hands dragging down his face as though to scrape away the weight of the night. His hair, damp and sticky from sweat, clung to his fingers as he dragged them through it. His breath came in slow, uneven bursts, each exhale tinged with the bitterness of failure.

Robert lingered near the doorway, one hand braced against the wall. His eyes flicked about the room absently, unfocused. His lips parted as though to speak, but no words came. After a moment, he closed them again, his expression grim.

Leofric finally broke the silence, his voice low and rough. "So this is failure, is it? Cold, damp, and sour as spoilt mead."

Robert huffed a hollow laugh, bitter and dry. "Nay, 'tis warm mead and regret, methinks."

Their words hung in the air, swallowed by the stillness of the kitchen. The fire crackled weakly, the stew bubbled faintly, and somewhere deep in the tavern, a door slammed shut. Robert flinched at the sound, his frayed nerves betraying him.

Leofric said nothing more. He merely sat, staring into the embers, waiting for the day to end ere it had truly begun.

Robert staggered to a seat beside him, barely holding himself upright. He clutched his head, the dull thud of a headache pulsing behind his eyes. "I am sorely in want of a draught," he muttered, though the thought of more ale made his stomach turn.

Leofric nodded, not trusting himself to speak. Leofric's gaze dropped to the floor, his thoughts circling back to every path they'd taken, every shadow they'd chased in vain.

Robert, silent beside him, clenched his fists as if trying to grasp something lost in the darkness of the night. Inns, forests, taverns—they'd searched them all and still found no trace of Sophia .

The door to the cooking quarters groaned open, and Henry entered, ready to attend to the food. He cast a glance at the bedraggled pair and shook his head in disbelief. "Thou look'st as though thou'st been dragged through a graveyard," he remarked, his voice sharp with a knowing tone.

"Verily, it doth feel much the same," Robert replied, his voice raw and laden with weariness.

Henry went to the bubbling pot and spooned them a serving of stew with a chunk of bread. The bread, though firm from the previous day, was hearty. The aroma of the food both comforted and overwhelmed their starved senses. Leofric tore into the bread, dipping it into the stew. The warm broth sent a wave of heat coursing through his chilled form.

They ate in silence, each bite heavy, the warmth of the stew doing little to ease the tension etched into their faces. Leofric stared blankly at his bowl, but the gnawing unease in his chest remained, untouched by the meal. Henry lingered nearby, his gaze softening as he watched them. "Adom did say thou wast with Robert last night," he murmured gently. "Fear not, for I am certain she will be found."

Leofric only nodded, his mouth too full to respond. He glanced at Robert, who had slumped against the table, eyes half-closed. The fire crackled softly, the only sound in the otherwise silent cooking quarters. Leofric leaned back, staring at the ceiling beams, each one as worn and tired as he felt. He exhaled slowly, the strain in his shoulders easing with each breath. "Tonight, we resume, after rest," he said softly, his words a fragile promise.

Henry's face twisted into an awkward grimace. "Thy father did seek thee this morning," he said, his voice heavy with hesitation. "He would have thee serve out front this night. Another revelry is to be held to mark the princess's return. I expect there shall be celebration all the week long."

Leofric's lips thinned into a tight line, his eyes narrowing with barely suppressed irritation. Festivities were the last thing he could endure while Noor Winterbourne remained missing. The thought of her out there, frightened and pursued in the shadows, gnawed at him. His grip tightened on the table, knuckles whitening.

"And where is Adom?" he hissed, his voice sharp as a dagger, eyes darting around the cooking quarters.

Henry shifted uneasily, rubbing the back of his neck. "Well, regarding that matter," he began, glancing at the ceiling. "A maiden, who was, uh, greatly enamored with Robert yesterday—she did burst in, most wroth that he had departed without a word." He laughed awkwardly, the sound forced and brittle. "One thing led to another, and Adom and Walter found themselves in, shall we say, an unlooked-for entanglement with the maiden." Henry's eyes darted toward the door to the server's chambers, his cheeks coloring with discomfort. "Before the day's first light, Adom and the maiden took their leave, declaring he would be absent for several days." Henry let out a nervous chuckle, thin and unsure.

He had heard Leofric speak of Noor Winterbourne often, though she had not set foot in the tavern since her father's passing. Her absence had done little to diminish the way Leofric spoke of her, though—always with a wistful edge, as if she were someone set apart from the rest. To him, she was rare, captivating, and altogether unattainable.

Only a few days ago, Leofric had glimpsed her again. That brief encounter had stirred something long buried within him, a hope he could barely name. Yet now, just as he had mustered the resolve to act, she was gone again, leaving him to wrestle with questions he dared not voice aloud.

Leofric's gaze turned icy, his jaw tightening until the muscles in his neck stood out like cords. He stared at the embers in the hearth, the dying glow flickering weakly against the blackened stones. His mind returned to the paths they had walked, the shadows they had followed, each leading nowhere. The frustration inside him churned like a tempest, each fading ember a bitter reminder of his helplessness. The princess's celebration felt like a shackle, chaining him to the mundane duties of the tavern. Each moment spent here was a heartbeat in which Noor's fate hung perilously in the balance—a cruel twist of fate keeping him from the search he longed to resume.

He reached for a piece of stale bread, tearing into it with his teeth, his grip tightening as if the act itself could release the anger coiled inside him. A growl rumbled low in his throat. With his mouth still half-full, he barked, "Inform my father that I am aiding Robert Winterbourne in the search for his sister!" His eyes blazed with determination, each word striking the air like iron against stone.

Robert stirred from his slumped position, eyes fluttering open with the sluggishness of one torn from deep sleep. "Sister?" he muttered, the word slipping from his lips, fragmented and uncertain. His face twisted in confusion, as though his weary mind were still tangled in dreams and shadows, unsure if Leofric's words were real or a figment of his troubled thoughts.

The air thickened with silence. Leofric's jaw clenched, and a flicker of dread crossed his eyes. Henry shifted uneasily on his feet, his gaze locking with Leofric's. A silent exchange of alarm passed between them, the tension coiling between them like a serpent ready to strike.

Henry's voice came out slow and measured, each word a cautious step over a minefield. "Pray tell, who hast thou been searching for, if not Noor?"

Robert's mind whirled with questions, each thought spinning like leaves caught in a violent storm. Had he, in his drunken haze, uttered Noor's name by mistake instead of Sophia's? Or was there something deeper, a reason Leofric was seeking Noor? His heart raced, doubt clawing at him, beads of cold sweat forming on his brow. "I've been searching for a maiden to whom I am closely bound," he muttered, his gaze flickering between Leofric and Henry, desperation gleaming in his eyes like a fragile candle in a howling wind.

Leofric and Henry exchanged bewildered glances, their brows knitting in confusion. They leaned closer, concern clear in their eyes, their questions sharp and urgent. "When didst thou last set eyes upon Noor?"

Robert's brow knit as he struggled to piece together the scattered fragments of memory. The truth struck him—he hadn't seen Noor in days. The last time he'd crossed her path was at the cottage, standing where the sunlight fell harsh against her face, and then again that evening when she and Sophia had returned from the market.

His thoughts had been elsewhere, tangled in the weight of everything he couldn't bring himself to say to Sophia.

He tried to recall more, but the details blurred together. Noor's movements that night had been brisk and efficient, her words few and biting, as though she were barely tolerating the company of others. He had been too distracted, too consumed by Sophia, to notice much else. He hadn't questioned Noor's sharpness or wondered at her quiet; she had always been difficult to read, and he had been too wrapped up in his own mind to see anything unusual.

"Why?" he whispered, the word barely escaping his lips. *Why dost thou think Noor is missing?* His stomach churned as doubt crept in, his thoughts racing with questions he hadn't asked until now. *Where hast Noor gone? How hath I not noticed her absence ere now? Why doth it take mine own friend to point it out to me?*

Leofric's face contorted in horror, the colour draining from his cheeks. A nauseating churn twisted in his stomach, dread swirling through him. *If Robert knew not of Noor's absence, might he have seen her last? Perchance she is not missing at all, but hath merely chosen to stand me up?* The thought gnawed at him, but a darker certainty settled in his gut like a lead weight: Robert's ignorance spoke volumes.

Leofric cast a desperate glance at Henry, eyes wide with a silent plea, hoping he might bear the burden of the terrible news. Henry's eyes widened in return, a sharp flicker of refusal flashing in them, a silent defiance that made it clear he would not carry this weight.

In that unbearable moment of tension, Robert's patience snapped. His hand flew to the hilt of his dagger, the leather-wrapped grip firm beneath his fingers. The hearth's flames cast shifting light across the quarters, the warmth doing little to soften the sharp edge of his voice. "Speak forth now, or I shall draw my blade!" he barked, his voice a growl of frustration and fear, his eyes flashing with a fury that bordered on madness.

The quarters fell into a hushed stillness. Robert's demand hung heavy in the air, a palpable force that pressed down on Leofric and Henry. The midday light filtering through the narrow shutters mingled with the flickering glow of the hearth, stretching long, ominous shapes onto the walls as the young men stared each other down, each breath laden with the tension of unspoken truths.

Leofric's eyes widened, confusion swirling in their depths. His lips parted, but the words faltered, caught on the edge of a precipice. "Dost thou mean to tell me that all my inquiries about Noor did not alarm thee?" he snapped, disbelief thick in his voice. He had assumed Robert knew of her disappearance, thinking their inquiries were shared concerns for her. But now, a harsh truth did smite him, leaving his wits to falter and reel.

Robert's grip tightened on the dagger hilt, and with a deliberate pull, the cold steel slipped free of its leather sheath with a faint, ominous hiss. The weariness that had dulled his movements vanished, replaced by sharp, urgent energy. "Any with eyes could plainly see that thou hast ever held a tender regard for my sister!" he snapped, his eyes blazing with a mixture of anger and fear. "I thought thou wast asking about her because thou wert finally going to court her!"

His breath came in ragged gasps, chest heaving under the weight of realisation. Fear clutched at his heart, freezing him in place as though an icy hand gripped his lungs. "I shall not ask thee again," Robert hissed, the dagger's tip gleaming under the shifting light. "Doth she fare well?" His gaze locked onto Leofric, demanding an answer, dread written plainly across his face, a plea for the truth that chilled the cooking quarters.

Leofric shook his head, disbelief hardening his features. "Sheathe thy blade! I am no foe, but a friend!" he barked, his voice cutting through the thick air. They had known each other since boyhood, and never before had there been cause to draw weapons. "I have but acted in good faith evermore." Leofric's tone softened as he continued, "Noor did come to Ye Olde Thistle & Thorn. She believed someone followed her, though the tavern was full, and she knew not who it might be." He gestured toward the service entrance. "She did slip out yonder way, hopin' to shake off whosoever might've been followin' her. She did not return. I have gone to Thornbriar Cottage a few times, yet neither thee nor Noor, nor anyone else, hath answered the door."

His voice trembled as his gaze met Robert's. "I deserve not the threat of thy dagger. If thou dost not return it this instant, I shall have no choice but to act!"

Robert's hand clenched tighter around the dagger. Anger and confusion surged within him, a whirlwind of emotions he could barely contain. His own sister, Noor, had been in danger while he was preoccupied with the fruitless search for Sophia. Guilt knotted in his chest, the image of Noor, determined and unshaken, facing whatever threat had followed her burned into his mind. His heart pounded in his ears, the dagger trembling in his hand.

The oppressive silence stretched until Henry stepped forward, breaking the tension. "Prithee, allow me to fetch thee a drink!" he said, his voice a calm anchor in the storm.

Robert's grip on the dagger loosened. He glanced at Leofric, the fire in his eyes dimming to a flicker of desperation. Slowly, with a shuddering breath, he lowered the blade. The tension in the cooking quarters eased as he sank onto the bench, the weight of his sister's fate settling heavily on his shoulders.

Robert slumped, the dagger now lying forgotten in his lap. The light from the hearth flickered across his face, highlighting the exhaustion in his eyes. The responsibility of protecting his sister felt like a burden too great, a reminder of all the ways he had failed since their father's death.

He turned to Leofric, his voice a hoarse whisper. "Forgive me, my friend. My anger was never with thee, but with myself." Each word came heavy with regret. His attempt to hide his shame had crumbled, leaving him raw and exposed.

Leofric waved a hand dismissively, a gesture of forgiveness already given. "It hath been a long and gruelling night, Robert, and with all thou hast endured, thy response is well understood." he said, taking another bite of bread, chewing thoughtfully. As he chewed, his thoughts wandered, reflecting on the weight that Robert bore. Leofric had never tasted the bitter pangs of true loss. He couldn't fathom the depth of Robert's sorrow, who must have carried the heavy burden of his parents' passing every single day. It wasn't just the tragedy of their deaths, but the crumbling of the life and security that his father's presence had once guaranteed.

The responsibility that had fallen upon Robert's shoulders after his father's death was a mantle Leofric could only imagine.

The bread in his mouth seemed tasteless, the warmth of the hearth too distant to chase away the chill of the reality they faced. Leofric knew that no words of comfort could truly ease the pain that Robert felt. The emptiness left by such losses was a void that no friend, no matter how loyal, could ever hope to fill.

As the silence stretched, Robert's thoughts began to drift, sinking into the mire of self-reproach and exhaustion. His mind, clouded by fatigue, wandered to Sophia. Could the tangled threads of Sophia's predicament be somehow knotted with Noor's sudden disappearance? An uneasy question settled in his mind, a gnawing doubt that made his thoughts sluggish and amorphous, refusing to coalesce into clarity, leaving him feeling utterly adrift and lost.

Leofric shifted uneasily, his shoulders tensing with the weight of unspoken thoughts. He recalled their conversation from the previous night, realizing now they had been speaking of different people. His face clouded over, a crease etching itself between his eyebrows as he pitched forward, voice heavy with unease. "Does Noor have any foes?" he asked, the question hanging heavily in the air. "Or... dost thou know where she might seek refuge, a place to hide herself away?"

In Robert's mind, the forest loomed, a dark and forbidding expanse, its shadows a bitter reminder of the long, fruitless night spent searching for Sophia. He envisioned the forest clearly in his mind's eye, a place where he and Noor had found solace many times, beneath the ancient canopy, where trees stood tall like sentinels, whispering secrets to those who sought their shelter. The weight of this realisation pressed down on him, a cold stone in his chest, knowing he had trodden paths Noor herself might have chosen for refuge. The image haunted him, the thought that they might have brushed past her hiding place, mere moments separating their search from finding her.

As the vision of the forest consumed his thoughts, doubt crept in like a chilling fog. If Sophia's disappearance had no connection to Noor's, then who could wish harm upon his sister? He heard Noor's fierce spirit and sharp tongue flashing in his mind, her defiance having made enemies among those they had crossed in their struggle to survive. Many days, they had taken what they needed to fend off hunger and cold, leaving behind angry whispers and dark glances from those they had wronged.

The notion that Noor might have stolen something of great value gnawed at him, the thought twisting in his gut. Perhaps, in his search for Sophia, he had overlooked the very clues that would lead them to Noor. The vision of each darkened hollow and mossy retreat now seemed to echo with the missed chance to find her. The imagined silence of the forest felt heavy and oppressive, filling him with the fear that Noor, in seeking sanctuary, had instead fallen into unseen dangers, her foes lurking where they least expected.

"We hath yet to search Mudlark Alley, nor its market." Robert said, his voice heavy with realisation. He thought of Mary's assurance, the way she had mentioned that another family had taken residence in their old mud hut. His mind flickered through images of the faces they had come to know over the past year, each one a potential ally or a source of news. The cramped alleyways, teeming with the hum of market chatter and the shuffle of feet, felt like unturned stones, brimming with possibilities and answers yet to be uncovered.

Leofric's face blanched at the mere mention of Mudlark Alley, his eyes widening with a flicker of dread. Images of its squalid lanes and shadowy corners swam in Leofric's mind—a place where the stench of decay mingled with the filth of forgotten souls, where the dead lay unclaimed in the streets for days, even weeks. He knew it as a realm of destitution beyond imagination. Mudlark Alley was a wretched place, where hope went to die.

"Mudlark Alley... I am not well-acquainted with it. Perchance it is best thou goest alone." Leofric stammered, his voice thick with palpable dread. As he spoke, Henry approached, teetering under the weight of three chalices of Thistle Ale, each one threatening to spill its amber contents with every tremor of his hand. Drops of ale traced dark trails down the sides, a prelude to the chaos that might ensue.

Leofric sprang forward, his movements sharp and purposeful. With a steady hand, he relieved Henry of two of the chalices, nodding his thanks. "I am much obliged." he murmured, his voice regaining composure as he turned towards the heavy oak table. He placed one of the chalices in front of Robert, the chalice landing with a solid thud on the worn wood, echoing the weight of the unspoken words between them.

Leofric paused, his brow furrowing as he wrestled with the question that clung to the silence like a shadow. At last, he broke the stillness, his voice soft and hesitant. "Pray thee, before we proceed... was it truly so plain that I did bear affection for thy sister?" He looked at Robert, his eyes clouded with confusion, troubled by the realisation that his affection had been laid bare for all to see.

For the first time in what felt like an age, Robert's face broke into a smile, a laugh bubbling up from deep within as if Leofric had just uttered a jest. He picked up the chalice, the cool metal pressing against his palm, and took a hearty sip, his eyes twinkling as he glanced at Henry, who was also watching with an amused expression.

"Oh, Leofric," Robert said, setting the chalice back on the table with a soft clink. "Whilst we were but lads, anon as Noor didst enter the tavern, thine gaze wouldst dart to her like an arrow to its mark. Thou wouldst speak of naught else, thy words turning ever to her, thine eyes following her every move. Thou wouldst prattle on about her, seeking any excuse to hold her attention." Though he jested, there was a ring of truth in his voice.

Henry, who hadn't known them as children but had seen enough since he began serving at the inn, nodded with a knowing smile. "Robert speaks true," he said, his voice carrying the weight of many observed moments. "It has ever been plain to see, your fondness for Noor. You've scarce a word of sense for anyone else when she's near."

Leofric's cheeks flushed, a shade deeper than the Thistle Ale, as the weight of their words settled upon him. The candour in their jest revealed a truth he had scarcely admitted to himself, and the warmth of their laughter echoed softly through the quarters, a rare moment of levity amidst the shadows of worry that loomed over them.

He tightened his grip on the chalice, trying to steady the slight tremor in his hands. His gaze flickered between Robert and Henry, shame in his eyes. The warmth of the cooking quarters, mingled with the earthy scent of stale bread and the lingering smoke from the hearth, seemed to press in on him, amplifying his discomfort.

"Was it plain to Noor?" he asked, his voice barely rising above a whisper, each word heavy with the burden of his unspoken feelings. "Did she speak of me?" The question lingered in the air, thick with unspoken tension, as Leofric's eyes darted from Robert to Henry and back, searching their faces for any hint of an answer.

Leofric's heart pounded in his chest, each beat echoing like a distant drum, the vulnerability of his inquiry leaving him feeling exposed. The wooden oak table, worn and scarred by years of use, stood between them like a silent witness to his raw admission, awaiting a response that could either offer solace or deepen his shame.

Robert shrugged his shoulders, the weariness etched into his face and the lingering fog of a hangover dulling his eyes. He ran a hand through his disheveled hair, a sigh escaping his lips as he thought of his sister. His voice came out rough, the fatigue evident. "If she were aware of thy feelings, she ne'er did speak of them to me." "Were I thee, I would not take it to heart, for she is not much inclined to show her feelings, nor her love." he murmured, each word heavy with the weight of sorrow and regret.

His bloodshot and weary eyes gleamed with a hint of mischief as he glanced at Leofric. "Dost thou remember," he said, lifting the chalice once more, "When did she draw her bow and arrow upon thee, for naming her the fairest maiden of them all?"

A ghost of a laugh trembled on his lips, a fleeting echo of simpler times brimming with youthful fondness. The memory was vivid—Noor's fierce eyes narrowing, cheeks flushed with indignation, as she notched the arrow and drew the string tight. Her hands, steady despite her fury, betrayed not a single tremor. The sheer panic that had gripped Leofric's face was priceless, Noor's bowstring taut and ready to loose its arrow.

Leofric's eyes widened for a heartbeat, a flush of colour rising to his cheeks as the memory flared vividly in his mind. His grip tightened around the chalice, knuckles blanching with a newfound intensity, reflecting the tumult of emotions swirling within—a mix of admiration and unease. His face relaxed, the deep creases smoothing as a gentle smile spread, infusing his eyes with a warm, comforting light. In that fleeting instant, his expression transformed, casting a glow of quiet compassion that seemed to ease the air in the quarters.

"Dost thou recall the time when two knaves brought trouble to your father?" Leofric asked, his voice lightening with the humour of the memory. "A mere nod between thee and Noor, and before thy father could intervene, you both were upon them, disarming them ere they could draw breath. There thou stood, their own daggers pressed to their loins, and not a soul dared to intervene."

A soft chuckle escaped Robert, his eyes brightening with the recollection. The tension in his shoulders eased, a smirk playing on his lips as the weariness momentarily lifted, replaced by a glimmer of youthful mischief.

Henry's eyes widened in astonishment, his mouth agape as he turned to Robert. "Is that true?"

Both Leofric and Robert shaking their head with a bemused smile, Leofric continued, recounting a few more tales of Robert and Noor's daring exploits, each story more audacious than the last. The cooking quarters filled with a warmth that seemed to chase away the lingering shadows of worry, the flickering hearth casting a comforting glow on their faces.

"Aye, she is quite the spirit," Leofric said, his voice now tinged with a quiet pride that overshadowed his initial surprise. A soft breath escaped his lips, his demeanor shifting from amused to resolute. The earlier warmth of his smile was replaced by a steadfast certainty, a fierce commitment lighting his features. "I do fret, yet knowing her, I am assured she shall fare well." he continued, his tone steady and unwavering, the confidence in her strength clear in every word.

With a slow, unsteady movement, Robert pushed himself up from the bench, his limbs heavy as if burdened by more than just the night's weariness. In a faltering movement, he slumped forward, his hands instinctively reaching out to grasp the table's edge, the sole thing holding him together. The dark circles under his eyes told of sleepless nights and a restless mind.

He glanced at Leofric, his gaze tired and distant. "I shall seek her once more in Mudlark Alley." he said, the words rolling off his tongue with the reluctant determination of a young man resigned to his task. "Upon finding her, I will bring thee word." His voice was low, almost a whisper, as if the very thought of his quest drained the last of his energy.

Without waiting for a reply, Robert turned towards the door, his steps slow and heavy, each footfall echoing the exhaustion that weighed down his spirit.

Leofric watched Robert's weary form retreat towards the door, each of his friend's heavy footfalls echoing through the quarters like a mournful toll. Determination etched itself onto his face like a bold scar, his features bunching up in worry as he inhaled sharply. His heart, pounding with unyielding fervor, refused to let the night's despair settle into defeat.

As Robert reached the threshold, his hand resting on the worn wood of the door, he paused, caught by the intensity in Leofric's voice. Leofric clenched his fists, knuckles whitening with tension. His chest rose and fell with quickened breaths, each one stoking the fire of resolve in his heart. "I shall not yield." he murmured, his voice scarcely more than a growl in the back of his throat, yet filled with a vow that resonated with Robert. "The Priest and then the Town Watch," he declared, his voice growing stronger, as if speaking the names aloud could summon their aid.

Robert, half-turned in the doorway, met Leofric's gaze. His tired eyes widened slightly, absorbing the intensity of Leofric's determination. A flicker of hope crossed Robert's face, mingling with his exhaustion. The air was thick with unspoken understanding as he stood beside the door, a steadfast companion in the darkness, their united front a formidable defense against the uncertainties that lay ahead.

Turning abruptly, Leofric fixed his gaze on Henry, the flicker of desperation glinting in his eyes like a smoldering ember. "Henry, dost thou know of a tracker, or any other soul who might aid us in this dark hour?" The question hung heavy in the air, thick with the unspoken urgency that tightened Leofric's grip on hope, like a drowning man clinging to a piece of driftwood amidst a storm.

Henry, taken aback by the intensity in Leofric's voice, swallowed hard. His face was a map of uncertainty, with the hearth's flickering light etching lines of concern that deepened with every heartbeat. "I—aye, I may know a man," he stammered, his voice trembling as he spoke. "Cedric the Huntsman... he's the best tracker in these parts. If anyone can find her, 'tis he."

Leofric nodded curtly, the lines of worry etched deep into his brow momentarily easing as a flicker of hope kindled within him. The determination in his eyes seemed to burn brighter, a silent promise that no stone would be left unturned in their search.

Robert, hearing the name and recognizing the gravity of the situation, straightened slightly. "Cedric..." he echoed; his voice filled with the faintest hint of renewed strength. With a resolute nod, Robert turned back towards the door, ready to step into the unknown with the unyielding spirit of a knight charging into battle.

<u>Rosewood Hall on Gentry Lane</u>
<u>Robert Winterbourne</u> Several
days hence...
<u>Chapter Twenty-Four</u>

Several days had passed since Henry enlisted the help of Cedric the Huntsman, while Leofric sought counsel from the Priest and the Town Watch, and Robert scoured Mudlark Alley to no avail. Noor's prolonged absence was unsettling and unlike her. As hope began to fade, Robert decided to visit the Ashbourne family, the name Sophia had claimed as her own, still unaware of her deception.

At the break of dawn, with the first rays of sunlight illuminating the sky, Robert stood before the imposing gates of Rosewood Hall on Gentry Lane. The Hall, a testament to opulence with its intricate stonework and lush gardens, held little interest for him. His mind was set on finding one of the maids, a young woman he and Leofric had spotted during their search for Noor and Sophia.

The iron gates of Rosewood Hall, entwined with curling ivy and weathered by time, stood slightly ajar, their ancient hinges creaking gently as a breeze whispered through. Robert, draped in a worn cloak, lingered just outside, his eyes keen and intense as he surveyed the grand manor. The noble family remained in their slumber, the wooden shutters of their windows tightly closed to keep out the chill of the night, while the servants, having been awake for hours, attended to their morning duties with quiet efficiency.

Despite the fatigue etched in his eyes, Robert's sharp mind remained vigilant. Known among the privileged as a scavenger, he was adept at reclaiming what others discarded. This reputation afforded him a cloak of invisibility, his presence seldom questioned by those who mattered.
He observed the maids as they moved about with practiced diligence, their white caps bobbing as they fetched water and tended to the day's early tasks. One maid, in particular, had caught his eye a few days prior during a previous visit. Today, she moved with purpose, carrying a heavy bucket of water towards the garden's fountain.

Robert took a deep breath, and as the gates creaked open a little more with the morning breeze, he slipped inside. He strolled along the cobblestone path with the practiced ease of one who belonged, keeping to the shadows cast by the garden's ancient oaks. The scent of damp earth and dew-laden flowers hung in the crisp air, and he advanced casually, blending seamlessly with the morning's quiet bustle. He let his gaze wander, but it was the maid who snagged his attention, her quiet presence commanding his focus like an unheard whisper. She continued her routine, seemingly unperturbed, setting down the bucket to rest for a moment. Robert approached her as if he were meant to be there, moving among the garden's statues and hedges with a natural familiarity.

Her eyes widened briefly in surprise when she saw him, but then a flicker of recognition softened her expression. Robert raised a hand in a friendly gesture, masking his intentions behind a facade of normalcy. The maid blinked, her initial surprise giving way to a tentative smile as she resumed her task. In the stillness of the early morning, amidst the fragrant blooms and wet grass, Robert spoke softly, his voice carrying the casual tone of everyday conversation. "Good morrow. Needest thou assistance with yon burden?" he inquired, gesturing toward the bucket. The maid's eyes darted away, catching the manor's elegant lines before snapping back to his face, her expression a tightly wound puzzle. She nodded, a slight relief visible in her stance.

"Dost mine eyes deceive me?" she asked with a playful smirk, as if recalling a shared moment of intimacy that he could not place. Robert, masking his confusion, played along, though he struggled to remember any formal meeting with her. "'Tis a pleasure to see thee once more," he offered, his voice laced with feigned confidence.

A joyful gleam sparkled in the maid's eyes as her lips curved upward, releasing a soft, carefree chuckle. "I have not seen thee since the Harvest Festival," she said, her voice light and cheerful. "We danced until mine feet could bear no more. Methinks I have glimpsed thee oft about, but did not wish to intrude. We had much merriment and perhaps a bit too much ale."

Robert's mind raced, trying to piece together the fragments of her recollection. He did not remember the festival or dancing with her, yet he maintained his guise, nodding as if the memory were shared. He spoke with a feigned ease, "Aye, those were joyous times indeed. I am gladdened to see thee again, despite the burdens of the day."

The maid laughed again, the sound clear and genuine. "The burdens are lighter for the company, good sir," she said warmly. Robert bent down to pick up her bucket, lifting it with a slight grunt as they began to walk. "I knew not that you served the Ashbourne family. Pray, tell me, what is it like to serve them?" he asked, his tone light yet curious.

The maid's eyes flicked briefly to the manor, a shadow crossing her face. "The lady o' the house be a hard one to please." She said, her voice dropping to a more hushed tone. "Lord Ashbourne is seldom here, always gallivanting around Briarwood, so he is little bother. One of the maidens is of age now and will soon no longer require a governess."

Robert nodded thoughtfully, hiding his deeper thoughts behind a mask of polite interest. "Another household informed me that Lady Sophia Ashbourne is to court and marry soon. How has she been?" He tried to keep his voice steady, though each word felt like a dagger to his heart.

The maid stopped, her brow furrowing in confusion. "They must be mistaken, good sir. There is no Sophia Ashbourne. All the Ashbourne maidens are already betrothed, and have been since birth." Shock ripped through Robert, the words striking him like a sudden chill. His breath faltered, and his eyes, though outwardly steady, revealed an internal storm. He forced a smile, a fragile mask that threatened to crack under the strain. "It seems I have been misinformed. Pray, pardon my ignorance."

By this point, they had reached the doors that the maid had been heading towards. Robert handed the bucket back to her, the weight of his thoughts far heavier than the burden he had carried.
    The maid turned to him with a grateful nod. "Thy help hath been much appreciated, good sir." She paused, her gaze lingering on the door, a silent plea for assistance. Robert stepped forward and opened it, the hinges groaning in protest.

"If there be any cast-offs or discarded wares, thou wilt find them in the estate's outbuildings," she said, inclining her head towards a distant structure, its silhouette stark against the morning light. Robert's eyes followed her gesture, the outline of the outbuilding hazy in the dawn's mist.

As he turned back to her, his expression turned quizzical, the furrows on his forehead like tiny fault lines revealing the turmoil beneath. "I have heard tell that one of the maidens hath been missing. I was uncertain of which household it pertaineth. I hear she hath returned. Might it be of thine?"

The maid's face clouded with a fleeting shadow of unease, her eyes shifting before she composed herself. "Nay, good sir. No maiden hath been missing from this household," she replied, her voice steady though her eyes flickered with a hint of anxiety. "Perchance thou art misinformed." She dipped her head slightly in a curtsey, turning towards the door.

Robert stepped away from the door, his feet moving as if on their own towards the outbuildings, the path blurring beneath his ripped boots. Every step felt like a gamble, his mind a whirlwind of what-ifs and maybes. Had Sophia spun a deceitful web, or was the maid hiding the truth? He cast a longing glance back towards the manor, hoping the maid would emerge, chase after him, and offer a different answer. But the door remained closed, and she, burdened with her tasks, did not come.

The morning air bit at his cheeks, doing little to clear his foggy thoughts. A pressing discomfort built in his chest, fueled by the thoughts that hung unspoken. In the face of growing uncertainty, the garden's bright hues seemed to curl up and wither, like a leaf shrinking from the sun, leaving behind a dull, muted atmosphere. Why would Sophia lie? What reason had the maid to deceive him?

Ahead, the outbuilding stood as a dark shape against the dawn's light. Noor, his twin, and Sophia, both entangled in this mess. He felt adrift, a small boat on a sea of confusion, each stroke failing to bring clarity.

With a heavy sigh, Robert pressed on, his heart aching with every step. The promise of answers felt like dust in his hands, leaving him with only the cold weight of doubt and the fear that the truth was slipping away. Desperation gripped him, a longing to storm Rosewood Hall, to demand the truth, to find his sister Noor and unravel the lies. Yet his gut told him the maid had spoken honestly; he had been blind to Sophia's deceit.

Every step toward the outbuilding was like a march into uncertainty, the hope of finding discarded clues growing dim. The path beneath his feet blurred, the surroundings mere shadows to his inner turmoil. He had sought clarity but found himself lost in doubt. As the outbuilding's shadow crept closer, a sense of unease settled in, like a sinister hand on his shoulder.

Robert's heart was heavy with realisation, each step deeper into the unknown stinging with the bite of betrayal. The promise of truth had turned to ash in his mouth, and he trudged forward, a man lost in a sea of uncertainty, the outbuilding a mere waypoint on a path to answers that seemed ever more elusive.

The Wretched and the Wicked

Cutthroat Row, Agathe and Lucian

Agathe's fingers skimmed the ridges of the scroll, her touch deft despite the gnarled shape of her hands. The raised markings formed words that only her fingers could decipher—a clever contrivance she had commissioned long ago, paid for with coin coaxed from gullible fools who dared to cross her threshold.

Within her hut, every detail was a deception wrought with care. Shelves bowed beneath dried herbs and knotted charms, their presence more for spectacle than purpose. Bronze bowls, blackened with soot, spoke of countless brews never made, while bundles of sticks dangled from the rafters, feigning arcane significance. It was a stage, nothing more. She played the witch well—had done so for years—and though it brought her little wealth, it had granted her a measure of comfort in her old age.

Her patched wool and linen garments hung loosely from her crooked frame, each stitch deliberately uneven to look hastily mended. A tattered shawl, stained with ash, draped over her hunched shoulders, the draft creeping under the warped door set the loose threads of her skirts swaying. Let them think her destitute—it served her well.

Her fingers stilled on the scroll, hovering as something unfamiliar threaded through the air. A sharp tang prickled her senses, distinct against the smoky warmth of the hut. Leather, well-worn and oiled. Steel, clean yet metallic. And beneath it, an elusive scent—dry, like sunbaked stone.

Her breath hitched as the sharp scent pricked her senses. A dry chuckle rasped from her throat, her lips curling in faint amusement. "Hmm. A serpent slithers in silence, yet silence hath a scent."

Stillness followed, deliberate and heavy. She might have doubted herself if not for the subtle disruption of the air—barely perceptible, but there. He was close, not yet close enough to strike.

Agathe leaned back in her chair, her wheezing breath rasping softly in the gloom. "Thou dost not creak, stranger," she rasped, her voice coarse as burlap sacks. "But neither art thou invisible."

No reply came. Her sightless eyes stared unblinking, opaque but unsettlingly aware, as though she could see far beyond the confines of the hut.

"Aye," she murmured, amusement thick in her tone. "Well-oiled leather, cold steel, and a shadow that clings like death. None in this den of thieves bears such a scent unless they've means to pay—or to kill. So, which art thou? A coin bearer or a blade wielder?"

The faintest shift reached her—a soft exhale, controlled but unmistakable to trained ears. Agathe tilted her head, the gnarled fingers that had stilled now drumming lightly against the scroll.

"Lucian Blackthorn," she said, the name rolling off her tongue with a dry, bitter amusement. "Still slithering through shadows, I see. Thou tread'st softly, yet thy reputation doth thunder louder."

A voice emerged from the darkness, low and sharp, its edge as dangerous as any blade. "Agathe. I had thought to find thee dead by now, yet here thou art, cursing my name."

Her laugh was dry and hoarse, rattling faintly in her chest. "Dead? Nay, serpent. Not yet. The blind learn to see what others cannot, and I see thee clear enough. Thy scent betrays thee as ever—steel, leather, and ambition steeped in blood." She gestured absently to the door, though her milky eyes remained fixed ahead. "Tell me, hast thou come for business or blood this time?"

Lucian stepped closer, his boots whispering against the floorboards. "Perhaps both," he said, a faint edge creeping into his flat tone. "I heard tell thou served the prince. For what purpose did he bid thee?"

Agathe's fingers tightened around the scroll, the parchment crinkling softly under her touch. She set it aside with care, her hands trembling slightly as they pulled away. Wheezing softly, she pushed herself to her feet, shuffling toward the clay pot hanging over the fire. Each step was slow, her bare feet rasping against the floorboards as though mapping the familiar path.

The firelight caught the gnarled shape of her hands as she reached for the wooden spoon resting on the hearth. Her thin fingers closed around it, knuckles sharp beneath her pale skin. With a quiet grimace, she grasped the clay cup from the hearth's ledge and poured the dark tea. Steam curled lazily upward as the liquid splashed softly into the cup.

"His Highness sought a charm to shield him from spirits," she said, her voice roughened by strain. "He doth fear the maiden he left to perish in the forest." Straightening slightly, she drew warmth from the clay cup, her bony fingers tightening around it. "He was searching for thee. Yet the other Shadow Serpents knew not where thou wert."

Her lips twisted faintly, her unseeing gaze fixed on the fire. "Curious, is it not? Were he but to call upon the Shadow Serpents, one would think he'd have summoned them ere the stabbing of the maiden."

Agathe turned, her slow steps deliberate. She set the cup before him, her fingers briefly skimming the rim to ensure it was within his reach. Her breath wheezed faintly, filling the room like an old bellows winding down. Lowering herself into her chair, she exhaled, the act draining what little strength she had left. Her gnarled hands folded in her lap, her silence deliberate—a calculated pause to draw him in.

Lucian moved with practiced ease, his boots barely brushing the floor. Agathe tilted her head, tracking the faint creak of leather and the subtle displacement of air as he approached. His presence claimed the space effortlessly, quiet confidence woven into every movement. The scrape of wood against the floor told her he had seated himself, his cloak settling with a faint rustle.

His gloved hand closed around the cup, the faint creak of leather accompanying the motion. The earthy, faintly bitter scent of the tea wafted between them as he took a deliberate sip. Though she could not see him, she felt his ease in her presence, the weight of his body settling into the chair like a man accustomed to command.

"Speak not of this to a soul," he said finally, his voice low and measured, "but I am in the service of Lord Reginald Hawkecliff. He hath sent me to slay the suitors of Princess Shorwynne of Eldoria. It seemeth he desireth her for his bride."

His words hung in the air. Agathe tilted her head, a faint smirk curling her lips. Her fingers tapped lightly on the edge of the table, the rhythm uneven as if weighing her response. A dry hum rasped from her throat.

"Alas, poor Princess Shorwynne," she murmured, her voice thick with wry amusement. Her milky eyes stared blankly at the fire, her expression tightening as she considered his words. "I hear many tales of Lord Reginald Hawkecliff." Her fingers curled around the worn wood of her chair, steadying herself. "Is he not more than capable of slaying her suitors himself?"

Lucian leaned back slightly, the faint creak of the chair marking his movement. His gloved fingers brushed the table lightly, the sound calm and calculated. "If he doth desire her hand in marriage," he said at last, his tone smooth but edged, "he must needs avoid any appearance of involvement in the slaying of her suitors."

The cup touched the table with a soft clink as he set it down, his movements precise but unhurried. The faint metallic chime of his concealed weapons shifting reached her ears, a sound so subtle most would have missed it. "Ah, hag, prithee, tell me of the maiden that the prince left to rot in the forest."

Agathe's unseeing gaze shifted slightly, her head tilting as though attuned to something beyond the hut. Her breath rasped in rhythm with the faint crackle of the fire, her fingers tracing a slow, deliberate pattern on the frayed edge of her shawl. "If mine memory serves," she said at last, her voice trailing like smoke, "the maiden's name be Noor Winterbourne..."

Her words lingered, unfinished, her brow furrowing as if in deep thought.

Across from her, Lucian shifted, the scuff of leather breaking the quiet. His gloved finger tapped the table once, the sound sharp and deliberate. His dark eyes narrowed, his lips pressing into a thin line as though restraining some inner irritation. "The prince," he said, his tone brittle with disdain, "a moron. A fool, he is."

The words hung between them, heavy with disdain, but Agathe remained still, the faint wheeze of her breath filling the silence like a distant echo. "Know her, dost thou?" she rasped, her voice low and deliberate, as if drawing out a truth already half-known.

Lucian's jaw tightened, his hand brushing the hilt of the dagger hidden beneath his cloak. His response came not in words but in the faint crease at his brow, his posture straightening slightly.

"Her name be Noor Winterbourne," he said finally, his tone clipped, each syllable weighted with displeasure. His voice carried a faint edge, each word clipped with displeasure, his disdain unyielding. His fingers tapped the table again, slow and deliberate, as though lost in thought.

"She would have been the next to strike fear as a Shadow Serpent," he admitted, his lips twitching faintly.

His voice shifted again, gaining an almost reflective cadence, the gruffness replaced by something nearly reverent. "Oh, Agathe," he murmured, leaning forward slightly as though confiding a rare truth. "She was truly a rare sort. Her skills in the hunt—aye, there was a certain pleasure she took in it, as though the very hunt coursed through her veins."

The firelight caught the faint gleam in his eye, a flicker of something not quite admiration but not far from it. His gloved hand gestured faintly, as though tracing the memory of her movements. "She could've been shaped well, given the right hand," he continued, his voice deepening with a quiet intensity. "She hath only just come of age—'tis the perfect time to mould her, fit for the grandest of the Shadow Serpents."

He settled back again, the faint creak of the chair marking his movement. The soft rustle of his cloak followed, a sound Agathe recognised, tied to countless meetings between them. His presence pressed against her senses, familiar yet weighty, like a stormcloud lingering by design.

"It be a shame," he said, his voice low but edged with dry humour, "that thou art not a true witch, for I wouldst ask thee to bring her back from the grave."

Agathe tilted her head, her unseeing eyes narrowing as if to pierce the darkness. Her breath rasped faintly, uneven in the quiet, but her lips moved with deliberate precision. "Only thee and Ysabeau ken that I am not a true witch. For what it be worth, if I were a witch, I would cast any spell needed to bring one back for thee. Thou and Ysabeau have shown me kindness."

Her fingers paused on the wood, the faint scrape of her nails breaking the silence. "Speaking of Ysabeau, she hath also been seeking thee. She came hither to see if I had heard aught from thee."

A faint pause followed, her lips parting slightly as though weighing her next words. Her unseeing gaze shifted again, this time with the deliberation of a hunter locking onto prey. "Ysabeau did say that Roric Darkmane, who spoke of a chambermaid by the name of Mary, hath been here in Cutthroat Row, asking for thee by name."

Lucian's lips twitched, his brow furrowing as his expression darkened. A spark of recognition crossed his face, quickly smothered by suspicion. His jaw tightened briefly before he exhaled through his nose, the motion sharp, almost irritated.

"Mary Winterbourne," he said, his voice cool but edged with curiosity. "Noor's sister. I suspect she doth seek answers of some kind. Yet..." His head tilted slightly, his gaze narrowing as though working through an unseen puzzle. "How came she upon Roric Darkmane?"

Agathe's fingers stilled on the edge of the wood, her nails pressing faintly into the grain. The faint wheeze of her breath shifted slightly, uneven for a brief moment before resuming its steady rhythm. Her head tilted slightly, unseeing eyes narrowing as though scrutinizing something beyond the hunt. "Roric Darkmane doth claim that she did say the king bade her go to The Rusty Sword and inquire for a blade," she said at last, her voice measured and deliberate, as though laying down a piece on a game board.

Lucian's hand tightened against the edge of the table, the faint creak of leather cutting through the quiet. His jaw shifted, the tension visible in the hard line of his expression. The wooden chair creaking under his weight, as though forcing himself into a controlled stillness. His exhale came sharp and deliberate through his nose, a subtle but unmistakable signal of his irritation.

"The king," he muttered, the word carrying brittle disdain, each syllable clipped. His tone remained low, but the edge sharpened with every word. "She is meant to draw nigh to the prince, not the king!"

Agathe's breath hitched, a sudden rasp breaking the stillness. The dry, stuttering cough that followed shook her frail frame, her shoulders jerking slightly with the effort. She pressed a hand to her chest, the sound rattling in her throat before subsiding. When she finally spoke, her voice was hoarse, her words dragging like a blade over stone. "Perchance the maiden doth draw near to both the king and the prince."

Lucian's gaze flicked upward, his eyelids lowering in a slow, disdainful roll. A faint huff escaped him, barely audible but weighted with disbelief. His lips pressed into a flat line as though stifling the urge to speak aloud what he clearly thought: Mary had no such cunning. The king, however, had a way of making maidens swoon, and Lucian saw no need to entertain such folly further.

His tone shifted, smooth and unhurried, as he moved slightly in his chair. "How fare things at Thorncrest Castle? Hath Ysabeau brought any tidings?"

Agathe wheezed faintly, her breath still uneven as she leaned forward, one hand fumbling in the folds of her robe. Her thin fingers grasped at the edge of a crumpled, stained cloth she pulled free from her pocket. She dabbed it against her nose with trembling hands, the material smudged with grime from her earlier work. Her words came in gasps, her voice rough and strained as she fought to speak. "Ysabeau still poisons the prince's chalice, aye, with drops of mercury each day. His irrational fears and paranoia grow ever more."

She paused, dragging the cloth across her nose again, the motion unsteady but purposeful. Her head tilted slightly as though recalling some troubling thought, her unseeing eyes narrowing faintly. "'Tis said the princess hath been drinking much and doth seem rather unwell."

A sudden knock echoed through the hut, sharp and urgent, the hollow thud reverberating off the worn wooden walls. Lucian's head snapped toward the sound, his dark eyes narrowing with alert curiosity. The tension in the room shifted as a boy's voice pierced the air, high-pitched and breathless, muffled by the barrier between them.

"Master Lucian!" the voice called, edged with a mix of urgency and resolve.

Lucian's brow furrowed faintly, the only sign of his surprise. Rising with fluid precision, his cloak whispered around him like shadowed water. He reached the door in two long strides, unlatching it with a sharp pull. A boy stood framed in the doorway, no older than twelve, his face streaked with soot and his oversized tunic hanging awkwardly from bony shoulders. A shock of unruly ginger hair flopped into his freckled face as he shifted from foot to foot, his wide eyes darting around the sunlit clearing outside the hut, like a wary animal.

"Ewan," Lucian said, his voice low and calm, the name carrying a weight of expectation. "Thou art not where we agreed."

The boy's chest heaved, his breath still coming in hurried gasps. "Forgive me, Master. I spied the old girl tethered outside," he said quickly, his words tumbling out like a confession. His gaze darted over Lucian's shoulder, catching sight of Agathe's hunched silhouette near the fire.

A folded missive, sealed with crimson wax, slipped from his trembling hand. He extended it toward Lucian, the movement brisk and purposeful despite the slight tremor in his fingers. "Lord Reginald Hawkecliff's list, Master," he murmured, his voice barely above a whisper, meant only for Lucian's ears.

Lucian's dark eyes flicked over the missive as he slipped it into the folds of his cloak with a single motion. "Continue," he said, his voice smooth, almost expectant.

Ewan shuffled his feet, his wide eyes scanning the clearing beyond the doorway as though searching for unseen watchers. He leaned in slightly, his voice tight with urgency. "On another matter," he said, each word weighted, "word doth reach mine ears that King Shepparton of Valoria seeks to visit Briarwood, with hopes of courting Princess Sophia. He hath sent spies forth to gather tidings of her disappearance."

Lucian's lips pressed together in thought, his gaze dropping briefly to the floorboards before he reached into his pocket. He drew out a small coin purse, plucking a coin free and holding it out between two gloved fingers.

"Thou hast done well," he said, his voice quiet yet approving. "Give the old mare a carrot and water her well."

Ewan's face brightened faintly at the gesture. He snatched the coin with a quick, dirt-smudged hand, his head dipping in a hasty nod. With a final glance toward the open clearing, the boy turned and hurried off toward the horses.

Lucian's hand lingered on the doorframe as Ewan's quick footsteps faded into the clearing. He shut the door with a sharp motion, the wood groaning softly before the latch clicked into place. Turning toward the table, he glanced down at the crimson-sealed missive in his hand.

The wax bore Lord Reginald Hawkecliff's crest, its edges smudged from Ewan's grip. Lucian's thumb pressed against the seal, the wax giving way with a sharp crack. The faint pop of wax breaking cut through the quiet as he unfolded the parchment.

He moved to the table, angling the paper toward the firelight. His dark eyes scanned the contents, the neat script stark against the aged paper. A list of names revealed itself, each written with deliberate clarity. The higher entries commanded attention, but it was the last name at the bottom that made him pause.

"Lord Edward Saint-Clair of Ironwood."

Lucian's breath caught for the briefest moment before he exhaled slowly, the name weighing heavier than the others. Saint-Clair was no ordinary target, and Lucian's blade did not move without purpose.

The parchment stilled in his hand, his brow furrowing as though weighing its significance. A slow breath escaped his lips, quiet but tense. Saint-Clair. Of all names, his presence here was unexpected—a weighty figure relegated to the bottom, like an afterthought, yet one that demanded notice. Agathe sat motionless by the fire, her unseeing eyes fixed ahead, the faint wheeze of her breath the only sign of her impatience. Her gnarled fingers drummed lightly on the arm of her chair, each tap deliberate but uneven, like the slow drip of water from a leaky roof. Lucian remained silent, his dark eyes fixed on the parchment in his hand. The crackle of the fire filled the room, stretching the silence until Agathe's lips pressed together in a thin line.

"Well?" she rasped, her voice cutting through the stillness like a blade on stone. "What tidings hath he brought?"

Lucian didn't answer immediately. He stared at the missive, his face unreadable in the firelight. With a sudden motion, he stepped toward the hearth, the parchment crumpling in his gloved hand. The flames hissed as he tossed it into the fire, the wax seal curling and blackening as the edges of the parchment turned to ash.

He stood by the fire, the parchment curling and blackening in the flames. His posture was taut, his shoulders rigid, as though the act had done little to ease the weight of its contents. His jaw tightened, the faintest flicker of something unspoken crossing his face. He turned sharply, the edge of his cloak catching the air like a shadow given form.

"I shall be away for a couple of weeks," he said at last, his tone cool and measured, as though the decision had been made the moment the missive touched his hands. He moved to the table, his gloved fingers brushing the wood lightly before coming to rest on its edge.

Agathe tilted her head slightly, her milky eyes narrowing. "To Eldoria?"

"And beyond," Lucian replied, his voice low, as though the room itself was unfit to hear more. His gaze flicked briefly to the fire, where the last fragments of the parchment disintegrated into embers. The list was clear—the men marked for death.

He would move through Eldoria and other lands, his blade cutting through those whose names adorned the list. Yet one name refused to be dismissed entirely, a quiet thorn buried deep in his thoughts. Saint-Clair. The matter could wait, but not forever.

Lucian straightened, his hand brushing his cloak as though sweeping the thought aside for now. His resolve was clear, even if the question of Edward Saint-Clair lingered at the edges of his mind. Without another word, he crossed the hut, his boots scuffing softly against the worn floorboards, leaving Agathe to the fading warmth of the fire.

Shadows of Longing and Desperation Chapter Twenty-Five A few weeks later

Weeks dragged on. Mary paced the castle, searching for Lucian Blackthorn, while Robert scoured the forest for Noor and Sophia, but found nothing. Sophia's lie about being an Ashbourne lingered in Robert's mind, leaving him questioning what else she'd hidden.

The search for Noor, involving Mary, Robert, and others, went nowhere. Hope dwindled, and though Mary clung to the possibility the Shadow Serpents might know something, it felt fragile.

At Thornbriar Cottage, Mary and Robert barely spoke. Mary worked tirelessly and visited the castle, while Robert drank his sorrows away at the tavern, returning too drunk to communicate. When their paths did cross, their shared grief was overshadowed by his intoxication.

It was another cold morning when the first rays of dawn slipped through the cracks in the shutters, casting light across the floor. Mary shivered as she pushed the blankets aside, the cold seeping into her skin. She glanced around the room, the dim light offering little comfort. *Another day to bear. Another day of naught.*

She reached for her maid's dress, pulling it on quickly. The coarse fabric scratched at her skin as she fumbled with the laces, her fingers stiff from sleep. *No time for idleness. The cold shall not best me.*

Once dressed, she grabbed her cloak from the end of the bed and wrapped it tightly around her shoulders. The warmth of it was brief but welcome, offering a little relief from the biting chill of the room. *If only warmth could come for my heart as easily.*

She moved slowly through the dim corridor, each step heavy with the weight of the cold. The door to Robert's chamber stood ajar, his bed undisturbed, a silent reminder of another night spent elsewhere. *Another night gone, and still, he is not here.*

Her thoughts flickered briefly to the tavern or the embrace of stranger, but she shook the image away. *No use in such thoughts. He drifts further from me, or perhaps it is I who drift from him.*

The stairs creaked beneath her as she descended, the house still and silent, save for the sound of her footsteps. *This place grows colder still. I wonder if it shall ever warm again.*

As she reached the kitchen, a burst of laughter shattered the quiet. Robert stumbled in, a maiden clinging to him, their drunken laughter filling the cottage. *Of course. Another maiden, another night of folly.*

The maiden's giggle rang out again, heedless of the hour or who might be slumbering. Robert, swaying unsteadily from the effects of drink, pushed the door shut with a careless shove, pinning the maiden against it. Their lips collided in a hasty, sloppy kiss, a tangle of limbs and breathless murmurs, their movements stiff and awkward from the cold. The chill in the air seeped through the cracks, but neither seemed to notice, wrapped in their drunken haze, their warmth fleeting and thin against the bitter morning.

Mary stood frozen, her heart weighed down by sorrow and resignation. *How far he has strayed, how lost he seems in these fleeting pleasures. The brother I once knew is buried beneath this... this cold, empty indulgence.*

She wanted to speak, to tell him, but the words failed her. Instead, she slipped on her tattered boots and walked past them, her steps resolute yet heavy, leaving Robert and his fleeting lover to their oblivion. The cold air wrapped itself tightly around her, the sting sharper than the distance between them.

She stepped out into the crisp morning air, the early light casting long shadows across the cobblestone path leading to Thorncrest Castle. The ground, still damp with morning dew, whispered beneath her worn boots as she made her way past the familiar cottages that lined the road. Each step was measured, yet bore the silent weight of unspoken burdens, her mind tangled in thoughts she dared not voice. Once, we were family. Once, we were close. Now, I am adrift, lost in a sea of silence.

The wind bit at her cheeks, but she didn't pull her cloak tighter around her. It was cold, yes, but the chill was a welcome companion—nothing was more painful than the warmth of memories she couldn't reach. The path before her stretched out endlessly, the quiet of the morning only broken by the soft crunch of her boots on the frost-covered earth. She kept her gaze fixed ahead, not looking at the cottages, nor the trees that reached bare limbs to the sky. She simply walked, one foot before the other, a rhythm that helped her forget, if only for a moment, the ache of a life lost.

Her breath escaped in visible puffs, the fog of it mixing with the cold air. She passed the small gardens of the cottages, each one meticulously tended, their flowers faded and dry in the winter months, offering no colour to the grey morning. Even in the dead of winter, the people who lived here kept their spaces neat, perhaps out of habit, perhaps because it was the only thing they could control in a world that often offered little else.

She paused for just a moment as she passed an old oak tree, its gnarled branches stretching out like a forgotten memory. It stood near a house long abandoned, its once grand structure now crumbled into ruin. The sight stirred something within her—a distant echo of times gone by. She could almost hear the laughter of a family that had once lived there, the quiet murmurs of life now silenced by time. The world had moved on, and with it, so had the echoes of the past. Still, the feeling lingered in quiet moments, like now. Her eyes closed for just a second, letting the past pass through her before she continued forward, each step carrying her further from the ghost of what had once been.

As she neared Baldwin's family cottage, her thoughts briefly lingered on the place. It stood at the corner of the path, modest and unassuming, a quiet refuge where Baldwin sometimes stayed. Though he lived mostly at the castle, serving as the prince's personal servant, he would occasionally seek solace at his mother's cottage, away from the demands of the royal court.

Baldwin walked a fine line between duty and kinship. His loyalty to the prince, steadfast and unwavering, was something Mary couldn't fully understand, especially after all she had seen of the prince's cruelty. Yet, Baldwin remained unmoved by the prince's faults, quick to justify and defend him. He serves the prince, yet in some ways, he remains untouched by the cruelty I despise.

Mary recalled their few quiet exchanges, moments of companionship that had grown unexpectedly comfortable. At first, his loyalty to the prince had grated on her, a reminder of the arrogance and cruelty she had come to hate. But over time, her view of Baldwin softened.

Her eyes lifted from the path as she neared the cottage, and she spotted Baldwin stepping outside. His dark hair neatly bound, his face serious, he looked up and caught her gaze. Despite their brief connection, something about his presence felt grounding, and for a moment, the distance between them seemed to shrink. It was a fleeting warmth, something she hadn't expected to find, but she could hold onto it, even if only for a moment.

"Good morrow, Mary," he called, his voice carrying a note of surprise and genuine welcome. He approached with the deliberate grace of one assured in his path, each step reflecting the quiet confidence of his servitude.

At least there be one soul who doth see me, without judgment. She thoughts. She gave a small, almost unreadable smile and nodded, as if they shared some silent understanding despite the difference between them.

For a fleeting moment, the weight of her burdens felt lighter, and the chill in the air seemed less biting.

"Good morrow, Baldwin," she replied, her voice soft, but steady, the warmth of a familiar companion evident in her tone.

Their brief exchange brought no answers but some solace. They continued walking together, the silence between them a quiet balm to the weight of their duties and obligations. Despite their differing loyalties, there was comfort in these quiet moments where the world outside could not reach them.

"I had word that His Majesty, the King, may be coming to Thorncrest Castle." Baldwin's voice broke through the stillness. His news was troubling—carried by a late-night messenger who had arrived with no further explanation. As the prince's personal servant, Baldwin's interest in royal matters was ever keen, especially when it might concern the prince before the prince knew.

Mary's heart fluttered, though the sensation was a twisted mix of anticipation and dread. She spoke calmly, each word controlled. "Is that so? Hast thou any inkling of what might bring the King to Thorncrest Castle?"

She had no word from the King since that fateful night. The silence stretched long, gnawing at her with doubts she could not quell. Why had he not spoken to her? Had she been but a fleeting conquest? Was his visit to the castle just part of his royal duties, or did he seek her once more?

Baldwin shrugged, the movement casual yet uncertain. "That, I know not. Nor when, nor how long he doth intend to stay. The prince doth fret at the thought of the King's coming. Their bond is much strained."

Mary's cheeks flushed with conflicting emotions. Thoughts of the King stirred a storm within her—excitement and insecurity warring inside her. She turned her gaze away, willing herself to remain indifferent, though the ache in her eyes betrayed her.

She glanced back at Baldwin, her lips pressing into a thin line. "Thou servest the prince; thou must know how intolerable he can be. Perhaps the King finds him impossible to befriend."

Baldwin replied, but his words faded into the haze of her own thoughts. Perhaps this was for the best. The King's distance, their separation—it was necessary, wasn't it? Their worlds stood too far apart. Yet, despite her reasoning, an ache settled deep in her chest, hollow and gnawing. She had convinced herself they were never meant to meet again, yet his absence weighed upon her more than she wished to admit.

Her feelings for the King, tangled with her need to speak with Lucian Blackthorn, drove her toward the one person who might be able to help.

Would Princess Sophia cast me aside, as I did unto her? Her fingers curled into fists, the cold biting at her knuckles. A shallow breath hitched in her throat, her pulse drumming against her ribs. She straightened her shoulders, but the weight in her stomach remained, heavy and unshakable.

Mary's lips twitched, the ghost of a smile barely forming before she forced it into place. "Gratitude, Baldwin. Thy counsel is most appreciated." Her voice was steady, but the effort behind the words was thin, fragile.

Baldwin inclined his head, his gaze unclouded by the suspicion that lingered in the eyes of others. Unlike the rest, he did not avert his gaze when she entered a room, nor did his voice drop to a whisper when she passed.

The other servants spoke to her only when duty required it, their words clipped, their eyes sharp with quiet disdain. Conversations halted when she drew near. Footsteps shuffled away before she could reach them. Even in the busiest corridors, she moved through the castle as though wading through an unseen fog of judgment.

But Baldwin remained. He neither flinched nor frowned in her presence. There was no wary glance, no hushed murmurs at her back. Perhaps he was the only one who did not cast her aside. Perhaps he was the only friend she had.

Thorncrest Castle

Princess Sophia

That same morning, as the sun climbed higher in the sky, many hours past dawn, Princess Sophia sat slumped in her chair, a portrait of sorrow. Rosalind stood behind her, gently brushing her long golden locks, cascading like a silken waterfall down the chair's back.

"Your Highness, it grieves me to see thee in such despair," Rosalind murmured, her voice tender with concern. "'Tis been weeks since thy return. Thou must reconcile with the unknown fate of Noor. The lad from Mudlark Alley be a memory best left to wither and fade." She spoke softly, though she knew her words would fall on deaf ears. She hoped that time would mend the princess's heart, each day a stitch in the fabric of healing.

Sophia's shoulders tensed as she exhaled sharply, a huff of frustration mingled with sorrow. She knew Rosalind spoke the truth, but the cold logic of reality could not thaw the despair that gripped her heart. Hope, stubborn as a flame, refused to die.

"Rosalind," she said, her voice a soft plea, "Did Mary Winterbourne receive my message yestereve?"

Rosalind's brow furrowed slightly as she continued her task. "Aye, each day thou dost inquire, I dutifully seek Mary in the servants' quarters and convey thy wish to see her. And each day, I am met with the same response." Her voice held a hint of resignation, knowing that Mary's refusals pierced the princess deeply.

Sophia's heart sank further. She stared at the reflection of her sorrowful face in the polished silver mirror, her eyes dulled by worry, cheeks hollowed by sleepless nights. She felt like a ship lost at sea, yearning for the faintest glimpse of land to guide her to safety.

The grand, opulent chambers felt more like a gilded cage. Once-vibrant tapestries, depicting brave conquests and revered champions, now haunted her, overshadowed by an unshakable sense of disconnection. Rosalind's gentle ministrations were a comfort, but they could not soothe the ache that had taken root in her heart.

Outside, the castle grounds bustled with life, sounds of daily activity drifting through the open windows, yet inside, Sophia felt the crushing weight of solitude. Every distant clang of the blacksmith's hammer or call of the stable boys seemed to echo her emptiness.

"Pray, Rosalind," Sophia began, her voice wavering, "Why doth Mary not come? She must surely ken how urgent my request is."

Rosalind paused in her brushing; her eyes soft with sympathy as she met Sophia's gaze in the polished surface before her. "Your Highness, I believe Mary is burdened with her own sorrows. She, too, searches for answers in the wake of loss."

Sophia nodded, her throat tightening with unshed tears. She understood Mary's pain, for it mirrored her own. She could not fault her for seeking solace in the shadows, away from the prying eyes of the court. But her voice was firmer now. "Very well," she said quietly. "I shall wait a while longer. Perhaps, in time, Mary will heed my call."

Rosalind resumed her gentle brushing, her touch soothing against the storm of emotions inside the princess. In the quiet of the chambers, Sophia allowed herself a moment to grieve, to hope, and to cling to the fragile thread that connected her to Noor.

Seeking to lift the heavy mood, Rosalind tried to steer the conversation toward lighter matters. "I know that thou art merely courting His Grace, Edward Saint-Clair, to fulfill a promise and ward off other, less desirable suitors," she began, a playful smile touching her lips. "But thou dost get on quite well with him, dost thou not?" She paused, a giggle escaping as she continued, "He is rather handsome, is he not?"

Sophia forced a smile, her thoughts turning reluctantly to Edward. He was kind, his presence a balm against the more aggressive advances of other suitors. But her heart, heavy with longing, remained with Robert. "His Grace is indeed kind," she replied, her voice carefully measured. "His eyes hold a certain charm, but it is merely a pact between us, nothing more."

Rosalind sighed, a dreamy look crossing her face as she spoke. "A pact it may be, but I see the way he gazes upon thee, the tender brush of his hand, as though he yearns to feel the warmth of thy skin. Would that he looked upon me as he does thee," she added wistfully.

Sophia turned her gaze to Rosalind, a shadow passing over her face. "He too plays his part in this charade of courtship. He seeks to mend his wounded pride and restore his good name. His father, Lord Geoffrey Saint-Clair, and his brother are hard upon him for my disappearance. It is naught but a ruse."

Rosalind, undeterred, looked at Sophia with a knowing smile. "Thou mayst call it a ruse, but I see the truth in his eyes. Edward is clearly taken with you, Princess," Rosalind said with a gentle smile. "How many men wouldst show such steadfast devotion? Were it only a pretense, he might have searched for Noor Winterbourne but once or twice, not every day as he has done."

Sophia's expression softened, a hint of doubt creeping into her heart. Outside, the clanging of the blacksmith's hammer and the chatter of stable boys faded into the background as the truth of Edward's feelings began to seep into her consciousness. Yet, despite the tender image Rosalind painted, the ache for Robert, the true object of her heart's desire, remained.

Rosalind, her eyes bright with conviction, resumed her task, brushing Sophia's hair with renewed vigor. She hoped that in time, the princess might see the depth of Edward's devotion, a devotion that perhaps ran deeper than mere duty or a desire to repair his tarnished reputation.

Sophia, quick to divert the conversation, averted her gaze with a mischievous glint. "I have observed the way thou dost look upon Sir Hector, my knight," she said, her eyes twinkling with playful judgment. "By thine own logic, dost thou not bear affection for him?"

Rosalind laughed, a soft blush colouring her cheeks. "Aye, my princess, a knight in shining armour is many a maiden's dream come true," she replied with a light-hearted sigh. Sir Hector was indeed a sight to behold, but she had no mind for courtship or the need of a husband. "Yet Sir Hector hath not bestowed upon me the fairest flowers or a rare diamond necklace as His Grace hath upon thee."

Sophia's smile widened, though she shook her head in mock exasperation. "Rosalind, I assure thee, 'tis but a mere pretense," she said, though her voice held a note of uncertainty that did not escape her handmaiden's notice.

"I have heard from mine good friends," Rosalind declared, the news fresh from Baldwin Honorcrest this very morn. "The King is to visit soon." Her eyebrow arched playfully. "Mayhap at the behest of His Grace?" Though her words carried jest, her words held weight. Edward Saint-Clair, amidst the throng of suitors vying for the princess's favour, had come to love her deeply. He knew their courtship had begun as a mere arrangement, but he harboured the hope that Sophia's heart had also softened toward him. His family's expectations weighed heavily on him, and he knew he had little time if he wanted to secure his place at court.

Edward had indeed penned a heartfelt missive, a plea to the King, seeking permission to ask for Sophia's hand in marriage. With each stroke of the quill, he poured out his heart, requesting not only the honor of Sophia's hand but also expressing his desire to obtain Lorendale Castle, or another estate of equal grandeur, to be their future home. He sought not only to prove his love but also to solidify his position and meet the lofty expectations set by his lineage.

The princess rolled her eyes at her handmaiden, a gesture of weary resignation. "I am to request that my brother, His Majesty, insist upon a betrothal between Lord Edward and myself," she said, her voice tinged with irony. She waved her hand dismissively, as if brushing away an annoying fly. "Lord Edward will, of course, decline the offer, as per our agreement."

Sophia's lips curved into a sardonic smile, the corners of her mouth barely lifting as she contemplated the farce of their arrangement. The flicker of candlelight caught in her eyes, narrowing slightly with a mixture of amusement and frustration.

Rosalind, with a gentle sigh, continued, "I do comprehend, Your Highness, yet if thou findest thyself compelled to wed, His Grace, Edward Saint-Clair is a far better prospect than many." She paused, her breath escaping in a heavy sigh. "Thou art prepared." Just then, a loud knock echoed through the door, causing Sophia to turn to Rosalind, her eyes widening in surprise.

Sophia's heart quickened as the sharp rap on the door echoed through the chamber, followed by the voice of a servant, clear and reverent. "Her Majesty, the Queen Mother," announced the servant.

Sophia, regaining her composure, turned to Rosalind with a nod. "Pray, tell my mother I am prepared," she said, her voice steady yet soft.

Rosalind, acknowledging the command, turned and moved to the door. She opened it slightly and curtsied deeply, her head lowered in deference. "Your Majesty, Her Highness is prepared to receive thee," she announced, her voice respectful.

The door swung open fully, and the Queen Mother entered the chamber, her presence an embodiment of regal grace. Draped in rich robes of deep burgundy, the soft rustle of brocade and the faint scent of lavender and rose heralded her entry. Her silver hair, meticulously braided and adorned with delicate pearls, caught the sunlight, casting a gentle radiance. Sophia's eyes widened, her breath catching at the sight of her mother. The Queen Mother's lips curved into a knowing smile, a blend of concern and authority in her expression. "Daughter," she said, her voice carrying the weight of her position, yet suffused with tenderness, "I come to speak with thee on matters most pressing."

Sophia rose from her chair, the heavy folds of her gown whispering against the stone floor as she straightened under her mother's watchful eye. Rosalind stepped back, her head bowed in deference, fully aware that the ensuing conversation would carry significant weight and likely influence the affairs within the castle.

The Queen Mother, Victoria, flicked her fingers, a sharp command that sent Sophia back into her chair. "I come bearing grave tidings," she began, her voice like cold iron. "Thou hast received a proposal from King Shepparton of Valoria, and many at court deem this match most suitable to strengthen Briarwood. His vessel is already at sea, and he shall arrive within three weeks, should the seas remain kind."

Sophia's eyes widened in horror, her face paling as the implications of her mother's words sank in. "Mother, thou dost jest!" she cried, her voice trembling with disbelief. "King Shepparton is a man thrice my age, and vile in demeanor. He must have been a hog in his past life!"

Victoria's expression softened, yet a sorrowful determination lingered in her eyes. "I jest not, my dear," she said quietly, her tone laced with regret. "Thou must choose a husband swiftly, lest thou be bound to such a loathsome man. The court favours this match, but thou mayest avert it if another suitor more pleasing to thee is secured."

Sophia's heart pounded in her chest, a thousand thoughts racing through her mind. The weight of her mother's words pressed down upon her, and she felt as if the very walls of the chamber were closing in. Her fingers clenched the arms of her chair, knuckles whitening with the force of her grip. The flickering light from the hearth cast shadows that danced mockingly around her, echoing the turmoil within.

Victoria's gaze, though stern, held a glimmer of compassion. She stepped closer, the rustle of her gown a soft whisper against the stone floor. "Thou art a princess," she said gently, "and with that title comes the burden of duty. Choose wisely, Sophia, for thy time grows short."

Tears welled in Sophia's eyes, shimmering like unshed pearls. "Mother," she began, her voice breaking as tears streamed down her cheeks, "surely the land or court would not condemn their princess to the fate of wedlock with such a wretched man." The very thought of marrying anyone but Robert turned her stomach, but a man like that struck a sickness that twisted her insides with each passing moment.

The Queen Mother, Victoria, gently placed her arm around Sophia, her touch a fleeting comfort. "Thou hast had many proposals, all of which thou hast declined," she said softly, her tone heavy with unspoken questions. Victoria suspected that another held her daughter's heart, but dared not ask, for such secrets carried grave consequences. "King Shepparton's proposal would see thee far from here," Victoria's gaze flicked momentarily to Rosalind before returning to Sophia, "and thou couldst take thy handmaiden, should she wish it. Else, thou wouldst be served by those of King Shepparton's choosing. His proposal may supersede any suitor thou art presently entertaining."

Her words hung in the air, laden with the weight of their implications. The spectre of King Shepparton loomed large, and Sophia's thoughts turned to Edward Saint-Clair, the one with whom she had found a tentative harmony. Victoria's own past echoed in her voice, a silent testament to the precarious position of an unwed maiden. "At the end of the day, 'tis the King's will that doth prevail." she continued, her voice lowering to a conspiratorial whisper as she leaned closer to the tearful princess. "His advisers shall surely seek to sway him towards King Shepparton."

The Queen Mother's eyes darted around the chamber before she spoke again, her voice barely a breath in Sophia's ear. "I have learned in secret that Lord Edward Saint-Clair hath written to thy brother, declaring his love for thee and his wish to propose. Mayhap thou shouldst consider playing upon this, whether or not thou returnest his affections. In his missive, he spake of residing in both Stowshire, an' if it be thy will, Ironwood, which lieth within the bounds of Briarwood."

Sophia's tears trickled down her cheeks, each drop a silent testament to the tempest within her. Her mother's words cut deeply, each one like a dagger, laden with the weight of her precarious circumstances. The news that Edward had secretly written to her brother struck her like a blow, leaving her breathless. Could it truly be that Edward sought her hand in marriage? Was it out of sincere affection, or driven by ambition, a desire for title and power, or a need to prove his worth to his father?

Questions whirled in her mind, each one tightening the knot of doubt and uncertainty in her heart. Yet, at this moment, the reasons seemed distant and indistinct. The thought of marrying Edward, regardless of his motives, appeared to be the only refuge from the bleak fate that awaited her with King Shepparton. She knew she must act swiftly, and the possibility of a future with Edward, despite its uncertainties, shone like a fragile beacon of hope she could not afford to dismiss.

Sophia drew in a deep breath, her chest rising and falling with the weight of her resolve. "I am grateful for thy counsel, Mother," she began, her voice steady yet laced with urgency. "Couldst thou not bear the favour and entreat King John to see that an alliance with Edward would be most beneficial? Perchance thou couldst persuade him that we care deeply for one another."

With a sudden surge of emotion, Sophia rose to her feet and threw her arms around her mother, her embrace fervent and desperate. For a moment, the Queen Mother was taken aback, her posture stiff with surprise. But then, she softened, wrapping her arms around her daughter, the bond of their shared blood warming the embrace.

"I shall do my utmost," she murmured, her voice gentle but firm, as she held Sophia close. The gravity of her daughter's plea weighed heavily upon her, and she resolved to speak with the King, her heart aching with a mother's desire to protect her child from an unwanted fate, knowing that both her children—Sophia and the King—faced different challenges but shared the burden of duty and expectation.

The Queen Mother stepped back, a shadow of concern fleeting across her visage. "There is more, Sophia," she began, her voice heavy with the gravity of her news. "Lord Geoffrey Saint-Clair hath sent word this very morn. His Grace, Edward, shall soon take leave for Ironwood. Matters of grave import demand his attention, and I shall inform thee upon his return." "I do pray His Grace returns from Ironwood anon, for I hold hope for this meeting 'twixt His Majesty the King and thee, to discourse of an union 'twixt thee and Edward. Fortunate for thee, the King and his men have journeyed southward to Briarwood, where the court may whisper into his ears of thee wedding King Shepparton, or any other suitor not to thy liking."

Sophia's heart sank, a shroud of dread enveloping her. This revelation meant Edward would no longer be searching for Noor; the urgency of her predicament squeezed her heart like a relentless vice. What if her mother had erred in her account of the proposal? She turned her face away, her hands clasping tightly together, the luxurious fabric of her gown gathering and crumpling under the strain of her grip.

The Queen Mother, her eyes softening as she observed the distress etched across her daughter's features, felt the immense weight of their world's burdens pressing down upon them. She reached out, her hand resting gently on Sophia's shoulder, a gesture of solace amid the gathering storm. "Be patient, my dear," she whispered, her voice a gentle caress. "We shall navigate this together."

Sophia nodded, yet her mind churned with a tempest of fear and doubt. The knowledge of Edward's impending departure, the looming shadow of King Shepparton's arrival, and the precarious uncertainty of her future pressed upon her like a heavy yoke. Each breath became a labor, her thoughts a maelstrom against the impending tide of duty and fate. "Is his grace still present? Might I have audience with him?"

The Queen Mother's brow furrowed, her hands clasped tightly in front of her as she stood still, her gaze fixed on a distant point. "Nay, it seems he was about to ready his steed once more," she said, her voice tinged with irritation. "He appears to have a fondness for the forest."

Frustration flash-fired in her eyes, and her mouth twisted into a tight, pinched line. Little did she know, Edward Saint-Clair's time spent in the woods was far from a casual pursuit. His focus was on finding Noor, as per his secret agreement with Sophia.

Edward Saint-Claire visits to Viper's Den's cottage

Edward urged his horse forward, the animal's hooves pounding against the frozen earth, each thundering step cutting through the chill of the mid-morning air. The sun was high but weak, casting long shadows across the forest floor, the cold biting at his face. His breath came in sharp bursts, clouding the air around him, but he ignored it, focusing only on the path ahead.

He was a blur of brown leather and thick wool, his cloak whipped behind him in the wind, the colours of House Saint-Clair dark and rich against the muted landscape of bare trees and frosty ground. His family's crest, a tree of iron and wood, was stitched into the cloak's lining, the branches rendered like ironwork, twisting and curling through the fabric, as if the metal itself held the power to root him in the very earth beneath him.

The horse's mane streamed behind him like a banner, and the animal's hooves struck the earth with a rhythm that matched Edward's heartbeat, steady and relentless. He had no time to spare. The forest blurred as he navigated through the trees, branches scratching at his face, the scent of damp earth and cold pine filling his nose.

The horse's breath steamed in the air as it galloped faster, leaping over fallen branches and weaving between towering trunks. The world around him seemed a blur of cold, iron-dark shadows, but Edward's focus never wavered. His hands gripped the reins tightly, knuckles white, as the wind tore at him and his horse plunged deeper into the forest, faster still.

Ahead, through the haze of frost and trees, he could see the silhouette of the clearing, the sun breaking through the canopy above. The urgency of his mission pushed him harder, the pounding of hooves echoing in his ears, until the branches seemed to stretch before him like the iron roots of his house's crest—unbending, unwavering, relentless in their pursuit.

Edward's horse thundered through the forest, its hooves striking the ground like a drumbeat, the distance between him and Viper's Den closing rapidly. The trees thinned, and there, just beyond a cluster of boulders and bramble, he saw it—the cottage.

Viper's Den's cottage appeared through the trees, squat and weathered, its stone walls gray and chipped, nearly swallowed up by the forest.

The dense forest pressed in around it, wild and untamed, as if the land itself was guarding the place.

But Edward wasn't alone.

The moment he saw the building, he felt it—the unmistakable presence of eyes on him.

Two figures emerged from the shadows by the cottage, their swords glinting as they drew them in a single, fluid motion. Their faces were hidden beneath dark hoods, but the sharpness of their posture betrayed the trained stillness of Viper's Den's guards. One of them made a slow, deliberate movement, his hand resting on the pommel of his blade, eyes fixed on Edward as the horse drew closer.

Edward's heart raced as he took in the situation. An archer. He hadn't seen him until now, but there, high above in the branches of a tree, a flicker of movement caught his eye. The archer's eyes gleamed from beneath a shadowed hood, the tip of his arrow drawn taut, aimed straight at Edward. The tension in the air thickened, the cold making every breath visible.

The guards were unmoving, their swords raised but not yet lunging, waiting for the right moment. Edward's eyes narrowed as his own hand reached for the dagger at his side, fingers brushing the cold steel. His horse slowed, sensing the standoff as much as its rider. The wind whispered through the trees, making the leaves rustle, but it was the sound of Edward's breath, shallow and focused, that filled his ears.

His free hand held the reins tight, his gaze locked on the guards. "I have come to parley with Bartholomew," he called out, his voice steady but carrying the weight of his command. The archer didn't waver. The guards' swords gleamed in the faint sunlight, and still, they didn't advance.

He had been searching for Noor for some time at the princess's request and keeping it secret, but it had gotten nowhere. So, a few days ago, he had sought the Shadow Serpents' help. A messenger boy had informed him to come meet Bartholomew here. He had never actually hired the Shadow Serpents before. His father had plenty of times, but not Edward.

As Edward's horse slowed to a halt, one of the guards stepped forward, his sword still raised but no longer aimed directly at Edward. He shot a quick glance at the archer above before lowering his weapon. The edge of his mouth twitched in a faint smirk, though the hardness in his eyes remained.

"Good morrow, Your Grace," one of the guards said, his voice steady, but with a barely concealed amusement behind it. He clicked his tongue, sending a sharp sound through the air, his eyes flickering with recognition, though his posture remained carefully respectful. "When Bartholomew informed me that Lord Saint-Clair would be coming, I did imagine it would be thy father."

Before Edward could respond, a stable boy, quick and nimble, rushed forward. His boots scraped against the frozen earth as he made his way to the horse. Standing ready, his hands extended, the boy waited as Edward swung his leg over the saddle, stiff from the cold.

The stable boy grasped Edward's arm with a grunt, helping him down. Edward's feet hit the ground with a soft thud, the frozen earth firm beneath his boots before the boy quickly steadied him. Despite his trembling hands, the boy was eager, guiding Edward away from the horse, careful to avoid any uneven ground.

Edward's boots crunched softly in the dirt as he dismounted, his posture straight, the pride of a lord apparent in every movement. His gaze locked onto the guard as he took a step forward, keeping his composure despite the eerily still air. His heart raced with a mix of irritation and arrogance, the usual confidence that came with his title pushing back any feeling of unease. But still, a part of him, hidden beneath layers of arrogance, felt the weight of the situation. The Serpents, after all, were dangerous.

Edward's eyes swept over the guard, lingering on the archer above. Edward had not come here to play games, yet he couldn't ignore the tension hanging in the air.

The guard held his position, the sword still in his hand, but now lowered—though not without an edge of readiness in his stance. His eyes flickered toward the archer, then back to Edward. "Bartholomew awaits inside, Your Grace," the guard said, his voice carrying that same steady, almost mocking tone.

Edward narrowed his eyes but didn't respond right away. Instead, his gaze flickered to the archer in the tree. The man's stance was rigid, his arrow still aimed at him. Edward clenched his jaw, not willing to show any sign of hesitation.

Edward's heart beat a little faster, but his hand remained at his side, close to the dagger he kept there. He wouldn't give them the satisfaction of seeing him flinch, not now.

The stable boy's breath came out in visible puffs, a cloud of mist vanishing into the air with each exhale. The cold stung his cheeks as he led the horse toward the stables, the rhythmic clop of hooves against the hard earth muffled by the thickening frost. Edward watched him for a moment, his eyes flicking back to the guard, who had yet to move.

The guard's gaze never wavered from Edward, his stance as rigid as the sword he held. The air around them seemed to freeze, both men standing still, each breath visible in the frigid morning air. Finally, with a curt motion, the guard turned on his heel, breaking the silence. He nodded once to Edward and walked ahead, the door to the cottage creaking open at his command.

Edward followed, the crunch of his boots against the ground louder in the quiet. The guard held the door wide, stepping back slightly. The cold air still lingered between them, sharp and biting. A gust of wind blew across the open space, and the guard exhaled sharply, his breath forming a brief mist before dissipating.

The guard's voice was cold as the wind itself. "This way, Your Grace."

Edward stepped forward, his jaw tight as he crossed the threshold, leaving the cold outside as he entered the warmth of the cottage.

His boots sank softly into the wooden floor, each step taken with the slightest hesitation. The fire hissed and popped in the hearth, its heat brushing against Edward's skin as he stepped inside. It smelled of wood and something more—something metallic that hung in the air like an unsettling presence.

As his eyes swept the room, something caught his attention. A severed human hand, resting on a table just off to the side, half-hidden beneath a pile of disheveled papers. It was still, unnaturally still, fingers curled in an unsettling way. Edward's stomach twisted, but his expression betrayed none of the shock that seized him. He shifted his gaze quickly, his body going rigid as he stepped deeper into the room, the unease settling in his chest as he tried to look past what he had seen.

Bartholomew, hunched over in the far corner, was cleaning his dagger, the motion deliberate and slow. He hadn't even bothered to look up at Edward's entrance, a calm indifference radiating from him. The air between them was thick with silence. Edward shifted his weight, his jaw tightening against the unease gnawing at him.

Without looking, Bartholomew spoke, his voice as smooth as the blade in his hand. "Your Grace, what bringeth thee hither?"

Edward, his face unreadable, steadied his breath, forcing the discomfort deep down. "I've come for answers," he replied, his voice steady, though the words felt harder than they should have. His eyes darted back to the severed hand for just a moment before he turned his attention back to Bartholomew, trying to mask the tremor in his chest. Everything about this place—these people—spelled danger. And he wasn't about to show weakness now.

Edward took slow, measured steps toward the fire, the heat from the flickering flames brushing against his cold, stiff skin. He reached out, letting his hands hover over the warmth, though the heat seemed to seep into him reluctantly, as if the fire itself were wary of his presence. The crackle of the flames was the only sound that filled the room for a moment, allowing him to gather his thoughts.

"Thou hast mine thanks for receiving me," he said, his voice carefully steady, though a slight tension lingered in his posture as he turned toward Bartholomew. The words were a courtesy, a mask, for Edward couldn't tell the full truth of why he had come. The princess had made him swear to secrecy, so he twisted the tale.

"A maiden came with me from Ironwood, a servant lass. I've not laid eyes upon her in nigh a few weeks. 'Tis not like her to vanish for so long," he continued, his gaze flickering toward the fire, unwilling to look directly at the Serpent. "I wondered, might ye have word of a dark-haired maiden, pale of skin? She's fair to look upon, and her tongue, sharp as any blade, mayhaps hath led her into trouble."

He tried to paint the picture of Noor as best as he could, despite having spent only a day with her. His description felt hollow in his mouth, the memory of her face—so fleeting—sharpened only by the weight of his uncertainty.

Bartholomew paused in his task, the rhythmic scraping of his dagger against the stone halting as he turned toward Edward. Bartholomew's eyes flickered with suspicion before he set the dagger down, his gaze locking onto Edward as he slowly wiped his hands on a cloth. A quiet smile tugged at the corner of his lips, but it didn't reach his eyes.

"Forgive me, mi lord," Bartholomew said, his tone measured and laced with a hint of mockery. "Might I ask, such a wealthy and powerful lord as thyself, venturing all the way to Cutthroat Row and further still into these woods, to seek but a mere servant?" He leaned back slightly, his eyes flicking to Edward, assessing him. "Most lords would hire a new wench, or at the least, bid another to seek her out."

Edward's eyes widened ever so slightly, the shock flashing across his face before he masked it with a quick, controlled glance. Few dared question him, least of all someone beneath his rank. The audacity of the question pricked at his pride, but he forced his jaw to relax as his mind scrambled for a response.

With a slight cough to mask his discomfort, Edward spoke quickly, his voice smooth but firm. "She hath a necklace of mine," he said, meeting Bartholomew's gaze. "'Tis worth more than mere coin to me."

Bartholomew's smirk grew wider, his eyes gleaming with dark amusement. "Ah, ye would have me seek her out, relieve her of the necklace, and be rid of her corpse?" he asked, his voice teasing but tinged with an underlying seriousness.

The words cut through Edward like a knife, and though his face remained stoic, a brief shiver of shock passed through him. The thought of it—of how easily Bartholomew could've done such a thing—flickered across his mind. He quickly shoved the unsettling thought aside, unwilling to show any hesitation.

"Nay, nay," Edward replied sharply, the lie already half-formed in his mind. His voice dropped slightly, becoming more insistent. "I but wish for thee to bring her unto me."

Bartholomew nodded slowly, his eyes glinting with dark amusement. "Ah, my grace," he said, his tone rich with mockery, "thou dost wish to handle her thyself? Pray, mayhap I fetch thee some thumbscrews?" He tilted his head slightly, a dark smile curling at the edges of his lips. "Thou canst place her fingers in the device, and with each turn of the screw, crush and break her bones. She shall ne'er dare to steal from thee again."

Edward's stomach tightened as Bartholomew's words echoed in his mind. *Thumbscrews for a stolen necklace?* The thought sent a cold shiver down his spine. In Ironwood, such a crime would be punished, but it was never to this extent. Thieves were taken to the square, their wrongs proclaimed for all to hear. They were bound, forced to make restitution, either by paying a fine or returning what was taken, and sometimes offering further recompense for the wrong done. But no one would ever think of subjecting a thief to such horrific punishment.

Edward had witnessed brutality before. He had fought in battles with his father, seen men struck down in the name of war. He had witnessed executions—heads severed, bodies left to rot as a grim reminder of the consequences of rebellion. Yet, in his experience, there was some order to the chaos of battle—a reason behind the cruelty. A thief, a common criminal, had never warranted such harsh retribution.

And yet here was Bartholomew, offering up something far darker, far more vindictive than anything Edward had seen in his years of warfare. What kind of man entertains such a suggestion for a stolen trinket?

The idea of a necklace being worth such punishment filling him with disgust. *These men, and their world, were naught but madness, cruel beyond the reach of my ken. In his mind, the theft of a necklace should never result in such torment.* The Serpents had no sense of justice—they simply acted as they wished, without mercy.

Edward's hand moved to his pocket, his fingers brushing against the leather pouch. He pulled it out, opening it with a slight tug. The pouch felt cold in his hand, and he poured half the coins into his palm, feeling their weight as he gripped them tightly. He looked up at Bartholomew, his gaze steady despite the tension in the air.

"The servant and I are well-acquainted, if thou understand'st. I am quite fond of her and wouldst not have her harmed. Shouldst thou or thy men lay hands upon her, know that I shall not be pleased if she be injured in the process," Edward said, his voice firm, though the words came with a thin veil of deception.

Without waiting, Edward stepped forward, holding the coins in his hand, offering them to Bartholomew.

"Thou shalt receive more when she is found," he added, his voice unwavering.

Bartholomew's eyes flicked to the coins, and he reached out, taking them from Edward's hand. His fingers brushed against Edward's briefly, a fleeting touch, and a small smirk tugged at his lips. *Foolish young lord, in love with his servant. How quaint. Methinks he hath mistaken his fleeting affections for some noble bond.*

It was no surprise that a lord might have a woman in his employ, but it was rare for one to pay so dearly to have a servant found.

Bartholomew's eyes lingered on the coins for a moment before his gaze rose back to Edward.

"And pray tell, my grace," he asked, a glint of mockery in his tone, "what name doth thy servant go by?"

Edward's mind froze for a heartbeat, the silence stretching around him like a thick fog. *I cannot share her name, can I?* He'd lied already, but this lie felt different, somehow more fragile.

He inhaled deeply, his chest rising as he fought to push the words past the knot in his throat. "If truth be told, I but call her servant afore the masses," he began, the lie thick on his tongue, "yet in private, I dub her mine own dearest. Her name, I know not, but long dark tresses she doth possess, and a tongue most sharp. Last seen, she was, nigh the edge of the forest and Ravenswood."

He glanced down at his hand, still holding the leather pouch. With a swift motion, he tucked it back into his pocket, feeling the weight of it against his side. A sheen of sweat appeared on his brow, just enough for him to feel it, but not enough to show. Would the man before him believe it? Edward's heart pounded as he wondered. He was a lord. He should have been the one in control. Yet, with each lie, the ground beneath him felt less sure.

Bartholomew's expression remained unreadable as he absorbed Edward's words. The silence thickened, the air between them heavy with something unsaid. The seconds stretched long and taut, like a bowstring pulled to its limit.

Finally, after what felt like an eternity, Bartholomew broke the silence. His gaze, sharp and calculating, never wavered as he looked at Edward. "If she be dead or harmed," he asked, his voice steady but low, "what wouldst thou have me do?"

Edward's gaze flicked to the severed hand on the table, his stomach twisting at the sight of it—a real hand, detached and discarded. He fought the urge to recoil, his breath catching for a moment. His eyes quickly snapped back to Bartholomew, unwilling to show any sign of the unease that gripped him.

"A'n she be dead, I wouldst see her body with mine own eyes," Edward declared, his voice steady, though the words felt heavy in his mouth. "An she be harmed, near to death, do what thou must to save her. But if 'tis but a few minor harms, I shall take her back to Ironwood and have a healer tend to her."

Bartholomew's lips curled into a faint, knowing smirk as he nodded, his gaze never leaving Edward. The subtle shift in his posture—slightly more relaxed—told Edward that the deal had been struck, and the words felt like a weight lifting, but only slightly.

"As ye wish, yer grace," Bartholomew said, his voice low and deliberate, carrying just the right amount of mockery. "I shall inform ye of any maidens with yer description."

Edward straightened, his mind still reeling from the unsettling moments. He nodded curtly, his posture stiff as he took a measured step back, the weight of the situation pressing down on him. Edward's gaze shifted toward the door. The cold air outside seemed less inviting, more a relief than a comfort, but it was the only way forward. He needed to leave the tension of the room behind him.

He moved toward the exit with deliberate steps, his boots making the only sound in the quiet cottage. As he passed Bartholomew, the tension in the air seemed to grow, but Edward made no motion to address it. His thoughts were elsewhere, already racing with what lay ahead.

At the door, he paused, hand resting briefly on the cold handle. He glanced back, catching Bartholomew's steady gaze, and gave a short, clipped nod before stepping out into the cold, the door creaking softly behind him.

Edward shivered, the cold biting into him as he stepped out into the open air. His breath misted in the chill, and the weight of the meeting still pressed on him. He had been expecting only the two guards, the archer in the tree and the stable boy. But as his eyes swept the area, something caught his attention.

A new horse stood near the others, its coat gleaming in the pale light of the morning. And the rider... Edward's gaze shifted, locking onto the man. The man sat tall in the saddle, silver locks falling beneath his hood, his attire unmistakably marking him as one of the Shadow Serpents. His presence was commanding, even from a distance. The black and red of his cloak, the way his posture demanded attention—everything about him screamed danger.

Edward's heart gave a sudden, uneasy lurch. The memory of Mary Winterbourne's words echoed in his mind: "The man with silver hair." Briarwood was full of folk with grey and silver hair—noblemen and soldiers alike—but something about this man felt different, more foreboding. Could it be the same man she spoke of? He couldn't be sure.

The man's eyes met his, unwavering, cold like the steel of a drawn sword. The two guards flanking him narrowed their eyes as they observed Edward, their stares cold, challenging, waiting for a misstep.

Edward cleared his throat, trying to push the unease aside. "Mine steed?" he ordered, his voice cutting through the tension.

One of the guards, face impassive, replied, "One moment, my grace." He turned his head sharply, shouting toward the stables. "Boy! To the horses!"

Edward stood still, his mind racing as he tried to assess the situation. The air felt thick with unspoken tension. The man with the silver hair didn't move, his gaze never leaving Edward.

Little did Edward know, the man before him was Lucian Blackthorn. As Edward stood there, Lucian inwardly scoffed. It had only been yesterday when Lord Reginald Hawkecliff had listed Lord Edward Saint-Clair among his marks.

Lucian couldn't help but scrutinize Edward, his gaze sharp and calculating. *His grace hath scarce become a man, mayhap a year or two past his coming of age. For what cause would Hawkecliff seek the boy's death? Princess Sophia hath returned, and surely Edward is her suitor once more, not another suitor for Princess Shorwynne?*

Lucian absentmindedly patted his horse, the old mare standing firm beneath him. *Perchance Hawkecliff doth believe the might shall fold if Edward be slain, mayhap he doth think to wed Princess Sophia in his stead?*

His thoughts lingered for a moment longer, before he finally spoke. His voice was calm, but laced with an undercurrent of something unreadable. "Lord Edward Saint-Clair, 'tis an honour to lay mine eyes upon thee. I be Lucian Blackthorn."

Edward's gaze shifted, his brow furrowing slightly as he took in the man before him. He had never seen Lucian Blackthorn, but there was something about him—a stillness, a quiet menace—that made Edward's instincts flare to life. The man's presence was like a shadow, heavy and watching, and Edward's skin prickled with the weight of it. Lucian's words were casual, but there was an edge, something unreadable beneath them, and Edward couldn't shake the feeling that they were more than mere pleasantries.

Edward blinked, momentarily caught off guard. Lucian Blackthorn. The name rang no bells, but the way the man stood—unmoving, calculating—suggested a life lived in the shadows of danger. Edward straightened his posture, masking his discomfort. "It is a pleasure to make thy acquaintance, Lucian Blackthorn," he replied, his voice firm despite the unsettling weight settling on his shoulders. "With much regret, I must now take my leave."

Before he could move, the stable boy appeared from behind the barn, leading Edward's horse with a fluid motion. The boy's feet made no sound on the hard earth, and his face was set in the focused calm of someone who had done this task a thousand times before.

Lucian's smile remained, but there was a coldness to it—something not quite right. "The pleasure be mine," he said, his tone shifting just enough to leave a sense of hidden meaning.

"It doth seem I have forgotten that I have a meeting in Stowshire. If it be thy will, mayhaps thou wouldst allow me to ride with thee, my grace?"

Edward's gaze flickered as the stable boy drew closer, leading the horse with quiet determination. As the boy reached Edward's side, he gave a brief nod before holding the reins steady, offering Edward an unspoken assurance that the steed was ready.

Edward's hand twitched slightly toward the reins, but his attention remained on Lucian. "I do not plan to ride to Stowshire just yet; I wish to ride in the forest," he said, his voice firm but betraying a small crack of uncertainty. It was not that he was unwilling, but Lucian's presence—left him on edge.

Lucian's lips curled slightly, a knowing, almost amused glint in his eyes. "Old maid here doth enjoy riding through the forest," he quipped. "We may be tardy for our meeting. Pray, when thou art ready."

The words hung in the air, both casual and challenging. Edward's gaze shifted toward the archer still perched in the trees, a shadow in the branches, and the weight of his father's warning resurfaced in his mind. *Shouldst thou ever make use of the Shadow Serpents, prithee, do not provoke their wrath.* His hand tightened on the reins, fingers flexing involuntarily as the realisation settled in. They were dangerous—these men and their games. But turning down Lucian now, with the archer above and the whole situation swirling, seemed far worse.

Edward sighed, his breath a puff of mist in the cold air. Edward glanced at Lucian again, feeling the weight of his unblinking gaze. It was steady, sharp, almost as if Lucian were gauging his every move, waiting for any sign of hesitation.

The tension between them stretched taut, but Edward's posture straightened as he mounted his horse, his movements smooth but deliberate. "Yet let us ride then," he said, his voice as steady as he could muster, though the unease crept beneath his words.

The stable boy stepped back as Edward mounted, his eyes never leaving the pair, his silence palpable. Edward spurred his horse forward, the crunch of hooves against the frost the only sound in the cold, still air. Lucian followed, his mount—an old mare—moving with steady grace as he urged her forward. The two men fell into line, their path toward the forest unfolding ahead.

As Lucian guided his horse forward, his eyes flicked briefly to Edward, his mind churning with unspoken calculations. *Lord Geoffrey Saint-Clair hath parted with much coin for our service,* he mused inwardly, his fingers tightening slightly on the reins. *Yet mine loyalty is ever fickle. Should I remain true to him, warning of his son's name upon Lord Reginald Hawkecliff's list, or doth the weight of Hawkecliff's purse sway me toward darker tides?*

The old mare beneath him shifted with a quiet, practiced grace, and Lucian adjusted his posture in the saddle, his thoughts a tangle of ambition and duty. He let the silence settle, allowing the steady rhythm of hooves to steady his mind as the wind whispered through the trees. *Is it fate, perchance, that I should cross paths with Lord Edward now?*

A week hence

Princess Sophia

A week had dragged by, each day a relentless torment that weighed upon Sophia like iron shackles. Her stomach roiled without end, twisting and heaving as if to purge the very anxiety that gnawed at her insides. Food had become an enemy, turning sour upon her tongue, and her nerves, wound as tight as a lute string, left her trembling even in stillness. Each night, she endured the ritual of her despair: bent over the basin, wracked by retching that left her throat raw and her body hollow.

The chambermaid had come before the first blush of dawn, moving with the silence of a spectre to kindle the fire and bear away the fouled linens. Yet the air in the chamber remained heavy, her suffering clinging to it like smoke. No fire could chase away the chill that seemed to seep from within, nor could the faint light of morning ease the shadow upon her heart.

An hour later, the door creaked open once again, Sophia barely stirred, her wide, sunken eyes fixed upon the ceiling's wooden beams as though they held the answers to her torment. Rosalind entered with quiet purpose, her hands steady as she carried a steaming cup of herb tea. The soft scent of chamomile and mint whispered through the room, a fleeting kindness against the bitter pall that clung to Sophia like a shroud.

"Good morrow, Your Highness," Rosalind murmured, setting the cup upon the bedside table with deliberate care. Her gaze lingered briefly on the freshly scrubbed basin, a flicker of something between pity and resignation crossing her features. "The chambermaid hath seen to the fire and carried away the basin," she said, her voice calm, though her movements betrayed the tension of a woman well-versed in navigating delicate ground.

With great effort, Sophia pushed herself upright, her limbs heavy and trembling as though they bore the weight of her dread. Her hands closed around the cup, the warmth seeping into her chilled fingers offering a faint reprieve. "I thank thee, Rosalind," she whispered, her voice fragile and hoarse, as though the very act of speech were an exertion. She raised the tea to her lips, but the rising steam only turned her stomach anew. Setting it aside, she cast a pleading glance toward Rosalind. "Prithee, tell me thou hast heard aught from Lord Edward."

The silence that followed was damning. Rosalind hesitated, her steady composure cracking for but a moment as her gaze flitted to Sophia's trembling hands. "Nay, Your Highness," she said at last, her voice low and careful. "No word hath yet come."

Sophia's chest rose sharply as her breath hitched, the pain of disappointment cutting through her fragile resolve. Her nostrils flared as she exhaled, the sound sharp against the oppressive quiet. She lowered her head, pressing a hand to her temple as the room swayed faintly around her. "Since the news of King Shepparton's cursed proposal," she began, her voice low and bitter, "I have sought solace in the wine cup. Yet never, even in the wildest nights with Robert, did I wake so stricken as this day." Her lips twitched in a wry smile that did not reach her haunted eyes.

Rosalind moved closer, her presence grounding yet tentative, as though afraid to disturb a fragile thread. "Your Highness," she said softly, her hand brushing Sophia's sleeve, "the weight thou bearest is great. But if thou canst sway King John—if thou canst make him see reason—mayhap there is still hope to be found." She hesitated, her voice faltering under the weight of her own doubts. "Come now, let us prepare thee for the day. Thy strength must not falter when thou dost stand before him."

Sophia struggled to rise from the grand canopy bed, the fine feather-stuffed mattress beneath her offering no comfort to her aching body. The silken sheets, though soft against her skin, felt suffocating in her restless state. Clutching the edge of the carved wooden bedframe, she groaned, her voice trembling with indignation. "King Shepparton doth prattle whilst he dines! Fragments of food dost scatter hither and yon!" she lamented, her words sharp yet unsteady. "Even Beatrice Eldridge, who wast compelled to court him, hath attested to his loathsome nature. Not only is his visage most grotesque, but his character is as vile and repugnant!" Her voice cracked, and she pressed a trembling hand to her face as a sob escaped. "He did oft vaunt of his many harlots and baseborn whelps, and whilst his late wife yet lived, he would have her partake in his foul wickedness, treating her as naught but a vessel for his loathsome seed."

Rosalind's eyes flickered with a momentary glint of disdain as she adjusted the folds of her gown. "Do not vex thyself over King Shepparton," she said softly but firmly. "King John will see reason."

Sophia's hands trembled as Rosalind moved to her side, steadying her with gentle but purposeful hands. Unable to hold back, Sophia leaned into Rosalind, wrapping her arms around her tightly. "We must sway him," she whispered, her voice hoarse and choked with desperation. "Else I know not what I might do." She pulled back reluctantly, her pale face a mask of fear and resolve.

"King John is a just man, and though his duties oft keep him distant, he doth care for thy happiness. Trust that thou canst move him to favour thy choice of husband." Rosalind's voice was low, meant to soothe as she moved to assist Sophia. With practiced hands, she untied the laces of Sophia's finely woven shift, slipping the garment from her shoulders. The cool air nipped at Sophia's skin, drawing a faint shiver that worsened the unease already coiling in her stomach.

The fitted bodice came next, its snug lacing designed to shape and support, yet now it felt oppressive to Sophia's trembling frame. As Rosalind worked, pulling the laces tighter, Sophia's head swam, and her breath grew shallow. The nausea that churned in her stomach threatened to rise, and her face turned ashen.

Rosalind hesitated, her hands pausing mid-motion as her gaze flicked to Sophia's paling lips. "Your Highness, perchance I should summon a healer," she murmured, her tone careful but firm.

"Nay," Sophia whispered, her voice thin but resolute, though it cost her to speak. She gave a faint nod, bidding Rosalind to continue despite the torment.

With steady hands, Rosalind resumed her task. Each deliberate tug of the laces felt like a test of

Sophia's fragile strength. The corset was secured at last, and the gown of deep blue was brought forward, its heavy fabric whispering as it slid over Sophia's shoulders. The weight of it settled heavily, a stark reminder of her rank and all it demanded.

Sophia stood motionless, her breath shallow as Rosalind smoothed the folds of the gown and tied its fastenings. Even the gentle tugs of the laces sent tremors through her frayed senses, yet she bore it in silence. Rosalind's hands moved to Sophia's hair, weaving it into a simple braid, her usual precision softened by the care she took to avoid causing further distress. When the braid was finished, Sophia exhaled shakily, the effort of sitting still leaving her as drained as a day's labor.

The stillness shattered with a sharp knock at the door, the sound echoing through the chamber like a thunderclap. Sophia stiffened, her wide eyes darting to Rosalind, who shared her unease.

"Who might it be?" Sophia asked, her voice tight with apprehension.

"I know not, Your Highness," Rosalind replied, already moving to the door. She opened it cautiously, revealing Sir Hector standing in the dim corridor beyond. The knight shifted awkwardly, his gaze briefly flicking past Rosalind to the richly appointed chamber.

"Good morrow, Sir Hector," Rosalind greeted, her tone polite yet wary. "What brings thee hither at this hour?"

Sophia remained seated, her trembling hands clutching the armrests as she fought to compose herself. Each beat of her heart throbbed in her temples, and the folds of her gown felt unbearably heavy against her lap. She glanced toward the door with shadowed eyes, her voice barely above a whisper. "Good day, Sir Hector," she said, the faint quiver in her tone betraying her effort to sound steady. "What news dost thou bring?"

Sir Hector inclined his head with a knight's practiced precision, his armour creaking faintly with the motion. "Your Highness," he began, his voice steady and formal, "a chambermaid hath informed me that thou didst request further aid for thy quarters this morn. She awaiteth in the corridor—shall I bid her enter?"

Rosalind stepped forward, her movements smooth and purposeful as she positioned herself between the door and Sophia. "Aye," she said quickly, her tone measured but firm. "We did request aid this day. Pray, send her in, Sir Hector."

Sophia nodded faintly, her lips parting as though to speak, but she held her tongue. Her grip on the armrests tightened, her strength reserved for holding herself upright as the chamber swayed faintly around her.

Hector gave a brisk nod. "At once, Your Highness." Without hesitation, he turned on his heel and strode out down the corridor, his boots ringing faintly against the stone. The door clicked softly as it closed, leaving the two women in uneasy silence.

Sophia exhaled shakily, her chest rising and falling in uneven rhythm. "Could it verily be Mary?" she whispered, her voice low, trembling with a fragile hope.

Rosalind's gaze remained fixed on the door, her expression calm but sharp with awareness. "We shall see," she said, her tone steady but edged with caution. She moved to stand beside Sophia, her presence a quiet reassurance.

Sophia's fingers dug into the armrests, her mind spinning with possibilities. She pressed her lips together, willing the nausea and dizziness to subside as the moments stretched on, taut with anticipation. The chamber felt smaller with each passing breath, the weight of the unknown pressing heavy on both women as they waited for the door to open once more.

Rosalind stepped to the small wooden chest beside the vanity, her hands deft as she opened it to reveal the princess's finest adornments. Gold gleamed in the soft morning light, and jewels of sapphire and pearl winked from their delicate settings. Rosalind selected a modest necklace of deep blue stones, its colour echoing the gown Sophia wore.

"Let us finish thy preparations, Your Highness," Rosalind spoke softly, her tone calm but unwavering as she returned to Sophia's side. She unclasped the necklace and gently looped it around the princess's neck, her fingers light and precise as they fastened it. The cool touch of the metal against Sophia's skin caused her to shiver faintly, but she said nothing.

"'Tis fitting," Rosalind said softly, stepping back to survey her handiwork. She retrieved a matching pair of earrings, offering them to Sophia with a small tilt of her head. "Shall I assist, or dost thou wish to place these thyself?"

Sophia's trembling hands rose slowly, but they faltered before reaching the earrings. Frustration flickered across her pale cheeks. "Pray, do it for me," she said, her voice barely above a whisper. "Mine hands lack steadiness this morn."

Rosalind nodded, her movements as steady as ever as she affixed the earrings, her touch careful so as not to pull at Sophia's tender skin. "There," she said, stepping back once more. "Now thou art ready, Your Highness."

Sophia exhaled softly, lifting a hand to trace the edge of the necklace. The weight of the jewelry, though slight, felt like another tether to her role—a role she could not escape. She spoke at last, her voice frail but steady. "Let us meet whatsoe'er doth await, Rosalind."

It seemed an eternity before Mary and Sir Hector finally arrived at Sophia's chamber. Mary's eyes widened at the sight of the guards stationed outside the doors. With guards at the princess's quarters and chamber as well, was the princess truly in such need of that much protection? She curtsied to Sophia, the motion feeling foreign and strange. She recalled when Sophia had disguised herself as a fellow peasant, a supposed runaway from a lesser household, spending time with Robert and even staying at the cottage—a choice that would have surely landed them both in trouble. Now, Sophia sat before her in one of Briarwood's grandest castles, adorned with gold necklaces, bracelets, and a gown of exquisite beauty. "You may come in," Sophia commanded, her voice steady. She turned to Sir Hector and said, "Your gallantry is greatly appreciated, good knight." Sir Hector nodded respectfully and withdrew, allowing Mary to enter the chamber with hesitant steps.

Rosalind curtsied gracefully. "Should I take my leave as well, my princess?"

Sophia offered a gentle smile, understanding Rosalind's intent. "Aye, Rosalind, thou mayest go."

Before leaving, Rosalind moved toward the side table where the untouched cup of herbal tea rested. She lifted it with care and carried it to Sophia. "Mayhap this will bring thee some ease, Your Highness," she said softly, offering the cup with steady hands.

Sophia hesitated, then accepted it with a faint nod. Her trembling hands brushed against Rosalind's steady grip as she tried to take hold of the cup. For a moment, she faltered, the weight unsteady in her grasp, but she managed to bring it carefully to her lap. "I thank thee, Rosalind," she murmured, her voice soft and strained.

Rosalind curtsied once more and departed swiftly, her movements precise and respectful. As the door closed behind her, Sophia felt another wave of nausea rise, but she forced it down, determined to keep her composure.

The door closed behind Rosalind with a soft thud, leaving the princess and Mary in the quiet chamber. Though it was daytime, the narrow window allowed little light to filter in, and shadows clung to the corners where the faint glow could not reach.

Sophia drew a shaky breath, her trembling hands resting in her lap as she steadied herself. Her gaze settled on Mary, uncertainty flickering in her eyes as she searched for the words to cross the divide between them. "Mary," she began softly, her voice laced with hesitation, "I am grateful thou hast come."

Another wave of sickness struck Sophia. She hovered her hand over her mouth as bile rose, managing to swallow it back. With slow, weak steps, she moved to the bed and sat near the bucket. "Forgive me, my strength is lacking this morn," she murmured, her voice strained. "I beg thee, tell me how Robert fares?"

Mary stood before her, the conflict within her a tempest. Her fury simmered beneath the surface, tempered only by the obligation to respect Sophia's royal station. Though she was still the princess, the hurt she had caused Mary's family deserved recognition. "He is as well as one can expect, Your Highness," Mary replied, her tone edged with restraint. "Considering our sister hath been attacked and is still missing."

Sophia's smile faltered, her expression clouded with concern. Guilt weighed heavily on her heart, each beat a reminder of her remorse. Sorrow wrapped around her like a shroud, knowing that her actions had unwittingly placed Noor in harm's way. "Lord Edward Saint-Clair hath spared no effort in searching for her," she said softly. "He hath even offered rewards for any word of Noor's whereabouts."

Mary's heart tightened. Resentment flooded her being. She couldn't escape the knowledge that it was the princess's decisions that had set this chain of events in motion. She forced a grateful smile, mustering the strength to thank Sophia, though her mind churned with conflicting emotions.

Blinking back tears, Mary fought to steady herself, pushing aside her turmoil to refocus on her purpose. With a voice thick with emotion, she made her plea to Sophia, her desperation evident in every trembling word. "I was hoping thou couldst arrange a private audience with the king for me."

Sophia's eyes flickered with recognition, subtly indicating her awareness of the rumours about Mary and the king. The memory of Sophia hiding behind a tapestry, watching her brother's fleeting glances at Mary, resurfaced. She nodded in understanding. "Of course, I shall do what I can," Sophia replied.

Noticing the tension in Mary's demeanor, Sophia sensed her discomfort. "Pray, take thy seat," she urged, gesturing towards a nearby chair. A vulnerable warmth flickered across her face, gradually pushing back the strain that had grown thick and heavy in the air. "If thou art to meet with the king, allow me to do thy hair. I remember how exquisite it looked on the day of the ball, and I am certain the king was captivated by thy beauty."

Sophia reached for her herbal tea, hoping it might ease her unsettled stomach. She blew gently at the steam before taking a careful sip, then placed the cup down again.

Mary's mind raced with conflicting thoughts and emotions. She wished to maintain a distance, to protect herself from the unpredictable nature of her feelings for the king. Yet, there was a flicker of longing deep within her, a desire to present herself in the best possible light for their possible meeting. With a resigned nod, Mary took a seat, allowing Sophia to help prepare her for the audience ahead.

Sophia slowly stood, fighting the sickness in her stomach, a strange exhaustion weighing her down. She wished to inquire more about Robert, but sensed that easing Mary into such a conversation would be wiser. Her fingers moved with practiced grace as she began to style Mary's hair, reaching for a simple ribbon and gently weaving it through, creating a modest yet elegant style.

As Sophia delicately wove her fingers through Mary's locks, a moment of silence hung between them. Finally, Sophia broke it, her voice soft. "How dost thou find serving Charles?"

Serving Prince Charles was sheer torment. He had openly confessed to stabbing her sister and faced no consequences. What he did to Noor and how he still forced her to serve him filled her with rage. Every day, the knowledge and helplessness haunted Mary. She could do nothing and tell no one; he promised to bring more harm to her family if she did. The thought of her beloved Robert in danger made her blood boil and her heart ache. She dreamed of the day she could exact her revenge but didn't trust Princess Sophia with her true feelings. Despite Sophia's kindness, Mary couldn't shake the feeling that the princess was part of the court's treachery. Masking her pain, she said, "Serving in the castle rather than in the fields takes much less toll on one's mind and body. Thy mother, the Queen Mother, surprises me. She is not at all what I had imagined."

Sophia's eyes softened as she replied, "I can only imagine what hard labour it must be to serve in the fields, enduring the cold storms. It must be truly dreadful." In truth, she had never known such hardship, having spent most of her life in the comfort of the castle. Her face remained serene, betraying none of her inner thoughts. With a light, airy laugh, she added, "Mine own mother surpriseth me at times as well."

Mary tilted her head slightly, her eyes lifting to meet Sophia's. "It is my understanding that thou and my brother have ventured into the forest," she began, her voice measured. She hesitated, carefully avoiding the word "hunt," as it was illegal without royal permission. The thought crossed her mind that, as the princess, Sophia's presence might itself grant permission, yet she chose caution. "It can be very hard labour in the forest, especially in such bad weather, dost thou not agree?"

Sophia's heart lifted at the mention of Robert's name. She knew she must explain to Mary that neither she nor Robert could speak to anyone else about their intimate relationship or their questionable antics. Such matters could have them all thrown into the dungeon, or worse, executed. For risking the tainting of the royal bloodline with a peasant was treachery of the highest order. She knew she had to say something but did not wish to frighten Mary. Seizing the opportunity to ask more, she spoke softly, "Aye, many a time the weather was frightful. Thy brother bore the brunt of it."

Her mind drifted to the moments Robert had shown her the secrets of the forest: identifying poisonous plants, those that healed, and those that killed. She remembered the exhilaration of learning to hunt and survive by his side. Her thoughts then lingered on the stolen moments of passion, her back pressed against the rough bark of a tree, their lips meeting with fervor despite the cold numbing their fingers. The memory was so vivid, she could almost feel the warmth of his breath, the softness of his lips once more.

With a heavy sigh, Mary summoned the strength to respond. "Your Highness," she began, "may I speak freely?" The request hung in the air, laden with the weight of unspoken truths and pent-up emotions.

"You deceived us by concealing your true identity and vanishing," Mary continued, her voice tinged with disappointment. "Robert had to learn from me that you were courting Edward Saint-Clair, a man of high standing that he can never compete with. I believe he feels more betrayed than protected."

Sophia's head drooped, tears welled up in her eyes. She couldn't bear the thought of Robert's pain. Her words flowed forth like a sorrowful stream, each one burdened with regret and longing. "If thou understood my duties and my yearning for freedom," Sophia whispered, "I had to forsake the royal life." Each syllable carried the weight of her desire to break free from Thorncrest Castle's confines, to shatter the chains of captivity. "I should have disclosed all truth to thee," she confessed, her voice heavy with remorse.

Sophia's voice quavered as she continued, her eyes brimming with anguish. "I did not wish to return! I was brought back hither against my will. Now mine own mother and the royal adviser have condemned me to this chamber, making me a prisoner within the very walls that once offered sanctuary.

Guards shadow my every step, as if I am a danger to be contained. I may only leave this chamber under their vigilant gaze." She gestured towards the door, her expression pained. "Didst thou see Sir Hector? He is to accompany me everywhere."

Mary's eyes narrowed as she observed Sophia. "Sir Hector is quite the sight to behold. He doth not appear as a mere hireling; nay, he hath the bearing of a well-to-do knight. A knight who would require much coin." She paused, curiosity edging her voice. "When thou took thy leave, when thou decided to be anyone but the princess, how much coin didst thou bring?" She wondered how the princess planned to survive outside the castle walls.

Sophia's eyes met Mary's without a flicker of hesitation. "I brought three hand-held sacks with me," she replied calmly.

Mary could not suppress the roll of her eyes, feeling a twinge of irritation. She was beginning to feel like Noor, who was usually the one to ask countless questions, not herself. "Bronze, silver, or gold?"
Sophia's brow furrowed slightly, as if she seldom dealt with bronze. "Why dost thou ask?" she inquired, tying the end of the braid she was working on in Mary's hair.

Mary recalled Noor mocking Sophia when she first heard of her, ridiculing her for wearing such pricey items that would surely draw the attention of thieves and muggers. She pressed on, "The items thou brought with thee, were they for trading shouldst thou run low on coin?"

Sophia's silence spoke volumes; the idea of trading her goods had clearly never crossed her mind. Mary did not wait for an answer, instead, she swiftly asked another question, "How much coin and how many items didst thou return with?"

Sophia's inner thoughts crumbled as she recalled her journey. She had spent many coins on lodging and nights out with Robert, and the rest was stolen when her chamber was ransacked. Though she did not wish to share this with Mary, she did not understand why Mary was asking so persistently. "Enough to flee Ravenswood town," she lied.

Mary, sensing the unease but maintaining a respectful tone, pressed on, "Oh, how lovely, Your Highness. Where didst thou plan to flee?"

Sophia's composure wavered for a brief moment. She had no clear destination when she fled, just a desperate need to escape. She quickly masked her uncertainty with a faint smile. "I thought to find refuge in the southern lands," she replied, hoping the vague answer would suffice.

Mary's gaze remained sharp, not missing the brief flicker of hesitation in Sophia's eyes. She remembered Noor's mocking words about the princess's naivety. Pressing on, she asked, "What didst thou intend to do in the southern lands, Your Highness?"

Sophia's mind raced, the pressure of maintaining her facade growing heavier. Panic sparked within her, but she squashed it, pulling on a mask of serenity to hide the growing anxiety. "To purchase farmland and live there," she said softly, trying to steer the conversation away from her failures.

Mary recalled Noor's derisive laughter when she spoke of Sophia's folly. Her eyes narrowed slightly as she asked, "And didst thou have knowledge of farming, Your Highness? What price doth one pay for farmland in the southern lands?"

Sophia forced herself to hold Mary's gaze, though her heart pounded in her chest. "I had hoped to gain knowledge," she replied, her voice steady but tinged with uncertainty. Her words faltered as though tripping over the weight of her own naivety, a feeble attempt to justify her choices. Mary, though careful to maintain a respectful demeanor, could not hide her frustration entirely.

"Your Highness, thou didst leave the castle with no plan and no knowledge of the hardships of common life, bringing Robert with thee without him fully understanding thy true station?"

Mary, trying to temper her frustration with understanding, spoke gently, "I cannot pretend to fathom the hardship thou dost face, being forced into a marriage. But didst thou not think that if thou hadst not encountered my brother, thou might have faced a far worse fate?" She paused, her voice laced with concern. "A fair young maiden wandering alone in the forest... thou couldst have crossed paths with thieves who would take all that thou hadst, including the very gown upon thy back. Or worse, someone might have taken thee by force, sold thee to a brothel, or locked thee away as their own wife, never to see the light of day again. Such a fate would be no better than a forced marriage, save that thou wouldst be deprived of seeing thy family or holding thy title."

Sophia's face paled as the dread crept over her. With each syllable, Mary rewrote the script of what might've been, her words rendering a desolate landscape that left her shaken. Mary's tone was earnest, her intent clear: to make Sophia understand the gravity of her reckless actions.

Sophia reached for her tea and took another sip, trying to steady her nerves. "I cannot speak to what might have befallen me had I not been so fortunate as to meet Robert," she said softly. "Whilst some forced marriages may turn out well, many do not. "Many a time have I laid bare mine plight before him, and he did seem to grasp it. A fool am I, for I know well that Robert hath lain with many afore me. His dealings have oft been fraught with complications, and though he knew not that I am the princess, he did seem to hold some faint understanding that I fled, bearing a noble title."

The princess may have her own battles, but she would never know the hardships of days of labor. She would never truly understand what it is to starve and watch her family cry on the floor as they succumb to hunger. She would never have to beg for shelter from the cold. Despite this, Mary kept her tone respectful and understanding. "Whether Robert doth understand the circumstances or not, it shall not ease the pain he might feel," she remarked with a hint of gravity.

Mary clenched her hands, the memory of her own family's suffering vivid in her mind. She wanted to ask about Sophia's relationship with Edward, but she knew better than to pry. The sight of

Robert's anguish was enough to make her hold her tongue. It mattered little whether Sophia's involvement with Edward Saint-Clair was of her own free will or not. The damage had been done, and the heartbreak endured by Robert could not be easily assuaged.

Sophia's sobs intensified as Mary's words sank deep into her wounded heart. Her voice cracked with pain as she confessed, "I ne'er meant for any of this to happen."

As she spoke, Mary could discern the love and longing in Sophia's eyes, and in that fleeting moment, she couldn't help but feel a pang of sadness for her. However, what could she say to the princess? It was done now; she couldn't afford to scorn her highness, as it could land her in trouble.

Sophia's fingers moved deftly, tying off the braid in Mary's hair with a simple ribbon. She stepped back, her gaze lingering briefly on her work. "Thy hair looks lovely," she said softly, her tone calm but distant.

The lingering emotions in the chamber seemed to intensify, creating an almost suffocating atmosphere. Mary awkwardly smiled in return, running her fingers over the braids. ""I thank thee, Your Highness," she replied.

Turning to the side table, she reached for the clay cup that Rosalind had left earlier. She gripped the cup firmly, its rough surface coarse against her fingertips, and raised it to her lips. Though the fire in the hearth crackled softly, its heat had not fully dispelled the lingering chill from the far corners of the chamber.

She sipped the tea, the bitterness sharp on her tongue. As the warmth slid down her throat, her stomach shifted uneasily, settling just enough to keep the nausea at bay. Lowering the cup slowly, she placed it back on the table with care.

She exhaled quietly, her breath trembling as if it carried the weight of her thoughts. "I must ask thee not to speak of Robert and my connection within earshot of anyone," she murmured, leaning slightly forward. Her voice lowered, each word deliberate, as though the air itself grew heavier between them. "It could mean ruin for me, and the consequences could be grave for us both."

Mary's gaze narrowed, concern etching lines across her brow, as Sophia's words hung in the air like an ominous cloud. The prince's blunt threats during their private encounters had made it abundantly clear. Mary knew all too well the severity of the consequences for a commoner—or anyone, for that matter—who dared to engage with a titled woman. The double standard favoured men, granting them freedoms denied to women. They could father illegitimate children with impunity, deciding at their discretion whether to acknowledge their offspring.

"Fear not, Your Highness," Mary responded, her voice steady yet tinged with quiet defiance. Each word she chose subtly pushed against the oppressive norms that bound them. "I knowest the law. I shall hold my tongue, lest trouble find me or any other."

Sophia's tense expression softened as she prepared to speak. But just as she poised to utter her thoughts, a firm knock reverberated through the chamber. From the other side, Sir Hector's voice announced, "Your highness, 'tis thy handmaiden."

Sophia's shoulders eased slightly as she beckoned, "Enter, Rosalind," her voice tempered with lingering relief from the earlier tension.

Rosalind, the princess's handmaiden, knocked gently on the door, drawing Sophia's attention away from her conversation. The morning sunlight filtered weakly through the high, narrow windows, its touch doing little to dispel the weight hanging over her. The impending arrival of the king cast a shadow over her thoughts, and with it, the matter of Edward's proposal weighed heavier still. A week had passed since she had last heard from his grace, the silence gnawing at the edges of her composure. She forced a smile, brittle and brief, as though trying to convince herself there was nothing to worry about.

Sophia's gaze fixed on the heavy oak door as it creaked open, revealing Rosalind's figure framed by the muted light from the corridor beyond. The hinges groaned in protest, the sound filling the room like an unwelcome reminder of what awaited. Mary rose gracefully from her seat, her sharp eyes flickering between Sophia and Rosalind, as if reading something unsaid in their faces.

Rosalind approached with a deferential bow, her steps quiet but deliberate. "Your Highness, I bear news from His Majesty's messenger," she announced, her voice calm yet tinged with something unspoken. Her gaze flitted to Mary briefly before settling on Sophia, and the silence that followed carried a weight Rosalind didn't dare name.

Sophia inclined her head, her brow furrowing slightly as though searching Rosalind's face for answers she wouldn't give. "Thank thee, Rosalind," she replied, her voice steady despite the tightening of her hands at her sides. "Inform Sir Hector that we shall descend to the lower chambers presently."

Rosalind curtsied and withdrew, her footsteps soft as she disappeared through the door. Sophia's eyes lingered on the space she left behind, her thoughts circling Edward's absence. *Surely, there is a cause for his silence. There must needs be.*

Her hand brushed against the silk of her gown, a nervous gesture she barely noticed as unease tightened in her chest. Edward was the best choice among the suitors pressed upon her—better, at least, than the ancient lords with their hollow eyes and greedy smiles. And yet, the very thought of tying herself to him left her heart aching for what could never be.

Sophia's brow furrowed with worry as she pondered the weight of duty and the constraints of her royal station. Would her brother, the king, decree that she marry King Shepparton, or might there be mercy, allowing her to pursue a union with Lord Edward Saint-Clair?

Her hands fidgeted with the fabric of her gown, as though trying to keep still, but the gentle caress of the silk only amplified her anxiousness.

She summoned a faint smile to mask her inner turmoil before turning to Mary. "Wouldst thou care to accompany us in greeting the king?" she inquired.

Mary's heart fluttered at the thought of seeing the king. Her pulse quickened with a mix of excitement and apprehension. Gathering her resolve, she accepted with a steady voice, "It would be an honour, Your Highness."

As they departed the chamber, sunlight spilled faintly through the narrow stone windows, casting elongated shadows along the cold floor. The heavy oak door groaned as it was drawn shut behind them, enclosing the chamber in quiet.

Two guards stood sentinel at the princess's chamber, their chain mail glinting faintly in the dim light of the corridor. They bore polished spears, standing rigid with stern gazes fixed on the hall beyond. Sir Hector, though younger than most knights, followed at a respectful distance behind the princess and her entourage. His robust stature and sharp features might have been striking, but Sophia found his constant presence an unwelcome reminder of the scrutiny that followed her every step, even in Thorncrest Castle, her own home.

*

<u>Thorncrest Castle's main gates</u>

The corridor stretched before them, dim and cold, the tap of Sophia's boots breaking the heavy silence. Rosalind kept close to her side, her hands clasped at her waist, her face betraying little but the faint crease of worry at her brow. Ahead, the great doors of the castle courtyard loomed, their iron bands glinting faintly in the muted light.

Sophia's pace quickened as they neared. Her head tilted slightly, her sharp gaze cutting toward the attendant lagging behind. A flick of her hand, almost imperceptible, sent him stumbling forward, his face flushing as he rushed to the doorkeeper.

Mary walked a step behind them, her fingers twisting the edge of her apron. She swallowed hard, her gaze darting toward the sentries flanking the gate. Their stony expressions and watchful eyes pinned her in place for a moment before she forced herself forward, her steps faltering only slightly.

The doorkeeper leaned into the peephole, his words muffled as he spoke to the guards on the other side. Sophia stood motionless, her chin high and her eyes narrowing ever so slightly. The faint scrape of metal on wood broke the silence as the doorkeeper withdrew, reaching for the iron key at his neck. His movements were slow, deliberate, the key catching in the lock with a hollow clank.

The doors groaned open, sunlight spilling into the dark corridor and bringing with it a sharp gust of cold air. Sophia raised a hand, squinting slightly as the glare struck her face. When her gaze adjusted, the faintest shadow of irritation crossed her features. Baldwin Honorcrest stood waiting, his polished boots and immaculate posture at odds with the rough stone courtyard behind him.

"Your highness," Baldwin greeted, bowing low, his voice smooth and practiced. He straightened with a slight smile, his eyes lingering on Sophia just long enough to gauge her reaction.

Sophia inclined her head, her expression unreadable save for the slight tightening at the corners of her mouth. "Baldwin." Her voice was clipped, the single word carrying an edge sharp enough to slice. *Doth he come to greet the king, or hath Charles bid Baldwin some foul task?*

Baldwin's smile didn't falter. He turned to Sir Hector, offering the knight an equally deep bow. "Good day, Sir Hector."

Hector nodded curtly, his gauntleted hand resting on the pommel of his sword. Baldwin's attention then shifted, his polished demeanor softening as he addressed Rosalind. "Mistress Rosalind," he said warmly, inclining his head. "A pleasure."

Rosalind's lips curved in a polite smile, though her eyes flickered with unease. She glanced briefly at Mary, whose hands stilled against her apron as Baldwin turned to her.

"Mistress Mary," Baldwin said softly, his tone gentler now. His gaze lingered a moment longer than necessary, as though recalling their earlier walk.

Mary hesitated, meeting his eyes briefly before looking away. The faintest of smiles touched her lips, fleeting and uncertain. Her grip on her apron tightened again as she shifted her weight, her shoulders stiffening. *By the saints, shall Baldwin betray me anon? Will he haste to the prince and speak of my presence here, and that I bide with the princess, awaiting the king?*

The cold air swirled around them, carrying with it the faint clang of distant bells. Baldwin's presence, though outwardly benign, hung over the group like a storm cloud on the verge of breaking. Sophia's gaze flicked toward the open courtyard, her impatience barely hidden beneath the steel of her composure. Beside her, Rosalind stood silent, her hands clasped tightly as though bracing for what lay ahead.

Mary cast a fleeting glance toward the doors, her breath misting in the chill air. The moment stretched taut, the yawning expanse of the courtyard a stark reminder of the unseen forces at work beyond the gates.

The gatehouse loomed ahead, its spires clawing at the pale winter sky. Beyond, a carriage emblazoned with the royal crest waited, its restless horses pawing at the frozen ground, their breath clouding the crisp air. A blast of horns shattered the courtyard's stillness, reverberating off the castle walls as the drawbridge creaked, groaning under the weight of unseen tension.

Sophia paused mid-step, her head tilting ever so slightly as her gaze met Mary's. No words passed between them, but the sharpness of the princess's glance spoke volumes. Mary stiffened, her fingers clutching the fabric of her apron as she matched Rosalind's pace, trailing behind the princess into the open courtyard. The chill cut through their layers, nipping at exposed skin as they moved into the light.

Sir Hector and a castle guard strode forward to flank the princess, their steel-clad boots striking the cobblestones with authority. Mary stumbled at Sir Hector's sudden movement, her lips pressing into a thin line as she regained her footing. Rosalind cast her a quick, knowing look but said nothing, her attention shifting as the sound of hoofbeats began to rise—distant at first, then steadily louder, like the drumbeat of an advancing storm.

The drawbridge lowered, its massive chains groaning under the strain. Beyond, the royal procession emerged, the powerful steeds at its head gleaming as sunlight caught the polished barding that adorned their flanks. Knights rode in tight formation around the king's carriage, their armour flashing like mirrors, their eyes scanning the surroundings with cold vigilance.

Baldwin Honorcrest, ever the dutiful attendant, took a step back, bowing swiftly. "I shall inform the prince and the Queen Mother at once," he murmured, his words clipped but deferential.

Sophia's lips barely moved as she muttered under her breath, her tone carrying just enough venom to make Mary glance sideways. "Let the prince rot in his chambers. His presence will not dignify the king's arrival."

Mary's mouth twitched, stifling the smile that threatened to break free. Rosalind glanced at her and gave a slight shake of her head, though her own lips curved with faint amusement. Baldwin, unbothered, nodded and strode off toward the castle, his boots clicking sharply against the stone.

The knights thundered across the drawbridge, the lead rider reining in his destrier with a sharp pull. Sir Eadric dismounted in one fluid motion, his dark cloak sweeping the ground as his boots struck the cobblestones. His gloved hand rested lightly on the pommel of his sword as he moved to the carriage door, his keen eyes sweeping the courtyard.

Mary leaned toward Rosalind, her voice low. "Requireth His Majesty truly so many knights? We be but an hour's ride from Ravenswood, if that."

"Guarded, always," Rosalind replied in a hushed tone. "This be not so many guards for a king. Oft doth he keep far more."

The clatter of wheels on stone signaled the carriage's stop. Alaric Stonebrook, the king's steward, darted forward, his movements quick and efficient as he reached for the door. With a practiced motion, he stepped aside as the king emerged, his mantle of deep royal blue shimmering with gold embroidery.

Mary drew a sharp breath. The golden crown rested firmly atop his head, catching the sunlight in brief flashes that gleamed against the rich blue of his mantle. The king stepped down from the carriage with measured grace, the weight of his crown matched by the presence that seemed to settle the air around him. Each movement was deliberate, his mantle brushing the cobblestones as his gaze swept over the gathered company, sharp and assured.

His every movement was deliberate, exuding the effortless command of one who had borne the weight of a kingdom for decades.

The king's gaze swept the courtyard, settling first on Sophia. A rare smile crossed his face, faint but genuine, the kind that might briefly ease the weariness etched into his features by years of kingship. "Sister!" His voice rang out, rich and affectionate, cutting through the tension as easily as a blade.

Princess Sophia, Mary, and Rosalind curtsied deeply, the hems of their gowns sweeping the cold stone as they lowered their heads in respect. Around them, the guards placed fists to chests in solemn salute, and Sir Hector, ever vigilant, inclined his head in acknowledgment of his liege. Even the doorkeeper, stooped with age and years of service, bent low, his key-laden chain clinking faintly with the movement.

As the king drew near, Sophia was trapped in the intensity of his gaze, his eyes flashing with an unspoken intent. "Thou look'st well," he said, his voice rich with warmth as his arms opened briefly in invitation. Sophia moved with practiced grace, closing the distance and accepting the embrace without hesitation.

Her shoulders easing as she embraced him briefly. "'Tis a boon to set mine eyes upon thee, Your Majesty! Thou hast been sorely missed."

When the king's eyes shifted to Mary, the young maiden stilled under his gaze. Her cheeks flushed as though the winter chill had returned, her hands twisting the fabric of her apron before she caught herself and stilled. His smile remained kind, yet sharp with the weight of authority, as he turned next to Rosalind. A faint nod and a fleeting smile spoke volumes, a gesture of familiarity that carried the ease of a man well-versed in diplomacy.

The king's attention returned to Sophia, whose gaze was steady, her posture immaculate. "To what do I owe the pleasure of this welcomed party?" he asked, his tone light yet probing, like a knight testing the strength of his opponent's guard.

Sophia inclined her head, her voice measured as she replied, "Your Majesty," her words dipped low, meant only for her brother's ears. "Mary Winterbourne hath sought an audience with thee in private."

The king's sharp eyes turned to Mary, his brow arching slightly as curiosity flickered across his face. Before he could respond, Mary stepped forward, her hands clasped before her as though to anchor her courage. "Your Highness," she began, her voice quiet but steady, "if it pleases thee, I would prefer our meeting to remain confidential."

The king regarded her in silence for a moment, his lips curling into a faint smile that hinted at intrigue. He inclined his head in agreement, his voice dropping to match the hushed tones of the exchange. "Very well," he murmured, the words carrying the weight of both command and promise.

He straightened then, his voice rising to fill the courtyard. "But first," he said, his tone regaining its commanding edge, "let us render due homage unto our most gracious host."

With a sweeping gesture of his hand, he motioned toward the towering castle doors. The procession fell into step behind him, the sound of their footsteps echoing faintly against the castle's stone walls. Guards in polished armour took their places, their swords glinting in the pale light as they moved with practiced vigilance. Danger lurked in every corner, but they stood watch, vigilant sentinels scanning the courtyard with an intensity that bordered on ferocity.

Sophia and Mary followed closely, Rosalind a step behind them. The tension in the air remained unspoken but palpable, each member of the party acutely aware of the protocols that governed their every movement. The guards stationed at the entrance bowed deeply as the procession approached, their disciplined movements a mark of respect for the royal party.

The king paused just before the doors, his figure framed by the looming stone archway.

Commanding attention without a word, he swept his gaze across the room, exuding an air of quiet strength that pressed pause on the entire gathering. "Shall we?" he said, his voice a touch lighter now, gesturing for the others to proceed.

Sophia exchanged a brief glance with Mary, her expression unreadable but not unkind. They moved back through the shadowed corridor, where the air hung cool and still. The dim light filtering through narrow windows high in the stone walls mingled with the flicker of torches mounted along the passage. Their steps echoed faintly as they approached the grand doors ahead.

Hastening back, Baldwin Honorcrest dipped into a quick bow, his breath uneven from his hurried pace. Straightening, he ran a hand over his tunic as though to steady himself, then clicked his fingers sharply to summon a nearby steward. William, the steward, stepped forward at once, his head bowed in deference. "Permit William to escort thee unto the guest chambers, Thy Highness," Baldwin said, his voice tight as he exhaled sharply, gesturing for the steward to approach.

The king waved his hand dismissively. "That needeth not be. Lead me unto the prince," he commanded firmly.

Understanding the king's directive, Baldwin Honorcrest nodded briskly and motioned for the king and his guards to follow him. They moved purposefully through the familiar stone corridors of the castle, their footsteps echoing softly against the walls. Light filtered in faintly through narrow, high-set windows, illuminating patches of the worn stone floor. Princess Sophia, Mary, and Rosalind followed close behind, their movements steady as they trailed the royal procession.

As they walked, the king glanced at the stone walls, saying nothing. "It seems little hath changed," he remarked quietly, his tone tinged with nostalgia. He touched the wall as they passed, his fingers briefly skimming the cold stone.

The faint marks etched into the stones—where torches had hung or furniture once stood—brought back fleeting memories of his childhood.

Sophia exchanged a knowing glance with Mary, recognizing the weight of her brother's words. This was not the grand seat of a king, but the home of his boyhood—a place tied to his past, not his crown.

Sophia leaned toward Rosalind, her voice low but sharp. "I fail to understand why Charles must be involved. Must we endure his presence at every turn?" She rolled her eyes in exasperation, her words carrying no effort to conceal her disdain.

Rosalind blushed slightly, though a flicker of amusement crossed her lips. "Treading lightly around Prince Charles can prove quite the challenge, Thy Highness. His presence always doth complicate our affairs unnecessarily." Her tone was measured, though her lowered gaze betrayed a reluctant fondness.

Mary trailed behind, her sharp gaze catching the faintest shift in Rosalind's countenance as she spoke. A cold knot of disdain coiled within her breast. Admiration for Charles? The very thought curdled the blood—nay, a man such as he deserved naught but contempt. Her jaw tightened, but she stilled at the king's gaze, heat rising unbidden to her face.

King John's sharp eyes flicked her way, narrowing ever so slightly. Mary's heart stuttered, her pulse quickening as though she had been caught pilfering from the royal table. Her cheeks burned, and she dropped her eyes at once, smoothing her skirt with trembling hands as though the motion might steady her. *Still thy thoughts, girl. He sees too much. Let not thy tongue betray thee further.*

The king's attention lingered a heartbeat longer before he resumed his purposeful stride. The echoes of their progress filled the corridor—the steady rhythm of boots on stone, the creak of Baldwin's worn leather, and the faint jingle of the guards' mail. Sunlight streamed faintly through high, narrow windows, its cold morning glow spilling across the polished stone walls.

As they neared the grand throne chamber, the company halted abruptly. Mary blinked, her brows furrowing as she caught sight of the Saint-Clair guards stationed with the royal guards and the royal usher. "Saint-Clair? What business have they here, and at such an hour?" She cast a sidelong glance at Sophia and Rosalind. The faint widening of Sophia's eyes and the sharp intake of Rosalind's breath mirrored her own astonishment, though neither dared to voice it.

The guards at the chamber's doors waited in sharp formation, their polished steel helmets gleaming faintly in the pale morning light that filtered through the high windows of the corridor. At the first sight of the king approaching, they sprang to attention, the subtle jingle of armour breaking the stillness of the hall. The royal usher, Roderick, stepped forward, bowing deeply before straightening with practiced ease.

"Your Majesties," he said, his voice steady and clear. Without hesitation, he turned, his fist striking the oak door with a resounding force that sent a low thrum reverberating through the corridor.

"Thy Highness," Roderick called to the prince within, his voice firm, each word deliberate, "His Majesty, the King, and Her Royal Highness, Princess Sophia, are preparing to enter."

A clipped response followed, sharp as steel. "The king and Princess Sophia may enter!" Charles's voice carried no warmth, its cold edge like frost against the skin.

At once, the guards moved with practiced precision, pushing the heavy doors open. The oak doors shuddered open, their sound rolling through the hall. Smooth stone floors stretched into the vast expanse, illuminated by the cool light spilling through narrow windows. The still banners of House Beaumont, bearing the royal crest—a golden lion crowned against a field of deep purple—hung high upon the walls, a silent reminder of the family's dominion.

Near the throne, Charles stood as a dark silhouette, his rigid stance unyielding, his gaze fixed somewhere unseen. Though this was not the king's main residence, the chamber bore the unmistakable marks of House Beaumont's heritage, the late king's legacy looming in every corner.

Mary lingered near the threshold, the chill of the stone floor biting through her thin shoes. Her stomach churned at the sight of Charles waiting within, his figure rigid, his gaze fixed somewhere unseen. To enter that chamber would be to face the viper itself, and she was no fool. Let the others risk their heads. She would remain here.

Beside her, Baldwin Honorcrest shifted, his boots creaking faintly against the floor. His posture betrayed no tension, yet his stillness seemed deliberate, as though he observed more than he let on. His eyes flickered briefly toward Mary, unreadable, before making his way to the doors. She dropped her gaze quickly, unwilling to meet his scrutiny. How many here knew her secret fears? How many could see them writ plain upon her face?

Rosalind stood nearby, her expression calm but her fingers tightly clasped before her. She leaned in slightly, her voice a whisper barely audible over the quiet hum of tension. "Thou art safe here, Mary."

Mary's jaw tightened, but she said nothing. *Safe? Not when he is near. Not when the serpent smiles and strikes without warning.*

The guards shifted as the royal party began their slow procession into the chamber. Mary remained rooted in place, her heart pounding as the heavy doors began to creak closed once more, sealing away the throne chamber and the horrors it contained. A faint tremor ran through her fingers as the muffled echo of Charles's voice reached her once more, cold and sharp, even through the thick wood.

Rosalind tilted her head slightly, her lips curving into a smile that seemed sweet but didn't quite reach her eyes. Her fingers played with the hem of her sleeve as she spoke, "I am heartened thou hast at last accepted the princess's invitation to parley with her." Her tone was as smooth as silk, but her gaze flickered, lingering just a moment too long on Mary. *Ah, but a mere handful of weeks.* The thought almost curled her lips further, but she forced the smile to remain steady.

Mary's brow twitched as her fingers adjusted her shawl. She felt the heat of a sharp retort rising but swallowed it down, the smallest flicker of disdain passing over her features. *Did the princess confide in Rosalind the reason why? Or doth Rosalind stand blind to all the princess's misdeeds?* Her jaw set, and she swallowed hard before clearing her throat.

"What tidings knowest thou of this meeting?" Mary asked, her voice even, though her nails dug faintly into the fabric of her gown. The king's visit loomed, its purpose cloaked in secrecy. For a week, the court had whispered of his arrival, yet the purpose of this meeting remained a shrouded thing.

Rosalind's eyes widened for a brief moment before she quickly lowered them, her hands stilling as if caught unprepared. A flicker of unease passed over her face before she smoothed it away with an airy laugh. "I am but a humble handmaiden, and Their Highnesses confer not with me on matters of state," she replied, her fingers brushing over the folds of her gown. "I remain as much in the dark as any other."

Mary's gaze lingered on her, weighing every word. The nervous laugh, the too-quick denial—it all smelled of falsehood. Yet she gave no outward sign of her doubts, merely tilting her head slightly as if considering the response. Rosalind was fair, delicate, with a softness to her manner that betrayed her youth. *She is of an age akin to the princess,* Mary thought. *The ease betwixt them speaks not of mere servitude. Nay, she is more than handmaiden—she is companion and confidante.*

Her lips pressed into a thin line before she let the sharper thought slip, her tone quick and cutting. "I wonder, doth Her Royal Highness ken thou dost fancy the prince?"

The words hung in the air like a dagger poised to strike. Rosalind's smile faltered, her fingers twitching against her gown as her composure wavered. "I—" she began, but the response died in her throat. Her cheeks flushed faintly, the pink creeping up her neck as she scrambled for footing. "Thou art mistaken," she said, her voice stiff, though the edge of uncertainty clung to it.

Mary arched a brow, watching Rosalind squirm with a detached curiosity. *So, the notion is not entirely unfounded,* she thought, though she said nothing more. Instead, she let her gaze drift past Rosalind, as if the conversation had already grown tiresome.

Rosalind shifted uneasily, her gaze darting for a moment before she steadied herself. Her lips tightened briefly before curving into a sharp smile. With a quick tilt of her head, she leaned closer, her smile returning—this time sharper, calculated. "If it please thee, Mary, may I inquire of thy bond with the king?" Her voice was smooth, her words wielded like a blade. "I have heard much gossip, which I strive not to heed," she added with a coy tilt to her tone, "but the manner in which thou dost look upon each other giveth weight to such whispers."

Mary froze, her jaw tightening as her chest twisted in panic. *"Gaze upon one another?"* The words echoed cruelly in her mind. She had avoided looking at him, had forced herself to avert her eyes whenever he was near.

Her lips parted, but the words she spoke felt distant. "He is our king, nothing more," she replied, her voice clipped. Yet her thoughts betrayed her calm. *Hath word traveled of the corridor? Of the ball, where the king did stay mine hand from striking the prince? Or mayhap of the morn thereafter, when we did wake together? When mine trembling fingers didst graze his bare chest with such a tender purpose? Where I lay, clad in his majesty's tunic, and he, with naught but the furred blanket to shield him?* Her mind raced, and her pulse quickened, each beat a drum in her ears.

Rosalind's smile softened, her tone lowering as she leaned in slightly. "Duchess De Valois, Madame Élisabeth, is a lady of title, land, and great influence among the nobles," she began gently, her words measured. "She seeketh thy king's hand in marriage." A flicker of unease passed over Rosalind's face as her gaze darted briefly to the shadows of the corridor. Her voice dropped further, a whisper meant only for Mary's ears. "Word hast it that she doth hunt for the maiden who danced with the king at the princess's ball. She useth all her power to uncover thy identity."

Rosalind placed a hand lightly on Mary's wrist, her grip steady and warm. "I tell thee this not to frighten thee, but to forewarn thee. The lady is relentless, and her gaze is set upon thee. Take heed, Mary, for all within Thorncrest Castle know who thou art, yet none have betrayed thee thus far. But I fear her reach is long, and her wrath unforgiving."

She placed a hand lightly on Mary's wrist, her grip firm despite its softness. "Thou must tread carefully."

Mary's breath caught, her chest tightening as Rosalind's words settled over her like a cold weight. *Duchess De Valois, Madame Élisabeth. Aye, I met her but once, yet once was enough.* Her beauty striketh like a blade, sharp and unyielding, the kind that turneth heads and hearts alike. She moveth as though the very earth bendeth to her will, untouched by toil, her every step measured, her every breath laden with purpose.

And I? Mary's nails pressed hard against her palms. She cast her gaze downward, spying the frayed hem of her gown, her hands roughened from labor. The ache in her chest quickened, burning hotter with each breath. *What claim have I against one such as her? A chambermaid, plain and common, against a lady of title and might?*

The thought of the king wedding such a woman did set her stomach to roil, though she scarce dared name the feeling. *Jealousy. Grief.* These words burned upon her tongue, and so she swallowed them, willing her thoughts to still. *Why should it matter?* she hissed inwardly, her bitterness rising like bile. *He is a king, and I but nothing—less than the dust beneath his heel.*

Straightening her spine, Mary exhaled slowly. "I thank thee," she said, her voice low but steady. "Yet I assure thee, the king is but my king, and I am naught but a chambermaid." Her words wavered slightly as she forced a polite smile. "This noblewoman wasteth her time." She dared not meet Rosalind's gaze too long, for the lie burned hot within her throat.

The memory of John filled her, unbidden—his touch, his kiss, the way his voice had softened as he whispered her name. She felt his presence as though it lingered in the air. *I wish it not, yet he is more than a king to me—words I dare speak only in the silence of mine own heart. His memory is as a wound, a pang no healer's craft may mend.*

Mary inclined her head politely, stepping back. "I bid thee farewell, Rosalind." Rosalind returned the gesture with a gentle incline of her head, though her gaze lingered, warm and conspiratorial. "Such meetings as these oft take some while," she began, her tone lilting as though savouring the words. "Yet this, Mary, is betwixt thee and me: the princess doth seem to think the king is much fond of thee. At her return ball, she did marvel at how thou and His Majesty did appear—"

Rosalind sighed dreamily, her expression softening, "Not only the princess, who doth speak much of love, but all who attend the ball—aye, even those from far-off lands that could not come—whisper they of such tales. 'Twas this, perchance, that hath stirred the duchess's envy."

Rosalind clasped her hands together, her smile growing as she stepped nearer. "And now, having witnessed the glances betwixt thee but moments ago, I do harbor no doubt the king shall seek thine audience at the soonest he may."

Her words hung between them, carried on a note of playful enthusiasm, her eyes bright as though she swooned over the notion herself.

Mary's cheeks flamed, the heat rushing to her face despite her efforts to stay composed. She cleared her throat, turning her head slightly to hide her blush. "Thou and the princess dost possess a wild imagination," she replied, her voice clipped and deliberate. Her hands fidgeted at her sides, smoothing invisible creases on her gown as though brushing the conversation away.

Without waiting for Rosalind's response, Mary turned fully, willing her voice to sound indifferent. "I thank thee for thy thoughts."

Mary's steps echoed softly in the corridor as she moved away, her pace measured and quiet. Behind her, Rosalind's voice mingled with the low murmurs of the guards, their words fading as distance grew between them. She glanced back briefly, careful not to draw attention, catching only a glimpse of armour glinting faintly in the morning light and Rosalind's still figure.

The castle corridors were cold, the morning chill clinging to the stones and seeping through her thin sleeves. She curled her hands into loose fists, her fingers brushing the smooth, worn fabric of her chambermaid's uniform as though the motion might steady her.

She turned a corner, her gaze flicking toward the throne chamber. Its heavy oak doors loomed ahead, flanked by unmoving guards whose presence seemed carved from stone. Voices bled faintly through the thick walls—too muffled to make out, yet enough to remind her how close she lingered to where she should not be.

Her focus shifted to the door she sought, nearly hidden in the shadows of the adjoining wall. It was small and plain, its wood dark with age, easy to overlook amidst the castle's grandeur. Mary quickened her steps, keeping her movements precise and unhurried, as though she belonged in every shadow she passed.

At the door, she paused, her breath steadying as she glanced back one final time. The corridor stretched empty save for the distant figures of the guards, who stood unbothered at their posts. Satisfied, she reached for the iron latch, the metal cold beneath her touch. With slow, practiced care, she eased it downward. The door yielded with a soft creak, enough to send her pulse quickening.

Mary slipped through, pulling it closed behind her with a muted click that vanished into the stone silence of the corridor.

The walls loomed close around her, the air heavy with the scent of dust and neglect. Scrolls were heaped in chaotic disarray, their brittle edges curling like leaves left too long in the sun. Some bore the marks of age, darkened and cracked, as if they had languished here since the reign of kings long past. Forgotten histories lay strewn across the shelves, their whispers lost beneath the weight of the years.

Mary's hand hovered just above the pile, her fingers trembling as though tempted to reach for one. Yet she hesitated, her breath caught in her throat. These parchments might hold royal secrets—deeds of valour, betrayals cloaked in shadow, or perhaps even the cruel machinations of the prince. The temptation was strong, but her purpose was urgent. With a quick intake of breath, she stepped forward, her movements careful yet swift.

She squeezed through a narrow gap between a leaning shelf and the stone wall, her maid's uniform snagging briefly on a splinter of wood. The cold of the stones bit through her thin sleeves, making her shiver as she pressed closer. At last, her ear met the unyielding surface, the chill seeping into her skin. For a heartbeat, she stilled, scarcely daring to breathe, straining to catch any sound that might drift from the throne chamber beyond.

Murmurs reached her, muffled and indistinct. She pressed closer, shifting slightly, her breath shallow. Had she risked too much for nothing? Her heart hammered with the weight of doubt and the ever-present fear of discovery. Her gaze darted to the door she had come through, her nerves taut as a bowstring. Any moment, someone might come searching.

Her hands felt along the stone, her touch hurried but meticulous. At last, her fingers found a tiny fissure, a hole no larger than a coin. She bent low, pressing her ear to it. Her breath hitched as the muffled voices sharpened into words. "Hand in marriage," one said, the cadence firm and deliberate. Another spoke: "Lorendale Castle." And then, the final phrase struck her like an arrow loosed into her chest: "The Cathedral of St. Reginald."

Her eyes widened, her hands trembling against the cold stone. Lorendale Castle—a fortress renowned across Briarwood for its grandeur and strategic value. It stood not far from Ravenswood, a place of power and prestige among the realm. And the Cathedral of St. Reginald? Its hallowed halls were ever kept for unions most sacred. Might this herald a wedding of royal blood?

Her stomach churned as another thought struck her, sharp and unbidden. What if they speak of the king marrying Duchess De Valois? The thought pricked at her mind like a thorn, sharp and unwelcome. Yet another possibility crept into her thoughts, one she could not ignore. The Saint-Clair guards stood outside—could it be the princess they mean to wed? No solace came from the thought, for either path seemed fraught with ruin. Her lips drew into a hard line, her breath catching in uneven bursts.

The very notion of such unions left her reeling, her chest rising and falling in shallow, hurried breaths. Whose heart shall shatter? Mine own, or Robert's?

She forced her gaze to the door once more. Duty pressed heavily upon her, a weight she dared not shirk. Charles's bedchamber awaited her care, and the prince's temper was as unforgiving as his cruelty. To linger here would court disaster. Yet the words she had overheard burned into her mind, their meaning coiling and twisting, refusing to relent.

The prince's chamber

The prince's chamber was cold when Mary arrived, the air biting against her cheeks and fingertips as though mocking her every step. Her breath misted faintly before her as she worked swiftly, her movements honed by repetition yet driven by an unshakable urgency. She crouched low before the hearth, her hands trembling as she struck flint against steel. The faint spark caught, and the kindling smoldered at last, the meager flame crackling to life. Smoke stung her eyes as she leaned close to feed the fire, coaxing warmth into the room where none belonged.

She did not linger to feel its heat.

Rising too quickly, Mary swayed for half a heartbeat before steadying herself against the stone wall, her chest tight. Her mind was not here—it raced elsewhere, tangled in half-formed thoughts she dared not name. The thud of her broom against the cold stone floor brought her back, the rhythmic sweeping breaking the heavy silence. Dust danced briefly in the pale morning light that spilled weakly through the narrow window slits, only to settle once more where it did not belong.

Her hands moved without pause as she crossed the chamber, heading for the small wooden door at the far end. Beyond lay the prince's private privy—a narrow, stone-walled space built into the castle's design. The cold air seeped through the cracks as Mary unlatched the door, the faint groan of the hinges stirring the silence.

The wooden seat, polished yet unremarkable, was built above the dark shaft leading to the castle cesspit far below. She worked quickly, wiping the edges of the seat and clearing away the faint traces of use—a task foul in its own right but far preferable to the indignity of hauling waste through the corridors.

Satisfied the space was clean, she latched the door shut and turned back into the chamber, briskly brushing her hands against her apron. The lingering chill of the privy clung to her, but there was no time to dwell on it.

There was no time to rest.

Dust still clung to the prince's ornate trunks, to the rich tapestries that lined the walls, their woven depictions of hunts and battles mocking her with stories she would never live. She worked over them quickly, her hands steady but her heart leaden. Her fingers caught on a tear in one fabric, the threads frayed from some forgotten slight. For half a breath, she lingered there, her touch delicate—almost tender—before shaking herself and turning to the bed.

The mattress was heavy, its stuffing dense with wool and feather down, though age had left it uneven in places. She hauled it upright with a grunt, the weight dragging at her shoulders as a faint layer of dust scattered onto the cold stone floor. Beneath her hands, the fur-lined blanket felt soft but carried the unmistakable scent of its use—warmth masking something less clean. Her feet shifted slightly against the uneven surface, where a fine woven rug softened the chill, its edges beginning to fray with wear.

She dared not think of who had lain there, or what whispers had passed in the dark beneath such costly coverings.

The garments were next—his tunic, his boots. They had been laid aside carelessly, as though their worth was naught. Mary wiped them clean with brisk, practiced motions, her fingers working the leather until the scuffs faded and the gleam returned. *A prince's boots should never bear a mark,* she thought bitterly, though her own feet ached in shoes near worn through.

Her final task brought her to the candles, their wax melted low, the wicks blackened with use. She replaced them swiftly, her hands brushing against cold metal as she worked. The room looked clean now, warm even, though none of it touched her. Mary stepped back at last, her gaze sweeping over her work. In pristine state, the prince would find no fault here.

"Yet, it did feel hollow," she thought to herself.

The fire burned quietly, its glow flickering against the stone walls, yet she took no comfort in its warmth. She could not linger; there were other chambers, other tasks. Turning sharply on her heel, Mary crossed the chamber, the hem of her gown whispering faintly over the cold, smooth stone. Her hand hovered on the latch for a moment, her fingers curling against the cold iron. She exhaled, steadying herself, before pulling the door open and slipping into the corridor beyond.

The chill met her at once, biting through the thin fabric of her uniform as if to remind her of her place. Her steps were quick, her pace unyielding. Another chamber awaited her—another fire to stoke, another bed to shake, another silent burden to carry.

Her thoughts threatened to stray, but she forced them down, locking them away as surely as one might bolt a door.

There was no time for sadness. Not now.

Serving the prince's chamber had taken near two hours, yet still, there was no sign of the king. Mary slipped out quietly, pulling the heavy door shut behind her. Aldric and Gareth, the guards stationed outside, stood watchful and silent. Their armour caught the faint daylight streaming through the high windows, and the muted clink of chainmail followed her as she passed. She dipped her head, her steps quick, though her heart stumbled under the weight of their gaze.

The corridor of Charles's quarters stretched long and unrelenting, bathed in pale morning light that spilled weakly through narrow slits in the stone. Tapestries hung still upon the walls, their embroidered hunts and battles lifeless as if holding their breath. Her worn shoes scuffed faintly against the stone, but she could not shake the feeling of being watched. *To the king's reserved quarters I go,* she thought bitterly, swallowing against the dryness in her throat. *Though I pray none hath yet seen to his chambers. The guards mayhap shall turn me away.*

At the far end, another set of guards flanked the arch leading to the spiral stairs. One tilted his head, squinting at her as though she were out of place. Mary's hands tightened on the hem of her gown, lifting it just slightly as she moved past. She kept her chin low, her pace quick, though the back of her neck prickled under their scrutiny.

The spiral stairs awaited, narrow and steep, the stone steps worn smooth from years of use. Sunlight trickled faintly down from the upper windows, bright but cold, a sharp contrast to the sweat gathering at the nape of her neck. Each hurried step sent a jolt up through her legs, but she dared not slow, her breath coming shallow as she climbed higher.

Reaching the upper floor, she emerged into a wide corridor—clean and still, with walls dressed in tapestries finer than those below. Here the daylight spilled freely through tall, arched windows, casting long bands of light upon the floor. The air felt colder here, sharper against her skin.

A guard stood to the side, his hand resting idly on the pommel of his sword. He grunted, barely shifting, though his eyes met hers with a flicker of suspicion. "What brings thee here?"

Mary gave the faintest nod of acknowledgment, her voice steady despite the thudding in her chest. "The king's chambers await tending."

The guard let out a low grunt, offering no challenge, and she moved on. Her steps quickened, the worn soles of her shoes whispering faintly over the cold stone floor.

Let no other servant have entered, she prayed, her lips moving faintly. *Let his chambers remain untouched.*

The doors loomed nearer, their gilded edges glinting in the pale light. She was almost there when another guard stepped into her path.

"Halt," he said, voice firm. His eyes narrowed, lingering on her a moment too long.

Mary froze mid-step, the weight of her task and the cold corridor pressing against her like an unseen hand. Her pulse thrummed painfully in her ears, and for a moment, she could not find her voice.

For an instant, her eyes locked with the guard's, caught in a stark, piercing stare. He knew her—Mary Winterbourne. The whispers had reached him as well, drifting through the stone halls like smoke. The Rumours about the girl who danced with the king had spread quickly, carried down the tongues of every servant and noble alike.

He'd been there that night at the ball. He'd seen her with Prince Charles at first, then later, when the king had taken her hand and danced with her in full view of the court. Whispers about that had spread like wildfire, the king's interest in her apparent to all.

Now, she stood before him in the corridor, her posture stiff, eyes lowered, her breath caught.

His hand tightened on the pommel of his sword, his voice low and steady as he spoke. "The king's chamber hath been seen to."

Mary's gaze flickered up briefly before her head dropped again, and her hands twitched. There was no answer. She stood still, her mouth parted, as if she had intended to speak but could not.

The sound of footsteps reached him then, faint at first, but rising quickly. The muted clink of armour, voices—a handful of guards were coming their way, the sound growing louder with every second.

Mary stiffened, the weight of their presence pressing down on her. She could not hide forever.

As she grasped the hem of her dress, her silence was palpable, a heavy stillness that commanded attention.

The guard's gaze never wavered, his face a mask, watching her every movement. The silence stretched between them, his thoughts running as fast as her heart must have been.

"What dost thou linger for?" he asked, his voice a little sharper now, suspicion clouding his words.

Mary swallowed, her lips parting but not forming words. She glanced behind her, clearly listening to the approaching guards but did not look up at him again. "I—I must tend to other duties," she muttered, her voice quieter than usual, but it was clear—she was trying to remain composed.

The guard did not step aside, his posture remaining firm. He was watching her, though his gaze flickered briefly to the approaching footsteps.

The sound of footsteps echoed down the stone corridor, heavy and deliberate. From around the bend, Sir Eadric appeared first, his armour gleaming in the daylight, the weight of his presence enough to shift the air. Alaric Stonebrook followed closely behind him, his eyes scanning the passage, and several royal guards trailed behind the king, forming a protective circle.

The guards were disciplined, their armour gleaming, boots striking the cold stone floor in unison. The faint jingle of their armour filled the hall, their formation tight to ensure the king's safety.

The low murmur of their voices was drowned by the sharp, commanding sound of the king's approach. King John stepped forward, his posture regal, every step purposeful. His gaze landed on Mary, and for a brief moment, his lips curved slightly, a warmth in his eyes as he recognised her. He nodded slightly in her direction, his lips curving into the faintest of smiles, clearly pleased to see her.

Behind him, the guards remained alert, keeping a watchful eye on the corridor, but it was clear that the king's demeanor was not one of mere formality. His gaze lingered for a moment, and for that instant, it was as though the rest of the world disappeared.

King John's lips spread into a genuine smile, and he took a step forward, his voice warm as he spoke. "Ah, Mary, I had but just sent one to seek thee."

Mary's heart fluttered briefly at the sound of his voice, but she quickly suppressed the feeling. With a swift motion, she dropped into a curtsy, her gown sweeping the floor as she lowered herself. Her hands rested lightly at her sides, the gesture smooth and practiced. Her gaze remained lowered, though her pulse quickened beneath the calm exterior.

Beside her, the guard who had been standing at attention shifted uncomfortably. With a sharp movement, he straightened his back, placing a hand over his chest, and bowed deeply. "Your Majesty!" he called, his voice thick with respect, eyes lowering to show deference.

Mary glanced briefly at him but said nothing, her thoughts still spinning from the brief encounter with the king, her breath caught in her chest. The space around her seemed to close in as she remained still, hands clenched at her sides, waiting for what might come next.

The king's hands moved gracefully, as he gestured toward the door. "Art thou content to parley in mine chambers, or dost thou wish to wait until after, and we may meet at a place of thy choosing?"

Mary's shoulders stiffened, and her breath caught in her throat. She glanced briefly at the king, then quickly lowered her gaze, her hands clasped tightly in front of her. "If ye be content to have me join thee, 'twould be mine honour to parley with thee in thy royal chamber."

A small nod from the king was all the encouragement she needed. The king gestured with a subtle flick of his wrist, his gaze steady, as though the motion itself was enough to summon her forward.

She stepped forward, her feet hesitant at first, but the weight of his presence drove her onward. His pace was steady and unhurried, and she matched it as best she could, the air between them thick with the unspoken tension of the moment.

The corridor stretched ahead, the sound of their footsteps mingling with the soft echo of the guards behind them. As they approached the king's chambers, Sir Eadric turned toward one of the guards walking with them, his voice low but firm. "Check the chamber," he ordered, his tone carrying the weight of command.

The guard nodded quickly and moved toward the door of the royal chamber, his hand resting lightly on the hilt of his sword. He pushed the door open slightly, peering inside to ensure there was no danger lurking within. After a brief moment, he stepped back, giving a slight nod to Sir Eadric, signaling that the chamber was clear.

With that, the king moved forward, his steps measured and purposeful, as Mary followed behind, her heart racing with the weight of the moment.

As the door creaked softly behind them, the king's gaze swept across the room, taking in the familiar surroundings. His fingers brushed against the back of a nearby chair as he walked deeper into the chamber, and Mary hesitated by the threshold. The soft crackle of the fire and the pale daylight streaming through the windows were the only sounds breaking the stillness between them.

Without a word, King John turned toward her, his eyes locking onto hers. A fleeting smile tugged at his lips before he motioned to a chair by the hearth, offering her a place. "Sit, if ye wish," he said, his voice gentle but commanding.

Mary stepped forward, her breath catching in her throat, and took the seat, careful not to make any sound. She kept her hands in her lap, knuckles white, betraying the tight grip she had on her composure.

Meanwhile, one of the guards stationed by the door stood watch, his hand resting idly on the pommel of his sword. Near the table, a cupbearer stepped forward, his movements precise and deliberate, the mark of a man well accustomed to his duty. He reached for the decanter of wine, tilting it slightly, watching as the deep red liquid caught the flickering light, its hue shifting like molten garnet.

He glanced at Sir Eadric, who offered a single nod. Without hesitation, the cupbearer lifted a silver chalice, pouring the wine with steady hands, careful not to let a single drop spill. He did not drink immediately. Instead, he held the chalice up to the light, tilting it slightly, observing the way the liquid clung to the sides before inhaling subtly, testing for any acrid or unnatural scent. Satisfied, he brought the rim to his lips and took a slow, deliberate sip, his features betraying nothing.

The chamber stilled, the weight of expectation pressing down on those within. He did not swallow at once. The wine lingered on his tongue as

he tested it for the telltale signs of foul play—the faint bitterness of nightshade, the metallic tang of arsenic, the slow-spreading numbness that certain poisons left behind. Time stretched, each second thick with unspoken tension as the flickering torchlight cast shifting shadows against the stone walls.

At last, he swallowed, but even then, he did not speak. His expression remained unreadable, his posture unmoving as he waited, listening to his own body, attuned to the slightest anomaly, the first stirrings of heat, dizziness, or unnatural tightness in his chest. Another moment passed. Then another.

When at last he exhaled, it was slow and measured. He lowered the chalice, placed it carefully upon the table, and turned toward Sir Eadric, his voice even, absent of hesitation. There was no further acknowledgment, no lingering presence. His task complete, the cupbearer stepped back with a practiced grace and bowed his head ever so slightly before turning on his heel. Without another word, he withdrew, his departure as silent as his entrance, leaving only the tension he had momentarily commanded in his wake.

Only then did Alaric Stonebrook step forward, reaching for the decanter. Without a word, he poured the wine into a separate golden chalice, the liquid swirling in rich, velvety ribbons, dark as spilled ink beneath the dim glow of the chamber.

The king's voice broke the stillness, deep and smooth. "Alaric, hath any man informed thee of our mother's whereabouts? She oft doth greet me upon mine arrival."

The king's hands moved to unclasp his cloak, his fingers working with practiced ease. Alaric paused, waiting until the king was settled before responding. "Nay, Your Majesty, wouldst thou have me send for her?"

The king nodded briefly, not looking at him. "Later will suffice. I was but curious."

Alaric moved forward with the chalices in hand, one in each of his palms. He placed them gently on the table—first the king's, then Mary's—before stepping back.

The king, still removing his cloak, gestured toward the table. "Drink not the wine until the time hath passed," he instructed Mary, his tone calm, but with an edge of command.

Mary froze for a moment, her shock evident. Up until that point, she was immune to the allure of drinking, but then he opened his mouth and her curiosity grew. Before she could offer any response, the king turned his attention toward the door.

"Thou mayest wait without; knock should there be a matter with the mine or the guard." The guards, Alaric, and Sir Eadric stood silent and still, their figures imposing in the pale light. A faint jingle of chainmail echoed as they moved, the subtle shifting of metal betraying their otherwise perfect stillness. Without a word, they inclined their heads in unison—a gesture of respect, precise and deliberate. Boots pressed lightly against the stone as they turned, their movements synchronized and purposeful. The soft scrape of leather and the faint chime of armour accompanied them as they made their way toward the door.

The heavy wood groaned faintly before closing with a muffled thud, leaving behind a chamber thick with silence and the lingering chill of their departure.

The king turned to face Mary, his movements deliberate, the faint crackle of the fire filling the silence. His steady gaze settled on her, gentle but expectant, carrying no judgment—only curiosity. "Pray, is this a matter of personal import, or doth it bear weight of greater consequence?"

Mary's breath hitched, her lips parting, but no sound came. She sat frozen, her voice stolen as though the air had thickened around her. Her gaze flicked to his, caught in the warmth of his eyes, and for a fleeting moment, the chamber seemed smaller, the fire brighter, the very world narrowing to just the space between them.

The words she sought refused to come. Her throat felt tight, her mind blank, as though she had forgotten how to speak at all. Stars above, he was waiting. Her hands trembled faintly in her lap before she clasped them tightly, willing them to still.

The king's brow arched slightly, but this time it was paired with a soft smile. The fire crackled softly, its warmth brushing against her face, though Mary felt only the cool sweat at her nape, the thundering of her heart in her ears.

Say something, her thoughts screamed, yet she sat rooted in place, starstruck by the man who sat before her—kingly yet kind, close enough to touch but still untouchable.

"Your Majesty," she began, her voice steady despite the storm of emotions roiling within. "I loathe to ask, yet I have received no word from the Shadow Serpents." She paused, swallowing hard as she gathered her thoughts, mustering the courage to continue. If any man could command the Shadow Serpents' attention, it was the king.

She held onto her hope, fragile as spun thread.

The king's smile faltered, fading like mist before sunlight, leaving behind a quiet weariness. "I am full of sorrow to hear such tidings," he said, his voice edged with frustration. "After that morn, I did take it upon myself to reach out unto the Shadow Serpents on thy behalf."

Mary's heart swelled, a flicker of warmth breaking through her worry. Yet the weight in the king's voice lingered heavy in the air, coloured with melancholy that made the chamber feel colder.

His jaw tensed, his frustration betrayed in the faint crease of his brow. "I do not wish to sound arrogant," he said, his tone cooling like tempered steel, "but if this Shadow Serpent cannot make time for the king, then methinks greater matters hold his attention."

The willingness to use his power for her sake stirred something unfamiliar—gratitude mingled with longing. She wasn't accustomed to kindness, nor to anyone stepping beyond duty for her.

The thought warmed her briefly, but doubt coiled at the edges. Her composure cracked. "I... I..." The words trembled on her lips as if her thoughts and voice refused to align. "I am truly... most grateful."

The king's gaze softened, though his brows drew together faintly, as though the silence whispered doubts he dared not voice. "I sent a missive," he said, his voice low but weighted. "Didst thou receive it? Or perchance thou wished not to reply?"

There it was—vulnerability, a sliver of uncertainty he seemed loath to expose.

Mary's breath caught, her eyes widening. A missive? The thought struck her like a blow, confusion swirling with panic. "I... Your Majesty," she stammered, her voice hushed, trembling with earnestness. "I assure thee, I have received no such missive. I would never ignore a missive from thee."

Her chest tightened, a storm of questions brewing within. If the missive was lost—or worse, withheld—then who had seen it? *I know not how to read, even were it thrust upon me,* she thought bitterly, the words unspoken yet heavy in her mind.

The king's brows, once furrowed in concern, suddenly smoothed out, a gentle calm washing over him. "I did think, mayhap, thou wert no longer inclined to seek mine presence."

The king's words struck a chord within Mary, stirring a mixture of emotions. A restless hankering had settled in, whispering to her that she had to find a way to confess to him the overwhelming hunger she felt to be near him once more. She held back her words, as she did not want to risk them getting back to Charles. "Your Majesty, I would be a fool not to seek thy presence. Pray, might I ask, what did the missive contain?" she asked, her voice barely above a whisper.

For an instant, the king's gaze wandered, his eyes clouding over as he formulated a thoughtful response. The suspense was almost unbearable as she waited for his answer. "The missive..." the king began, his voice tinged with a touch of vulnerability. "It did convey mine earnest longing to see thee once more, and to pass more hours in thy most pleasing company."

"Ne'er hath such a missive reached mine hands," Mary confessed, her voice tinged with regret. Mary squeezed her eyes shut; her heart was pounding in her chest as she gathered the courage to decline the king's invitation. She took a deep breath and spoke softly, "I would have declined, Your Majesty."

The king looked at her with a mixture of confusion. She felt the need to explain herself, to make him understand that she was not worthy of his attention. "I come from humble birth, Your Majesty," her voice trembling but faint. "As thou well knowest, I am not fit to stand before one of such noble station." She nervously continued, listing numerous reasons why they should not sup together.

The king moved then, leaning forward in his seat, closing the space between them. Mary froze, a jolt of something unnameable rushing through her—excitement, fear, longing. His eyes pinned her in place, his voice a gentle but firm punctuation to her stream-of-consciousness chatter. "Mary," he said, his words carrying a weight that stilled her tongue. "Thy background doth not define thy worth, nor doth it diminish the captivating essence that draweth me to thee."

Her breath caught in her throat as his words sank in. Longing dripped from her voice like honey as she lifted her eyes to his. In that moment, all her doubts and insecurities began to fade away, overshadowed by the undeniable connection they shared.

Their faces mere inches apart, the air was charged with anticipation before their lips met in a fierce, passionate kiss. As his touch grazed her, a shiver ran through her, and her heart did skip a beat, yearning for more. When their lips touched, a fiery energy surged through her veins, erasing all coherent thought and leaving only a primal longing.

For a moment, they were lost in the intensity of the kiss, but then came a sharp knock at the door. Mary pulled back in shock, her heart racing.

Alaric eased the door open just a sliver, the faint creak of the hinges breaking the silence. He did not step inside but leaned slightly, his voice calm and precise as he called out, "Your Majesty, the guard is well. Thou mayst drink the wine."

Without waiting for a response, Alaric withdrew, the door clicking softly shut as he sealed the chamber once more.

The king let out a low, slightly annoyed laugh, the sound rumbling like distant thunder, as he reached for his chalice. Fingers curling around the gilded stem, he lifted it with casual grace, the faint clink of metal against the table breaking the quiet. He took a slow sip, his gaze never wavering from Mary.

"I must admit," he said, the words softened by the hint of a smile tugging at his lips, "I have been much eager to lay mine eyes upon thee. During mine absence, 'tis thy face that hath consumed mine thoughts."

With deliberate care, he set the chalice back upon the table, the motion unhurried but decisive, the faint scrape of its base meeting the wood lingering in the air.

Then, without a word, he reached across the small space between them, his hand settling around Mary's. His touch was warm, steady—a stark contrast to the icy flutter that jolted through her.

"We cannot," she whispered, her voice a frail breath, swallowed by the weight of the stone walls. Her words trembled, hollow against the pull of him. The air between them crackled, laden with the scent of oil and wax, warm as the embers smoldering in her chest. Yet even as she spoke, her lips betrayed her, brushing his again in a tender surrender.

A groan escaped him—a low, rumbling sound that stirred the stillness. His hand slid to her hip, fingers pressing through the fabric, steady and unyielding. She shivered, the heat of him seeping through her as his other hand threaded into the golden tangles of her hair, a slow, deliberate motion that sent tingles sparking along her scalp.

The king moved as if he might devour her whole, mouth seeking hers with fervent hunger—feasting, claiming, lingering. Her pulse leapt, hammering against her ribs as though it might break free. She was softening, sinking into him, powerless to resist the pull of his hands, his touch, the low growl of his breath mingling with hers.

But Mary tore away, breathless. Her lips burned, tingling with the remnants of him. The heady rush surged wild through her veins, a force she barely controlled. Her voice cracked as she spoke, each word a brittle plea against the enchantment binding them both.

"We cannot, Your Majesty!" Her chest heaved as if she had run leagues. "I came only to inquire what more may be done to find my sister."

The words hung in the air like mist, and she dared to meet his gaze. Hurt—quiet and sharp—lingered there, though he turned away, hiding it behind the straight line of his shoulders. For a moment, silence reigned, save for the faint hiss of the hearthfire.

"I must take my leave." Her voice wavered as she pulled back, her limbs reluctant to obey.

The king sighed, a sound heavy with both weariness and longing. Yet he nodded, a motion at once regal and resigned. His hand caught hers—gentle but insistent—as though afraid to let her vanish into the void.

"As you wish," he murmured, the words falling soft as dust. His voice lowered, a whisper woven with something that sent a shiver trailing down her spine. "But before thou goest, I would ask thee to reconsider my invitation to supper."

Mary stilled. That whisper lingered in the small space between them, its weight settling deep.

"Forgive me, Your Majesty," she replied, her voice a tight braid of longing and restraint. "It would be an honor. But 'twould not be fitting, given our present... circumstances." Her throat burned as she spoke. She stepped further back, her palms clenching at her sides. "I pray thou dost understand."

A faint smile touched his lips, though his eyes burned with something she could not name. Slowly, he closed the space between them, one hand lifting to cradle her chin. His touch was a whisper of warmth, calloused fingers tracing her skin.

"I told thee, I care not for titles or station." His voice was low, quiet—dangerous, perhaps, in its gentleness. "A king may heed counsel on matters of war and realm, but in matters of the heart, I shall choose as I will."

Mary's breath caught as he leaned in, his words brushing against her like velvet and iron. "And if that doth not convince thee," he continued, softer still, "what if we do not name it courting? Nay, but a simple meal, whereupon we may speak of thy sister and how best to bring her home."

The flames in the hearth danced, their flicker caught in his gaze. Those eyes—earnest and perilous all at once—could bend steel if he willed it. Mary's resolve wavered, her heart thrumming loud in her ears. Her cheeks flushed, and a smile, rebellious and faint, curved her lips.

"Very well." Her voice betrayed her, hushed and unsteady. "If I agree, none shall learn of our feasting together. Dost thou understand me, Your Majesty?"

The king's answering smile was swift, triumphant, though tempered by a promise unspoken. The fire crackled, its warmth pressing against them both. "If that is thy will." He nodded. "No one shall know, Mary. Our secret shall be protected. I promise thee that."

Mary's chest rose with a measured breath, her voice no stronger than a whisper. "I accept, Your Majesty. I would be honoured to sup with thee."

"Morrow it shall be," he declared, his voice ringing with the authority of one who rarely heard refusal. "At Ravenstone Castle, then?"

Mary's hands clenched briefly at her skirts, her gaze fixed on the floor. "I shall be there, Your

Majesty," she replied, the words uneven on her tongue. After a moment's pause, her voice steadied, though each word seemed to cost her. "Yet I must humbly ask—pray, inform thy most trusted guards of mine humble standing, a mere chambermaid, and that 'tis but for us to converse on a matter of import. Let them guide me through the servants' entrance, lest I—" She faltered, her throat tightening around the rest. *Lest I invite their mockery.*

For a moment, silence hung between them, broken only by the faint hiss of burning wood. Then the king laughed—a sound warm and low, rolling over her like an unexpected comfort. "If that is thy wish, then so it shall be." His voice softened, words spoken as though sharing a secret. "On the morrow's eve, Mary, I shall await thee eagerly."

"Until then," he murmured, the final words a hush against the chamber's still air.

Upon the close of that day

Mary & Charles

Thankfully, Mary's long day at Thorncrest Castle was drawing to a close. She was preparing to leave when Charles suddenly blocked her path. One step closer, and the air thickened with tension; her spine turned rigid, cold dread rippling through her.

Before she could react, he yanked her forward, her arm colliding painfully with the unforgiving stone. The cold seeped through her sleeves, biting into her skin like frost on a winter's night.

His breath, heavy with the stench of ale, clouded the air between them as he leaned closer. "The guards speak of thy meeting with the king in his chambers," he snarled, his voice a low growl. His hand clamped around her wrist, squeezing hard enough to make her wince.

"Speak truth!" he barked, his tone laced with venom. "Dost thou conspire against me with Princess Sophia?"

Mary turned her face away, willing herself not to recoil from the drunken heat of his breath. She struggled against his grip, her voice a sharp hiss. "Thou didst order me to win his favour, Your Highness! I act only in accordance with thy will."

His fingers dug deeper into her skin, his knuckles white with fury. For a moment, she thought he might strike her. Then, just as quickly, he released her with a sneer, stepping back as though her presence disgusted him.

"Is it working?" he jeered, his tone mocking. "Hath the king succumbed to thy wiles, or dost thou lack the wit to charm him?"

Mary rubbed her wrist, the skin throbbing where his grip had bruised her. Her breath came in short, uneven bursts as she fought to keep her composure. "His Highness invited me to supper," she said carefully, choosing her words with precision. "But his attentions seem… scattered. Thy hopes may yet be misplaced."

Charles's eyes narrowed, suspicion darkening his expression. He loomed nearer, his gaze sharp and unrelenting. "Thou must do more," he hissed, his lips curling into a cruel smile. "Thou art naught but a servant. Serve me well, or I shall find another who can." He snapped, "An ye be of no use to me, ye know well what shall befall thee and thy last living kin."

Mary clenched her jaw, her knuckles whitening as her fists curled at her sides. The heat of her anger surged beneath the icy grip of fear, but she held her tongue. Her voice was measured, her expression devoid of emotion. "As thou commandest, Your Highness."

Charles lingered, swaying slightly, the drink making his movements uneven. He waved a dismissive hand, nearly stumbling as he turned. "See that thou dost not disappoint me," he slurred before staggering off into the shadows of the corridor.

Mary stood alone, her pulse pounding in her ears. The dim light of the corridor flickered weakly against the stone walls as she leaned back against the cold surface, trying to steady herself.

A tempest of fury churned within her, yet she locked it away, refusing to let it show.

Her heart thundered in her chest, but her face betrayed nothing. With a quick tug at her apron, she straightened her back and pushed forward. She couldn't afford to falter—not when the weight of Charles's scrutiny still clung to her like a shadow.

Her fingers brushed the cold stone wall as she moved down a narrow passageway, her footsteps barely breaking the stillness. The flickering torches lit the walls in uneven patches, the shifting shadows dancing erratically as she moved. She glanced behind her, unable to shake the sensation of being followed, but the corridor was empty.

Ahead, other maids whispered in low voices, their presence a small relief, though her nerves refused to settle. She joined them at the head of the stairs, their chamber uniforms swaying as they descended in uneven pairs. The cold air of the lower levels hit her like a wave, damp and heavy with the faint smell of ash and cooked meat from the kitchens.

By the time she reached the servants' quarters, her legs ached from the strain of a hurried pace she dared not betray. The large chamber, dimly lit by a few guttering candles, was far quieter than usual. Those who remained spoke in muted tones or worked silently to finish their tasks. Mary kept her head down, weaving past benches and hanging cloaks as she made her way to the alcove where the maids changed.

She waited her turn, hands clenched tightly at her sides. The maids ahead of her spoke in whispers, their voices blending with the faint rustle of fabric. When her moment came, she pulled at the ties of her uniform with stiff fingers, the trembling of her hands betraying her nerves. The memory of Charles's grip lingered like a bruise on her skin, the ache a sharp reminder of how easily his power could reach her.

Mary shed the royal garments in a hurry, her breath shallow and uneven. She grabbed her simple dress and cloak, the threadbare wool coarse and thin against her skin. The scant folds offered little warmth, barely warding off the bite of the night's chill. Without a word, she stepped back into the stream of servants heading toward the exit.

Two guards stood by the wooden door, their eyes sharp despite the late hour. One reached out an arm, blocking the path as another maid stopped to murmur her name and duty. Mary's pulse quickened. She forced herself to walk slowly, her steps measured as the line inched forward.

The guard's eyes lingered on her for a moment before he nodded and lowered his arm. She passed beneath his gaze, her breath catching as the door creaked open.

Outside, the courtyard was dark, the pale light of distant lanterns doing little to soften the shadows. Maids ahead of her murmured quietly as they disappeared into the night, their cloaks drawn tight against the cold. Mary kept her steps even, though her heart felt like it might burst from her ribs.

She stole a glance back toward the castle. The door shut with a final groan, sealing her exit, but the uneasy feeling did not leave her. Charles's drunken rage still weighed heavily in her mind. If he stumbled into the halls again and decided to follow, there would be no walls to protect her now.

The dirt path yawned ahead, uneven and unforgiving beneath her aching feet. The cold gnawed at her fingers, chapped and raw from a day of endless toil. She clenched her hands into fists, desperate to keep the biting chill at bay, forcing her focus on the rhythm of her steps—each one dragging her farther from the castle and closer to the fragile safety of the cottage.

Her breath misted in the frigid air, vanishing into the dark as she braced herself for the descent down Thorncrest Hill. The frost-slicked path gleamed faintly under the weak light of the moon, every step a gamble against the icy ground threatening to give way beneath her.

Her muscles throbbed with each step, the relentless cold creeping through her layers and biting at her joints. The steep slope turned each footfall into a test of balance, the ground shifting treacherously beneath her weight. The other maids had already vanished into the night, their figures swallowed by shadows, leaving Mary alone with the bitter wind and her spiraling thoughts.

Behind her, the castle loomed like a silent threat, the memory of Charles's drunken grip still lingering on her wrist. She quickened her pace, the sting of the cold and the ache in her legs nothing compared to the dread that coiled tight in her chest.

The dark silhouettes of cottages lined the road like silent sentinels, their windows tightly shuttered against the night. She passed them one by one, each darkened dwelling a stark reminder of how far she still had to go. Her pace stayed steady, though her feet screamed with every step. The path seemed endless, a stretch of dirt and frost pulling her farther from the safety of the castle but no closer to the cottage.

The wind tore through the twisted branches of the old trees, their gnarled limbs clawing at the air as if trying to snare her. Above, an owl's mournful cry pierced the silence, its sound lingering like a warning. Her breath caught in her throat as her chest tightened, the oppressive quiet wrapping around her. The futher she walked, the darker the tunnel of shadows became, the trees pressing closer together as if conspiring to block her path.

Her legs burned from the steep descent, each step a battle against the unrelenting slope. The icy ground shifted beneath her boots, and when her foot slipped on a patch of frost, she barely caught herself, her heart slamming against her ribs. The cold gnawed at her exposed hands, her cloak little more than a token shield against the wind that tore through her layers.

The cottages thinned, their comforting shapes giving way to darker woods. Her breath misted in quick bursts, uneven and shallow. She glanced over her shoulder, her skin prickling as though unseen eyes bore into her. Nothing but the restless sway of branches met her gaze, but the feeling wouldn't leave—a gnawing dread burrowed deep into her chest.

A sudden rustle from the underbrush froze her mid-step. She turned her head sharply toward the tree line, where a faint amber glow flickered through the darkness.

A pair of glowing eyes stared back at her, unblinking. A fox, its thin frame and sharp features cutting an eerie silhouette against the dark. It let out a low, sharp yip that sliced through the quiet before vanishing into the shadows. Mary shivered, the sound trailing behind her like a whisper she couldn't shake.

The path stretched on, darker and more desolate with every step. The sky above was a blank void, the stars hidden behind a veil of clouds. Only the faint light of the moon broke through now and then, casting fleeting glimpses of the path ahead. The castle walls were long gone, swallowed by the mist, leaving her utterly alone.

Her legs dragged, each step heavier than the last. Her thoughts spiralled, twisting tighter with every moment—Noor, the Shadow Serpents, the king. The weight of it all pressed against her chest like a stone, suffocating and relentless. Ahead, the outline of Thornbriar Cottage appeared, barely visible through the gloom. Relief flickered for a moment, but the sight felt more like a mirage, the kind that might vanish if she dared to hope.

Her feet stung from the cold, her body trembling from exhaustion, but she forced herself forward. As the trees began to thin, a flicker of light caught her eye—a candle glowing faintly through the shutters of her cottage.

Relief surged through her, only to be swallowed by a cold wave of dread. She stopped mid-step, her breath hitching. Someone was inside.

She looked down at the ground. Fresh muddy footprints trailed up the path to the door. Her stomach knotted as her breath turned shallow, each one catching in her throat.

Whoever had lit that candle—they hadn't left.

Noor had been missing for weeks. Robert was often out at this hour, his late-night drinking common, but if not him, then who? She approached the cottage, the thought weighing on her.

Her chest constricted as though a hand clutched at her ribs, squeezing tighter with each labored breath. Her cloak, pulled snug against her shoulders, did nothing to ward off the crawling chill spreading through her. She glanced up at the door. Its dark frame loomed in silence, daring her to approach.

She gripped the rough wool tighter, her fingers twisting into it. The faintest creak of a branch behind her froze her in place. Her pulse pounded in her ears, drowning out the whispering wind. It took a long moment before she willed her legs to move again.

The cottage door grew closer, the faint light from within seeping through the cracks in the shutters, thin and pale against the night. The faint warmth teased her from afar, but it only pulled at the knot forming in her stomach. The light was wrong.

Her hand hovered just over the door handle, trembling. She brushed the cold wood and swallowed hard. A sound—a rustle of movement or maybe just her own breath—echoed faintly behind her, and she froze. The seconds dragged, but nothing followed. She forced her hand down.

The handle turned stiffly in her grip, the door creaking with a low groan as it eased open. Candlelight spilled across her boots, and the cold air around her stilled as if it too had stepped inside.

The chamber flickered with shadows, cast long and sharp by the single burning candle on the table. Wax dripped slowly down its sides, pooling like a frozen tear. The floor bore muddy prints, their edges fresh and dark against the worn boards.

Her gaze darted to the shoes near the door—Robert's, tattered and caked in grime. Relief rushed forward but stopped short. The prints were too large, each step deliberate, trailing deeper into the cottage.

She hesitated on the threshold, her fingers brushing the door for balance. The fire crackled faintly in the hearth, but its warmth failed to reach her. Her eyes flicked to the chair in the corner, empty and still. Noor and Robert's absence hung heavy in the air, pressing against her like the weight of unseen eyes.

Mary stepped inside, the boards groaning beneath her weight. Her breath hitched as her gaze followed the footprints leading toward the staircase. Her knees wavered, but she held herself upright, one hand clutching the back of the nearest chair for support.

The shadows stretched longer, darker, as her heart hammered against her ribs. Someone else was here. The footprints stopped her cold. Her breath hitched. She took another step forward, the candlelight wavering against the shadows that seemed to close in around her.

Panic clawed at her throat as she followed the muddy trail, halting at the base of the stairs. "Robert!" Her voice echoed through the empty house, laced with fear. The silence answered back.

She grabbed the candle from the table, its flame flickering against the cold draft creeping from above. Hand shaking, she cupped it protectively, rushing toward the staircase, each step heavy with fear.

The wooden steps groaned under her weight, each creak a sinister whisper in the stillness. Her breath came in shallow gasps, mingling with the faint smell of wax and damp air. Thoughts of Charles's threats and the cruel image of Noor, stabbed and abandoned by the prince, tore through her mind, urging her onward.

At the top of the stairs, she paused for a brief, heart-stopping moment. The corridor stretched ahead, dark and unfathomable. The candlelight barely pierced the gloom, casting long shadows that seemed to mock her. Teeth clenched, she pressed on, her steps quick and desperate, the floorboards groaning beneath her feet.

Approaching Robert's chamber, her heart gripped with fresh fear, a vice tightening around her chest. With a surge of urgency, she flung the door open. Relief flooded her—so powerful her knees nearly buckled.

The fire in the hearth crackled warmly, its glow dancing across the chamber. Three empty flasks lay discarded on the floor, their contents long consumed. The clothing and boots of Ellyn and Mari were scattered about, remnants of the evening's revelry.

Robert lay sprawled on the bed, his chest rising and falling in peaceful slumber. The cheap blanket covered his lower half, while Ellyn and Mari, their bare skin visible in the dim fire, slumbered beside him.

Mary's breath escaped in a quiet sigh, her voice barely audible. "Sleep well, brother." The words were meant as reassurance, to herself as much as to him. Her fears lifted, if only for a moment.

With trembling hands, she gently closed the door, fingers lingering on the handle as she tried to calm the flutter of her heart. Each breath came a little easier now, but the memory of her fear lingered, a shadow that wouldn't fade.

Mary bent down, joints clicking as she did so. Muddy footprints splattered the dark corridor, tracked in by someone who had abandoned all pretense of stealth. Haste or carelessness had left a trail of filth on the worn wooden floorboards, eerily illuminated by the flickering candlelight.

Her breath hitched. Robert's boots were downstairs—these prints were far too large to be the maidens'. Panic twisted tighter around her heart, every shadow now seeming to hold a lurking danger.

Her pulse raced, each beat pounding in her ears. Her gaze shifted sharply, every shadow feeling like it might move. The air felt thick, each creak of the old cottage magnifying her anxiety. She could almost hear whispers of unseen threats closing in on her.

Fear trembled in her chest, but she pressed on. Each step was tentative, as though the ground itself might give way. The cold, damp air stuck to her skin, the fear in her gut growing heavier with every step. In the half-light, the corridor warped into a monstrous shape, its familiar contours turning dark and unfamiliar, as if the walls were alive.

Near her chamber, the silence grew oppressive. The hairs on the back of her neck prickled, as though unseen eyes were watching. Her pulse raced, every beat screaming for escape. She could feel something—or someone—lurking just beyond the reach of her flickering candlelight.

Her hand shook as she reached for the door, its cold surface rough under her fingers. She stopped, straining to hear, her breath coming in quick, shallow gasps.

Mary's desperation outweighed her caution. She rushed inside, her steps hurried and unsteady. She set the candle down with a hasty thud, its flame flickering wildly as she lunged for the dagger hidden beneath the straw bed. Her fingers fumbled, trembling as they sought the familiar hilt.

Finally, she seized the dagger, her hand unsteady. She spun to face the door, chest tight with fear. Her arms trembled, the dagger wavering in her grasp. The candlelight flickered weakly, casting only vague shapes in the darkness.

A deep, menacing voice echoed from behind the door. "Now, who bade thee go to The Rusty Sword?"

The intrusion jolted Mary to her core. Her hands shook as she raised the dagger, the tip unsteady. "Reveal thyself!" she demanded, her voice breaking with fear, the uncertainty gnawing at her insides. The door inched closed as the unseen figure pushed it gently. Her heart raced as the door continued to move.

As the figure stepped closer, Mary squinted, trying to make out the features. Her panic intensified until, finally, he stepped into the candle's glow. Her eyes landed on a face creased by time, forever altered by the ravages of an unyielding quest. Her initial terror gave way to a conflicted relief. It was the man with silver locks, Lucian Blackthorn, the very one she had been searching for.

Mary gasped, her breath catching in her throat as her eyes welled with tears. "I... I did not know if thou wouldst come or not," she stammered, her voice quivering like a leaf in a storm. The words tumbled out in a frantic rush, her gaze flickering nervously to the door as though expecting someone to burst in. "None o' the servants shall utter a word o' thee. They seem afeared of ye." Her mind flashed back to the servants' furtive glances, their whispers drowned in fear whenever she spoke of him. They avoided her gaze, their silence a heavy weight that pressed upon her chest. No matter how she probed, not one would speak of him—only the hollow echoes of their frightened looks remained.

Her thoughts turned sharply to Ysabeau. "Ysabeau, methinks, be either addled in her wits or doth feign all knowledge o' me an' hers ever crossin' paths," she muttered, a bitter chuckle escaping her trembling lips. The old woman had been too quick to dismiss the truth, and Mary could not shake the feeling that Ysabeau knew far more than she let on—far more than anyone dared to say.

Her lips trembled, "I beseech thee," fear taking hold once again. "Tell me, dost thou know news of my sister?" she pleaded, lowering her dagger, her voice shaking. Rumours whispered through the ranks of the Shadow Serpents spoke of Noor's brutal stabbing, the countless wounds meant to ensure her demise. A select few of the Shadow Serpents had been dispatched to feed Noor's body to flesh-eating creatures. Should she cling to life, they were to make certain she met her end.

Yet there was talk, murmured in hushed tones, that things had not gone according to plan. In this instance, he found a grim satisfaction in their failure. Normally, he would grunt in frustration at the ineptitude of the sword hires, cursing their lack of skill and precision. If it were up to him, he would have sent them straight back to training, ensuring they learned the harsh lessons of their incompetence. Though he was uncertain of what Noor's fate might be, he had learned after the fact that the prince had required the services of his organisation.

No flicker of emotion betrayed his ice-cool exterior as his toneless words lashed out, striking her where it hurt. "Thy kin hath been stabbed many a time, and the blade was laced with poison. They say she now lieth with a healer, who hath used myrrh and sundry herbs to mend her. Only time shall reveal if she doth endure."

Mary's heart tightened, and she stumbled to her bed, sinking onto it with a heavy sigh. It was good to hear that Noor might still live, yet the crushing reality remained that she had likely suffered in ways Mary could scarcely bear to imagine. In her mind's eye, Mary pictured Noor's eyes widening at the first stabbing—a moment of pure shock as the blade sank deep. But there would be no respite. Each subsequent thrust would tear anew, rending flesh and shattering any fragile sense of hope. Pain and shock would surely wage a savage war within Noor's body: every strike a fresh torrent of agony coursing through her nerves, every heartbeat a plea that would go unanswered. No part of her could escape this brutal symphony of torment. Each renewed strike denied her the mercy of a swift end, compounding terror upon terror until even the simplest act of drawing breath would have seemed a cruel luxury. Mary's own heart faltered, robbed of its former sparkle. Tears welled up in her eyes as she looked at him. "Why, prithee tell, for we be but humble folk, content to mind our own meager affairs in Mudlark Alley. Why hath the prince wronged her so?"

Seated before him, her body trembling with sorrow, he displayed no inclination to console her, as though entirely unaffected by her tears and the looming dread pressing down upon her heart. In a voice devoid of warmth, he sternly demanded, "Now, prithee, answer my question forthwith!" His gaze pierced through her.

Mary's eyes fell to the cold, hard floor, unable to meet his glare. A chill raced through her veins as he ominously withdrew a dagger, its blade gleaming in the candlelight and causing her to flinch. Though terror clutched at her throat, she knew she must tread carefully—naming the king outright could seal both their fates. Hers was a world of secrets and perilous whispers, and she did not wish to drag a royal name into such a deadly game if there were any other way.

Her voice trembled as she forced herself to speak, heart hammering as she sought words that might deflect his wrath without so much as casting the king's name beneath its shadow.

"What doth it matter?" she managed to utter, her words barely audible beneath the weight of her fear. The question hung in the air, a feeble shield against his demands, her trembling heart praying he would not force her to utter that name.

Lucian's fury settled into a chilling calm, a pale and rigid mask devoid of any human warmth. His gaze fixed on her without a single blink, a steady, clinical calm that suggested he could peel away layers of flesh and thought at will, reading whatever secrets lay beneath. When he spoke, his words fell softly, yet each one cut deeper than a blade could. "Dost thou require me to visit Robert's chamber?" he asked, his tone eerily polite, as if the cruelty beneath it were a private joke shared only with himself. The quiet menace of that question coiled through the air, pressing against her lungs until drawing breath itself felt like an act of defiance.

He knew only the most powerful would dare traffic with Robert; such knowledge, meted out sparingly, did not simply circulate among common tongues. That he could even mention such a thing suggested the depths of his reach, of the subtle darkness he would unleash should it suit his purposes. He doubted the prince would share that secret with her—and yet here he stood, offering a thinly veiled threat that cast its long, silent shadow over her quivering heart.

Fear and desperation flooded her being. "The king!" she blurted out, her voice cracking. "Pray, it was His Majesty, the King," she pleaded, clinging to a fragile hope for mercy.

Lucian paused, his lips twisting into something that might have been a smile if not for its utter lack of warmth. He repeated the title as if tasting something sour: "The king?" His eyes drifted downward, fingers tapping once against the hilt of his dagger—not a nervous habit, but a methodical, counting gesture. Twice, he had seen the king's envoys at The Rusty Sword, and the timing of their visits lined up all too neatly with Mary's own. He let the silence breathe for a moment, then slid his blade back into its sheath with a quiet precision.

He turned his gaze back to Mary, a tightening of his jaw and a narrowing of his eyes conveying quiet disapproval. "Thou art playing a dangerous game," His voice emerged low, carrying the weight of a cold warning, withdrawing a leather flask from beneath his cloak. He drank without haste, as though savoring the moment. "The prince be filled with jealousy and possessiveness. Should he discover the king's hand in such matters…" He let the words trail off, refusing to give voice to the name of the Shadow Serpents, though both of them knew exactly what he meant. The silence that followed felt heavier than any blade.

"Game?!" Mary's voice shook, pitched higher than she intended. "Games are fashioned for mirth—at least a morsel of delight. Yet all I see is peril, a cruel snare set by royal kin!" Her fists knotted in her skirts as if to hold herself steady. "Mark me, there is no jest in this. I would be free of their schemes!"

His next words came crisp and unyielding, each syllable as pointed as a dagger's tip. "Like it or not, thou art part of it. A pawn surrounded by pieces of greater might."

The mention of Noor's plight pressed like a storm cloud over the small, candlelit chamber. Lucian took another measured sip from his flask, the faint sound of liquid and leather breaking the heavy silence. "Thou wouldst do well to remember," he said, "that 'tis the prince thou must woo, not His Majesty."

A frustrated hiss escaped Mary's lips, her eyes flashing. "Why must I woo anyone?" She turned her face away, as though the very thought had a foul scent. "I despise the prince, a vile creature undeserving of the title he holds! And His Majesty… 'tis folly to dream of a future with a king!" Her pulse pounded, recalling Noor's sufferings. "Noor's life hangs by a thread, all by Prince Charles's doing!" Her voice trembled with fury as she clenched her hands, wishing for strength she lacked. "Were I capable of it, I would see the prince undone, not stoop to court him!"

Lucian's lips curled into a weary sneer, the candlelight playing off the silver strands of his hair like tarnished coins. "Many have tried," he said, voice low and sardonic. He knew all too well the coin earned from thwarting those who sought the prince's end. "If Noor endures, she shall not return to Ravenswood, that much is certain. She must remain hidden, beyond the reach of curious eyes." He paused, letting the words sink in. "I spoke not with her, yet even a brief glimpse revealed a startling promise in the girl."

Mary's face tightened, anguish churning in her stomach. The thought of her sister's exile clung to her like damp wool. She raised her head, meeting his gaze at last. The candlelight picked out a tremor in her stare, as if every unsaid plea hovered, trembling, in the dark rim of her irises. "Whither should we seek our concealment?" she demanded, each word a plea for something more than cruel fate and the unspoken dangers lurking in every silence.

Lucian shrugged, as though her plight weighed no more than a stray mote of dust. "That duty rests with thee," he said, lifting his flask and drinking with a measured slowness. "Seek thy haven beyond these borders. Eldoria, for instance—" he paused, letting the name hover in the dim air. "I have walked its roads many a time, felt its sunlight upon my skin. 'Tis a land warmed by kindness and gentle breezes. Near Lake Seraphine, blankets are but a needless burden. Some whisper the waters possess healing virtues."

At that name, Eldoria, Mary's face lit with a faint, wistful glimmer. She had heard traders and travelers conjure its image in quiet corners of Mudlark Alley: a paradise tucked beneath cobalt skies, where fields stretched green and unending. Yet Eldoria lay cruelly distant, costly and perilous to reach. *And what of Noor? If she yet liveth, 'twould seem she shall be in no state to brave the treacherous seas.*

Desperation tightened in her chest. Her trembling fingers hovered near Lucian's sleeve, finally catching lightly at the worn fabric. "Pray thee," she managed, voice cracking under the weight of her plea. The candlelight reflected tears not yet fallen, and she searched his face for a flicker of understanding. "We must have audience with Noor."

At once he jerked his arm free, as though her touch carried a contagion. His lip curled. There was no warmth in his gaze, only a flinty hardness that made her body tense, as if she'd grazed against steel sharpened just for her. Mary recoiled, blood rushing in her ears. "I shall see to it," he said at last, his tone low and edged with steel. "But rest assured, thou art under watchful eyes. The prince hath spies that mark thee, as a hawk doth its prey." The chamber felt smaller then, as if unseen watchers crowded its corners.

His brow lowered, words dropping to a quieter pitch. "Keep thy distance from His Majesty," he warned. "Consider well the ruin that will unfold if the king and Charles clash o'er thee." The unspoken truth was plain: though the king's fairness was heralded, he shared the prince's blood, and no one could predict what shape his wrath might take.

Fear prickled along Mary's spine. She drew a shallow breath, her voice snagging on something unspoken. After a moment's hesitation, she forced the words past the tightness lodging beneath her tongue, each syllable emerging like a strained whisper against the silence. "What course remains for me?" she asked, her voice trembling like a leaf in a bitter wind. "The prince doth command that I sunder the king's heart—" Her voice faltered, eyes lowered. "I cannot! I have striven with all mine heart to keep afar, yet the ache doth gnaw upon my very soul. How am I to bear such torment?"

Lucian fixed her with a hard stare, his eyes cold and unforgiving. "Then thou must learn to endure the pain," he said harshly. "For if thou dost not, it will be the prince who will make thee suffer, and those thou carest for."

Mary stared at him in disbelief, her heart pounding in her chest. "I cannot merely forsake all that I hold dear." she protested weakly, her voice catching in her throat. The suffocating sensation of his words wrapped around her like a tightly wound coil, squeezing out all air, all hope.

In the flickering light, his face hardened, lines etched like fault lines on a shifting terrain, freezing her in place. "What dost thou cherish, I prithee? Thou dost despise this humble cottage, and thy purse is as empty as thy ambitions. Thy heart doth sway toward the king—aye, A KING! Let me remind thee, thou art but a peasant! Thou hast naught but folly to cling to! What thou shouldst hold dear are thy kin, and thou must see them to safety forthwith!" "If thou continuest down this path, it will not end well for thee," he warned, his voice slicing through the air. The faint sound of liquid sloshing accompanied his deliberate swig from the flask before he placed it back on his belt with a metallic clink.

Mary's heart thundered, the rhythmic pounding echoing in her ears. "I knowest," she whispered, her voice quivering. Her eyes fogged, refusing to cry, as the burden of her troubles settled on her like a suffocating blanket.

He shifted, the leather of his boots creaking softly against the wooden floor. "A messenger will be dispatched," he said, a grudging note of reassurance in his tone. "Their mission will be to relay the healer's decision regarding thy request to visit Noor."

The flickering candle cast dancing shadows on the walls, the flame wavering with each movement. "I thank thee," she whispered, the words barely audible over the heavy silence that filled the chamber. Her breath hitched as she watched his figure retreat, each step a soft thud against the worn floorboards.

As he moved further away, the shadows seemed to swallow him whole, his form melding with the encroaching darkness. A dying flame's final shudder tossed eerie silhouettes across the walls before the darkness closed in, and he was gone, erased from her sight like a fleeting thought.

A shiver coursed through Mary as sorrow took hold, wrapping her in an icy embrace. Her movements slow and sluggish, she reached for the candle again, the fragile flame casting a dim light that barely cut through the darkness. The flickering light seemed to beckon her, its gentle dance a siren's call to her exhausted soul.

Mary's grip on the candle faltered, her fingers rigid as ice. Her eyes, devoid of warmth, stared into the flickering flame with a hardened resolve. *"Pray, let us kindle the fire,"* she thought, the words sharp and unwavering in her mind."

The darkened chamber closed in around her, its shadows threatening to overwhelm; yet the pale, lambent glow of the candle urged her onward, step by hesitant step. The chill crept in on her, fogging the air with each exhale as her bones and heart radiated cold.

With each step, the small light wavered, casting fleeting, dancing shadows that only emphasised the vast emptiness around her.

She reached the fireplace, the hearth cold and unwelcoming. Kneeling before it, she held the candle close, the flame trembling as if in sympathy with her trembling hands. The kindling and logs waited, patient and inert, as she fumbled to arrange them. Her fingers, numb with cold and sorrow, moved slowly, setting the pieces in place.

As the first sparks caught, a tiny, hopeful flame began to grow, casting a warm glow that gradually spread. The firelight pushed back the shadows, inch by inch, filling the chamber with a tentative warmth. Mary watched the flames dance, their flickering movements a fragile promise of comfort.

Mary's body coiled in shock as she heard another voice in her chamber. "Who wast thy guest?" Though startled, the voice was familiar, one she knew well. She did not turn, her hands rubbing together in a desperate attempt to gather warmth from the newly kindled fire.

"Oh, Robert! Thou dost startle me!" she replied, her tone laced with weariness. "I am surprised that thou hast taken notice or that thou art home at all. Thou hast been drinking at taverns until thou art kicked out, and when thou art here, thou dost always indulge with many different maidens."

The fire crackled, its light casting flickering shadows on the walls. She could hear the creak of floorboards as her brother stumbled closer, his unsteady steps and slurred voice betraying his drunken state. With her eyes fixed on the flickering flames, she felt the chill of the outside world slowly fade, replaced by a sense of comfort that spread through her like a soothing balm.

"Thou art ever the observant one, sister," he said, his voice heavy with the effects of ale. "And what of thy mysterious visitor? Dost thou make secret pacts now?"

Her hands stilled, the rough fabric of her cloak brushing against her fingers. She drew a deep breath, steadying herself before speaking. "No secrets, Robert. Only matters that concern our survival, something thou might consider more oft."

He let out a humourless chuckle, the sound grating in the confined space. "Ever the dutiful one. Pray, enlighten me. What business hath brought thee such a guest?"

She turned then, her eyes meeting his, the firelight reflecting in their depths. "Tis not thy concern," she said firmly, her voice steady. "But know this, brother: our sister Noor is missing, and thy indulgences and wayward ways will only hinder our efforts to find her."

The words hung in the air, heavy with unspoken fears and the weight of their shared burdens. The fire crackled louder, its flames dancing wildly as if in response to the tension that simmered between them.

"Mayhap thou art right," Robert muttered, his bravado faltering as he swayed slightly. "But tell me, Mary, what dost thou plan to do about it?"

Mary's resolve hardened, the fire's warmth emboldening her spirit. "I shall do what I must, Robert. For Noor, for thee, and for myself. Even if it means making alliances with those I despise."

Robert's eyes, bleary with drink, narrowed in confusion and concern. "Alliances, sayest thou? With the prince, or perchance that strange man?"

Her jaw clenched, the thought of Prince Charles igniting a spark of defiance within her. "I shall forge alliances with whomsoever I must." she answered, her voice a mere whisper but carrying the weight of her determination. "I shall do whatsoever is required to find our sister, e'en if it meaneth treading through the very flames."

The two fell silent, the only sound the steady crackle of the fire and the soft rustle of their breathing. In that moment, amidst the flickering shadows and the cold stone walls, Mary felt a flicker of hope. It was fragile, like the flame before her, but it was enough to kindle the strength she needed to face the trials ahead.

Robert stumbled over and sat heavily beside her, the scent of ale strong on his breath. He too extended his hands toward the fire, seeking its warmth. "I have sought Noor, I do swear it." he slurred, his voice thick with the effects of drink. He turned his head slowly towards Mary, his eyes glassy and sorrowful. "I know we see each other but little, yet Leofric and I did search far and long. Henry even sought to hire Cedric, the finest huntsman in all of Ravenswood. The passing months hath tempered our hopes, leaving naught but disappointment in their stead. It hath been weeks. Dost thou fault me for drowning mine sorrows?"

Mary's heart ached at his words, a blend of frustration and sympathy welling up inside her. A subtle widening of her eyes was the only giveaway of her concern as she took in the somber landscape of his face, its deeply etched crevices an uncanny echo of her own tired features. His features twisted in anguish, the fire's gentle light amplifying the despair that leaked from his every pore.

"I would not burden thee with mine own failings," Robert continued, his voice breaking. "Our father and mother we lost to the plague, and no coin had we for a proper burial. They were cast into the common pit, as all others who perished, without so much as a token of honour. A man ought to provide for his kin's rest, yet I could not. And now, Noor is gone—vanished as though she were but a shadow. Nor can I account for Sophia, who hath disappeared as well. My heart is nigh unto breaking, Mary."

His voice trembled, the pain of their shared losses evident. "Ale and maidens be the sole diversions that yet remain unto me," he admitted, his eyes reflecting the fire's glow. "They dull the ache, though but for a fleeting while."

Mary felt a tear escape down her cheek, the weight of their collective grief pressing down on her. She placed a hand on his shoulder, squeezing gently. "I understand, Robert," she whispered, her voice heavy with emotion. "We have both borne far more than our share of sorrow. Yet must we remain steadfast, for Noor's sake and our own. We cannot permit our grief to devour us."

Robert nodded slowly, his gaze returning to the fire. "Aye," he murmured, his voice barely audible. "for Noor."

The chamber remained silent, save for the crackling of the fire and the occasional sniffle from both siblings. They sat together, united in their shared pain, drawing what little comfort they could from each other's presence.

"Thou must not repeat my words, brother," Mary cautioned, her eyes scanning the chamber for any signs of eavesdroppers. She inched closer, the warmth of the fire a poor match for the shivering dread that spread through her like ice water. Bringing her lips close to Robert's ear, she whispered, "The man who was here is a perilous sort, bound to a shadowed order known only to those of wealth and might."

Robert's face shifted from drunken indifference to shock. His gaze locked onto Mary's, and for an instant, he hesitated, reading the lines of her face for any whisper of a jest. The weight of her words seemed to sober him slightly, his expression growing more serious.

"If he be so perilous, why dost thou harbour him within thy chamber?" Robert's words stumbled, softened by the lingering haze of drink, yet a flicker of worry crept into his tone, like the fraying edge of a cloak too often mended.

Mary straightened, her gaze steady and unwavering. "Because, Robert, at times must we forge bonds with those we dread, that we might shield those we hold dear. Noor's fate doth hang by a thread, and this man, perilous though he be, holdeth the means to uncover tidings that might reunite us."

Robert's brow furrowed, his confusion clear. Yet beneath the haze of ale, a spark of excitement ignited. With a questioning enthusiasm, he drew near, "Mary, this is wondrous news! But why or how art thou mixed with such company?"

Mary took a deep breath, the weight of her actions pressing down on her. "'Tis not by mine own choice, brother. The prince's wiles have pressed me to the wall. I seek any means to guard Noor's safety, though it should bind me to those I would lief keep afar."

Robert's eyes, though still bleary with drink, sharpened with judgment. Worry and annoyance warred for dominance on his face, but his eyes gave him away, revealing a concern that he couldn't shake. "Thou avoidest my question, sister," he said, his tone accusatory. "How art thou mixed with such company?"

It was as if her breath caught in her throat. "His Majesty the King." She snapped her eyes back to the fire, unable to bear Robert's judgmental gaze.

Robert's shock quickly turned to incredulous laughter. "The king?" he repeated, disbelief evident in his voice. "Mary, hast thou taken leave of thy wits? Folk such as we doth not address the king. Pray, how camest thou into his presence?"

The very reminder of the king filled her heart with both longing and sadness. "Robert," she began hesitantly, as if sharing a shameful secret, "His countenance doth haunt mine every thought. I muse but on the hour when mine eyes may once more behold him. 'Twas at Thorncrest Castle we first did meet, when I didst take up the post of chambermaid. I knew not his station then. By fortune we did chance upon one another, and with each meeting, he proved himself ever the charmer—and aye, most fair to look upon. When his true rank was revealed, I did feel myself a proper fool."

Her voice wavered, the memory of their encounters tugging at her emotions. She dared not meet Robert's eyes, instead keeping her gaze fixed on the flickering flames that danced in the hearth.

Robert's face froze, a jolt of surprise twitching at the corners of his mouth as concern swept in. He opened his mouth to speak, but no words came. His eyes locked onto his sister's, and for an instant, the entire universe distilled down to that single, aching connection – and the mind-bending news she'd just dropped on him. "The king? My, my, Mary! Thou hast shown no interest in any man for years, and now dost thou tell me that thou art sweet upon the king?"

Shoulder to shoulder, their eyes met in a moment of unspoken connection. Her heart raced with uncertainty as she began to speak. "Noor liveth still, and that, in sooth, is a blessing in itself," she said. "However," she paused, her voice quivering ever so slightly, ""she remaineth ensnared in a grim struggle for her very life."

Robert gently clasped her hand in his, his voice filled with unwavering conviction. "Noor hath ever been resilient; I do know she shall yet prevail." he affirmed, his words resonating with confidence.

A mischievous twinkle sparked in Robert's eye as he changed the subject back to Mary's want for the king. He couldn't resist playfully teasing Mary about her infatuation with the king. With a smirk, he quipped, "The king, thou dost claim? My fairest sister, bewitched by His Majesty? Verily, Noor shall rise from the ashes but to mock thee alone. "Nay!" A faint blush crept 'cross Mary's cheeks. "'Tis not quite as thou thinkest," she hastily interjected, her voice tinged with a mix of embarrassment. "I merely... hold a profound admiration for His Majesty."

Robert's brow arched in amusement, a smirk playing at the corners of his lips. "Admiration, dost thou say?" he echoed, his tone laced with playful disbelief. "One doth detest too much."

Feeling embarrassed by his words, Mary gently turned away, her eyes briefly avoiding his gaze. The tremble in her voice betrayed her best attempts to mask the emotion etched on her face. "Pray," she whispered, her words tinged with embarrassment. "I know how foolish it sounds."

Robert's chuckle faded as he saw the sincerity in her eyes. He squeezed her hand reassuringly. "Perhaps it is foolish," he said softly, "But 'tis also brave. To care for one so beyond thy grasp... it requires courage. And I know thou hast that in great abundance."

Mary gave him a small, grateful smile, her heart slightly lighter despite the heavy burdens they carried. "What might our sire and dame proclaim? The both of us, bewitched by the king and the princess?"

Robert's brows furrowed, his gaze unfocused. A look of puzzlement crossed his face, freezing on hers. "Princess?" he slurred, his voice thick with drink and bewilderment.

Mary let out a tense laugh, her cheeks flushing with a mix of frustration and hurt. "Yea, dear brother, I know that Sophia is the runaway princess. Why didst thou keep this from me? It hath brought upon much trouble."

A sluggish smile played on his lips, wavering between amusement and confusion. His speech slurred, each word trailing into the next as he tried to grasp the weight of Mary's revelation. "Forgive me, sister," he hiccuped, swaying slightly, "but surely mine ears deceive me! Forsooth, didst thou not name Sophia a princess?" He let out a hollow laugh, shaking his head as if trying to dispel a persistent fog. "Ha! A jest, perchance, or hast thou truly gone madder than I this eve?"

Mary tilted her head, her brows knitting together as she struggled to comprehend. Her eyes searched his face for any sign of jest, but found none. "Sayest thou this in jest? Dost thou truly know that Sophia is a princess?"

Robert's face contorted, the flickering firelight casting unsettling shadows across his features. His drunken stupor seemed to shatter in that instant, eyes widening in horror as the gravity of Mary's words settled in. The jovial veneer melted away, revealing a glimpse of fear and realisation beneath the haze of his inebriation. He blinked rapidly, struggling to maintain his composure, the truth of Mary's seriousness cutting through his drunken facade like a sharp blade.

Mary's face reflected sudden horror, her eyes wide with disbelief. "Thou didst hear correctly, Robert," she said, her voice a mix of exasperation and worry. "Princess Sophia, sister to the King and Prince Charles, dost thou truly declare that thou knewest not?"

Robert felt the ground shift beneath him, confusion swirling like a tempest in his mind. "Sophia... a princess?" His voice trembled, the reality of her true identity crashing over him like a cold wave. "She didst inform me that she hailed from the household of Ashbourne." A laugh of despair escaped his lips, sharp and bitter, as if mocking his own naivety. "After her disappearance, I hath ventured to Stowshire many a time. I even forged bonds with the maids, and 'twas then I did uncover that it had all been naught but a falsehood."

His heart raced, and a lightheadedness crept in, blurring the edges of his vision. "Though I know she hath deceived me of her ties to the House of Ashbourne, ne'er did I imagine she were the princess!"

"The princess? Yet we laid with one another?" The thought crashed into him, sending a jolt through his body. His breath quickened, heart racing as the weight of truth pressed down on him like a vice. *"I was a fool! I heeded not Noor's dire forewarnings."* A wave of nausea rolled through him, and he brought his hand to his forehead, pressing against the skin as if to steady the turmoil within.

I wot well I tread upon perilous ground, he thought, a cold sweat trickling down his back. Panic clawed at his throat, tightening it as he struggled to grasp the enormity of his actions. *Yet to lie with the princess be naught but treason.*

His vision swam, shadows flickering at the edges of his sight, and each breath felt shallow, as if the air itself conspired against him.

Mary's heart sank further. She had been certain she had already told him. Had he been so deep in his chalice that he had forgotten? Or was she losing her mind in the midst of all their troubles? "I told thee afore, Robert, did I not?" she whispered, her voice trembling. "Didst thou not remember?"

"I remember not! Art thou certain thou didst tell me? Or perchance I was inebriated and could not grasp thy words." Robert's shoulders slumped, the weight of his grief pulling him down. "All those nights we did spend in discourse and mirth... I knew not she could be so deceitful. Not one soul didst recognise her as our princess. We visited many a tavern; how is it that we were all so blind?"

Mary placed her hand on his, her touch gentle and reassuring. "I beheld her this day, brother. Her eyes, clouded and dimmed by the heavy burden of her own deceit, did reveal an anguish almost tangible. Her affections for thee were genuine, yet she hath no choice but to return to her duties as princess." Mary could not bear to add that those duties included marriage, knowing it would only deepen his hurt.

Robert's eyes filled with tears, his sorrow overwhelming. Though unspoken between them, he understood what Mary meant by duties: Sophia would be wed. "I would have done aught for her," he whispered. He sought to console himself with the thought that, at the very least, she was safe. Turning his visage to the floor, he concealed the signs of his weeping. *"What am I to do with this love that hath no place wherein to rest?"* His inner thought echoed, *She did flee because she must wed; now she hath returned to her duties, duties that bind her to wed.*

Mary squeezed his hand, her heart aching for him. "My dearest brother, in due time, all shall be well. It may appear as if thou shalt never love again, yet I assure thee, thou surely wilt." They sat in silence, two siblings broken-hearted over another pair of siblings—royalty destined to wed not for love but for duty. The thought of their loved ones being forced into such painful and loveless unions gnawed at Mary, stirring a longing she struggled to suppress—a longing for a love unbound by duty and royal obligation.

Robert nodded, his grief still raw, but he did not wish for his sister to see him so vulnerable. "I shall return to my slumber, for two most favoured maidens await me in my bed. What care I for the princess and her deceit?" His words tumbled out in a bitter sigh, eyes shadowed with the pain of betrayal and lost love.

Mary watched him as he stumbled to stand, her heart heavy with sorrow for both their losses. Regret and determination wrestled within her, each breath a reckoning. Robert refused to meet her gaze as he walked away, his steps unsteady.

"Morrow, we shall take our leave," he declared, his voice rough and weary. "See if thou canst find the man to send a message of Noor elsewhere. Noor detests the cottage; she will not wish to return hither. We can make a home in the forest until she is well."

Mary nodded, though Robert did not see. "Aye, brother," she whispered to his retreating figure. The fire crackled softly, its warmth a stark contrast to the cold resolve settling in her heart. Memories of the king's noble presence flickered in her mind, igniting a yearning she dared not fully acknowledge.

She waited a few moments, allowing the silence and the heaviness of the moment to linger. Her gaze settled upon her bed as she found herself lost in thoughts of the king once more. It felt as if her legs refused to move, as if making those extra steps was too much to bear.

Summoning a strength she did not know she possessed, Mary forced her way to the bed, each step a relentless battle against her own fatigue. She lowered herself onto the straw-filled pallet, the rough texture of the straw poking through the coarse fabric cover. She tugged at the scratchy blanket, pulling it tightly around herself. The scant bedding offered little solace, its frayed edges a testament to her weary heart's desolation.

As Mary lay in bed, her mind raced with thoughts of what to do next. They had no coin, no horse, and no real plan. She worried about Noor's health and how long it would take for her to be strong enough to travel. A constant hum of uncertainty thrummed in her brain, making it impossible to shake off the din of doubt. Yet beneath it all, a silent hope persisted—a hope that one day, her own heart might find solace in love once more, perhaps even with the king who occupied her dreams.

Mary tossed and turned, her heart filled with dread for her dear sister, wounded and frail. The future, once a promised land, now seemed a precarious terrain, full of unknowns and threats. In an attempt to soothe herself, Mary hummed a tune, a lullaby to calm her fears and ease her pain. She let the syllables trill on her tongue, their musicality transporting her to a place of serenity, a temporary escape from the burdens she bore.

As she continued to repeat the lines, she felt herself slowly drifting off to sleep, finding a measure of peace in the comforting embrace of the melody. Her dreams became a refuge from the chaos, a chance to rediscover a sense of calm where tomorrow looked a little more promising, and where perhaps, her heart could find the love it so desperately yearned for.

End of Part Two. The story continues in Book Three.

The second volume of The Downfall of the Winterbournes closes, yet the tale is far from over. If this story hath moved thee—be it to laughter, fury, or the edge of thy seat—I would be most grateful if thou wouldst share thy thoughts.

Scan the QR code to leave a review on Amazon and share thy thoughts. Thy support is invaluable, and for it, I thank thee.

Printed in Great Britain
by Amazon